# THE LURE OF TREASON

Bishop Edmund Loris was aware that many would regard what he was about to do as treason. He did not. As bishop and priest, he was duty-bound to root out evil and corruption. And the source of corruption lay in the Devil's brood called the Deryni.

They must be eradicated—every last one of them. And though Loris' mind recoiled at the thought of raising hand against an anointed king—Kelson, whom he himself had crowned—the thought of not acting against a servant of Darkness on the throne repelled him more.

For the sake of every soul in Gwynedd, the Deryni heresy must be stamped out—and Edmund Loris would use whatever means necessary to accomplish that end.

"A RICH FEAST OF MEDIEVAL CHIVALRY, ROMANCE AND MAGIC—THE BOOK THAT ALL KATHERINE KURTZ'S FANS HAVE BEEN AWAITING."
—MARION ZIMMER BRADLEY

# THE BISHOP'S HEIR

### VOLUME I OF
### THE HISTORIES OF KING KELSON

## KATHERINE KURTZ

**A Del Rey Book**
**BALLANTINE BOOKS • NEW YORK**

All rights reserved under International and Pan-American Copyright
Conventions. Published in the United States by Ballantine Books,
a division of Random House, Inc., New York, and simultaneously
in Canada by Random House of Canada Limited, Toronto.

Library of Congress Catalog Card Number: 84-4935

ISBN 0-345-30097-1

Manufactured in the United States of America

First Hardcover Edition: October 1984
First Ballantine Books Edition: August 1985

Map by Shelly Shapiro

This one is for my Sibling,
JEANNE MARIE BROWN,
and the rest of the Brown Clan:
David, Graham, and Adriane

# CONTENTS

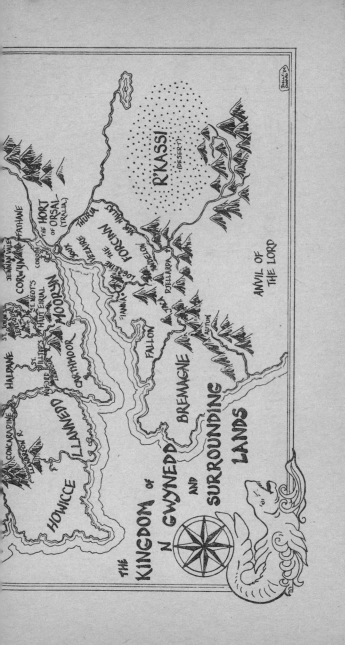

# PROLOGUE

*And he put on the garments of vengeance
for clothing, and was clad with zeal for a
cloak.*

—Isaiah 59:17

Edmund Loris, once the Archbishop of Valoret and
Primate of All Gwynedd, stared out to sea through the
salt-smeared windowpanes of his tower prison and allowed
himself a thin smile. The rare display of self-indulgence
did nothing to diminish the fury of the wind shrilling at
the ill-fitted glass, but the letter secreted in the breviary
under his arm gave its own grim comfort. The offer was
princely, befitting even the exalted status he had enjoyed
before his fall.

Exhaling softly of his long-hoarded bitterness, Loris
bowed his head and shifted the book to hold it in both
hands, wary lest the gesture seem to make it too precious
in the eyes of his jailers, who could look in on him at any
time. For two years now they had kept him here against
his will. For two years his existence had been defined by
the walls of this monastic cell and the token participation
permitted him in the life of the rest of the abbey: daily
attendance at Mass and Vespers, always in the company
of two silent and all-too-attentive monks, and access to
a confessor once each month—seldom the same man
twice, and never the same one any two months in succession. Were it not for one of the lay brothers who brought
his meals, whose fondness for intrigue Loris had early
discovered, he would have had no contact whatsoever
with the outside world.

The outside world—how he longed for it again! The two years spent in Saint Iveagh's were but an extension of the outrage which had begun a full year before that, with the death of King Brion. On just such a chill November day as this had Brion Haldane met his doom—blasted from life by the hell-spawned magic of a Deryni sorceress, but leaving an unexpected legacy of forbidden powers to his son and heir, the fourteen-year-old Kelson.

Nor had young Kelson hesitated to seize his unholy patrimony and use it to overturn almost everything Loris held sacred, not the least of which was the Church's stand against the use of magic in whatever form. And all of this had been done under the guise of his "Divine right" to rule and his sacred duty to protect his people—though how a king could justify consorting with the powers of evil to effect that protection was beyond Loris' comprehension. By the end of the following summer, with the help of the Deryni heretics Morgan and McLain, Kelson had even managed to turn most of Loris' fellow bishops against him. Only the ailing Corrigan had remained true—and his faithful heart had given out before he could be subjected to the humiliation Loris finally endured. The rebel bishops actually believed they had done a great kindness by allowing Loris to attend the travesty of a trial at which they stripped away his offices and banished him to a life of forced contemplation.

Bitter still, but heartened by the prospect of a chance to set things right, the former archbishop tapped the edge of his book lightly against his lips and thought about its secret contents—yet another communication from folk with similar cause to feel uneasy at what the new king had wrought. The wind whining in the roof slates of Saint Iveagh's sea-girt towers sang of the freedom of the open seas whence it came, bearing the tang of salt air and the cries of the wheeling gulls that circled the abbey during all but the darkest hours of night, and for the first time since his imprisonment, Loris allowed himself to hope that he, too, might soon be free. For many, many months, he had feared never to taste freedom again except in death.

Oh, he was not fool enough to think there would not

be a price—but he could afford to promise anything, for now. With care and craft, he might play more than one side to his advantage, perhaps eventually becoming even more powerful than before his fall. Then he would make himself the instrument of God's retribution, driving the cursed Deryni from the land once and for all.

And the Deryni taint was in the very blood of the king—perhaps in *all* the Haldane line, not in Kelson alone. In the very beginning, Loris had thought Kelson's forbidden magic strictly the legacy of his Deryni mother— that poor, conscience-hounded lady who even now kept strict seclusion in another remote abbey, praying for the soul of her Deryni son as well as her own and devoting her life to penance for the evil she carried. She had confessed her guilt before them all, that solemn day of Kelson's coronation, prepared to sacrifice life and even soul to protect him from the sorceress who had already been responsible for his father's death.

But Queen Jehana, though she had the will, had not the power to fight Kelson's battle for him; and in the end, the young king had had to face the challenge with his own resources—prodigious resources, as it happened, easily equal to the challenge, but frightening in their implications. While granting that his mother's Deryni blood might have made its contribution, Kelson had publicly claimed sacred right as the source of his newfound abilities. Loris had feared otherwise, even at the time, for he remembered stories about the boy's father.

In fact, the more Loris thought on it—and he had had ample time for *that* in the last two years—the more convinced he became that Brion and hitherto unsuspected Deryni ancestors were as much to blame for Kelson's condition as Jehana. The full extent of the taint could only be guessed. Certainly both Brion and his father before him had harbored Deryni at court from time to time. The detested Morgan and McLain were but the most recent and blatant of many such—and the latter a priest all the while, hypocrite to the core—on both of whom Loris wished only the vilest of fates, for the two were largely responsible for his present situation.

As for Brion, who could deny that the late king once had faced and killed a Deryni sorcerer in single combat? Loris, then but a parish priest of rising prominence, had heard of the incident only at second and third hand, but even in the first throes of public jubilation at the king's victory, he had been chilled by the recurring suggestion that Brion's opponent, father to the woman eventually responsible for his death, had fallen not alone to Brion's sword but to strange powers wielded by the king himself. In the taverns for months afterward, haunted eyewitnesses with tongues loosened by ale whispered fearfully of magic worked upon the king by young Morgan before that fateful confrontation—the unleashing of awesome forces which Brion *said* were benign, the royal legacy of *his* father—but even that admission cast grave suspicions on the king, so far as Loris was concerned. Though a man of honest if rigid religious conviction, he was not naive enough to concede that purity of intent and fervence of faith—or Divine favor to an anointed king—had been Brion's salvation, though he kept his misgivings to himself so long as Brion lived.

Now Loris knew that only power such as the Enemy himself wielded could have given Brion victory against such odds, and over such a foe. And if that power had been granted, or even merely released, by one of the accursed Deryni, then its source was clear: an evil legacy from years of dark alliance with that unholy race. The double inheritance of evil from Brion and Jehana was doubly damning in their son. Kelson was beyond redemption, and must be eliminated.

Nor, by the same logic, were Brion's brother Nigel and his brood to be spared—for though uncontaminated by Jehana's blood, still they, like Kelson, traced their ancestry back through the generations of Haldane kings who had carried forward some other variant of Deryni curse from the time of the Restoration. The land must be freed of this evil, cleansed of the dark Deryni taint. A new royal line must be raised to rule in Gwynedd—and what better source, and who with better legal claim, than the old royal line of Meara, human to the core, one of whose supporters even now offered assistance to Gwynedd's rightful Primate, if that Primate would support Mearan independence?

With a shiver, Loris slipped his breviary into the breast of his homespun woolen robe and drew his meager cloak around his shoulders—he, who had worn fine linen and silk and furs before being deprived of his office! Two years of the sparse, simple fare of the *Fratri Silentii* had pared a handspan from an already trim waist and honed the hawklike features to even sharper definition, but the hunger which gnawed at Loris now had nothing to do with physical appetites. As he laid one hand flat against the window glass, his eye was caught by the amethyst on his finger—sole reminder left him of his former rank—and he savored the words of the letter next to his heart.

*Meara will bow no more to a Deryni king,* the missive had said, echoing his own determination. *If this plan meets with your approval, ask shriving of a monk named Jeroboam who shall come within the week to preach, and be guided by his advice. Until Laas. . . .*

Laas. The very name conjured images of ancient glories. It had been the capital of an independent Meara a hundred years before the first Haldanes came to Gwynedd. From Laas, sovereign Mearan princes had ruled as proudly as any Haldane, and over lands by no means less fair.

But Jolyon, the last Mearan prince, had sired only daughters by the time he lay dying a century before, and the eldest, Roisian, was only twelve. To prevent the rending of his lands by avaricious guardians, regents, and suitors, Jolyon willed his coronet and the hand of Roisian to the strongest man he could find: Malcolm Haldane, newly crowned King of Gwynedd, a respected former adversary.

But Jolyon's final act found little favor with Meara's native sons; the prince had read his nobles well. Before Malcolm could even bed his young bride, dissident Mearan knights abducted both of the queen's sisters and proclaimed the elder, Roisian's twin, Meara's sovereign princess. Malcolm put down the ensuing rebellion in less than a month, capturing and hanging several of the ringleaders, but he never did locate the stolen princesses—though he encountered their heirs many times in the years which followed. He moved Meara's territorial capital from Laas to the more central Ratharkin the following summer, both for greater ease of administration and to lessen the importance of Laas as a symbol of former Mearan sovereignty, but the ancient city remained, from time to time, a rallying point for cadet lines of the old royal house which waxed with each new generation and as swiftly waned whenever Haldane expeditions swept into the principality to quash the beginnings of revolt—and execute pretenders. Malcolm and his son Donal were scrupulous about their periodic "Mearan housecleaning," as Donal called it, but King Brion had taken such action only once during his reign, shortly after the birth of his own son. The venture, while necessary, had been so personally distasteful that he had avoided even considering the need for a repeat campaign a generation later.

Now Brion's softness was likely to cost his son a throne. The current Mearan Pretender had no cause to love King Kelson, for she had lost a husband as well as a child the last time a Haldane flexed his strength in Meara. It was even rumored in Meara that an impassive Brion had watched the baby prince put to the sword—a lie promulgated by Mearan dissidents, though it was true that the child had died. Soon afterward, the self-styled Princess Caitrin of Meara, descendant of Queen Roisian's twin, took as husband and consort the ambitious younger brother of one of Gwynedd's earls and disappeared into the mountains to breed rebellion and more pretenders—until Brion's death brought them out of hiding. It was one of Caitrin's agents who had contacted Loris.

Sighing, Loris pressed his nose against the glass of his prison and watched an autumn squall-line crawl toward the shore from the northwest, well aware that many would regard what he was about to do as treason. He did not. It was a means to an end. If he had learned one thing in more than half a century of service to his faith, it was that the integrity of Holy Mother Church depended upon temporal dealings as well as spiritual ones. Higher loyalties than those binding him to any temporal lord bound him to his future course, for as bishop as well as priest he was duty-bound to root out evil and corruption. Inevitably, the source of that corruption lay in the devil's brood called the Deryni.

The Deryni must be eradicated—every last one of them. The time was past for leniency, for trying to save their souls. Though Loris' mind recoiled at the thought of raising hand against an anointed king—Kelson, whom he himself had crowned—the thought of not raising hand against a servant of darkness on the throne repelled him even more.

The boy had put on a bold charade, but blood would always run true, in the end. For the sake of every soul in Gwynedd, the Deryni heresy must be stamped out—and Edmund Loris would use whatever means he must to accomplish that end.

# CHAPTER ONE

*He made him a lord of his house, and*
*ruler of all his substance: to bind his*
*princes at his pleasure.*

—Psalms 105:21-22

The Bishop of Meara was dead. In more stable times, that fact might have elicited little more than academic interest on the part of Duke Alaric Morgan, for his duchy of Corwyn lay far on the other side of Gwynedd, well beyond the reach of any Mearan prelate's influence. Bishops there were whose passing would have meant a personal loss to Morgan, but Carsten of Meara was not one of them.

This is not to say that Morgan had regarded Carsten as an enemy. On the contrary, even though the old bishop had been of a very different generation, bred in an age when fear of magic had made far greater men rabid in their intolerance of such as Corwyn's Deryni duke, Carsten had never succumbed to the open hostility displayed by some. When, on the premature accession of Kelson Haldane to the throne of Gwynedd, it had become increasingly clear that the young king was somehow heir to magical abilities which the Church had come to condemn as heretical over the years—powers that Kelson intended to use for the protection of his kingdom—Carsten had retired quietly to his episcopal holdings in Meara, rather than choose between his fanatically anti-Deryni archbishop and his more moderate brethren who supported the king despite the questionable status of his Deryni soul. The king's party had eventually prevailed, and the deposed Archbishop Loris languished even now in the secure Abbey of Saint Iveagh, high in the sea cliffs north of Carbury. Morgan himself thought the sentence far too lenient to balance the harm Loris had done human-Deryni relations by his venom, but it had been the recommendation of Loris' successor, the scholarly Bradene of Grecotha, and was actively supported by the majority of Gwynedd's other bishops.

No such majority prevailed in the consistory Morgan now watched in the chamber below, assembled in Culdi to elect old Carsten's successor. The unexpected vacancy in the See of Meara had touched off old, old controversies regarding its tenure. Mearan separatists had been agitating for a Mearan-born prelate for as long as Morgan could remember, and had been agitating in vain through the reigns of at least three Haldane kings. This was the first time that young Kelson had had to face the ongoing argument, but with the king less than a fortnight past his seventeenth birthday, it was not likely to be the last. Even now, he was addressing the assembled bishops in the chamber below, outlining the factors he wished them to consider in weighing the many candidates.

Suppressing a cough, Morgan shifted forward on the hard stone seat in the listening gallery and eased aside the heavy curtain to peer down. He could see only Kelson's back from this angle, stiff and formal in a long scarlet court robe, but Conall, Prince Nigel's eldest son and second in line to the throne after his father, was visible in profile to Kelson's right, looking very bored. The bishops themselves seemed attentive enough, but many of those watching from the tiered benches along the walls wore stormy faces. Morgan could identify several of the principal aspirants to the vacant Mearan See.

"We wish, therefore, to reassure you that the Crown will not interfere unduly in your election, my lords," the king was saying, "but we enjoin you to consider well the candidates who shall come under your examination in the coming days. The name of the individual eventually chosen matters little to us, personally, but the peace of Meara matters a great deal. That is why we have spent this past season progressing through our Mearan lands. We recognize that a bishop's principal function is to provide spiritual guidance—yet we would be naive in the extreme if we did not also acknowledge the temporal power wielded by the incumbent of any such office. All of you are well aware of the weight your opinions carry in our own secular deliberations."

He went on, but Morgan released the curtain with a bored sigh and folded his arms along the railing, allowing his attention to drift as he laid his head on his crossed forearms and closed his eyes.

They had gone over all of this before. Morgan had not been along on the royal progress, having business of his own in Corwyn, but he joined the king as soon as word arrived of old Carsten's death. His first night back in the royal entourage, Archbishop Cardiel had briefed him on the political ramifications and acceptable successors, while Kelson listened and Duncan occasionally added his own observations. Duncan was down there now at Cardiel's side, poised and attentive in his clerical black—at thirty-one, young even to be serving as a bishop's secretary, much less an incipient bishop himself, though he had shown sufficient promise even a full five years ago to be appointed the then-Prince Kelson's chaplain and given the rank of Monsignor.

Not that Duncan would be Carsten's successor—though many might have feared that, had they known of his impending change of status. Fortunately, most did not. The bishops knew, of course. Cardiel had determined to make Duncan his assistant even before Carsten's death, and had spearheaded his election as one of the first items of business when the convocation convened a few days earlier.

But partially because Duncan's secular status already presented complications in the deliberations ahead, and partially because he wished to delay his formal consecration until the following Easter, no public announcement had yet been made. Duncan's very presence at the convocation, ostensibly as secretary for the proceedings, had been enough to raise eyebrows among the Mearan clergy and lay observers in attendance.

Nor did Mearan uneasiness spring from the fact that Duncan, like Morgan, was Deryni—though the Deryni question had certainly presented problems of its own in the beginning, and doubtless would continue to be a factor of varying importance. For nearly two centuries, no known Deryni had been permitted ordination to the priesthood. Discovery that *Duncan* was Deryni and *had* been so ordained had sparked a panicked flurry of ecclesiastical speculation as to how many *other* Deryni might have served in the clergy secretly, to the possible detriment of un-countable human souls to whom they might have ministered—and how many might be serving now? No one knew how virulent the infection might be, if Deryni consorted unbeknownst with decent Christian folk. The very thought had sent men like Edmund Loris into near-apoplectic fits on more than one occasion.

Fortunately, cooler logic than Loris' had eventually prevailed. Under the physical protection of a part-Deryni king, both Duncan and Morgan had managed to convince a majority of the ecclesiastical hierarchy that *they*, at least, did not fit the image of evil for so long attributed to Deryni—for surely evil men would not have put them-selves so thoroughly at risk to save their king and kingdom from another of their race.

But while Morgan could quickly return to a status not unlike that which he had enjoyed before the death of Brion—known and sometimes feared for what he was, but nonetheless grudgingly respected, if only for the threat of what he might do if provoked—Duncan's situation required more delicate handling. Once he and Morgan had made peace with the bishops, the Deryni priest had spent many agonizing weeks reconciling his own conscience on the matter of having accepted ordination to the priesthood when he knew it was forbidden to Deryni. He had re-sumed his priestly function only after Kelson's victory at Llyndruth Meadows.

In Duncan's favor, at least, was the fact that few out-side the confines of consistory and court definitely *knew*

he was Deryni; and whatever rumor and innuendo might
be whispered beyond that circle of intimates, scrupulous
avoidance of any public display of magic had enabled
Duncan not to confirm anything. He was not known to
*be* Deryni by most; he was only known to *consort* with
them—Morgan and the king, in particular. Arilan, now
the Bishop of Dhassa, was Deryni too; but among the
bishops only Cardiel knew that—as did a meager handful
outside the episcopal ranks—for neither Arilan nor Duncan
had had to reveal their powers against Wencit at the Llyndruth Meadows confrontation two years before. Morgan
did not fully trust Arilan, but he was sure he and Cardiel
were largely responsible for Duncan's cautious acceptance among the clergy. Certainly, Duncan could not have
been elected bishop without their support.

What gave the Mearans cause to distrust Duncan, then,
had almost entirely to do with Duncan's secular status;
for following his father's death without other heir, Duncan
had assumed the ducal and county titles of Cassan and
Kierney—titles which had once belonged to Old Meara.
To Mearan separatists, working to establish a powerbase
for a Mearan restoration, a Cassani duke loyal to the
crown of Gwynedd was merely a political annoyance
across the northern border, to be worked around and
watched, as Duncan's father had been watched for years;
but if that duke was also a high-ranking priest, and Meara's
only bishopric fell suddenly vacant, matters instantly
became more complicated. A Cassani royalist duke who
*also* became Bishop of Meara would wield both spiritual
and temporal authority over *two* vast areas.

Indeed, Duncan's election to *any* bishopric would be
viewed with suspicion in Meara; for even if he himself
had no aspirations in that direction, his politically moti-
vated wishes could carry great weight in the selection of
the man who *was* chosen to occupy the Mearan See.
Monsignor The Duke of Cassan represented a threat, then,
for all that he seemed to be an innocuous-looking priest-
secretary seated quietly beside the Archbishop of Rhemuth.

Smothering another cough, Morgan glanced down at

the consistory chamber again—Kelson was winding up his speech—then allowed his gaze to drift lazily over his own form, reflecting on the effort which had gone into making *his* image less threatening in the past two years. Gone was the somber black attire which a younger, more arrogant Morgan had affected in those days as Brion's shadow and confidant. Cardiel had told him quite frankly that such affectations only tended to reinforce the sinister notions most people still entertained about Deryni.

"Why dress as the Adversary?" Cardiel demanded. "You've shown amply by your actions that you're a servant of Light, not Darkness. Why, with your pale hair and fair features, you could have come off my chapel ceiling: one of the Lord's messengers—maybe even blessed Michael himself!"

And Lord Rathold, his wardrober at Coroth, had badgered him no less mercilessly about his ducal image.

"You *must* think of your people, Your Grace!" Rathold had said stubbornly. "You dress like a common soldier, when you have your way. No one wishes to think he serves an impoverished master—or to have others think it! 'Tis a matter of pride!"

And so, unless there was a need for stealth, the sable leathers had been put aside and replaced with color: a deep burgundy cloak at first, as a self-conscious concession to his rank as King's Champion—he could not bring himself to adopt the crimson Kelson favored—but worn over muted, conservative grey, with little embellishment. Deep blues followed, and eventually greens and golds and even particolors—the rich jewel-tones rather than bright shades. Eventually, he even learned to like them.

His body squire had chosen verdant hues for him today: a blue-green cloak collared and lined in silver fox drawn over a nubby wool robe in a slightly lighter shade, ankle-length and slit front and rear for riding. The borders and cuffs were stiff with dozens of his Corwyn gryphons worked in gold bullion, the throat clasped with a silver penannular brooch which had been his mother's.

He still wore a mail shirt beneath his finery, as he always had: fine, supple chain which would turn aside all but the most direct dagger thrust. But where once the metal would have gleamed openly at wrists and throat, boldly belligerent and just a little to ready for trouble, now it was hidden beneath an undertunic of rich, slubbed silk, with soft wool between the chain and his skin. The scabbard of the sword at his left hip was mounted with silver-set Cassani cairngorms the size of a man's thumbnail—Duncan's birthday gift to him two months before: civilized splendor, even if the blade the scabbard sheathed was as serviceable as ever.

A shorter blade was thrust into his right boot-top, the hilt never far from his gloved hand, and he still carried a narrow stiletto in a wrist-sheathed strapped along his left forearm, underneath the mail. Around his neck he wore the gilded captain-general's chain Kelson had given him at last year's Christmas Court, each link engraved with Haldane lions and Corwyn gryphons chasing one another's tails. The old Morgan would not have understood the joke.

He sighed and shifted, and the sound of the chain chiming against the stone railing brought him back to awareness of his surroundings. Kelson's voice in the chamber below had been replaced by another while Morgan daydreamed, and a quick glance between the curtains confirmed that the speaker was Archbishop Bradene. Seconds before the door latch lifted, Morgan sensed the king approaching even as he quested outward with his mind. He was already rising to incline his head in a slight bow as Kelson stepped inside.

"Well, no sense trying to take you by surprise," the boy remarked with a rueful smile. "You always seem to know it is I. How did I do?"

Morgan shrugged and returned the smile.

"The part that I heard was fine, my prince. I must confess that my attention wandered, toward the end. We went over this so many times in Droghera."

"I know. I nearly bored myself as well." Kelson flashed a more wistful grin as he drifted over to peer through the curtains as Morgan had done. "Still, it had to be said."

"Aye."

As the king stood there poised and listening, Morgan was reminded once again how much had changed in the past three years. Kelson had grown more than a handspan since that day Morgan had come to help a grief-stricken boy of fourteen keep his throne. The boy was a man now—still not as tall as Morgan, but already taller than his father had been, if more slightly built. In other ways than size, he would also be a bigger man than Brion. Already he knew more of his magical heritage than Brion ever had, and more of the ways of people.

The eyes were the same, though—the grey Haldane eyes that could pierce all subterfuge and read a man's soul, even if the vigor of merely human potential were not enhanced by Haldane magic. The silky black hair was Brion's, too, though Kelson wore it far longer of late than his father ever had—short across his forehead, but almost brushing his shoulders on the sides. A golden circlet chased with an interlace design bound the long part off his face, but the back was rumpled where it had caught the high-standing collar of his formal court robe. Kelson raked the fingers of one hand through the snarls and glanced aside at Morgan with a mischievous grin as he let the curtains fall back into place.

"I've a mind to do something that I know will vex you," he said, beginning to shrug out of his heavy outer robe. "Would you be terribly cross if I went off and left you here for a few days to supervise the bishops?"

Adopting the bland expression as well as the stance of a valet, Morgan caught Kelson's robe before it could slip to the floor and laid it aside, gathering up the fur-lined cloak of scarlet that the king had worn earlier in the day.

"I shan't deny that listening to a pack of bishops argue is among my least favorite occupations—or that I should prefer you didn't go too far afield, this close to Meara," he said neutrally. "On the other hand, you generally have good reasons for the things you want to do. Where, specifically, did you plan to go?"

Still grinning, the king took off his circlet long enough to rub his forehead where the band had pressed, before turning to back into the cloak Morgan extended. In the process, one long strand of hair caught on the wire of the great ruby winking in his right earlobe, and he tossed his head to free it as he settled the circlet back on his head.

"Why, Morgan, you're beginning to sound like a true courtier," he said, adjusting the cloak on his shoulders and snapping the clasp as Morgan freed his hair from the sable collar. "I need to go to Trurill, though. I'd planned to include it in my progress this summer, but Carsten's death interrupted that, as you know. It occurs to me that this might be my last chance to poke about before the rains start."

"Why Trurill, in particular?" Morgan asked. "Do you have reason to suspect trouble there?"

"No. But if Meara should go more sour than it already has, I'd like to be certain of my border barons. Brice of Trurill *says* he's loyal—*all* of them do, when I'm nearby and they're this far from Rhemuth—but in another few weeks, he'll be beyond my reach until the spring."

Morgan grimaced, personal distaste for the job Kelson was leaving him giving way to very real concern for the royal safety.

"Are you sure this isn't just an excuse to get out of an onerous job?" he murmured. "I hasten to remind you that the troops we brought from Rhemuth are not accustomed to the ways of the bordermen. Up here, they fight an entirely different kind of skirmish. If Brice *isn't* loyal—"

"If he *isn't* loyal, then I need to know," Kelson interrupted. "I'm taking Duncan's Jodrell as guide. He's familiar with the area." He paused to grin. "And of *course* it's an excuse to get out of an onerous job. You don't think I'd be fool enough to go into the borderlands without you if I really thought Brice was vacillating, do you? You taught me better than that."

"I should like to think so," Morgan returned, little reassured. "I just hope you're as good a judge of character as you think you are. I've met this Brice. He's a tricky devil."

"Tricky enough to lie to me and get away with it?"

"Probably not. But he might not tell all the truth, either.

Half-truths can sometimes be more dangerous than outright lies—and Truth-Reading isn't much defense against that."

Kelson shrugged. "That's true. But I fancy I know enough to ask the right questions."

Morgan said nothing, but he was thinking that sometimes Kelson did now know quite as much as he thought he did. The boy was more experienced than many other young men of far more years, and mature for his age, God knew—he could not have survived the past three years if he were not—but he sometimes tended to take his newly gained maturity for granted and to over-estimate what could be done. Age and further experience would compensate for that in time, but meanwhile, the king sometimes gave Morgan the odd, anxious moment.

Still, Morgan supposed that Kelson could not get into too much trouble this close to Culdi, and with the local barons aware that the king's champion was not far away and expecting a prompt return. In all ages, fledglings must be permitted to try their wings—even if the trying sometimes turned their mentors prematurely grey. Morgan was suddenly grateful that his hair was already light, so Kelson would never know the extent of the anxiety he caused.

"You aren't really worried, are you?" Kelson asked after a few seconds, when Morgan did not speak, apparently sensing the other's reservations. "Nothing is going to happen. Ewan is dying to get away to the mountains for a few days—I think he dislikes being cooped up at court even more than you do—and I thought I'd take Conall along, as well. Maybe a little patrol work will teach him patience. It's a courtesy call, Alaric—that's all. I want to see how Brice operates when he isn't expecting me to see."

"Do as you wish, then," Morgan muttered. "You will, anyway. I don't know why I bother worrying."

Kelson grinned, a boyish quirk of a smile which was quite at odds with his regal attire and bearing.

"I think you do. *I* do, if you don't. And the day you stop worrying is the day I'll start." He touched Morgan lightly on the shoulder.

"Just keep our wayward bishops in line for me, Alaric. I'll be back in a few days."

By the following afternoon, Kelson was beginning to wonder whether he had truly gotten the better end of the bargain. He had expected the weather to hold for at least another week; but as he and his warband rode west along the river toward Trurill—a full two dozen knights and men-at-arms, in addition to squires and servants—the air grew increasingly still and oppressive. An annoying drizzle set in just before noon, dampening dispositions as well as armor and equipment. Conall, riding beside his royal cousin, spent nearly all of their brief meal-break complaining about the weather, but at least the more important grumbling of the men was mostly good-natured. The road was still good, the rain only settling the dust as they resumed travel. At midafternoon they entered an area of sparse forest, where the drizzle subsided to a less irritating drip as it filtered through the trees.

They heard the sound of fighting long before they came upon it. The shrill whinnies of horses in distress warned them first, setting their own blooded warhorses to prancing and snorting with anticipation. As shouts and the clash of steel began to reach them, Duke Ewan signalled a halt and sent two advance riders spurring on ahead to investigate. Kelson, who had been chatting with several of his younger knights halfway back along the column, eased his mount forward at once, tugging distractedly at a gauntlet cuff.

"Jodrell, were you expecting any activity along here?" the king called softly, as he drew rein beside their guide.

The young Kierney baron only shook his head, still poised in a listening attitude. When the outriders did not return within a few minutes, Kelson silently signalled Saer de Traherne to begin stripping the waterproof cover off the Haldane battle standard.

"What are we waiting for, Ewan?" Conall fretted, standing in his stirrups to peer ahead into the forest gloom. "If there's trouble, we should try to stop it!"

Old Ewan, sitting his horse ahead of the two Haldanes

and at right angles to them, squeezed his eyes to calculating slits as he glanced in their direction, armored hand
already fingering his sword hilt. His bushy red beard protruded beneath his helmet quite without discipline of razor
or scissors.

"*Their* trouble, not ours, Your Highness—unless, of
course, we insist upon charging into things without knowing what we're about. Hush ye, now, so I can listen."

Still the silence was broken only by the continuing
sounds of the distant fighting and the closer noises of the
Haldane great-horses held in check, bits and chains jingling, leather creaking, mail clinking softly as the knights
strained to hear. Kelson surveyed the two dozen mounted
knights settling helmets on heads and taking up shields
behind him, then shifted his attention back to Ewan.

"What do you think?" he whispered.

Ewan slowly shook his head. "I dinnae know yet, Sire.
We're on the edge of Trurill holdings, eh, Jodrell? That
means that Trurill levies are likely on one side of whatever's dusting up."

The border baron nodded. "Aye, Your Grace—though
it's God's good guess who's on the other side. I'd wait
for Macaire and Robard, if I were you, Sire."

"I fully intend to."

"But, can't we—" Conall began.

"No, we can't," Kelson murmured, giving Conall a
warning look as he twisted to take the shield that his squire
had brought forward. "Jodrell, check the men, please."

Conall started to object again as Jodrell reined his horse
out of line and headed quietly back along the column, but
another sharp look from Kelson silenced him. The prince,
only a few months younger than Kelson, had been along
on the Cardosa campaign two summers before, but he still
had much to learn about strategy and the art of command.
It was a common failing, and not entirely Conall's fault,
for though Gwynedd common law declared fourteen to
be the legal age of manhood, in fact few boys were actually
called upon to function as adults for several more years.

Chivalric custom recognized this, even if the law did
not, denying the knightly accolade to those under eighteen

except on rare occasions. Even Kelson, who could have made himself such an exception as king, had declined to be knighted until his eighteenth birthday. If Conall gained sufficient experience in the coming year, his knighting *might* be moved forward a few months to coincide with Kelson's; but meanwhile, he remained in the subordinate rank of squire, royal though he was.

That was little comfort to Kelson just now, weighing Conall's inexperience against the possible dangers of the coming skirmish. He could not help remembering Morgan's warning about the difference of fighting styles and wondered whether the Deryni lord could have known he was foretelling the future. Border fighting favored quick, lightly mounted and armed raiding bands, not the heavier horses and armor to which Conall was accustomed and with which the warband was equipped. Should the terrain ahead boast closer maneuvering room than what lay immediately around them, the inexperienced among Kelson's company might find themselves at the disadvantage despite their numbers and superior armor.

Still, Kelson supposed he could let his untried cousin at least *think* he was performing an important function, while still keeping him relatively safe and under watchful eyes. As he adjusted the angle of his helm and secured the chin strap, he cast a stern glance at the impatient Conall, then relented and nodded to Traherne. Immediately, Conall was kneeing his charger between the two of them and reaching out for the royal standard, tight-jawed but triumphant as his gloved hand locked around the polished staff.

"No heroics, now," Kelson warned.

"Don't worry."

The crimson of the banner's field seemed almost subdued against the deep green of the surrounding forest, but the golden Haldane lion shimmered like a living thing as Conall gave the silk a shake and set the butt of the staff in his stirrup rest. The prince's grin was infectious, and Ewan and Traherne as well as Kelson found themselves smiling in response as muffled hoofbeats approached. Kelson cast about for hidden dangers as a returning scout burst through the trees and reined his horse to a sliding halt, but he sensed nothing other than the body of men ahead.

"Liveried men-at-arms, Sire—lightly mounted, against what appears to be a band of brigands," the man reported. "Maybe twenty on a side, but none of them are particularly well armored."

"Whose livery?" Kelson demanded.

"Trurill, Sire. Two swords in saltire over a third in pale, all on a blue field."

Kelson glanced at Ewan, who nodded confirmation.

"Those'll be Brice's lads, right enough. Do we have maneuvering room, son?"

"At least as good as here, Your Grace. Part of the area is an open glade. Robard has stayed to watch they don't shift while we're planning."

"Well done." Kelson drew his sword and glanced back at his waiting men. "Very well, gentlemen, I think it's time to show ourselves. If we can manage without bloodshed, so much the better. Traherne, I want you on Conall's other side. Jodrell, you ride on my right. Ewan, deploy the men."

With an economy of silent hand signals, Ewan gave the necessary orders. As ever, Kelson was impressed with the efficiency and polish which came with more than thirty years' experience as a field commander. The jingle of harness and the wet, sucking sound of the horses' hooves on the moss-covered forest floor temporarily covered the battle sounds as the knights peeled off to either side and fanned out in perfect parade ground formation, Ewan and one of the senior knights each taking a wing. Kelson urged his bay forward at the trot, sword at the ready, he and his escort marking the center of a deepening crescent intended to engulf attackers and defenders alike. Ahead, through the trees, he began to see the signs of battle.

"Yield, in the king's name!" he heard Ewan cry, as the royal knights burst upon the skirmish. "Hold, in the name of Kelson of Gwynedd!"

# CHAPTER TWO

*They all hold swords, being expert in war:*
*every man hath his sword upon his thigh.*
                                    —Song of Solomon 3:8

Kelson's first impression, as he and his warband burst
into the clearing, was one of brawl rather than battle.
Though most of the Trurill men were armed with swords
or the short horse-spears favored by bordermen, their
opponents seemed limited to cudgels, quarterstaffs, and
the occasional dirk. Nor did the Trurill men appear inclined
to overpress their advantage. Even as the Haldane ring
tightened, Kelson saw a Trurill retainer grab his opponent's plaid and yank him off his pony, cracking him across
the back of the head with the pommel of his sword when
he just as easily could have killed him. Several of both
sides lay unmoving or groaning feebly on the ground, but
few seemed seriously injured.

Trurill livery and leathers swirled and surged chaoti-
cally around Border tartans strange and familiar, loose
ponies and an occasional terrified highland sheep creating
additional hazards for the few men who continued to fight
from the ground. The ponies' whinnying and the frantic
bleating of the sheep made vocal counterpart to the grunts
and exclamations of the struggling men.

The confrontation was quickly over. With shouts of
"*A Haldane!*" the royal knights closed, shouldering their
greathorses deftly between the smaller, lighter border
mounts to break up individual skirmishes, flat-blading
recalcitrants who tried to keep on fighting, and sometimes
bowling over horses and surprised riders of both sides.

Kelson and the rest of the royal party held back as a reserve, but their help was never necessary. The closest Kelson came to action was the startled leap his horse made when one of the sheep suddenly bolted between its front legs.

Soon the brigands began dropping their weapons and raising their arms in surrender. With a shout, the Trurill men rallied to surround them. As Kelson's warband pulled back to sit their horses quietly at the perimeter of the clearing, still encircling captors as well as prisoners, the Trurill men began ordering the prisoners to dismount and to bind them, a few starting to see to the injured. Ewan, scanning his own command for injuries and seeing none, kneed his charger to Kelson's side and saluted with upraised gauntlet.

"Well, that was a pleasant enough romp, Sire," he said in a low voice, nodding toward the borderers. "You there— Trurill Sergeant!" he called in a louder voice. "Attend us at once!"

At his command, one of the older, better armored Trurill men glanced back at him, then broke away from the rest of his band and rode slowly toward the royal party, eying the Haldane standard with something akin to suspicion. He gave perfunctory salute with his sword as he reined in before them, glancing first at Kelson and Conall, then at Ewan.

"You are well come, sir," the man said, sheathing his sword. "By your plaid, I make you a highland man. Would you be The Claibourne, then?"

But before Ewan could reply, the man glanced less certainly between Kelson and Conall once again. "And you, my lords—I thank you for your assistance. We see few Haldanes this far west."

*And doubtless wish to see fewer still,* Kelson thought sourly, as he also sheathed his sword and removed his helmet.

He supposed he should not be annoyed that the man did not recognize him. Other than his own brief foray into Culdi two years before for the ill-fated wedding of Kevin McLain and Morgan's sister Bronwyn, Kelson doubted any other Haldane had penetrated this deep into the western borderlands for several years before his father's death. His progress of the summer just past had been confined primarily to Meara itself, and the flatlands of Kierney and Cassan. And even were bordermen not notorious for their indifference to lowland titles of nobility, how could a mere border sergeant be expected to know his king by sight?

"I am Kelson," he said patiently, pushing back a sweat-stained arming cap from damp black hair and handing off his helmet to a waiting squire. "It appears that the presence of this particular Haldane was rather timely. You are—?"

The man dipped his head in dutiful if chilly respect.

"Gendon, my Lord King, in service to the Baron of Trurill."

Kelson favored the man with the same sort of cool, impersonal nod which he himself had received, then scooped damp tendrils of hair from his face with the back of one mailed gauntlet as he glanced over the prisoners being secured by Gendon's men. How to unbend the man?

"Gendon, eh?" he said neutrally. "Tell me, Master Gendon, what brought about this little set-to? Actually, I'm not sure you needed our help at all. They weren't very well armed."

"They're outlaws, my lord," came the surprised reply, as if that explained everything. "They raid across the borders for livestock—sometimes even women and children."

"Oh?"

"Well, we try to stop it, of course, my lord," the man went on a little defensively. "The baron posts a regular patrol, as is his duty, but a man can slip off into these hills with half a dozen sheep and never be seen again. The young Laird MacArdry says this particular lot have been plaguing Transha as well."

"The young laird—you mean Dhugal, the chief's son?" Kelson asked, his more personal interest suddenly piqued.

Gendon raised one eyebrow in surprise. "You know young Dhugal, my lord?"

"You might say that," Kelson replied with a grin. "I don't suppose you've seen him lately?"

"Lately? Aye, my lord. Every blessed day."

But as Gendon gestured toward his men and twisted in his saddle to look, clearly taken aback at this lowland king's apparent recognition of highland relationships, Kelson had already spotted the object of his inquiry: a slight, ramrod-straight rider wrapped in a grey, black, and yellow plaid which only partially hid the russet leather of a neat Connaiti brigandine. He was talking to a Trurill man balancing on one leg beside his horse, gesturing for someone else to come and assist the man. A mail coif partially obscured the hair which would have made a beacon of his presence out of war harness, but the shaggy brown-and-white spotted border horse he rode was well known to Kelson, though its markings were common enough not to be remarked during the heat of battle— doubtless the reason Kelson had not noticed them earlier.

The MacArdry heir became aware of the royal scrutiny at about the same moment Kelson first saw him. One look at the riders sitting beneath the royal standard was enough to make him break away and urge his mount into a trot toward the king, grinning hugely.

"Dhugal MacArdry, what the devil is *that*?" Kelson shouted, pointing a gauntleted finger at the other's steed and grinning almost as widely as he. "Surely, 'tis no *horse* that looks so strange!"

The young MacArdry drew rein and almost flung himself from the saddle, pushing his coif back from bright copper-bronze hair as he thumped to both knees before the king's horse.

"Why, 'tis the beast who threw Your Grace the first half-dozen times you tried to ride her!" Dhugal replied. His sword hung from a baldric over his left shoulder, rigged to be drawn from the left, but he half-drew it with his right hand and offered the pommel in salute, face glowing with pride.

"Welcome to the borders—my King! It's been too many years."

"Aye, and I shall trounce you for a knave if you don't

get off your knees at once!" Kelson said happily, signalling the other to rise. "I was your brother before I was your king. Conall, look how he's grown! Ewan, you remember my foster-brother, don't you?"

"Aye, Sire—and the mischief with which both of you used to terrorize my pages' school! 'Tis good to see you, Master Dhugal."

"And you, Your Grace."

As Dhugal let his sword slip back into its scabbard and stood, and Kelson jumped down from his tall R'Kassan stallion, Conall also nodded in tight-lipped response to Dhugal's slight bow in his direction; the two had been rivals in those earlier days. Though nearly as tall as Kelson, the young border lord looked hardly older than when he had left court four years before, a sprinkling of freckles across his nose and cheeks only adding to the childlike first impression. Large, square front teeth flashed bright white as his face creased in a pleased, open grin, the smudge of reddish mustache across his upper lip hardly more than adolescent down. But the eyes which met Kelson's were no longer those of a child.

The two young men embraced exuberantly, thumping each other on the back and then drawing apart to study the other more soberly. Kelson did not resist as Dhugal took his hand and pressed fervent lips to the back of the gauntlet in homage before looking back at him.

"How *are* you, Dhugal?" he murmured.

"I am well, my prince, now that you are here," Dhugal replied softly, in the cultured court accents he had learned so many years before. "We have heard stories here in the west, of course, but—" He shrugged and grinned broadly. "Well, frankly, I did not think to see Your Grace in person until the day I came to claim my earldom. The borders and highlands have never been a favorite haunt of Haldane kings."

"The borders are loved by *this* Haldane," Kelson said, flashing with fond remembrance on the image of Dhugal's elderly father, who had fostered Dhugal to court when he was seven and Kelson nine. "And praise God it did not take your father's death to bring us back together after all. How *is* old Caulay?"

"He does as well as one might hope," Dhugal replied, a trifle more subdued. "He's not travelled since your coronation, though. I've spent the past three years standing in for him, learning a proper border soldier's trade. I—don't suppose my apprenticeship can last much longer now."

"His illness is worse, then. Dhugal, I'm sorry," Kelson murmured. But before he could continue, Gendon, the Trurill sergeant, cleared his throat.

"Your pardon, Lord King, but young MacArdry does have duties. Dhugal, there are wounded."

"Aye, Sergeant, I'll see to them directly." Dhugal gave Kelson a short bow of apology. "By your leave, Sire."

"Of course. My men will assist."

Most of the injuries were slight—the minor cuts and bruises expected of any rough and tumble altercation—but a few of the men, Trurill and prisoners alike, sported more serious wounds. One man was dead, despite the apparent restraint shown by all. Kelson detailed his battle surgeon and the squires to work with the bordermen and, when it became clear that Gendon did not intend to return to Trurill that night, gave orders for camp to be made. Conall he assigned to Ewan's supervision, to observe how the old duke integrated his command with Gendon's.

Kelson himself wandered in the forming Trurill camp with only Jodrell for escort, saying little but watching everything with interest. Recalling Dhugal's comment about the "stories" which had come westward in the past three years, he wondered what preconceptions these highland men might have about him as a result. In the eyes of men such as these, that Kelson was a Haldane was reason enough to suspect him. What further suspicion might have been generated by tales of his magic?

But when he tried chatting with a few of them, he sensed that their reticence had as much to do with his lowland origins as with his rank or any vague uneasiness they might have because he was part Deryni. They were respectful enough, in their rough, border way, but they offered no more than was asked for, never volunteering information.

The prisoners volunteered no information either, though that was hardly surprising. Nor was the information which *was* extracted, sometimes forcefully, of anything but local interest. Kelson Truth-Read a few of them while others asked the questions, but there seemed no point in flaunting his Deryni abilities when the interrogators were getting exactly the same answers he was. The distance between these men and himself had little to do with magic, but the loneliness was just as real. Eventually he found himself watching Dhugal from behind and signalled Jodrell not to speak.

Dhugal was kneeling beside the most seriously wounded of his own men, Kelson's squire Jatham assisting him, unaware of the royal scrutiny. His plaid lay discarded in a heap beside him, sword and baldric atop it, and Kelson could see that he had unbuckled the front of his brigandine for greater ease of movement as he bent to his surgeoning duties.

Dhugal's patient was a sturdy mountain lad hardly older than himself but half again as large, sporting a gash from wrist to elbow which would probably render him useless as a swordsman in the future, if he even kept the arm. His other brawny arm was pressed across his eyes, the bearded face beneath it drained of color. As the squire poured water over the wound and Dhugal loosened the tourniquet above it just slightly, bright blood pumped from deep within. Even from where he stood, Kelson could see that the cut had severed deep muscles and probably arteries.

"Damn!" Dhugal muttered under his breath, tightening the tourniquet again and muttering an apology as his patient sucked in breath between his teeth in pain. Neither he, his assistant, nor his patient seemed to notice Kelson's presence as he picked up a needle trailing a length of gut threat.

"Ye must nae move now, Bertie, if we're tae save yer arm," Dhugal said, his earlier court accents blurred with the lilt of the highlands now, as he positioned the bloody arm to his liking and shifted Jatham's grip. "Hold him steady as ye can, lad."

As Bertie braced himself and young Jatham clamped down at wrist and bicep, Kelson touched the squire's shoulder and nodded as he looked up, startled. Dhugal, too, blinked as he suddenly became aware of Kelson's presence.

"Why don't you let me take over here, Jatham?" he said to the boy, smiling and signalling him to move aside. "He's a little big for you to hold. Go with Baron Jodrell."

As Jodrell and the boy withdrew, Kelson dropped to his knees across from Dhugal and rinsed his hands in the basin of clean water near the patient's head, permitting himself a little smile as Dhugal stared at him in amazement.

"I was beginning to feel useless," Kelson explained. "Besides, it looked as if young Bertie, here, nearly outweighted you both. Hello, Bertie," he added, as their patient uncovered his eyes to squint at him suspiciously.

"Well, then," Dhugal grinned, the lilt of the highlands muted to only a slight blurr as he shifted to court dialect. "Last I heard, you weren't a battle surgeon."

"Last I heard, neither were you," Kelson countered. "I suspect we've both learned some things in the past few years. What would you like me to do?"

Dhugal made a grim attempt at a chuckle. "Hold his arm steady, then—just there," he said, repositioning the arm and guiding Kelson's hands into place as his patient continued to stare.

"Unfortunately," Dhugal went on, "battle surgeoning isn't one of the things I've had time to learn as well as I'd like—more's the pity for friend Bertie, here. Just because I've made something of a reputation patching up horses, he's convinced I can put *him* back together, aren't ye, Bertie?" he added, lapsing into border dialect again for just a few words.

"Ach, just watch who yer comparin' to a horse, young MacArdry," Bertie replied good-naturedly, though he hissed through his teeth and then tried to curl up on his side in reflex as Dhugal probed in the wound.

Moving nimbly, Dhugal helped Kelson immobilize the arm and again attempted to place his first suture, shifting from court speech to border dialect and back again with ease, though his face reflected the strain of the other.

"Bertie MacArdry, ye may be as *strong* as a horse, in smell if not in muscle," he ranted, "but if ye wish sommat besides a sleeve-filler, ye *must* lie still! Kelson, you've got to keep his arm from moving, or it's little use. I can't control his bleeding if he thrashes around."

Kelson did his best, slipping easily into the old cama-raderie he and Dhugal had enjoyed so long ago, as boys, and which remained so comfortable now that they were men. But as Dhugal continued to probe, and Bertie gasped and tensed again, Kelson glanced over his shoulder and, in a moment of sudden decision, shifted the back of one bloodied hand to the man's forehead, reaching out with his Deryni senses.

"Sleep, Bertie," he whispered, slipping his wrist down over the man's eyes and feeling the tense body go limp. "Go to sleep and remember nothing of this when you wake. No pain. Just sleep."

Dhugal's hand faltered and paused in midstitch as he sensed the change come over his patient, but when he looked across at Kelson there was only wonder—not the fear the king had come so often to expect in the past few years. After a few seconds, Dhugal returned to his task, working more quickly now, a faint smile playing across his lips.

"You have, indeed, learned a few things in four years, haven't you, Sire?" he asked softly, when he had tied off the last of the internal sutures and cut the gut thread close to the knot.

"You didn't use my title when we were boys, Dhugal, and I wish you wouldn't in the future, at least in private," Kelson murmured. "And I would have to say that you've learned a few things yourself."

Dhugal shrugged and began rethreading his needle with bright green silk. "You probably remember that I was always good with animals. Well, after Michael died and I had to come home from Court, one of the things they had me study was surgeoning—part of the training of a laird, they said: to be able to patch up one's animals and men."

He flushed out the partially sutured wound again, pausing when Bertie moaned and stirred a little—and Kelson had to reach out with his mind once more—then dusted the raw flesh with a bluish grey powder and had Kelson press the lips of the wound together from either side. Carefully, meticulously, he began drawing them together with neat, green silk stitches.

"Is it true that Duke Alaric healed himself at your coronation?" Dhugal asked after a moment, not looking up from his work.

Kelson raised one eyebrow, wondering why Dhugal was asking.

"Is that one of the stories that's come west?"

"And others—aye."

"Well, it's true," Kelson said, a little defensively. "Father Duncan helped him. I didn't see it happen, but I saw the result—and I *did* see him heal Duncan later on: a wound that should have killed anyone else."

"You actually *saw* this?" Dhugal asked, pausing to stare at Kelson.

Kelson shivered a little, and had to look away from the blood on his own hands to shake the memory.

"They took a terrible chance," he whispered. "We needed to convince Warin de Grey that Deryni weren't necessarily evil. Warin claims that his own healing comes from God, so Duncan decided to show him that Deryni can heal, too. He let Warin wound him in the shoulder, but it was almost too severe. I hate to think of what would have happened, if it hadn't worked."

"What do you mean, 'if it hadn't worked?'" Dhugal asked softly, his needle half-forgotten in his fingers. "I thought you said he and Morgan could heal."

"They can," Kelson replied, "only they don't really know how they do it, and the gift isn't always reliable. Maybe that's because they're only half-Deryni. From Father Duncan's research, we now believe that some Deryni were able to do such things on a regular basis during the Interregnum, but the art apparently has been lost since. Only a small percentage of Deryni had the healing gift, even then."

"But that Warin fellow can do it?"

"Yes."

"And he isn't Deryni?"

Kelson shook his head. "Not so far as we've been able to tell. He still insists his gift comes from God—and maybe it does. Maybe he's a genuine miracle-worker. Who are we to say?"

Dhugal snorted and resumed his work. "That sounds more capricious than being Deryni, if you ask me—working miracles! For myself, I think I'd gladly settle for being able to do *your* trick."

"*My* trick?"

"To knock out a patient painlessly before trying to work on him. From a battle surgeon's point of view, that's a blessing, no matter *where* the ability comes from, though I suspect ecclesiastical opinion would argue the point. No reflection on friend Bertie's courage, but if you hadn't done—whatever you did—he wouldn't have been able to hold still for me to do this. I suppose it *was* some of your . . . Deryni magic?"

Almost hypnotically, Kelson watched the bloody hands move up and down, drawing the wound closed with Dhugal's own almost magical ability, and he had to shake his head lightly to break the spell.

"I think you have your own kind of magic," he murmured, looking across at Dhugal in admiration. "And thank God you don't seem to be intimidated by mine. You have no idea what a relief it is to be able to use my powers for something like this—which is what they were intended for, in the beginning, I feel sure—and not have you be afraid."

With a smile, Dhugal tied off the last of his sutures and cut the thread, then looked up at Kelson with a keen, frank appraisal of the borderman.

"I seem to recall that we once swore a blood-oath to live as brothers all our lives," he said softly, "and to do whatever good we might. Why should I fear my brother, then, simply because he has been given the means to do greater good? I know you would never harm me—brother."

As Kelson caught his breath in surprise, Dhugal ducked his head and returned to his work, sluicing clean water over the sutures and then binding a handful of dried sphagnum moss over the wound.

That, at least, Kelson felt he understood, as he washed his hands and dried them on a corner of their patient's tunic. He was not sure he understood the other kneeling across from him, but he did not think he cared to question what had just passed between them. He had forgotten what a comfort it could be to confide in a friend of his own generation. Conall was his age, and Payne and Rory only a little younger, but that was not the same. They had not been tempered with adult responsibilities the way he and Dhugal had. Morgan and Duncan understood, of course, and perhaps his Uncle Nigel, but even they were somewhat removed by age and experience—and they were not always around. He found himself heaving a sigh of relief as Dhugal finally rinsed his hands and dried them on a blood-stained grey towel.

"That's it, then," Dhugal said, peering tentatively under one of his patient's eyelids and glancing at Kelson inquiringly. "I think I did one of my better repair jobs, but only time will tell for sure. He's still lost a lot of blood. Best if he simply sleeps through the night."

"We'll see that he does then," Kelson said, touching the sleeping man's forehead and making the necessary mental adjustments. "I'd have someone rouse him every few hours to drink some wine—Duncan says that helps to restore the lost blood faster—but otherwise, he shouldn't stir until morning."

As the two of them stood, Dhugal gathering up his sword and plaid, Kelson signalled one of his men to attend. Dhugal gave brief instructions, but then he and Kelson moved off slowly toward the edge of the camp which had formed around them while they worked. Wordlessly, Kelson took the sword and plaid while Dhugal began adjusting his armor.

The two were nearly of a height, side by side, Kelson perhaps a few fingers taller and a little heavier, though neither had yet come into their true man's growth. Before, Kelson had thought Dhugal's copper-colored hair cut short, but now, as Dhugal pulled off his mail coif and ran fingers under the neck of his brigandine in the back to free his hair, Kelson saw that it was even longer than his own, drawn to the nape of the neck in border fashion and plaited in a short braid tied with a leather thong. He took the coif as the young borderman began buckling the front closures of the brigandine, leaning against a tree to watch indulgently until Dhugal, with a roguish grin, reached out to finger a strand of Kelson's shoulder-length hair.

"So that's what comes of having no wars for the past two years," Dhugal said, dropping the lock and taking back the sword to loop its baldric over his shoulder. "Decadently long hair, like any common borderer. I wonder how you'd look in a border braid?"

"Why don't you invite me home to greet your father and sample highland hospitality, and perhaps you'll see," Kelson returned with a smile, giving him back his plaid and coif. "If I haven't already scandalized my men simply by being Deryni, then playing at being a wild border chieftain will surely turn the trick. You've changed, Dhugal."

"So have you."

"Because I've acquired—magic?"

"No, because you've acquired a crown." Dhugal lowered his eyes, fingering the leather-lined mail of the coif. "Despite what you said before, you *are* the king now."

"And does that make a difference?"

"You know it does."

"Then, let it be a positive difference," Kelson said. "You yourself admitted that with the power I've been given, both temporal and—other—I now have the power to do greater good. Perhaps some of the things that we only dreamed about when we were boys. God knows, I loved my father, and I miss him terribly, but there are things I'd have done differently, if I'd been faced with some of the things he had to face. Now I have that chance."

"And does *that* make a difference?" Dhugal asked.

Kelson shrugged. "I'm alive—and my father is dead. I've kept the peace for two years now."

"And the peace is being threatened in Meara. That's part of what this was all about, you know." Dhugal gestured around him at the resting men and the knot surrounding the prisoners across the glade. "We've always had a raiding problem in the highlands—it's part of our way of life—but some of these men, on both sides, are at least sympathetic to the Lady Caitrin's cause." He made a face. "She's my aunt, you know."

Kelson raised an eyebrow. "*Is* she?"

"Aye. My Uncle Sicard's wife. Sicard and my father haven't spoken for years, but border blood runs thick, as you know. Some wonder that we don't support them, being so far from central Gwynedd and all. I'm surprised you didn't catch some inkling of that during your progress this summer. Isn't that the sort of thing you're supposed to be able to do now, with your new powers?"

The question was not at all hostile, but it was clear that Dhugal was fishing for reassurance, as uncertain as any of his men about just what a Deryni king could and could not do.

"I'm not omnipotent, Dhugal," Kelson said quietly, looking the other in the eyes. "I can tell whether a man is lying, with very little effort—it's called Truth-Reading—but to actually learn the truth, I need to ask the right questions."

"I—thought that Deryni could read minds," Dhugal whispered. And though he did not break eye contact, Kelson needed no Deryni senses to know what courage that took, operating from ignorance as Dhugal was. That Dhugal trusted him, there was no question; but despite his earlier protestations that he was not afraid of what Kelson had become, certain fears could only be allayed by experience—and that, Dhugal did not have yet.

"We can," Kelson murmured. "But we don't, among our friends, unless we're invited. And the first time, even among Deryni, it almost requires some kind of physical contact."

"Like the way you touched Bertie's forehead?"

"Yes."

Dhugal let out an audible sigh and lowered his eyes, self-consciously wrapping his plaid around his shoulders like a mantle and fussing with a brooch to secure it. When he had adjusted it to his satisfaction, he gave Kelson a brief, bright smile.

"Well, then. I suppose we ought to see whether the others have gotten anything else out of the prisoners. You won't forget what I said about highland loyalties, will you?"

Kelson smiled. "I told you how *I* go about learning whether a man is lying. How do *you* do it?"

"Why, we highland folk have the Second Sight, don't you know?" Dhugal quipped. "Ask anyone in my father's hall about Meara, and her greedy would-be princess."

"Well, then, if it's Meara, I suppose I'd better be back there, come spring," Kelson replied. "And with men beside me who understand what's happening. Maybe even men who have this—Second Sight. Would your father let you come to court, do you think?"

"If you asked it as king, he'd have no choice."

"And what is *your* choice?" Kelson asked.

Dhugal grinned. "We were like brothers once, Kelson. We still make a good team." He glanced over his shoulder at the sleeping Bertie and back again. "What do *you* think?"

"I think," said Kelson, "that we should ride up to Transha in the morning and find out what he'll say."

# CHAPTER THREE

*And thou shalt put the mitre upon his
head...*

—Exodus 29:6

The rain which had been only an annoyance to Kelson,
in Transha, had turned to storm by the time it reached
Culdi the following afternoon. Stamping mud from the
soles of thigh-high riding boots, Morgan paused just inside
the doorway to the guest apartments at Culdi Abbey to
shake more water from his streaming leather cloak. He
and Duncan had intended to ride in the hills nearby as
soon as the afternoon session of the consistory adjourned,
but the unexpected storm had neatly stymied that plan.
Now the iron grey R'Kassan stud moping down in the
bishop's barn would have to wait another day, and perhaps longer, he and his master both growing surly and
restless from the forced inactivity. It hardly seemed fair,
especially with Kelson out enjoying himself.

Blowing on gloved fingers to warm them, Morgan
stalked on along the corridor toward Duncan's temporary
quarters and indulged a brief fantasy about a rainstorm
in Transha, too. The notion brought a smile to his lips.
None of the servants were about when he let himself into
the common room Duncan shared with his master,
Archbishop Cardiel, so he built up the fire himself and
set wine to mull, spreading his sodden cloak on a stool
to dry and shedding cap and gloves. Half an hour later,
Duncan found his friend ensconced in a deeply recessed
window seat which overlooked the cloister garth, boots
propped indolently on the stone bench opposite and a

steaming cup all but forgotten in one hand. His nose was pressed to the rain-streaked window glass, free hand shading his eyes against glare.

"I see I was right," Duncan said, casting off his black cloak and rubbing his hands briskly before the fire. "When I saw how hard it was raining, I guessed that even you wouldn't choose to ride in this kind of weather. What *are* you looking at?"

"The ambitious Father Judhael," Morgan replied, not moving from his vantage point. "Come and see."

Duncan needed no second invitation, for Judhael of Meara was probably the single most controversial candidate being evaluated by the bishops. Though unimpeachable on ecclesiastical grounds, and personable enough as an individual, his family connections inspired more suspicion than confidence among those aware of the politics which went with the Mearan See, for Judhael was nephew to the Pretender Caitrin. Just now, he was standing outside the door to the chapter house, deep in conversation with old Creoda of Carbury, Bishop of the new See of Culdi since last winter and host for this convocation. Only when the two had moved off down another corridor and disappeared from sight did Duncan draw back from the window.

"I don't like that," the priest said softly, glancing at Morgan with tight-lipped disapproval. "Old Creoda can change with the wind. You remember how he stayed by Loris almost to the end, two summers ago. When the bishops decided to phase out his old see, I thought for sure they'd retire him. Who would have guessed they'd give him Culdi instead?"

"Hmmm, I shan't argue that," Morgan agreed. "He certainly wouldn't have been *my* choice for a see so closely associated with a Deryni saint. But perhaps they thought Carsten would balance him, with Culdi being so close to Meara. I doubt anyone expected that Carsten wouldn't last out the year."

Duncan raised an eyebrow. "No? But then, no one asked me. Carsten's health had been frail for some time. Everyone in Kierney and Cassan knew that. Still, there was no real trouble in Meara while he was alive. Now that he's gone, most of the Mearan clergy are suddenly talking about Judhael for his replacement. Now, *that's* one I certainly don't fancy being appointed to the See of Meara."

"Judhael?" Morgan toyed with one of the links of his captain-general's chain, tapping the engraved gold against a front tooth as he nodded. "Nor do I. It's entirely too much like a real throne. Even by separatist standards, he's too far down the succession to press his own claim to the Mearan coronet, but as Bishop of Meara, he could certainly exert a great deal of influence for his aunt and *her* sons."

"Those sons—" Duncan snorted. "Sometimes I think we'd be better off if old Malcolm had killed off all the other Mearan heirs when he took the coronet and married Roisian. Perhaps that sounds cold and unpriestly, but it might have prevented a lot more bloodshed later on."

"Aye. And our Mearan princelings are only a little younger than Kelson: just old enough to be ambitious about asserting their mother's claim. And Judhael on a bishop's throne could be the foot in the door. The very thought gives me the shakes."

"You'll get no argument from me on *that*," Duncan replied. "The sad thing is, he's well qualified for the job. His record as a priest is spotless, and he has all the right administrative abilities to make a very good bishop."

"Or the focus for a separatist revolt," Morgan said. "Still, credentials like his will make it very difficult to ignore his candidacy. And let's face it: the man had no more say about being born into a cadet royal house than you and I did about being born Deryni."

"More's the pity."

With a sigh, Duncan turned away from the window and sat down in a high-backed chair whose shadows nearly swallowed his black cassock, stretching out his legs toward the fire. Morgan followed him, lifting mulled wine in wordless question and only refilling his own cup when Duncan shook his head. As Morgan sat in another chair beside him, Duncan rolled his head in Morgan's direction and looked at him searchingly, folding his hands and tapping joined forefingers against his cheek as he rested his elbows on the chair arms.

"I'm beginning to be really concerned, Alaric," the priest said softly. "We've interviewed a lot of candidates, but none of them match up to Judhael. Oh, some are better in one area or another, but none of them average out as well."

"What about that one they interviewed this morning?" Morgan asked. "What was his name—Father Benoit? He seemed well qualified to me."

Duncan shook his head. "A fine priest, but far too naive to cope with the Mearan situation. He's someone to keep in mind for the future, and he can be groomed for the episcopate in some subsidary post, but that doesn't help us now. No, what we need is a good compromise candidate—and I'm not sure he exists. He needs to be the king's man, but he also ought to have at least some familiarity with Mearan politics. The only men who seem to fill both requirements are either too young or too inexperienced. They can't all be like Arilan, I suppose: auxiliary bishop at thirty-five, and with his own see before he was forty."

"No, I suppose not," Morgan said. He took a thoughtful pull at his wine, then cocked his head at Duncan. "Has it occurred to you that perhaps the bishops have expanded the episcopal structure a little too quickly?—reviving three old sees and only abolishing one—that you've used up your reserve of men qualified to promote? Plus, you've lost—what?—four bishops in the past two years? Five, if you count Loris."

Duncan grimaced. "Count that a blessing, not a loss, cousin. Anyway, he's safely locked away at Saint Iveagh's, so I don't think we need to worry."

"Let's hope not. Wouldn't *that* muddy the waters, if he got out?"

"Don't even think it. They say he hasn't changed a bit, you know," Duncan went on, in a more confidential tone. "I hear he nearly had apoplexy when he heard Arilan had been made Bishop of Dhassa."

"Did he, now?"

"Oh, you needn't pretend to be surprised," Duncan replied with a droll grin. "Who, of all the so-called rebel bishops, was largely responsible for his fall, after all? And even if Loris doesn't know for *sure* that Arilan's Deryni, think about it. A suspected Deryni in one of the oldest sees in Gwynedd? It would have been bad enough if he'd only stayed the assistant in Rhemuth."

As if the mere mention of Arilan's name had conjured his presence, the door opened at that moment to admit Bishop Denis Arilan, closely followed by Cardiel. The two looked inordinately pleased with themselves as Duncan and Morgan divested them of their soggy cloaks, Cardiel shaking rain from his steel grey hair and smoothing back little wings of it over his ears with both palms as he sat in the chair which Morgan held for him. As the darker-haired Arilan also sat, leaning forward lazily to poke at the fire with a piece of kindling, Cardiel glanced at Duncan, who was setting new cups on the hearth by the pot of mulled wine.

"Duncan, a messenger's just arrived for you in the inner courtyard," he said. "A lad wearing your ducal livery. He's taken an amazing number of dispatches off a packhorse."

Grinning, Duncan turned over his hosting duties to Morgan and rose.

"Ah, well, I suppose they've found me. I was rather afraid the correspondence would catch up with me, if I stayed too long in Culdi. Will you excuse me for a moment, sir? I suppose I really ought to see what he's got."

Cardiel said nothing as he waved permission, but as Duncan left the room, Morgan was once again struck by an undercurrent of something brewing beneath the surface, another hint of the self-satisfaction he had sensed when the two first entered. He wondered about it as he handed Cardiel a steaming cup, aware, as their fingers brushed, that Cardiel was the source of most of it, but he did not even consider probing deeper with Arilan present. The Deryni bishop had a knack for knowing when he or Duncan were using their powers in ways of which he did not approve—in almost any way, it sometimes seemed. Of late, it often made Morgan ill-at-ease even to be around Arilan, though that was not the case today.

"Well, I'm glad Duncan's messenger arrived when he did," Cardiel said, as Morgan passed Arilan a second brimming cup. "We wanted to discuss something with you privately, very quickly before he comes back. What would you think of Duncan being consecrated bishop a little sooner than we'd planned?"

Morgan nearly dropped the cup he was refilling for himself.

"You're *not* thinking of making him Bishop of Meara after all, are you?"

"No, no—not of Meara," Cardiel reassured him quickly. "Just my assistant, as we'd already decided. We *have* found a candidate for Meara, however. If we take him, I'm going to need Duncan's help more than ever."

Morgan made no attempt to hide his sigh of relief. Still shaking his head slightly, he hooked a three-legged stool closer to the two and sat, his back to the fire.

"Sweet *Jesu*, I confess I thought you'd taken leave of your senses for a moment there. Are you *really* going to pass over Judhael?"

"Not—exactly," Cardiel replied. "That is, we're not going to consecrate someone else bishop instead of him. We've been aware from the beginning that any bishop not to the Mearans' liking was going to have his hands full, trying to learn his job and cope with Mearan hostility both at once. But suppose we were to put someone in Meara who's already experienced? That would eliminate half the problem from the start."

"You'd transfer an existing bishop, then," Morgan guessed, running swiftly down the list of prelates in his mind.

Arilan lowered his cup to nod. "That's correct. And there can be no question about passing over Judhael in favor of a man who already knows how to run a diocese."

"Except that all your diocesan bishops are already occupied," Morgan said, even more mystified. "Where are you going to find this paragon?"

Cardiel smiled. "Henry Istelyn, Bradene's assistant."

"Ah."

"He's already been handling a great deal of work behind the scenes for Bradene for the past two years," Arilan said. "Furthermore, when he was first made an itinerant bishop, several years ago, he spent a great deal of time in Kierney and the border areas. He probably knows the people better than anyone besides Judhael himself—or Duncan, of course. But we've already agreed that he's to be otherwise occupied."

Morgan nodded thoughtfully. From Gwynedd's point of view, the selection of Istelyn made perfect sense—but simply choosing a logically qualified candidate did not eliminate the very practical political repercussions which were likely to result if anyone besides Judhael were posted to Meara.

"You're saddling Istelyn with a heavy responsibility," he said. "What makes you think the Mearans will accept him? They have their minds set on Judhael."

"That's true," Arilan agreed. "However, even if they object—"

"Which you know they're going to do, if it's anyone else—"

"*Even* if they object," Arilan continued, "it's too late in the season to mount any kind of major military campaign to try to oust him. Ratharkin will be secure enough through the winter, if we leave him a detachment of episcopal troops for local security. And with the king planning to campaign in Meara next year . . ."

At Morgan's still-doubtful expression, Cardiel spread his hands helplessly.

"There isn't going to *be* a perfect candidate, Alaric— not one who will please every faction. And we could certainly find a lot worse than Istelyn. Incidentally, when is the king due back? Naturally, we'd like his concurrence before we go ahead with any formal announcement."

Morgan raised an eyebrow, still unconvinced. "I had word this morning that he expects to be back in a few days. He's headed north to see the Earl of Transha."

"Transha—that's The MacArdry?" Cardiel asked.

Arilan nodded knowingly. "I remember when his younger son was fostered at court a few years ago: a bright lad, about Kelson's age, as I recall. What was his name?"

"Dhugal," Morgan replied. "In any case, Kelson apparently ran across him over Trurill way, so he's decided to ride back to Transha with the boy and pay a courtesy call on the old man."

"Well, I suppose a few days won't make any difference, one way or the other," Cardiel said. "There are still details to work out on Istelyn—such as finding out whether he's even willing to take on Meara. This assumes, of course, that Kelson has no objection."

Before Morgan could reply, a sharp cry and the sounds of a scuffle in the corridor outside suddenly intruded, punctuated by a mental scream: Duncan's. Morgan was on his feet and moving before the others could even glance in that direction. As he burst into the corridor, he saw Duncan struggling with someone at the far end, but by the time he could reach them, Duncan was letting the body of his attacker slide to the floor. There was blood everywhere.

"Are you all—"

"Don't touch me," Duncan gasped, cradling a bloody right hand against his equally bloody cassock and wobbling to his knees. "There was *merasha* on the blade." He glanced woozily at his motionless attacker. "Christ, I'm afraid I killed him."

*Merasha.* The very word took Morgan back for just an instant to a chapel that was no more, and a barb on an altar rail gate, and the terror of being in the drug's grip, helpless to use his powers, at the mercy of men who would have killed him because of what he was. Duncan had gotten him out and nursed him through the worst of the physical effects of the ordeal, but the memory had never been fully exorcised, especially that final, haunting image of the stake wrapped with chains, which they had passed as they made their escape. It had been intended for him.

"Never mind him," Morgan replied, stepping over the

body to crouch cautiously beside the wounded priest. "Where are you hurt? How much of that blood is yours?"

Drawn by the disturbance, others were congregating in the corridor to gawk, servants and priests and even a few guards from the courtyard outside, forcing Cardiel and Arilan to push their way through to reach Duncan's side. White-faced, Duncan only shook his head and drew in his breath between clenched teeth as he gingerly eased open his right hand. The palm was slashed almost to the bone where he had tried to ward off his attacker's knife with his bare hand, but more terrifying, by far, was the wave of queasy disharmony that he radiated as Morgan reached out in instinctive mental probe and as quickly recoiled.

"Careful of the blade," Morgan warned, though Arilan had already stopped with his hand poised above the knife as he, too, sensed the drug's effects.

Taking care to avoid the blood, which might carry traces of the drug to affect them as well, the two Deryni turned over the dead assassin. Bright scarlet stained the front of the blue Cassani livery and steamed where it had pooled on the cold stone beneath the body, welling from a second mouth which gaped beneath a beardless chin. The bloody face could not have been more than fourteen.

"Why, it's a boy!" Cardiel murmured.

"As God is my witness, I had no choice," Duncan whispered, closing his hand again and slumping back to sit on his heels. "Until he actually cut me, I thought he was legitimate."

"You don't know him?" Arilan asked.

"No—but I wouldn't expect to recognize every last page or squire in my service. And with—with the *merasha* in me, I was afraid that if I didn't kill him while I still could, he might be able to outwait me, until I was helpless with the drug. Why did he do it?"

Morgan shook his head, reaching out gingerly with his mind as he slid a hand around the back of the boy's neck, where there was less blood. Sometimes it was possible to read just a little from a dead man's mind, if he had not been dead too long, but Morgan could detect nothing beyond a few hazy images of dim childhood memories, fading even as he read them. While Arilan and a monk began gathering up the scattered dispatches, he carefully searched the body for anything which might give them a clue as to the boy's identity or origin, but there was nothing. Duncan was beginning to weave as Morgan glanced over at him again, his blue eyes glassy from the drug, keeping them open only by the sheerest force of will. Cardiel had an arm around his shoulder to support him, but it was obvious that Duncan was slipping fast into the chaos of the *merasha*. Whoever the assassin had been, he had known his quarry to be Deryni.

"Thomas, why don't you take Duncan back to your quarters and see to his wound?" Arilan suggested softly, touching a hand to Cardiel's shoulder and including Morgan in his glance. "I'll see to the clean-up here and try to find out more about our boy-assassin."

Cardiel nodded, he and Morgan helping Duncan to stand.

"Very well. You might check with the guards who let the boy into the compound. Perhaps someone may have recognized him. It would also be interesting to know whether he was the original messenger sent with the dispatches, or if the real one is lying dead in a ditch somewhere—or, at the least, relieved of his livery."

Duncan went completely limp as Cardiel finished speaking, and Morgan and the archbishop together had to carry him back to the episcopal apartments. An hour later, washed and bandaged, Duncan was sleeping soundly in his own room, an exhausted Morgan running himself through a brief spell to banish fatigue.

"I'll try to heal him in the morning, when he's over the worst effects of the drug," Morgan whispered, as he turned at last from Duncan's bed. "It's a nasty wound, but I didn't think it was a good idea to put my fingers into all that *merasha*."

His hands were trembling as he took the cup of wine which Cardiel gave him, for going into Duncan's *merasha*-muddled mind had been a great personal trial, as well as a physically taxing one, forcing him to relive much of his own terrifying experience. He still kept flashing on the worst of it, unless he kept his mind on short leash. He knew he would have nightmares for days to come.

But Cardiel's touch on his shoulder conveyed genuine compassion and even understanding as he guided Morgan to one of the cushioned chairs beside the fireplace. Morgan guessed that the archbishop was remembering his own part in the later aftermath of that ordeal, when Morgan and Duncan had come to him and Arilan in Dhassa and disclosed all in desperate confession, seeking to make peace with the Church which had declared them excommunicate for what they had done to escape.

Morgan sat and sipped silently at his wine for several minutes, staring blindly into the fire and feeling himself gradually unwind, then laid his head against the back of the chair and closed his eyes until Arilan returned. The fatigue-banishing spell did not seem to have worked very well, even though he tried it several times.

"I've been questioning some of the guards," the Deryni bishop said, sitting beside Morgan after he had looked in on their patient. "Apparently the boy came from Ballymar, up on the north coast. He was trained in Duke Jared's household and page to one of the local barons for a while, but was dismissed. One of my informants seemed to think it had to do with Mearan sympathies."

"Mearan sympathies?" Cardiel murmured. "How old *is* the lad?"

"Older than he looked," Arilan replied, "and old enough to risk paying for his actions with his life. What puzzles me is why he tried to kill Duncan. It can't be over the Mearan bishopric. Everyone knows that Duncan was not a candidate."

Duncan and Meara. Suddenly Morgan sat up straighter, remembering the conversation he and Duncan had observed between Judhael and old Creoda. They had assumed that Judhael was campaigning for his coveted bishopric. What came to Morgan now was an oblique approach to Judhael getting what he wanted, but its further potential was yet more chilling.

"No, it wasn't about the bishopric—at least not

directly," he said softly, reviewing the genealogical relationships in his mind just to make sure. "But Duncan is
Duke of Cassan and Earl of Kierney. That makes him
almost a prince in his own right—and his lands have not
always gone by their present names."

Arilan's deep blue-violet eyes lit in sudden comprehension. "The other half of ancient Meara," he said with
a nod. "Now, wouldn't *that* be a power base, if one wanted
to break away from one's overlord and establish an independent holding? The two Mearas reunited!"

"And Duncan has no direct heir," Cardiel added, catching the gist of what they were suggesting. "Who *is* his
heir-at-law, Alaric? You? You're cousins, aren't you?"

Morgan grimaced. "Not in the right degree for this, I
fear—and I say that not out of any greed to amass more
titles and land, but out of concern about who comes ahead
of me. There are three, actually—though I'd only thought
about the first two until today. Neither Duncan's father
or his grandfather had any brothers, but his grandfather
had two sisters. The younger, my paternal grandmother,
produced one son: my father. The elder sister also produced a son, however; and he married the Princess Annalind of Meara."

"Queen Roisian's twin sister," Cardiel whispered.
"Then, Caitrin's eldest son is Duncan's heir!"

Morgan nodded. "Ithel; and after him, his brother
Llewell. The girl isn't in the succession, though any eventual son of hers would be, if her brothers failed to produce
heirs." He paused to moisten his lips as the two bishops
stared at him expectantly.

"You're still wondering who the third heir is, then. I'm
surprised you haven't guessed." He paused. "Caitrin also
had a sister, and that sister had a son. Who else could he
be but your good Father Judhael of Meara?"

As Cardiel's jaw dropped in disbelief, Arilan slapped
an open palm against the arm of his chair and swore softly.

"I'm not saying he had anything to do with the attack
on Duncan, mind you," Morgan went on. "I simply point
out that if it had succeeded, Judhael and his kin certainly
stood to gain. All we really know about his politics at this

point is that he wants very badly to be Bishop of Meara. If one of his Mearan cousins were Duke of Cassan and Earl of Kierney, that might make the whole thing fall together. The Bishop of Ballymar would have no choice but to support the candidate of his new duke's choice: Cousin Judhael. And with Judhael in the bishopric, that's added leverage to put his aunt on the throne of Meara—a united Meara, once she's gone and her son succeeds her in the south. It's ingenious, really."

"Its diabolical, if you ask me," Cardiel muttered, "not to mention treasonous. Denis, there must be something we can do. Perhaps we ought to call Judhael in and question him."

Arilan considered the suggestion, running his pectoral cross back and forth distractedly on its chain, then lowered his gaze.

"On what grounds, Thomas? We've been interviewing the man all week. Other than the fact that he's ambitious, he almost shimmers, he's so pure. What Duke Alaric has just outlined is a theory only—an incredibly brilliant one, if we were Mearan—but we have no proof it has occurred to Judhael."

"Well, use your powers to find out, then!" Cardiel blurted. "What good are they, if you don't use them?"

As Arilan sighed patiently, preparing to go into the argument he had used so often when trying to explain things Deryni to Cardiel, Morgan forced himself to put the temptation from his own mind. He had wrestled with this particular ethical problem before, not always successfully.

"Ultimately, it's a matter of ethics," Arilan finally said, echoing Morgan's rationale. "I *have* used my powers all this week, Thomas—to gauge whether our candidates were lying about their qualifications. That I could do without their knowledge, and without revealing myself as Deryni." He smiled, "Besides, they suspected Duncan was Deryni, and that helped to keep them honest: wondering whether he could read their minds—which he couldn't, of course, under those conditions, but they didn't know that."

"Then, let Duncan be present, if you feel you need a decoy," Cardiel insisted. "Or Alaric, since Duncan is temporarily out of action. Between the two of you, you should be able to get at the truth."

"And if he really is just a godly man, with ecclesiastical ambition but no interest in politics?" Arilan asked. "Then we've made another enemy for Deryni."

"Then, make him forget, afterward, if he's innocent!"

"And that begins to enter *really* hazy areas of conscience," Arilan replied. "Truth-Reading is one thing. Using our powers to detect whether a man is lying can be justified, since it doesn't force action against a person's will. To *make* someone tell the truth, however—well, I think that requires more than just a vague suspicion that he may be hiding something. So does making him forget. Sometimes such measures can be justified in a life and death situation, or where the subject is willing, but where does one draw the line?"

"Are *you* so unsure of that line, then?" Cardiel snapped.

"Of course not. At least I pray to God that I'll never be tempted to cross over and misuse my powers. But it was abuse of power that gave us the atmosphere of the past two hundred years. It's what the Camberian Council was created to prevent."

Morgan looked up sharply at that, for Arilan had scrupulously avoided discussion of the mysterious Camberian Council for the past two years. His reaction apparently reminded Arilan that he was beginning to speak of things best left unsaid to humans, even one as close as Cardiel. The Deryni bishop paused to regroup, shaking his head as he laid a hand on Cardiel's arm.

"Listen to me, Thomas. I'm flattered at your confidence in me, but you mustn't think all Deryni are like me, or Alaric, or Duncan, or you may get hurt one day. We've tried to be very careful not to do anything which might frighten you unduly, but you have to admit that we've made you more than a little nervous on more than one occasion—and you know and trust us. Think about the ones who don't have a strict moral code like the one we follow. How many feet in the door does it take to produce a Charissa or a Wencit of Torenth? Or an Interregnum? Alaric knows what I'm talking about, don't you, Alaric?"

Grudgingly, Morgan had to agree, though sometimes Arilan's scruples seemed to him to be rigid almost to the point of crippling. But in front of Cardiel was not the place to pursue that old argument. Cardiel himself required additional persuasion, but eventually he, too, had to admit that forcing Judhael to the question was premature.

"I still think Kelson should be told what has happened," Cardiel said stubbornly. "And I don't think it should wait until he gets back in three or four days, either. That was fine when we were only talking about Istelyn, but now—"

For that, at least, Morgan had a Deryni solution.

"Not *all* of our powers are forbidden, Excellency," he said quietly. "It's possible I might be able to reach Kelson in his sleep, later tonight. He won't be expecting it, but I can try." Cardiel nodded happily as Morgan went on. "If that doesn't work, I'll leave for Transha in the morning, after I've seen to Duncan—unless you have a better idea, sir?" he queried, glancing at Arilan.

The Deryni bishop shook his head. "No, none. Given the bond I know binds you and Kelson, I shouldn't be at all surprised if your plan works. However, I also know how difficult it is to make the link at such a distance and without preparation at both ends. If you don't succeed, we'll make the time you need to get there physically."

Arilan's confidence in his ability helped to take the edge off Morgan's earlier resentment at having to back off on questioning Judhael, but now that his own course was set for the next few hours, he needed some time alone. When he had assured himself that Duncan was resting more easily, and slipped briefly inside the priest's mind to deepen his sleep, he took his leave of the two prelates and headed for his own quarters. He tried not to think about how close Duncan had come to death, or the mortal helplessness Duncan had suffered under the influence of *merasha*, concentrating instead on the calm he would need if he hoped to succeed in reaching the king.

But distraction in the form of Judhael of Meara met

him as he passed the open door of the chapel in the guest
wing. Morgan stiffened as he saw him, mentally berating
himself for even having glanced inside. Judhael and another
vaguely familiar-looking priest were just coming out. The
temptation at least to test whether Judhael had heard about
the attack on Duncan was too enticing to resist.

"Your Grace," Judhael murmured, as Morgan loomed
in the doorway and blocked his exit, all diffidence and
courtly courtesy to the king's champion.

"Father Judhael," Morgan acknowledged. "I wonder
whether I might have a word with you in private," he
said, glancing pointedly at Judhael's companion. "Perhaps
we could step back into the chapel."

Judhael looked puzzled and a little uneasy, but he agreed
readily enough. When one aspired to high office in the
confirmation of the king, one did not decline the invitation
of the king's friend and confidant. He watched dispas-
sionately as Morgan closed the chapel door behind them,
inclining his head and preceding him down the short aisle
when Morgan gestured toward the front of the chapel.
Both men genuflected and signed themselves when they
reached the altar rail, Morgan and then Judhael easing
onto the kneelers which lay along its length. Morgan bowed
his head for a moment as if in prayer, letting Judhael's
curiosity and apprehension grow, then glanced at the priest
sidelong.

"You're acquainted with my cousin, Father Duncan
McLain, I believe," he said softly.

Judhael cocked his head and stared at Morgan in surprise.

"Why, I'm aware that he is secretary to the Lord
Archbishop of Rhemuth, Your Grace. He's been keeping
the accounts of the interviews this week."

"That he has," Morgan murmured, opening his mind
to Truth-Read. "Are you aware that he was set upon by
a boy with a knife earlier this evening?"

Judhael's eyes widened at the news, then shuttered
behind a quickly composed mask of concern.

"Father McLain is a priest like myself, Your Grace,"
he said in a low, uninflected voice. "I am sorry to hear

that someone would attempt his sacrilegious murder, but it grieves me far more to think that you might believe me involved in any way."

"You have no knowledge of it, then?" Morgan asked, a little taken aback to realize that Judhael was telling the truth.

"None, Your Grace."

"I see."

No knowledge whatsoever. Judhael really had not known. Morgan gazed searchingly into the priest's eyes for several seconds, not doing anything but looking—though Judhael might construe what he liked, and hopefully panic enough to let slip some additional bit of information—but Judhael met his gaze with no more uneasiness than anyone might have exhibited when stared at by a Deryni, the extent of whose powers were uncertain.

"Just one more question, then," Morgan said, choosing his words carefully. "When was the last time you heard from your aunt?"

Judhael hardly batted an eye.

"Last Christmastide, Your Grace. Why do you ask?"

Last Christmastide, long before Meara's bishopric became vacant, Morgan noted. Nor was there any duplicity in Judhael's answer. Not only was Judhael innocent of knowledge about the attempt on Duncan, but he did not seem to be involved in any machinations his aunt might have planned for his insertion into a bishop's see—though Judhael surely had his own ambitions.

Morgan dared not push the issue any further, however. Judhael was beginning to look more anxious, and the only way to go from here was to actually force a deep reading on the priest—and Arilan would very likely skin him if he got wind of it, after his earlier lecture to Cardiel.

"Very well, Father. I'll leave you, then. Thank you for your time. If you've a mind to ease a soul, you might whisper a prayer for the boy with the knife. I'm afraid he died unshriven."

He signed himself slowly and deliberately, not taking his eyes from Judhael's, then rose and glided back up the aisle. Judhael was still kneeling, face buried in his hands, when Morgan glanced back just before going out.

He walked for a while after that, reviewing what he had done and finally inquiring among the guards as to what had happened to the body of Duncan's attacker. He found it in the infirmary, covered with a blanket, and he stared at the face of the dead boy for some time, wondering who had sent him.

# CHAPTER FOUR

*Thou hast made us to drink the wine of
astonishment.*

—Psalms 60:3

Farther north and east of Culdi, nearer the coast, an
early dusk began to settle as Kelson and his warband
urged their weary horses along the final stretch approaching Castle Transha, cloaks pulled close against an increasingly bitter drizzle. Dhugal, riding at the king's side, had
set them a brisk pace since leaving the Trurill patrol at
midmorning, pushing to reach the shelter of his father's
castle before dark. They slowed as the grade of the road
got steeper, Dhugal expectantly searching the rain ahead
until the vast pile which was Transha gradually took shape,
almost black against the darkening sky. The young border
lord grinned as he glanced aside at the king.

"We're nearly there now," he said cheerily. "My father's
castellan should have everything prepared. We've been
observed for the past hour, you know."

"Oh?"

Surprised and a little taken aback, Kelson turned to
look at Dhugal in question, for he had been scanning the
craggy hills with Deryni senses as well as sight for nearly
that long, and had detected nothing.

"Don't worry," Dhugal went on with a chuckle. "I didn't
see them either. But then, I'm not as experienced as Ciard
yet. He signalled me when we made our last rest stop."

Ciard. Of course. He had been the only other MacArdry
retainer riding with the Trurill patrol, so of course had
come with them. Kelson remembered him well from the

days of Dhugal's fosterage at court. Glancing back thoughtfully at the middle-aged gillie riding a few ranks behind, he recalled being told that Ciard O Ruane had been made Dhugal's personal attendant and bodyguard by the MacArdry chief himself, shortly after Dhugal's birth. Kelson had never known him to be far from his young charge's side. The man's almost uncanny ability in the field had mystified Kelson even in the old days; and Deryni perceptions gained since their last contact had added no further explanation.

"Ciard. I might have known," Kelson muttered aside to Dhugal, as he returned his attention to the narrowing trail ahead. "I suppose next you'll be telling me he does it with that borderer Second Sight you mentioned yesterday."

"Why, I thought your kind knew all about such things," Dhugal replied with another chuckle. "You really needn't worry, though. I personally guarantee my people's loyalty—though I should warn you not to be surprised if your welcome seems a little cool at first. Even if you weren't the king, you *are* a lowlander. Both make you an oddity this far west."

*And being Deryni makes me odder still*, Kelson added in his own mind, completing what Dhugal had not said. Despite Dhugal's assurance, he could not suppress a faint itch between his shoulderblades.

The air tasted increasingly of salt as they approached the castle's outer defenses, and the gulls screeching overhead gave odd counterpoint to the dull clop of mud-clogged hooves and the muted jingle of harness. Ewan and Conall followed directly behind, the rain-soaked Haldane standard flapping wetly against Conall's gloved hand and occasionally lifting enough on the rising wind to actually be read. Dhugal had advised them not to furl it, so that there could be no mistaking their identity. The rest of the warband also followed by twos, Ciard with one of Ewan's gillies and then Jodrell, Traherne, and the rest of the column—knights, squires, and servants.

They came within easy bowshot of the outer curtain before Kelson at last spotted lookouts manning the battlements high above, barely silhouetted against the grey sky. Torchlight flickered at some of the arrow slits piercing the stone of the barbican gate, betokening human habitation there as well—a suspicion confirmed by Kelson's Deryni senses—but no one appeared at closer hand. The column slowed almost to a stop as they neared the gatehouse.

"They know who you are, but not why you're here," Dhugal murmured, as the heavy doors swung outward and chains clattered on windlass drums, raising the heavy portcullis. "One can hardly blame them for being wary."

"I suppose not."

As soon as there was headroom beneath the portcullis, Ciard kneed his pony past them with a scrambling of unshod hooves and jogged into the gatehouse passage, seizing a torch from a wall bracket before leading on across the drawbridge beyond. He reined in and looked back as he reached the other side, gesturing for them to follow, and Dhugal set heels to his own pony at once. Kelson glanced upward as he and the rest of the column followed Dhugal through the gatehouse, and was rewarded with a glimpse of a red-cheeked border face watching from a murder-hole high above. The man gave a nod and touched two fingers to the front of his highland bonnet before disappearing, but Kelson sensed that the salute was as much for Dhugal as for him.

The hollow clatter of the horses' hooves on the drawbridge gave way to the more solid ring of steel on flint paving as they reached the other side of the ditch protecting the outer ward, and as they resumed climbing, Kelson reflected that if ever a castle had been designed to take all advantage of its natural defenses, Transha was it. The road spiraling upward to the left rapidly became a steep, narrow killing zone, the seaward side sheering off in a heart-stopping plunge to the surf crashing far below. On their unshielded right, the keep itself rose forty feet above their heads, the gaps along the crenellated wall providing easy vantage points from which to bombard an approaching enemy. The way was wide enough for two border ponies side by side, but the Haldane greathorses were obliged to go single file. Sea gulls swooped in for a closer look at the intruders, veering off with angry cries when a horse would snort or a cloak would flap. The smell of the sea was strong, even when they had passed beneath a second gatehouse.

"Bring light for the young master and his guests!" Ciard cried, turning his pony in a tight circle and waving his torch as the Haldane column clattered into the inner ward. "'Tis I, Ciard O Ruane. Th' young master is home. Where is Caball MacArdry? Bring light, I tell ye!"

His voice brought immediate response. As torches flared all around the perimeter of the yard and voices began to buzz, a breathless stableboy came scurrying to take his pony. Kelson sat his greathorse beside Dhugal and the spotted pony and watched Ciard stride toward them. Behind them, the yard was filling with the rest of the Haldane warband, but Kelson signalled them to remain mounted before himself swinging to the ground. Dhugal was already there to take his reins, giving both their animals over to Ciard before setting his hand under Kelson's elbow to guide him toward the stair leading up to the great hall.

"Ho, Caball!" Dhugal called, as the door to the hall opened and a knot of tartan-clad men began to descend the stair. Some of them had pulled an edge of plaid over their heads against the rain, and a few bore torches. The leader wore the two feathers of a clan chieftain in his cap, and his bearded face split in a pleased grin as he came hurrying down to meet the unexpected visitors.

"Master Dhugal!"

"My father's castellan," Dhugal murmured aside to Kelson, as the men reached the bottom of the stair. "Caball, is all prepared to give fair guesting to the King's Majesty? Sire, I present my kinsman Caball MacArdry, who speaks for the clan and The MacArdry. How *is* my father, Caball?"

"The MacArdry's leal greeting, Lord King," Caball replied, touching his cap in salute and making his nod include his young master as well as his sovereign. "Dhugal, Himself will be heartened to see ye hame sae unexpectedly." He returned his attention to Kelson. "We cannae offer more than simple border fare on sae short a notice, but The MacArdry looks forward tae greetin' ye himself, when ye hae refreshed yerself, an' extends his hospitality tae yerself an' yer men tae sup with him in his hall."

"Please tell the MacArdry that I look forward to seeing him as well," Kelson replied, inclining his head graciously. "I've not had that pleasure since he came to see me crowned, and Dhugal tells me he's not been well of late. I'm sorry to hear that."

The castellan dipped his chin in clipped acknowledgment, rain dripping from his beard.

"As for the fare," Kelson went on with a disarming smile, "we've been in the field for several days. Any hot meal and a roof over our heads will be most welcome."

Caball seemed to unbend a little as he glanced back at Dhugal. "I think we can do that much for ye, sir—an' perhaps a mite better. Dhugal, we'll bed th' King's Grace an' such others as he wishes in yer quarters. The men can sleep in the hall with our own garrison, when supper's done."

"Prince Conall will be with us, then," Dhugal replied, looking to Kelson for confirmation, "and perhaps Jodrell and Traherne—or Duke Ewan, of course, unless they'd prefer to sleep with the men. Will that be satisfactory, Sire?"

"Ewan of Claibourne?" Caball murmured, head jerking up to search the riders behind the king. "By yer leave, sir, I'll make th' rest of the arrangements with him. Dhugal, take His Grace in out of the rain."

He and his henchmen were already moving past them before Kelson could do more than nod, border affinity for another highland man drawing the castellan instinctively toward Ewan's distinctive tartan mantle, his casual salute in Kelson's direction almost an afterthought. Kelson was only bemused, used to the brusque manners of bordermen from his dealings with Dhugal and his attendants as a boy, but an affronted Prince Conall kneed his greathorse nearer the king in shocked outrage.

"Do you intend to let him treat you that way?" he demanded in a loud stage whisper, bending beneath the dripping Haldane standard to peer at Kelson. "He dismissed you like a servant!"

"He asked my leave. Don't make a scene," Kelson warned, as he laid a hand on his cousin's reins. "The man has a job to do."

"Yes! To show proper respect for his overlord!"

"No disrespect was intended," Kelson replied, "and standing in the rain is no time for formality. I am not offended."

But Conall was, and he continued to fume and mutter to himself all the way up the newel stair behind Dhugal and Kelson, not ceasing his complaints even when the three of them reached a snug little room at the top of the tower. Kelson's squire came to help them off with their boots, but Conall continued to reiterate his displeasure about border disregard for rank and precedence, ending with a graceless remark about the accommodations. Kelson sent the squire out of the room before taking Conall to task, afterward apologizing to an uncomfortable Dhugal. The air was charged with resentment as the three young men began stripping off rain-sodden harness and tunics to wash for supper.

In the sullen silence of the next little while, Kelson could not help noticing the contrast between Dhugal's casual dismissal of the incident and Conall's petulant formality. His cousin's behavior had embarrassed him greatly. The squire soon returned with their meager baggage and helped Conall dress in a fresh court tunic which was far too ornate for this casual highland setting, but when Kelson tried tactfully to mention that to Conall, his cousin renewed his tirade about stiff-necked bordermen and declared that he would show them all how a proper prince behaved, donning a silver circlet of rank as he stalked out the door. Kelson sent the squire after him, hoping he could prevent Conall from insulting any other bordermen he encountered, and pulled a clean woolen singlet from his own pack in silence.

"I really am sorry about Conall's boorishness," he said after a moment, as Dhugal's head emerged from the neck of a saffron-colored shirt. "I hope it's only the folly of youth."

"Youth?" Dhugal made a rude noise, his courtly veneer vanishing in border frankness. "Kelson, he's a year older than *I* am. If respect is what he values, he'll never win it with behavior like that. He's second in line for the throne, too."

Kelson crouched to help his foster-brother finish arranging the pleats of a great kilt on the floor, unable to disagree.

"That's true, in theory," he said, watching Dhugal lie down on the kilt to belt it around his narrow waist. "Thank God his father comes first—and I've never heard anyone say an unkind word about Nigel. Perhaps by the end of next year there will be a new heir altogether. Still, you're right about youth being no excuse for rude behavior. Conall can be a terrible boor."

Dhugal, sitting up to brooch part of the plaid to his shoulder with an amethyst the size of plover's egg, looked up from the gem's clasp with a start to stare at the king.

"Bugger Conall! What do you mean, a new heir? Kelson, you aren't betrothed, are you?"

"No, no, not that, yet," Kelson replied with a chuckle. "But don't look so shocked. I'm seventeen and I'm a king. It's expected. Nigel and Aunt Meraude have been badgering me for over a year, and Morgan nearly as long."

"Morgan, too?"

Kelson shrugged wistfully. "Well, all of them are right, of course. The succession has to be secured. I've lost count of the princesses and countesses and other eligibile girls I've had to inspect in the last year. Every lordling in Gwynedd with a marriageable daughter or sister between the ages of twelve and thirty has been finding some excuse to bring her to court. Even Morgan is threatening to trot out some R'Kassan princess for Twelfth Night. She's a relative of his wife."

"His wife?" Dhugal stared even harder, though now he, too, was grinning. "So that's what it's all about! Morgan's gotten married, so now he thinks everyone else ought to be. Who's the lady?"

Kelson shook his head and grinned. He kept forgetting how isolated Transha was from the capital and its doings.

"You *are* out of touch, aren't you? You *did* know I'd made him Lord Protector of the South, didn't you?"

"No."

"Did you know that Torenth has a regency again?" Kelson ventured.

"A regency? What happened to Prince Alroy?"

Kelson sighed, trying to keep at least some of the old worry out of his voice.

"A fall from a horse, around Midsummer. He broke his neck. From what I've been able to gather, it was clearly an accident, but he'd just come of age. So some folk are saying I arranged it—the way Clarissa *arranged* my father's death."

"You mean, with magic?" Dhugal whispered.

Kelson nodded. "They don't know me very well, do they?"

"But, what possible motive could you have, even if you *were* able to—*are* you able to kill someone with magic, Kelson?"

"If you mean, do I have the ability to kill someone with magic, the answer is yes—I have the power and the knowledge to do so," Kelson said quietly, "I've—had to do it once already. I killed Alroy's father and uncle that way—and the Earl of Marley. I'm not proud of it, but there was no other way at the time. And I'd do it again to protect my kingdom."

He swallowed uncomfortably. "As for motive. I'm afraid I have that, too. Keeping a minor on the throne of Torenth lessens the chance that Torenth will move against me in anything but border skirmishes, at least until the new king is of age. Liam, Alroy's next brother, is only nine. That gives me nearly five years to get things settled in Meara, before I have to worry seriously about Torenth again— maybe more. I didn't kill Liam's brother, though."

"I believe you," Dhugal said.

The three words were spoken quietly, with little inflection, but Kelson knew that they were true. Four years had passed since he and Dhugal last had met, but he could sense that the old closeness had not weakened with the passage of the years and all that had gone on during them. He glanced down at his hands, the hands which literally held the power of life and death over so many, then shook his head, knowing he would never be able to put aside the knowledge of his power.

"But, enough of all this," Kelson continued more brightly. "You asked about Morgan, and Morgan's wife. He married Richenda of Marley a year ago last spring. They have a little daughter who's nearly a year old now. Briony, she's called."

"For your father," Dhugal murmured, nodding approvingly. "I like that. But Richenda of Marley—wasn't she the Countess of Marley? Didn't you just say you'd had to kill her husband?"

"Yes. But she wasn't responsible for her husband's treason," he said softly, "Nor was their son. I confirmed young Brendan in the Earldom of Marley when he turned six this past summer. I've made him Morgan's ward, until he's of age, and Richenda his regent."

"And what will he say when he's older, and he learns who killed his father?" Dhugal whispered. "Suppose he comes to hate you for it?"

"I suppose I hope that by then, he'll have learned why I had to do it," Kelson said with a sigh. "Bran Coris' was one of the first lives I had to take. Unfortunately, it won't be the last. At least I've learned a few things since then— not that they'd make any difference if I had to do over again." He sighed again, a gesture of finality.

"But that's done. There's no sense brooding about something I can't change. One thing I hope I *can* change is the reception I got when I rode in here an hour ago."

Dhugal laughed aloud, the solemnity of the past few minutes dispelled.

"Now, that *will* be magic, if you can accomplish that. You saw them, Kelson. They're bordermen. Most of them have never been to court, and never will. You can't expect to earn their respect overnight."

"Not overnight, no. But I do have an idea for making a start, perhaps."

Half an hour later, two young bordermen emerged from the tower room where only one had entered. Dhugal's comment about his long hair the day before had given Kelson his inspiration. He had decided not to hazard a great kilt such as Dhugal himself wore, for he was disinclined to trust a garment which depended on only a belt to discipline so many pleats, so he had chosen a set of Dhugal's rust-colored border leathers instead—close-fitting trews and sleeveless doublet over a saffron wool shirt like Dhugal's. A length of grey, black, and yellow MacArdry plaid was caught across his chest baldric style and secured at the left shoulder with a deeply chased silver ring brooch, and soft indoor boots of buckskin encased his feet in comfort. Instead of the golden circlet which would have adorned his head at any normal court function, he wore a border bonnet like Dhugal's. His black hair made a borderman's braid shorter by a handspan than Dhugal's copper one, but that, plus the clothing, transformed the king from a polished young lowland noble into a darker echo of the chief's son. Now, if only old Caulay would play along.

He began to hear the skirl of pipers tuning as he followed Dhugal down the newel stair and along the passage toward the castle's great hall—dissonant and whining at first, but then catching and carrying a traditional border air, one of the few he knew. The music put a new spring in his step as he and Dhugal emerged near the entrance to the hall, and he could hear Dhugal whistling softly under his breath.

Border henchmen, servants, and a few Haldane men alike milled in the anteroom outside the open doors to the hall, but in Dhugal's company, dressed as he was, no one paid Kelson any particular notice. Seizing a torch from a fire-blackened cresset, Dhugal led him through the press and quickly through a nondescript wooden door just beyond the entryway, signing for silence as he continued up a steep, narrow intramural passageway which paralleled the great hall. When Kelson judged them to be about halfway along its length, Dhugal stopped and uncovered two narrow squints cut at different angles in the stone, carefully holding his torch below and close to the wall to shield its light. Using each squint in turn, Kelson could see nearly all the length of the hall below, though the entrance and the dais at the other end were out of range.

"It looks like most of your men who aren't on duty are already seated," Dhugal murmured, gazing downward with Kelson. "You can see how they've all kept to themselves, though. A lot is going to depend on how you're received."

Kelson nodded as he studied the hall. Since, by border custom, all clansmen were more or less of equal rank, there were no separate arrangements for nobles and men-at-arms. He saw Duke Ewan moving down the hall with a surly-looking Conall—to be seated at the high table, Dhugal assured him—but other than them, almost all the rest of the royal entourage seemed to be crowded on either side of a long table parallelling one side wall—carefully isolated, Kelson noted, from the rest of the clansmen and their women. Hospitality, it seemed, had its limits.

He was thoughtful as he followed Dhugal farther along the passageway and around a bend, the pipers' jig hardly intruding at all now on his thinking as he gazed through another squint looking toward the high table. From there, he was able to survey everyone on the dias, including the Earl of Transha.

Caulay MacArdry had aged in the three years since Kelson last had seen him, but though time had robbed the old border chief of much of his mobility, it clearly had not touched his other faculties. A gillie had to help him into his chair at the high table, for he could no longer walk without assistance, but the arms emerging from his fine saffron shirt were still corded with muscle, tanned nut-brown from the high summer sun and wind of the Transha highlands. Kelson could see the muscles ripple as the old man hefted a full wineskin and drank unerringly from a stream of red without spilling a drop.

His wiry grey hair was drawn back in a borderer's clout and bound with a ribbon woven in the colors of his clan, but the full beard flowing onto his chest still showed a little of the chestnut gleam of his youth. The brown eyes were clear and alert as he conversed with Duke Ewan, seated on the other side of Conall, at his left hand; but he kept glancing at the far end of the hall as if in expectation.

"Is he looking for us?" Kelson asked softly, glancing aside at Dhugal. "Hadn't we better go on in?"

"Yes, but not in the way you're thinking," Dhugal replied. He grinned slyly as he seized a fold of Kelson's sleeve and drew him back into the passage. "Let's go. Just follow my lead, and do what I do."

Soon they were emerging behind the screens which separated the kitchen from the dais in the great hall, Dhugal nudging the king through one of the bays to move with him among the gillies serving the high table. The men deferred to their chief's son, but they hardly gave Kelson a second look other than to avoid running into him as he stuck to Dhugal's side. They were too busy watching Conall, seated on the chief's left, and Jodrell, who had pulled up a stool at the end of the table to sit and speak to Ewan between them. The old Duke of Claibourne had been readily accepted among them, for he came of the same clan system as themselves and understood their customs, but the others were lowlanders, like the knights and men-at-arms seated in the hall below. Conall, defiantly aloof in court dress and the silver circlet of his rank, looked particularly out of place.

But Kelson sensed Dhugal's intentions now. As the younger boy worked his way closer to the high table, gesturing toward the place of honor at old Caulay's right and easing onto the bench to the right of that, Kelson controlled a smile and followed. With casual nonchalance, he slipped into the place between Dhugal and the old man and leaned an elbow on the table, merely raising an eyebrow at a gillie who ducked between him and Dhugal to pour wine for both of them and started to question.

Some of his own men began to recognize him at that, however, and as more and more of them got to their feet with much clatter and scraping of wooden benches against stone floor, the commotion caught old Caulay's attention. As he turned to ascertain the reason for it, he was astonished to see a strange young borderman sitting at his right

hand. The pipers' skirling wheezed to a halt as all eyes
turned toward the MacArdry chief.

"The Haldane gives fair greeting to The MacArdry of
Transha," Kelson said gravely, inclining his head in respect
as Caulay's jaw dropped. "My brother Dhugal bade me
sit at your right hand, sir, and I am right honored to do
so, for his father must be my father, since I have none
anymore."

Stunned speechless, Caulay stared into the grey Haldane eyes as the buzz of questions grew among his people,
seeing the strange mixed with the familiar. The last Haldane old Caulay had seen had been a boy of just fourteen,
on the occasion of his coronation. The lad before him was
young, but he was a man, with the frank, direct gaze of
his other border chieftains. As he glanced beyond the
stranger at his son, Dhugal rose and came to kiss his
father's cheek with a grin.

"I've brought m'brother home tae sup with us, Da,"
he said in his broad border accent. "He would count it a
great favor if ye could put his other rank aside for a night,
for he would do honor to our house an' blood for sake o'
the bond he shares wi' me. Will ye nae greet him as a
kinsman an' a son?"

For an interminable instant, Kelson feared that Caulay
would not go along, that the close-knit bonds of border
kinship would force him back into the royal role he was
so often obliged to play. But then the old man's face split
in a pleased grin and he held out a huge hand to Kelson,
the brown eyes warming.

"Aye, and it's pleased that I am to see ye, son," he
said softly. "I left ye a boy, and ye've come back a man.
Will ye nae give yer old Da the kiss of peace?"

Solemnly Kelson placed his hand in Caulay's and rose,
inclining his head in proper salute, borderer to hosting
chief, acutely aware of the eyes upon him. When he bent
to kiss the old man's cheek, however, a ragged murmur
of approval rippled among the bordermen and the pipes
struck up a dutiful salute, this time punctuated by drums.

It was not the most spontaneous of welcomes, but it
was a start. Pretending not to notice Conall's sour looks

farther down the table, and the confused expressions on most of the rest of his retinue, Kelson took his seat, smiling. Brion would never have done this, but Kelson was not Brion. They would just have to adjust to the fact that he was going to develop his own style. He laughed at a joke Dhugal murmured in an aside, and when Ciard came to serve them roast fowl and beef on a trencher of hearty highland bread, he dug in with his fingers in proper border fashion.

He and Caulay made casual small talk through the meal, Kelson touching on some of his experiences of the past three years and the old chief proudly recounting Dhugal's skill as a future border chief. Only passing comment was made on his own failing health.

Out of respect for his host, Kelson veered away from politics or any other subjects of possible controversy, intending to save such conversation for more private surrounds, perhaps later that night. But just before the sweet was served—a sticky confection of crushed almonds and biscuit and honey—Caulay made passing reference to his brother Sicard, whose wife was the Mearan Pretender.

"What's she like, the Lady Caitrin?" Kelson asked, trying to keep too much interest out of his tone. To his relief, Caulay was neither offended nor reticent, wine having loosened his tongue to the point of amiability.

"Ach, she nurses an old dream whose time passed lang ago," Caulay said. "I did nae ever like her. She's of an age wi' me—no spring hen-chick, she—but she has fierce bairns an' a fiercer mate. She an' my brother—!"

He spat contemptuously, and Kelson raised an eyebrow in feigned surprise.

"You and Sicard had a falling out?"

"Ye might say that," the old man allowed. "Truth is, he an' I were never close. I'm nae close to the bairns, either—leastways not the boys. Ithel an' Llewell, they're named—though I expect ye know that. About your age, they are—mayhap a year or so younger. The girl, though—"

"Not another daughter," Kelson breathed, almost to himself.

Old Caulay immediately caught his drift, however, and laughed uproariously as he clapped Kelson on the shoulder.

"Ach, I see they've been pushing ye to choose a mate, haven't they, lad? Well, a man could do far worse than sweet Sidana. Her name means 'silk' in the old tongue, an' she has all the grace the boys an' their mother lack. Pretty she is, as well as heiress to a great name, wi' fine sleek hair that reaches to her knees—brown as a chestnut burr it is—an' eyes like a bonnie fawn. Fair white teeth, too, an' hips tae bear a man many fine sons, though she can nae be more than fifteen."

"You sound as if you're trying to marry her off," Kelson said with a smile. "Are you trying to tell me something?"

Caulay's shoulders lifted with a coy shrug, even though he was shaking his head no.

"Weel, 'tis not I who'd presume tae barter a bride for my king, son," the old man said. "But if a man wanted tae resolve an old, old rift an' bring peace tae his people, he could do far worse than marryin' Sidana. If I thought it would help, I'd marry Dhugal to her—or praise God, if I were a younger man, an' could find a willing priest, I'd marry her myself, an' she my own dear niece."

Kelson smiled wanly, remembering what he once read about incest of an only slightly closer degree toppling a throne two centuries before—though there had been a Deryni question in the case of Imre and Ariella, as well.

But Caulay's theoretical solution would certainly have no such repercussions, even if it were to occur. For that matter, he supposed *he* and Sidana were distantly related—his eyes glazed a little as he tried to sort out the generations of cousins through a common great-great-grandfather—though they were certainly outside the bounds of consanguinity proscribed by the Church.

"I don't think it will be necessary for you to make the sacrifice," he reassured Caulay, with a faint, droll grin.

"Ach, o' course not. 'Tis a Haldane husband she'd be needin', not another borderer, tae muddy matters further. If not Yer Grace, than perhaps yer young cousin, there—"

The old man glanced down the table where Conall had moved to sit between Ewan and Jodrell, brooding over his wine cup.

"Nah, on second reflection, Conall would nae do," Caulay went on more soberly. "She would nae be happy with the likes o' him—though methinks yer young cousin has ambitions o' his own. Power can be a great temptation, son. But I need nae tell ye about that, do I?"

Surprised, Kelson glanced at Conall and then back at Caulay.

"Conall?"

"Ach, I dinnae mean to cast a shadow on yer cousin, lad. But Sidana is a fair marriage prize, an' could give her husband a fair claim to Mcara. With the right persuasion, from the right man, her brothers might even be moved to abandon their claims."

Kelson chuckled grimly and shook his head, running a finger along the rim of his cup.

"I'm trying to avoid that kind of persuasion, Caulay," he said softly. "I don't *want* to have to march into Meara the way my father and grandfather did, and solve things with a sword. But I don't intend to give up what's lawfully mine, either."

Caulay's bearded face clouded and he dropped his gaze to stare into the depths of his goblet. "That may be the only way, son," he whispered darkly. "Young Ithel wants a throne. He won't be content to rule over an exile court in Laas, once his mother is gone."

"You speak as if that might be imminent," Kelson breathed, gently reaching out to read the truth of Caulay's words. "Is Ithel plotting something?"

"I dinnae know particulars, I dinnae care to know." Caulay took a long pull at his wine and shook his head. "It's only some rumors I've heard. What young man does not have ambition? I dinnae care to say more."

Chilled, Kelson nudged his cup aside and stared at Caulay. The old man was telling the truth, as far as he went, but what were the rumors he had heard? If Ithel of Meara was actively plotting a revolt . . .

"I need to know, Caulay," he murmured, as he touched his wrist and started trying to Mind-See. "If you know something—"

"I know nothing!" Caulay whispered, eyes flashing as he yanked away his wrist. "An' if ye press me for nothing, then—"

The skirl of pipes began outside the hall just then, and Caulay broke off and shook his head apologetically, taking another deep draught from his cup. While Kelson searched for a tactful way to reapproach the subject, two pipers marched in from the far end of the hall, preceding a white-robed old man brandishing two evergreen boughs like bushy swords. Conversation died away as they entered, even the rowdier of the clansmen putting aside their cups to brush caps in salute as the old man passed. The women standing curtseyed, and even the children serving table stopped where they were to render appropriate respect.

"Kinkellyan, the chief bard," Dhugal murmured in his ear, as the old man came between the two pipers and continued toward them. "This could be very important. Stay seated for now, but pay very close attention."

As the man reached the lowest step of the dais and stopped, crossing the boughs over his head in salute as he bowed, the music ended and Dhugal stood, raising a cup in answering salute to the man in white.

"Bright moon and starshine on thy path, noble bard. The MacArdry and all his kin welcome Kinkellyan to the hall of Transha."

The old man inclined his head and murmured a phrase Kelson did not quite catch, sweeping the narrow boughs in his hands to either side as if to open an embrace. Kelson thought he had heard his name, but he could not be sure. Dhugal replied with an answering phrase in the border tongue, then bowed and glanced at his father. Old Caulay seemed to have forgotten his previous agitation, and bowed low over his place at table as he, too, raised his cup in salutation.

"Kinkellyan offers you his bardic blessing and asks

that you be afforded the enduring friendship of the clan,"
Dhugal murmured to Kelson out of the side of his mouth.
"The MacArdry has accepted on your behalf. Stand up
and bow, and then do whatever seems appropriate after
Kinkellyan and I have finished."

As Kelson obeyed, Dhugal bowed to his father and left
the table, descending the dais to enthusiastic hammerings
of fists on tabletops by all his kinsmen. Kelson's men
looked mystified, except for old Ewan.

In slow, almost ritual mime, Dhugal took the boughs
from the old bard and bowed again, then crossed them in
saltire above his head and pivoted slowly on the balls of
his feet until he faced Kelson, bending to lay them that
way on the floor as the pipers skirled a few introductory
bars. The tempo changed as he straightened and set his
hands on his hips, rising again on the balls of his feet, and
Dhugal began to dance.

Kelson felt his own feet stir as he watched, for the
pipes seemed to beckon almost magically. For just an
instant, as Dhugal moved from the first quarter to the
second, his eyes locked with Kelson's in a linking so
profound that memory surged across the link almost as
surely as if Dhugal, too, had been Deryni and deliberately
sent his thought winging into Kelson's mind—the two of
them, half a lifetime ago, facing one another over crossed
swords, not evergreen boughs, treading out the measures
of the dance Dhugal now performed as it was meant to
be done. All at once Kelson knew what Dhugal had
meant—*do whatever seems appropriate*—and he found
himself edging out from behind the table and down off
the dais to where Dhugal spun and leaped.

The pipers never faltered as the king came onto the
floor. Kelson could sense the expectation of the audience
all around, some pleased, some thoroughly mystified, but
the old bard looked not at all surprised, though he raised
a white eyebrow. Dhugal was just finishing the first set
of measuring steps around the ends of the boughs, piv-
oting and rocking, with first one arm and then the other
raised above his head, but when he saw Kelson ease into
the quarter which was about to be opposite him, he grinned

and gave a nod, setting balled fists on his hips to repeat the first set as he completed the figure. Kelson caught the very first step of the repeat by letting his feet carry him as they had so many years before, mirroring Dhugal a little stiffly at first, but then with growing confidence as those in the hall, clansmen and lowland knights alike, looked on in astonishment.

As they shifted into the next set of figures, beating out a more emphatic rhythm as they danced within the quarters instead of all around the edges, feet never touching the branches, Kelson could sense that throbbing link again, melding his movements with Dhugal's. With rare abandon, he let his world shrink down to flying feet and evergreens and Dhugal's joyous grin. He was only dimly aware when the men and women around them started clapping and stamping in time to the music, urging them on, sharing the magic which had nothing to do with being Deryni.

Kelson was panting with exhaustion by the time they began the final set of figures, but he did not falter, springing lightly from quarter to quarter, heel and toe, until finally the rhythm changed, the music ebbed to a single sustained note, and he and Dhugal were bowing to one another on opposite sides of the evergreen cross, hands set on hips. The hall went wild.

The clansmen and their women continued to cheer as the two grinning young men half-collapsed against one another, both of them gasping for breath. Other than Ewan, most of Kelson's other retainers looked stunned, though a few had relaxed enough to join in good-naturedly, not the least of whom was Baron Jodrell. Conall sat sullenly between him and Ewan, his arms folded and lips set in grim disapproval, but at the center of the table the MacArdry chief was beaming, his earlier agitation apparently forgotten. As Dhugal and Kelson stumbled up the dais, arm in arm, he held out a newly filled cup in both hands.

"*Air do slainte!*" he cried, the others taking up the shout as Dhugal and then Kelson drank deeply from the cup. *To your very good health!*

The cheering subsided as Dhugal held up an arm for

silence, and he was still a little breathless as he turned Kelson to face his people, one arm still around the king's shoulders.

"Kinsmen, this is my foster-brother, Kelson," he said with a grin. "As you can see, he is a brother of our blood, as well as one of my choosing. That he is also my king is a great joy to me, and I freely give him my allegiance as lord as well as brother and kinsman. Will you honor him the same, for my sake?"

The renewed shouting and cheers were all the confirmation Dhugal needed. As Kelson stood back, pleased, still panting from the exertion of the dance and wondering just how he had managed to bring them around—these dour mountain folk who were usually so slow to admit a lowlander to their midst—Dhugal turned and knelt at his feet, slipping his joined hands between Kelson's and touching them to his forehead in homage.

In ragged succession, Dhugal's borderers joined him in salute, sinking to one knee in their places. A few even smiled, inasmuch as any borderer did when obliged to follow lowland custom. A handful remained dour and grim, but all of them knelt. The rarity of the concession was not lost on Kelson.

"My brother, I thank you," Kelson said, smoothly raising Dhugal and signalling the rest of them to rise. "And to you, my border kinsman, my profound thanks as well. Please believe that I understand the honor you have done me. And if there be some of you who yet have your doubts about this upstart lowland lord who comes among you, I cannot blame you. Nor will I try to change your opinion by my words. My actions, I hope, will speak for me, in that I shall always strive to be your true and gentle lord."

His own men pounded on the tables in approval, but Kelson held up his hand again for silence.

"But though I be lowland born, yet am I a borderer like yourselves, by choice and chosen blood, as my brother Dhugal has said. I would assure you, therefore, that whenever possible, I shall place the considerations of the clan above my own concerns, an' it be not against the interests of the other folk I have sworn to protect and defend. In token, therefore, I ask that you host me not as king tonight, but as kinsman, and that you join with me in toast to our noble chief: The MacArdry—long may he guide his children in peace and plenty. *Air do slainte!*"

It was the one border phrase Kelson could remember, and he blessed old Caulay for having refreshed his memory earlier, but it produced the desired response. This time there was no restraining the men of Transha. The hall erupted in echo of the traditional border toast, even the most dour of the old chieftains raising their cups with more thoughtful expressions. Soon the pipers struck up another dance tune and the floor filled with other dancers eager to tread a few steps with their new young kinsman. Some of the girls were very pretty. Kelson answered their first few invitations with laughing good humor and an honest attempt to follow, but the dance with Dhugal had exhausted both his knowledge and his energy. He soon had to bow himself out and retreat to the safety of his place by the chief. Dhugal remained on the floor.

Caulay was jovial company for what remained of the evening, but he downed three cups of wine to every one of Kelson's and quickly began to show the effects. Any serious return to their discussion was impossible under the circumstances, so they were soon reduced to rambling exchanges about the dancers, Dhugal's escapades and prospects for the future, and an increasingly maudlin tendency on Caulay's part to dwell on his failing health. By the time people began falling asleep at table and bedding down in the hall for the night, Kelson had managed to diminish the effect of his own alcoholic consumption to a dull buzz, but Caulay was on the verge of passing out. Dhugal was less steady on his feet than Kelson, but not really drunk, either.

"I think he's about had enough, don't you?" Kelson murmured, when Dhugal returned to the table to refill his cup during a piper's slowly skirled lament.

Dhugal looked down at his father, steadying himself on the edge of the table as he watched old Caulay bobble and grin, then signalled to a gillie who towered at least a head and a half above either him or Kelson. The man scooped up his chief with no more effort than Kelson might have picked up a three year old, and carried him tenderly out of the hall and up the newel stair with the two young men following behind, Dhugal with his arm linked in Kelson's for stability. When they had gotten the old man to bed and the gillie had gone, Dhugal sank down in a window seat and sighed, glancing up at Kelson with a tired grin.

"Well, you certainly left your mark on Transha tonight. The clan will be talking about you all winter—and speaking well, too."

Kelson smiled and leaned against the window embrasure, tossing his bonnet to the seat beside Dhugal. The climb to the laird's chamber had finished clearing his head, and now the considerations of earlier in the evening came flooding back. To have won the confidence of the clan was a fine thing, and part of what he had set out to accomplish, but he still had not learned all he needed to know about Caulay's Mearan kin. And if Ithel of Meara was plotting...

"I wonder, will they speak well of me when they remember that I'm part Deryni?" he mused, trying to decide how best to approach what he wanted to ask. However he phrased it, Dhugal was going to be either frightened or insulted.

Dhugal frowned. "What difference does it make? And what makes you think of it now?"

"It isn't all a bad thing, you know—being Deryni," Kelson continued, testing. "You saw that when I put that trooper to sleep so you could sew up his arm. It does have its positive uses."

Dhugal swallowed with an audible sound, suddenly far more sober than he had been, all the gaiety gone.

"Why do I have the sudden feeling that something very scary is about to happen. You're warning me, aren't you?"

"Not—exactly." Kelson glanced down at Dhugal's upturned face, then over at the sleeping Caulay.

"Dhugal, I've never even been *tempted* to take unfair

advantage of a friendship before," he said softly, "but damn it—he hasn't told me everything he knows."

"What do you mean?"

Kelson shook his head. "Oh, I don't mean to imply a deliberate deception. I think he just doesn't want to get involved—and one can hardly blame him. Sicard is still his brother, after all. Unfortunately, Sicard is also the father of a boy who may just try to take away my throne— and Caulay hinted of conspiracies at dinner, just before he clammed up."

"Surely, you're not suggesting he'd keep such knowledge *from* you, if there really were a danger?" Dhugal asked.

"I don't know," Kelson replied. "I do know that your father has information I may need—and that I have the means to *take* it, if I must, without his knowledge and without hurting him."

"With magic," Dhugal supplied. His face had stiffened to a taut mask as Kelson spoke, and now the honey-amber eyes reflected cold resentment, as well as a little fear.

"Kelson, I can't stop you," he continued, after a long, slow breath. "If that's what you're determined to do, there isn't a thing I can do to prevent it."

"I know that. That's why I'm asking if I may. He wouldn't remember it," Kelson added. "He need never even know I talked with him tonight."

"And if you had to use what you learned against him?" Dhugal asked.

Kelson sighed. "I hope to God it never comes to that," he murmured, eyes downcast. "You know I would never deliberately do anything to hurt you or your family. But if information that I gained had to be used to stop a war, to save innocent lives—well, what would you do?"

Only after a long pause did Dhugal's answer come: halting, reluctant—and resigned.

"I suppose I—would do what I had to do," he whispered.

# CHAPTER FIVE

*They have set up kings, but not by me:*
*they have made princes, and I knew it*
*not.*

—Hosea 8:4

*I would do what I had to do.*

Dhugal's words put responsibility squarely back on
Kelson—where it had always rested, with the other bur-
dens of the Crown, but this particular responsibility was
unique to a king endowed with magic. Kelson found himself wondering whether his father had ever had to make
such a demand of a friend. Somehow he could hardly
imagine Brion using his powers for much of anything,
even though he knew his father had slain the Marluk with
magic and obviously had taken the necessary measures
to ensure that his legacy passed to Kelson.

But Haldane magic was not the same as that derived
from being born Deryni—and perhaps that difference was
the source of some of Kelson's uneasiness just now, for
he had the limitations as well as the benefits of both sorts.
The Haldane legacy came full-blown to each successive
male heir in the senior royal line, its potential sealed by
the previous king and triggered in the heir by ritual whose
essential elements apparently had altered little in nearly
two hundred years. It was of Deryni origin, to be sure,
but it was a somewhat artificial construct, so far as Kelson
had been able to learn, crafted by the great Saint Camber
for the defense of Cinhil Haldane against mad Imre, to
end the Interregnum, and perpetuated in Cinhil's descendants ever since.

Such magic dealt primarily with protection—holding and keeping what was Haldane. But it was power to be called up without training and without real understanding, a compendium of set spells whose use and, indeed, very existence generally became apparent only when the need arose—difficult to call to mind of one's own inclination. A few casual skills there were of Haldane origin, like Truth-Reading and extending one's physical endurance, duplicating some Deryni functions, but the more subtle and satisfying uses of magic—and the ones most open to abuse—lay within the province of Deryni only. Indeed, most of the magic readily accessible to Kelson came from his Deryni blood, not Haldane sources: mostly what Morgan and Duncan had been able to teach him about that aspect of his heritage—and much of that still lay in the realm of theory.

Now his meager experience with the two of them must be melded with the impersonal knowledge at his beck and call from Haldane sources, and techniques chosen to fit the very personal situation here before him. Several times in the past two years he had watched Morgan do this kind of thing—and had done it himself under Morgan's guidance once or twice—but this was different: himself, alone, questioning someone he cared about—not some hostile prisoner, from whom the truth must be dragged by force. With Caulay's natural discretion already lowered by the wine, Kelson was not too concerned about the actual procedure, but he *was* concerned about alienating Dhugal. The friends he could trust, who were not afraid of him, were few and precious.

"If it should come to that, then I suppose *I'll* have to do what I have to do," he finally whispered, meeting Dhugal's eyes miserably. "That's one of the more unpleasant parts of being king. In the meantime, I'm afraid *this* is something I have to do." He paused a beat. "You don't have to watch if you don't want to. You can leave, or I could—put you to sleep, blur the memory. Neither of you has to remember."

Dhugal's jaw tightened visibly, the sun-amber eyes scared and a little desperate.

"If that's what you want, I'll—bow to your wishes, of course, but—dammit, Kelson, I *won't* let myself be afraid of you! God knows, I don't understand what you've become, and if you'd rather I didn't watch, I—I'll let you put me to sleep or whatever you feel you have to do. I don't want to leave, though."

The courage and blind trust blazing in Dhugal's face as he looked up precluded all further discussion. Kelson's grateful "Stay, then," was more mouthed than said, but Dhugal understood. His shaky smile and Kelson's quick, answering grin were all the further comment necessary. Together they moved back into the room where Caulay slept, Kelson no longer worried.

The old man snored on obliviously as Kelson sat down on the right side of the bed and drew a few deep breaths to compose himself, centering as Morgan had taught him. He did not touch Caulay, for he did not wish to alarm Dhugal in these early stages. Dhugal, initially skittish, claimed a stool on the opposite side of the bed and settled down to watch; but gradually even he responded to the calm and stillness radiating from the king. Like Kelson, his breathing soon slowed to a shallow, even cadence, nimble surgeon's fingers intertwined passively in the lap of his kilt, thumbs brushing tip to tip.

Reassured, Kelson shifted attention from his own slow breathing to that of Caulay, gently spreading his right hand across the old man's forehead and letting his thumb and little finger rest lightly on the closed eyelids for a few seconds. He could sense the blur of the alcohol as he sent his consciousness cautiously into Caulay's, but he quickly bypassed that to make the necessary connections for what must be done, closing his eyes as he felt his way through wine-drugged dreams.

"Listen only to me, Caulay," he whispered.

Dhugal's tiny start of surprise caused Kelson to glance up momentarily, and instinctively he sent a tendril of reassurance in the other's direction. He did not think Dhugal sensed it on any conscious level, but the young border lord seemed to relax again almost immediately, releasing a guarded sigh as he leaned forward to gaze at his father's placid face.

"Stay deep asleep and hear only my voice," Kelson went on, returning his attention to the old man. "You can hear every word I say, even though you're asleep, and you'll want to answer my questions as fully as you can. Do you understand?"

"Aye," came the blurred highland voice.

As Dhugal glanced up at him in wonder, Kelson sat back and gave him a faint smile, crossing his arms casually on his chest.

"He's going to do just fine," he murmured to Dhugal in an aside. "That's very good, Caulay. Let's talk about your brother, first of all. Do you know where Sicard is right now?"

Caulay grimaced in his sleep. "Aye."

A precise answer to the question asked, but nothing volunteered. Loosening control a little, Kelson reframed his question.

"Good. And where is that?"

"Ach, I suppose he's in that keep o' his in Laas—he an' his schemin' wife," Caulay said. "I didnae like her from the day I first set eyes on her, but he *would* marry her."

His voice was more animated now, the tone so casual and glib that he might have been back at table, confiding opinions over a cup of good ale, except that his eyes were closed.

"The Lady Caitrin?" Kelson asked.

"Aye. Cate Quinnell—an' she callin' herself a princess!" Caulay went on contemptuously. "They've become a brazen lot, an' that's for sure—high an' mighty, where they think ye cannae see them. 'Tis said they keep court as if she were a queen, and not upstart pretender."

Kelson nodded and relaxed control just a little more. He did not like the implications of what the old man was conveying, but the delivery was just about perfect.

"As if she were a queen, eh?" he repeated softly.

"Weel, surely ye knew, lad—an' ye must nae allow it

tae go on. They say she takes liberties due only a sovereign. She that steals yer homage also steals yer honor."

Kelson could sense Dhugal bristling indignantly, but he stayed him with a gesture. This was not the time for righteous outrage. If Caulay was using homage in its legal sense, the situation in Meara was even more serious than he had been led to believe. Homage implied the granting of land in return for service—the military service of knights. If Caitrin of Meara was receiving homage as suzeraine of Meara—

"Caulay, what liberties has she taken?" Kelson asked, glancing at Dhugal's stunned face.

"She swears knights tae her service, wi' the promise o' land when Meara is free again," Caulay replied promptly. "An' new knights hae been made. Even the two boys hae been knighted, an' they younger than yerself!"

Kelson felt his own anger rising to match Dhugal's, and he had to push it down with a conscious effort.

"Who knighted them?"

"My brother," came Caulay's response, though not quite so promptly, this time. "I wouldna' hae thought it possible—my own kin, that swore faith tae yer father, God bless 'im. I couldnae believe it mysel', when I heard the news. Young Ithel brags that he is a knight now, and will one day be Prince of Meara of his own account. Would he hae died at birth! He is nae true MacArdry, an' that's for sure!"

"I see." Kelson probed gently for a physical image of the upstart Ithel. "Tell me about this Ithel, then. I want to know everything you can remember."

And in Culdi, Alaric Morgan prepared to enter his own kind of grim, dark concentration, opening a red leather case half the size of his fist and dumping out a handful of polished cubes carved of ivory and ebony. They clicked against each other and the table top with solid, satisfying *snicks* as he set them down, reflecting dark and light as Morgan brought a single candle closer on the table before him.

Quickly he arranged the cubes in the traditional pattern: four white in the center, forming a single larger square;

the four black set one to each corner, not quite touching. The champion's signet on his right hand gleamed as well, as he poised his fingertips above the center of the white square, but he ignored it for the moment as he set his thoughts in order.

The odd black and white dice were called Wards in the parlance of those who knew about such things, named, like the most secure perimeter fortifications of a castle, for their function of defense. To set wards was to create a magical sphere of protection encompassing the area defined by the four points at which the individual wards were placed, containing the energy within and restraining the entry of disruptive forces. Such protection was all but essential when one intended a magical operation such as Morgan planned— for to reach Kelson at such distance, and without prior preparation, would require that Morgan place his body in deep trance, oblivious to physical sensation or danger, while his mind ranged forth in search of the king.

"*Prime*."

As he spoke the *nomen* of the cube in the upper left corner of the white square, he touched it with his fingertip and sent power into its matrix. Instantly the cube began to glow from deep within—milky, opalescent white.

"*Seconde*."

The process was repeated with the cube at the upper right, with similar results.

"*Tierce. Quarte*."

He was halfway through his preparation, the four white cubes forming a square of ghostly white light. He could feel the power drain. Slowly and deliberately he drew deep breath: tangible cue to trigger the reversal of polarities from white to black, positive to negative, male to female, the other side of the balance. The pull this time would be subtly different, slightly more difficult to channel, but well within his abilities. Breathing out softly, he brought his fingertip toward the black cube resting near the upper left of the white square.

"*Quinte*."

A tiny spark jumped between his fingertip and the cube just before they touched, green-black fire kindling from within. Quickly, before his momentum was lost, Morgan shifted his attention to the upper right black cube, bringing his forefinger nearer.

"*Sixte*."

Again, the eerie glow.

When the process had been repeated for *Septime* and *Octave*, all eight of the cubes shimmered with internal light, four white and four black. Now for the mating of opposites, the balancing of energies to build the watch-towers.

Rubbing a hand across his eyes, Morgan sighed and picked up *Prime*, shifting his balance points again and readjusting control as he brought the cube near its black counterpart, *Quinte*. He could feel the tug of the opposites attracting as he closed the distance, the black cube almost seeming to rise that last fraction of space to meet the white as he spoke the word of power.

"*Primus*."

The two cubes fused in a single, silvery grey oblong. One down. Breathing deeply, Morgan pushed the completed first ward a little to one side and plucked *Seconde* from its fellows, mating it to *Sixte*.

"*Secundus*."

Again, the silver-glowing rectoid.

When he had completed *Tertius* and *Quartus*, he set the four wards on the floor around his chair like tiny, glowing towers and sat down again, feeling for the balance points in his mind a final time before he set things into motion. Commanding now, he pointed to each of the wards in turn and spoke the words, sensing the surge as the elements meshed and flared.

"*Primus, Secundus, Tertius, Quartus, fiat lux!*"

It was like suddenly being inside a tent of pale, silvery light. The very air around him seemed to shimmer. As he lowered his arm and sat back in his chair, he could feel the wards like an insulating cocoon, shielding and protecting.

Satisfied, he adjusted the candle again and laid his hands along the arms of his chair, positioning the signet on his right hand to catch the light. It was a tangible symbol of the faith binding friend to friend, protector to sovereign; the golden Haldane lion etched on the curve of the gold-set onyx oval seemed to stare at him in the dimness. Morgan used it now as a focus, willing himself to still and center, conjuring the king's face over the lion's.

He could feel his breathing slowing, his pulsebeat steadying, and gradually his vision began to narrow until only the ring was in his gaze. Doggedly he held Kelson's image before his mind, letting his eyelids droop lower, lower, until they closed and the image of Kelson alone remained. Awareness of his body receded as the mental image sharpened, and as he stretched his senses northward, all his concentration was centered on the ring, the face, the mind.

After a long while, almost at the limits of perception, he at last sensed what he had come to find.

And in Transha, immersed in his questioning of Caulay and the concentration needed to maintain control, Kelson pushed aside the first vague brushing at his mind. He and Dhugal listened with horrified fascination as the old man wove a tale of treachery far more widespread than either of them had dreamed.

But as Caulay reiterated the rumors he had heard of knights gone over to the Mearan Pretender and of Ithel Quinnell's growing popularity, a hint of Morgan's urgency began to penetrate—though not its source, at first. The king tensed as it brushed for the first time at a conscious level, momentarily shutting out Caulay's rambling as he tried to track it down. When it proved too elusive, he laid a hand on the old man's wrist, shaking his head.

"Enough, Caulay. Hush for a minute," he whispered. He closed his eyes to listen better.

Nothing. Then the lightest of feather-brushes. He sensed it might be Morgan, but even when he turned all his concentration toward picking up the next touch, he could not be sure of more than the touch sensation.

"What is it?" Dhugal whispered, leaning closer on his stool. "Is something wrong?"

Carefully, Kelson shook his head, trying not to lose

the all too tenuous contact hovering at the edge of consciousness.

"Not here," he murmured. "Someone's trying to reach me, though—very far away and very faint. And it's urgent."

A little catch of breath from Dhugal's direction, and the sense of awe and apprehension mixed. Then: "Do you know who it is?"

Kelson nodded slowly, still straining to make it clearer. "Morgan, I think, I can't—quite—pull it in."

"Morgan? But you said he was in Culdi."

"He is, so far as I know. And at this range, for me even to be aware of this much is incredible."

Slowly he opened his eyes to look across at Dhugal, though he kept tenuous touch with the continuing call. The sense of urgency persisted, as did the growing conviction that the source was Morgan. After all he had done already, Kelson knew he had no chance of bringing the contact through on his own, but there just might be another way. It was much to ask, however.

"What is it?" Dhugal breathed. "Why are you looking at me that way?"

"Did you mean what you said before, that you wouldn't let yourself be afraid of me?" Kelson countered.

Dhugal turned a little pale beneath his coppery hair, and Kelson could sense the queasy apprehension rising in his chest.

"What are you going to do?" Dhugal whispered. "No, make that, 'What are you going to do to *me*?' You need me for something, don't you? To help you reach Morgan."

"Yes." Kelson glanced briefly at the sleeping Caulay. "I need one or both of you to augment my strength. His might be enough, but I'd like you in the link as well."

Dhugal swallowed hard, making no attempt to hide his fear.

"M-me?"

With a sigh, Kelson managed a none-too-patient nod. He was finding it increasingly difficult to concentrate on reassuring Dhugal and still maintain whatever contact he had with whoever was trying to reach him, but a slightly different approach was already taking shape in his mind.

"It's the not-knowing that's the worst, isn't it?" he guessed. "You see Caulay, obviously unconscious, and you're afraid of what might happen to *you*—and that you wouldn't even know. Loss of control."

"I—suppose so."

Nodding again, Kelson stood and came around the end of the bed, staying Dhugal with a gesture when he eased off the stool and started to back away.

"Let's try something a little different from what I originally had in mind, then, " he said, climbing onto the stool and motioning for Dhugal to come behind him. "This shouldn't be nearly as frightening. I need physical contact to make my link with you, but there's no reason *you* can't control that instead of me. It will make *my* part a little trickier with you completely conscious, but I'm willing to give it a try, if you are."

"What do I have to do?" Dhugal replied warily.

"Just stand behind me and put your hands on my shoulders. Let your thumbs rest on the back of my neck."

"Like this?" Dhugal whispered, as he gingerly obeyed.

"That's fine."

Kelson took Caulay's flaccid left hand and cradled it against his knee, then glanced over his shoulder as he straightened.

"Now come a little closer, so I can lean against you for support. It's going to seem like I've fallen asleep— rather like what I did to Bertie yesterday—and I don't want to fall off the stool. Don't laugh!" he added, as he sensed Dhugal's surprise. "I really am going to be somewhat at your mercy."

He could feel Dhugal's whole body tense behind him. Then, in a very faint voice:

"Kelson, I'm not sure I can do this."

"Yes, you can," he said patiently. "Dhugal, there's absolutely no danger. If you *should* freeze up, which is most unlikely, the worst that can happen is that I won't make the contact. Now, trust me, all right?" He reached back to touch Dhugal's forearm in brief reassurance. "Take

a few deep breaths to relax now, and try to let your mind
go blank."

He followed his own instructions and felt Dhugal's cautious response.

"That's right. Another deep breath now, and let it out
slowly. Close your eyes. Imagine all the tension flowing
out of your body as you exhale. Let yourself drift now,"
he continued, as Dhugal edged into light rapport. "You're
doing just fine. Soon I'm going to bring your father into
the link, but if he can't provide enough power I'll need
to draw from you as well. You may not even be aware of
it. At most, you'll feel a slight sort of a tickling sensation
in your head. Breathe again now, deeply...."

While he let Dhugal continue settling, Kelson turned
his attention briefly to Caulay, reaching out tendrils of
control as Morgan and Duncan had taught him and tying
in the potential. He had not expected it to be enough, so
he was not disappointed. At least he was able to confirm
that it was Morgan he was seeking, and that Morgan sensed
a mutual effort to bring the contact through. He could
feel Dhugal's untapped potential towering at his back,
fiercely supportive but still a bit too tentative for comfort,
and knew he would have to go a little farther than he had
told Dhugal he would.

Gently he reached out with his senses and brushed
Dhugal's mind, keying the triggers which would enable
him to slip Dhugal into a light control trance despite what
he had said, for he could not afford to have Dhugal falter
in midcontact. Gradually Dhugal's head nodded lower,
lower, until finally his chin was resting against the top of
Kelson's head, though he was not truly asleep—only
drifting in a placid, twilight state.

After another few heartbeats, Kelson turned his attention back to the waiting contact, opening his mind to fill
with Morgan's message.

*Well done, my prince,* came Morgan's whispered
thought in his mind. *I really wasn't certain I could reach
you. Who else is in the link?*

*Caulay and Dhugal,* Kelson replied. *And Dhugal is
still partially conscious, so try not to let anything surge,*

*or he's going to feel it and scare himself to death pulling out.*

He caught the impression of laughter, like tinkling silver bells, and then a more sober note.

*A brave lad and a true friend,* Morgan sent. *Why don't you bring him back to Culdi with you?*

*I'm needed already?* Kelson queried.

*Aye. Cardiel asked me to contact you. He and Arilan have in mind to promote Istelyn to the See of Meara, and they'd like your official opinion. I told them I thought you'd approve, but you ought to do it in person.*

The logic of the request was apparent, and the importance of the summons beyond question, but Kelson sensed something more, vague and less pleasant, lurking beneath the surface. Dhugal stirred, perhaps sharing some of that uneasiness, and Kelson had to tighten his control just a little.

*What's wrong?* he asked. *What is it you haven't told me?*

*Someone tried to kill Duncan earlier this evening—* merasha *on the dagger.*

*What?*

*One of his own retainers—hardly more than a boy, really. Unfortunately, he's dead.*

*And Duncan?*

As his own shock and concern reverberated in the link, he could feel Dhugal tense and try to withdraw. Relentlessly he clamped down on the controls, determined to hold the link just a little longer, even if doing so frightened Dhugal.

*He's all right!* Morgan's reassurance came lancing through. *A bad slash on his palm that I can probably heal in the morning, and the expected aftereffects from the drug, but no permanent damage. Just get back as soon as you can.*

The emotion behind Morgan's thought was controlled, but very powerful. Despite Kelson's attempt to buffer its intensity, Dhugal recoiled at the alien sensation; the link began to quiver. No longer trusting the luxury of worded communication, Kelson sent agreement and an urgency to break contact for Dhugal's sake—and was out of the link, as much pushed as of his own volition. As he twisted around to grab the trembling Dhugal by the wrists, he continued to catch the ragged after-echo of Duncan's pain as it had come through Morgan's perception—only now it was coming from Dhugal.

"Stop it!" he whispered harshly, giving Dhugal a shake and trying to force reason past the panic. "Look at me, Dhugal! Take a deep breath and listen! Let it go! You're all right! *Duncan* is all right. Will you—"

As his mind probed at Dhugal's, bright pain seemed to explode behind his eyes, rebounding against his swiftly raised shields and somehow echoing back to Dhugal with even greater force. Dhugal cried out, doubling up and sinking to the floor despite Kelson's attempt to support him, then lay there sobbing blindly—dry, wracking heaves as he gasped for breath, rocking in Kelson's arms.

Kelson was stunned. As he held the shuddering Dhugal and tried to comfort him, he could find nothing to account for the reaction. With the breaking of the link with Morgan, Dhugal should have felt nothing further.

But when Kelson at last tried another tentative probe, the reason became abundantly clear.

"*Shields!*" he whispered, withdrawing as quickly as he could and thrusting Dhugal far enough away to stare at him in shock. "Mother of God, Dhugal, where did you get shields? Can you hear me, Dhugal? You've got *shields*! Dhugal, are you all right?"

Groggily, Dhugal uncurled and managed to sit up, holding his head with one hand and leaning against Kelson's knee for support. Kelson did not press him for further response, only waited while Dhugal got his bearings and gradually raised his head, dragging a sleeve across his tear-stained face. His gaze was still a little glassy as he looked up at the king, and he seemed to be having trouble focusing.

"Dhugal, what happened?" Kelson breathed.

Dhugal made a brave attempt at a smile. "I was about to ask you the same question. God—my head hurts!"

"Somehow you managed to pick up some of what Morgan was sending me," Kelson whispered. "Then you slammed down shields on the link. How did you do that?"

"Do what?"

"Shield. Most humans can't. Everything was fine until Morgan told me about the attack on Duncan, and the *merasha*."

"What's *merasha*?" Dhugal asked blankly.

"Oh, sweet *Jesu*, of course you don't know. It's a drug. I don't know where it comes from. But it muddles Deryni senses so that we—can't use our magic. I've never had it used on me, but Morgan has—and now Duncan. And I know it was used to make my father vulnerable to Charissa's magic, so she could kill him."

Dhugal shivered. "It sounds terrible."

"So was what happened when you tried to back out of the link! And you've got shields, for God's sake! *He* doesn't," he stabbed one hand toward the sleeping Caulay in a gesture of frustration, "and you didn't seem to, either, until we started getting that rebound from Duncan. What the devil happened? Can you remember anything at all?"

Dhugal rubbed at his temples and winced. "I can't think with you yelling at me."

"I'm not yelling at you, I just have to know what happened," Kelson said, a little less emphatically. "You scared the hell out of me."

"I scared the hell out of me, too."

Cautiously Dhugal took a deep breath and let it out slowly, not looking at Kelson as he tried to ease himself back to memory of the pain.

"It's still mostly a jumble," Dhugal finally went on haltingly, "but I do remember that after you stopped talking, I got sort of—drowsy."

"That was my fault," Kelson muttered. "I confess I did a little more than I'd told you I was going to. But that shouldn't have made you react the way you did. What else do you remember?"

"I—have a vague impression of General Morgan laughing. . . . Something about bishops, too—and—and then a terrible pain in my head."

"That must have been Duncan and the *merasha*," Kelson said, nodding. "Somehow, you got farther into the link than I thought—just enough to channel some of the emotion. I wasn't expecting shields, though. Caulay doesn't have them."

"He doesn't have my knack with animals, either," Dhugal countered, almost a little irritated, "and he used to be as good a tracker as Ciard." He paused. "Maybe it does have something to do with the Second Sight, though. Maybe—maybe shields go along with that."

"Maybe," Kelson replied.

But Dhugal's comment about the animals had struck a responsive chord in Kelson, so that the part about the Second Sight barely even registered. He recalled his father telling him how Morgan could charm deer to the very gates of the city if he wanted to, and some passing mention he remembered of Morgan's sister Bronwyn being able to call the birds from the sky. If their ability came of being Deryni, then what about Dhugal? Dhugal was also good with animals—and that would certainly account for the shields.

"Let's try this again," he said, slipping his hands to either side of Dhugal's head before the other could object. "Try not to fight me. This is the only way we're going to find out more about what we're up against."

But Dhugal gasped and tried to pull away at once as Kelson's first probe clashed against the shields again.

"God, what are you doing to me?"

"I don't want to hurt you," Kelson answered. "Try to relax. I'll ease up while you do, but you've got to help me. Don't fight me, dammit! The more you struggle, the more it's going to hurt!"

But the pain of Kelson's probe had already pushed Dhugal beyond reason again, contorting him into a shuddering fetal ball. Kelson tried several approaches, but the shields refused to budge. He could also sense Dhugal's heartrate rising dangerously. He would have to stop.

"I'm sorry," he murmured, as he withdrew altogether. "God, I wish I knew where you got those shields!"

He doubted Dhugal had heard him, but he kept repeating his apology while he waited for Dhugal to come around, kneading the rigid shoulders until finally Dhugal stirred, uncurling enough to turn frightened, pain-dulled eyes on him.

"I'm sorry," Kelson said again. "I didn't *want* to hurt you. I really am sorry. Are you all right?"

Dhugal nodded groggily and sat up with Kelson's help, lifting a hand in reassurance.

"It isn't your fault. It's mine. I did try to do what you asked, but it hurt so much—"

"I know." Kelson glanced away, reviewing everything one more time, then shook his head and sighed.

"Well, it isn't going to do us any good to just sit here and make apologies to one another. It's no one's fault. I certainly wish I didn't have to leave for Culdi tomorrow, though." He raised an eyebrow hopefully. "I don't suppose you'd consider coming with me?"

"Because of—what just happened?"

Kelson nodded.

"I can't." Dhugal swallowed and turned half away, fiddling with a fold of his kilt. "It's my father, Kelson. You've seen how he is. Winter's just beginning. I couldn't leave him here alone."

"He wouldn't exactly be alone," Kelson ventured. "Your sisters are here, and he has a whole clan family. Or is that really the reason?"

Dhugal drew a deep breath and let it out slowly, avoiding Kelson's eyes. "That's most of it. If he dies—no, make that *when* he dies—I'm going to be Chief of Clan MacArdry, as well as Earl of Transha. I have responsibilities to my people. It—makes things very difficult if the new chief isn't around when the old chief passes."

Chilled, Kelson glanced up at the bed towering above them, though he could not see its occupant.

"Caulay's dying?"

"I doubt very seriously that he'll last out the winter," Dhugal said quietly. "He *looks* strong, but his heart—well, let's just say that if he were a horse, I probably would have put him down months ago. There's—something wrong in his brain, too. He couldn't even talk for a while after he lost the use of his legs, though that came back after a few months."

"I'm truly sorry."

"So am I." Dhugal gave a resigned sigh. "Unfortunately, that doesn't change anything. I doubt even your Deryni healers could have done much for him. The least I can do is be here at the end, if that's possible. Of course, if he does last out the winter, I have another problem. Come spring, my place is at your side, leading the MacArdry levies.

"But we'll worry about that then, if it happens," he concluded brightly. "As for the other, let's not worry about that until then, either, shall we?"

With a helpless shrug, Kelson rose and helped Dhugal to his feet.

"If you wish. Much as I'd like to have you at court through the winter, I certainly can't fault your reasons for staying here. I don't suppose there's any real urgency about—what's just happened. Whatever's going on in your head has probably been that way for some time, so I doubt much will change by waiting until spring to find out more."

He and Dhugal moved silently back into the embrasure of the window seat, where Kelson pushed one of the moveable lights farther open and looked out to sea, inhaling deeply of the salt air as Dhugal stood beside him.

"Strategically, nothing much is going to happen until spring either," the king continued, after a few seconds. "Look out there. The storms are already brewing. In another month, the rains will more than double the travel time in this part of the kingdom; in two, the snows will have doubled it again. Even your cousin Ithel, as much as he may want my throne, can't move any kind of effective army under those conditions. No, we have the winter to decide how to handle this. There may be some minor local disturbances, but no serious threat for at least five months."

Grim-lipped, Dhugal glanced back into the room, at the great bed wrapped in shadows and the man snoring noisily beneath the sleeping furs.

"When there *is* a threat, I shall be there, my brother," he said softly. And he held up his right hand with the faint scar etched across the palm.

The gesture moved Kelson more than almost anything

else which had happened that night—and there had been many moving moments. Wistfully he raised his own right hand and matched the faint scar across his own palm to the one on Dhugal's. The memory of the making of those scars came flooding back all in an instant, as if the two of them stood once more by the sacred well, high on a wind-scoured hilltop at the edge of Candor Rhea. Kelson had been ten, Dhugal nearly nine.

"Are you sure you really want to?" Dhugal had asked, as they washed their grimy hands in water from the well. "My people count an oath as strong as blood, when blood has been shed. And what will your father say?"

"I don't care what he says, after it's done," Kelson had replied. "He can't undo it, can he?"

"No. Nothing can undo it unless one of us is dead."

"Then we don't have to worry," Kelson had said with a grin, "because you and I are going to live forever, aren't we?" He paused a beat. "Does it hurt much, do you know?"

Dhugal had looked a little greenish under his freckles.

"I dunno," he confided. "My brother Michael made blood-oath with his friend Fulk when they were younger than we are, and he said it hurt *terribly*—but I think Michael makes things up to scare me sometimes." He swallowed. "It's only a little cut, after all. If we're going to be knights, we have to learn not to be afraid of getting wounded, don't we?"

"I'm not afraid," Kelson had retorted, handing Dhugal his silver-mounted dagger. "Here. Do it!"

He had actually been very much afraid, and so had Dhugal, but he had not allowed himself to flinch as Dhugal's inexperienced hand drew the blade across his flesh. Fascinated, Kelson held his wrist and watched the blood well in his palm, only dragging his eyes from it when Dhugal laid the black-carved hilt of his own dagger across Kelson's bloody fingers. The pommel had clasped a water-pale amethyst, and he remembered the blood staining it a darker hue as he drew the blade across Dhugal's palm in a wound to match his own.

"Say the words after me," Dhugal had whispered, clasping his bloody hand to Kelson's and looping a handkerchief to bind them. "I take you as my brother, of blood and of life."

"I take you as my brother, of blood and of life," Kelson had repeated.

"I call to witness the four airts—those are winds," Dhugal added.

"I call to witness the four airts," Kelson agreed.

"That so long as I have breath, I will stand by my brother with my life and my honor...."

With a little smile, the adult Kelson clasped his free hand around their joined ones and nodded.

"I'll expect you in the spring, then, my brother," he said quietly, not wanting to break the mood. "Do your filial duty through the winter, and keep the peace here in Transha for me, and then come to me at Culdi as soon as the passes are clear."

"I will, my lord," Dhugal whispered. "And God keep us both safe until then."

# CHAPTER SIX

*They only consult to cast him down from
his excellency: they delight in lies: they
bless with their mouth, but they curse
inwardly.*

—Psalms 62:4

By special request of the Archbishop of Rhemuth, the
bishops at Culdi met in closed convocation early the next
morning. In Duncan's absence, Istelyn was drafted to
serve as secretary for the proceedings. No one was more
surprised than he when Cardiel proposed him as the next
Bishop of Meara.

To the relief of Cardiel and Arilan, support for Istelyn's
candidacy quickly grew. Once the stunned Istelyn's praises
had been sung by a bemused Archbishop Bradene, who
had more cause than any other man to know Istelyn's
work, hardly a prelate in the room did not join actively
in his support, for Istelyn's nomination provided an ele-
gant solution to the Mearan problem. By noon, when the
entire community met for High Mass, Archbishop Bradene
was able to announce a unanimous decision from the pul-
pit. With few exceptions, the news was received with
relief and general approval.

One of those who did not approve of the bishops' choice
was Judhael of Meara, though his public reception of the
news was gracious and obedient. As soon as was seemly
after Mass, however, he tapped discreetly on the door of
his patron, Creoda of Carbury. The bishop's secretary
admitted him at once.

"You could have warned me," he said, when the sec-

retary had shown him into Creoda's presence and the
formalities had been observed.

Sighing, Creoda motioned Judhael to take a seat across
from him, staying the priest-secretary with a similar gesture. Judhael sat. He was a youngish-looking man of
ramrod-straight carriage, with hair gone prematurely silver, in stark contrast to his clerical black. The pale, sea
blue eyes measured Creoda accusingly, the hands also
betraying his agitation as he played with a ring on his right
hand.

"These things happen," Creoda muttered. "If it's any
consolation, you reacted precisely as you should have.
Cardiel sprang the recommendation on us at an early
meeting this morning. There was no way to warn you
between then and Mass. I'm sorry."

"So am I." Judhael worried at his ring a moment longer,
then glanced aside at the fire in the stone fireplace. The
silver signet on his hand was more befitting a secular lord
than a cleric.

"What happens next, then?" Judhael asked. "Is this
the end of it? Will the king ratify Istelyn's appointment?"

"I don't know, to all three questions," Creoda replied.
"Istelyn has been in the king's favor for several years, so
I doubt there will be any objection on the part of His
Majesty. That does not necessarily spell an end to things,
however."

"No?"

Creoda snapped his fingers in the direction of the secretary and held out his hand for the folded square of
parchment which the man immediately produced. Judhael
sat forward expectantly, but Creoda took his time unfold-
ing the missive.

"This came late last night," the bishop said, holding it
at arm's length and squinting at the text before handing
it over to Judhael. "The gist of it is that our brother in
Saint Iveagh's is prepared to support you, and awaits the
guide who will escort him to freedom."

"And how much is that support worth, now that someone else has been chosen for the See of Meara?" Judhael
said bitterly, as he scanned the closely penned script.

"It will be as useful as it needs to be," Creoda replied. "At very least, he can pull the ecclesiastical factions together for the reunification of Old Meara."

"You really think he still wields that much influence?"

"He might surprise you," Creoda countered. "Granted, he's a bit fanatic for some people's tastes, but I have always known him to be an upright and godly man. His treatment at the hands of the king rankled many, myself among them. He *was* our elected primate, after all."

"And a fanatic," Judhael reminded his superior, as he handed the missive back to the priest beside him. "You yourself have conceded that."

Creoda shrugged narrow shoulders and smiled a thin, smug smile. "Please, Father. Grant me credit for *some* common sense. Just because one describes our one-time master as a godly man does not necessarily mean one thinks he should be primate once again."

"Not primate?" Judhael stared at the bishop in blank astonishment. "But, I thought—"

"Don't think, Father." Creoda replied softly. "Let me do the thinking. There are other things at stake besides your Mearan See. The less you know, the better."

"But—"

"It is said that the king can force a man to speak the truth, Father," Creoda went on. "And God alone knows what unholy things his Deryni friends can do. But one cannot speak of what one does not know, now, can one? My silence is for your protection as well as mine, my son."

Judhael's face turned pale beneath his silver hair, and he hugged his arms across his chest as he suppressed a shiver.

"Dear God in heaven, you're right! General Morgan stopped me on the way out of chapel last night. I couldn't avoid him. He wanted to know whether I had any knowledge of an assassination attempt on McLain."

"An assassination attempt?"

"You weren't behind it, then?"

"Certainly not! What happened?"

Judhael looked confused as he shook his head. "I don't

know for certain. Apparently there was a boy with a knife. It can't have been too serious, though. McLain attended Mass this morning. I saw him sitting next to Morgan."

"So he was." Creoda stared into space for a few seconds, then shook his head. "No matter. It doesn't concern us. Any number of people might want a Deryni priest dead."

"Or a Deryni duke," Judhael added. "He's that, too, don't forget. My aunt and my cousins wouldn't mind."

When Creoda looked puzzled, Judhael continued a little disdainfully.

"Can you have forgotten, Excellency? Because it has no immediate ecclesiastical significance doesn't mean it isn't important. As Duke of Cassan and Earl of Kierney, Duncan McLain has no direct heir. By strict right of succession, his lands should pass to Ithel after he dies— not that the king would allow it."

"Ah, then, Morgan felt you had a motive," Creoda breathed. "Which, in fact, you did. That's why he wanted to question you. Aren't you glad you knew nothing to tell him?"

"I'll confess to that. He did want to know how long it had been since I'd heard from my aunt. And he has to be aware how my elevation to the See of Meara could have helped the cause of Mearan independence."

"That is hardly any secret," Creoda observed dryly. "But, very well. We must assume that in the future he'll be even more observant—which simply confirms my instinct that you should know as little about the rest of our plans as possible, until the deeds are done. Do you agree?"

"I have no real choice, it seems."

"No, you do not. Therefore, for the time being, I advise you to bide your time, support Istelyn with grace—and stay as far as possible from Morgan or any other Deryni. There are too damned many of them around, as it is."

Judhael inclined his head in assent.

"Good. I think you'd best return to your quarters now," Creoda went on. "And stay there, as much as possible. No one will think it odd if you keep to yourself for a few days. I gather that the king is expected back tomorrow or the day after, and I anticipate a mass exodus to Ratharkin for Istelyn's investiture shortly thereafter. I hope we will be ready to make our move soon after that."

"I shall bow to your judgment, Excellency," Judhael murmured, kneeling in formal leave-taking to kiss the bishop's ring and receive his blessing.

When Judhael had gone, Creoda glanced aside at his secretary.

"Is Gorony's messenger still waiting in the next room?" he asked.

"Yes, Excellency."

"Very well. Ask him to come in, then, and bring your inks and vellums. We have work to do."

Two days later, the king returned to Culdi. A delegation of bishops met him outside the city gates and conducted him with due ceremony to the chapter house, where Istelyn was formally presented as bishop-elect of Meara. Messengers had been sent ahead on several different roads to intercept the king and apprise him of the bishops' intentions, so an informed Kelson was able to grant his royal approval on the spot. He dined with Istelyn and a few other intimates that evening, then retired with Morgan and a mostly-recovered Duncan later that night; the three of them exchanged details of what had transpired in the days of Kelson's absence. The following morning, the entire royal party made the day-long ride to Ratharkin, to witness Istelyn's installation the following day.

That night, however, while king and court rested in Ratharkin and the new bishop-elect kept vigil with several of his brethren in a nearby monastic chapel, a man in monk's robes made his way along the silent corridors of another monastery far to the east and north, close by the sea. The prisoner of Saint Iveagh's paced impatiently as metal picked at the workings of his door lock from the other side, fearing at each new scrape or click that the sound would raise the alarm. The face which greeted him, when the door swung back at last, was that of the monk who had confessed him earlier in the week: the preacher

Jeroboam, whom he had been told to expect. Jeroboam inclined his head for Loris' blessing, then signed that he should remove his sandals. The bare feet of the two made no sound as they descended the tower newel to make good their escape.

It was the hour between Matins and Lauds, when all the abbey slept. Only now might they hope to traverse the abbey's corridors without danger of meeting someone. As they skirted the night stairs, closed by the monks' dorter, Loris hardly dared to breathe. Once past, he could breathe, but their route became a maze of unfamiliar turns and jogs. He had no idea where he was.

Another descending stair gave way to downward-sloping corridor, then to rock-hewn tunnel, then to rough sea cave—and a harrowing descent of the remainder of the cliff face by rope, to board a waiting curragh. Loris clung to the sides of the tiny craft and prayed as the curragh left the shelter of the cove and headed out through the swells, not relaxing until a ship suddenly loomed out of the fog ahead, spars stark and skeletal in the darkness. As he scrambled aboard, the master of the ship tugged at his forelock and gave silent signal for the crew to begin rowing.

"God prosper Your Excellency in your work," said a muffled voice, kneeling shadow-vague to grasp the newcomer's hand and kiss it.

"Gorony?" Loris whispered, raising the man to peer and then embrace him. "Gorony, Gorony, I feared never to see you again, or to taste freedom! Oh, I am well blessed with such service!"

Gorony pulled away far enough to incline his head in thanks, smiling contentedly. "I had powerful allies, my lord. But not powerful enough, I fear, to prevent your enemies from making our task more difficult from this point on. The Lord Judhael was *not* elected to the See of Meara. Tomorrow morning, Bradene and Cardiel will invest Henry Istelyn in Ratharkin, before the king and most of his court."

"Istelyn? Damn!" Slamming one fist into his other palm, Loris half turned away from Gorony, moving farther into the bow. The wind was freshening as the ship ghosted further from the shelter of the sea cliffs, and canvas rustled and snapped as the crew hoisted the sail aloft and caught the air.

"Do you know how it happened?" Loris asked, after taking a moment to subdue his anger.

Gorony shrugged. "Not in detail, Excellency, but one gathers that the Deryni McLain had a hand in it. Incidentally, I regret to report that our diversion was unsuccessful. McLain still lives and will himself be consecrated bishop at Easter, to serve Cardiel."

"A viper in the episcopate!" Loris spat vehemently over the rail. "What about our agent? Did he talk?"

"Apparently not. McLain killed him during the attack. Fortunately, not even Deryni can make the dead speak— especially when *merasha* is involved."

"Ah, then the boy *did* manage to wound him."

"Aye, though not deeply enough to do real damage: a slash across one palm, from what I hear. Apparently Morgan was able to heal that, though not right away, with the *merasha* in it. McLain was quite up to attending Mass the next noon, and seemed to bear no sign of the wound."

"Blast him for the Deryni heretic he is!—that both of them are!—and *that* is going to be a bishop!" He indulged an explosive sigh, then glanced at Gorony more mildly.

"How does this change our plans, then, my friend? You've worked miracles enough, simply to get me out of Saint Iveagh's, but there's no way we can reach Ratharkin in time to prevent the investiture."

"That's true, my lord. However, by the time we *can* reach Ratharkin, the king and his court will be on their way back to Rhemuth. For all the winter, Meara's new bishop will be guarded only by his garrison—and most of them owe obedience to the Bishop of Culdi or to Judhael himself."

"Do they, indeed?" Loris breathed.

"Even so, my lord," Gorony replied, smiling. "Nor does Bishop Creoda's support end with the gaining of your freedom. He proposes to help you depose Istelyn and then consecrate Judhael in his place. The king won't even know for several weeks, if things go as they should—and the snows will make it almost impossible to do anything about it until spring. By then, you and the Princess Caitrin should be firm allies."

When Loris had digested the information, he nodded. "Creoda, too, has served me well. Have we a third bishop available, to make the validity of Judhael's consecration beyond question?"

"We hope to—ah—'persuade' Istelyn to assist," Gorony said carefully. "His cooperation would lend us credence in the eyes of royalist supporters in the city, and perhaps ease the situation through the winter. Failing that, Mir de Kierney and several of the other itinerant bishops are remaining within easy access of Ratharkin. Once the city is secured, you shan't lack for bishops to do your bidding."

"How many?" Loris asked.

"For now, perhaps as many as seven, not counting Judhael or yourself. Three hold titled secs." Gorony paused. "I should add that none of these know that you are involved besides Creoda and Judhael, though the cause of Mearan independence binds them all. However, I think they can be persuaded readily enough to support you, once it's learned you plan to champion the Princess Caitrin."

Loris snorted under his breath, then glanced around behind them before looking at Gorony. "Do you think I care a whit about *her*, Gorony? It's my see I want back—and I want the Deryni who took it from me. I want them very badly."

"I believe you may just get your wish, my lord." Gorony smiled. "You'll find these bishops far more biddable than the last lot—and by starting with a united Meara, there's nothing to prevent the creation of more bishops who will do as you ask them. Meara can be but the first step."

"Ah, Gorony, you do understand quite well, don't you?" Loris murmured appreciatively. "I'll not forget, I promise you." He sighed as he glanced out at the blank sea ahead. "How long before we make landfall? I am eager to be about our work."

"Tomorrow, dawn. From there, it's two or three days' ride to Ratharkin. We expect no opposition. Why don't you rest, my lord?"

"Thank you. I believe I shall. And I may even sleep—now."

Sleep had fled Saint Iveagh's not long before, however, the abbot suspending the Office of Prime for the first time in thirty years. The old monk who knelt trembling before the abbot and the brethren hastily assembled in Loris' empty chamber was nearly weeping, his voice barely audible, even though the abbot had already dispensed all in the room from the Order's Rule of speaking in a whisper save during Divine Office.

"I cannot explain it, Father Abbot. He is simply gone. He asked to attend Vespers, so that he might hear Brother Jeroboam preach, and I myself locked his door when he returned. Here is the key." He extended it in both hands, not looking up. "I will swear on whatever holy relics you require that it has not been out of my possession."

Another monk stepped forward from the ranks and knelt beside the distraught man.

"It is true, Father Abbott. Brother Wenceslaus had the key when he returned from escorting Father Loris back to his room. He and I kept vigil in the Lady Chapel until Compline. Both of us looked in on Father Loris before retiring, but he seemed to be asleep—and he often omits the early morning offices. There was no occasion to check on him again until we came to rouse him for Prime."

The abbot, rumpled and disheveled in a hastily donned mantle pulled over his sleeping gown, sank wearily onto a stool and sighed.

"Then, he could have been missing for many hours," he murmured. "How *can* this have happened? Brother Wenceslaus, please believe that I do not hold you personally to blame, but could there possibly have been a second key?"

Another brother, bending to inspect the door latch by the light of a candle another monk held, tut-tutted primly to himself and shook his head as he glanced up at the abbot.

"I doubt there was another key, Father Abbot. The lock shows definite signs of tampering—perhaps one of the tinkers who paid us visit in the last few days." He paused a beat. "Or some other stranger. I don't suppose anyone has questioned Brother Jeroboam?"

The abbot shook his head miserably. "Unfortunately, I am informed that Brother Jeroboam is also missing. Alas, it appears the good preacher was not what he appeared. That we did not recognize this is the fault of no one in this Order, but the fact remains that the prisoner entrusted to our charge has escaped. We have failed in our duty."

As he sighed again, the assembled brethren hung their heads guiltily.

"Well, there is no help for it but to tell the king, my brethren—and told he must be, though I weep at the shame of it."

"The shame is all ours, Father Abbot," one of the monks murmured.

"Yes, yes." The abbot shook his head and sighed a third time. "Search a final time, my brothers. Perhaps we will find some further clue as to how this was accomplished. Meanwhile, I shall draft a letter to the king. Brother Hospitaller, I shall need a messenger to leave for Rhemuth at dawn. Do you see to his provisioning."

"Yes, Father Abbot."

At a noon Mass that same day, the Feast of Saint Andrew, the Most Reverend Henry Istelyn of Rhemuth was officially proclaimed Bishop of Meara and invested with the symbols of his office. Enthroned in his cathedral of Saint Uriel and All Angels, flanked by his archbishops and brother prelates, and witnessed by King Kelson, he received the homage and obedience of every Mearan clergyman present, no one's more gracefully or humbly offered than Judhael's. The king himself begged the favor of the new bishop's first blessing, for he had fond memories of Istelyn's loyalty during the campaign against

Torenth, and he and his closest confidants knelt with bowed heads as the age-tried words were spoken. That night there was feasting in the bishop's hall.

The citizenry seemed reasonably content with their new prelate, but just to ensure a peaceful winter, Kelson gave Istelyn the loan of twenty sergeants and men-at-arms from his own warband; Cardiel gave a like number of episcopal troops. These were to augment the garrison remaining from the tenure of the deceased Bishop Carsten, which had already been swelled by a score hand-picked from Bishop Creoda's levies. Creoda himself offered to remain in Ratharkin for a few weeks to assist Istelyn's peaceful assumption of the real reins of power. It was a brotherly gesture which no one had cause to question.

The worsening weather allowed no over-long lingering on the part of the king, however. With Istelyn apparently stable in his new-gained office, Kelson must return to Rhemuth to resume the governing of the rest of his kingdom. Troubles there might be during the long winter to come, but the king felt his new bishop tolerably well protected. He was merry as he rode out the Ratharkin city gates the following morning, he and his party in good spirits despite the light rain which was falling. Several of the other bishops who had come from Culdi for the installation intended to travel with the royal party until it was time to head off for their own holdings, so the journey had taken on almost a festival air. As the cavalcade made its way south, to broach the mountain passes near Cùilteine before bad weather should force a longer route, neither Deryni nor human in the royal van dreamed of the treachery brewing in the city they left behind—or the further treachery afoot but a few days farther north.

# CHAPTER SEVEN

*The words of his mouth were smoother*
*than butter, but war was in his heart; his*
*words were softer than oil, yet were they*
*drawn swords.*

—Psalms 55:21

In the predawn stillness of the following day, the curragh carrying the once and future Primate of Gwynedd pulled away from a ship standing to off the Transha coast and glided silently toward a sheltered cove. The fragile craft bobbed and bucked as it ploughed through the breakers closer to shore, and its two passengers gripped the hide-covered gunwales a little anxiously, huddled deep in heavy mantles against the icy spray. As sand hissed under the keel, two seamen leaped into the surf to pull the craft farther onto the beach. Torches emerged from the early morning fog, gradually revealing armed men, darkly clad. Beyond, just audible above the crash of the surf, horses stamped and snorted and harness jingled.

"Hello, the boat," a low voice from among the torches called.

As Loris stood a little unsteadily, the curragh teetered in the surf.

"Brice?"

Immediately, the band's leader and one of the torchbearers detached themselves from the rest and came forward.

"Welcome to freedom, Your Excellency," said Brice of Trurill. He handed Loris out of the boat and bowed

101

over his gloved hand. "I hope your journey was not exceptionally tiring."

Loris staggered a little on the wet sand as he found his land legs, but Brice steadied him with a hand under his elbow as together they trudged up the steep incline of the beach. His companion assisted Gorony from the boat. As soon as both men were ashore, the seamen began pushing the craft back into the breakers. Offshore, the waiting ship briefly showed a light.

"My thanks for your assistance, my son," Loris murmured, puffing a little from the exertion of the climb. "Your service shall not go unrewarded. Is everything in order?"

"All in order, Excellency. We've purposely kept your escort small, to avoid arousing undue attention, but Gendon managed to locate several of your former guards from Valoret. All of us are sworn to your service."

He gestured toward his comrades, waiting dark and faceless by the fidgeting greathorses, and as one, they bowed their heads in homage. With a satisfied nod, Loris raised his right hand in benediction and murmured the words of a blessing. Brice and Gendon also bowed their heads to receive it. When he had done, one of the men brought a pair of horses forward. Brice, after donning a helm with a baron's coronet embossed around its crown, himself held the renegade archbishop's stirrup so he could mount.

"What is our destination?" Loris asked, as he swung up and gathered the reins in gloved hands.

Baron Brice of Trurill smiled as he mounted his own steed.

"We ride to Ratharkin, Excellency, where more of your allies await us."

Loris' answering chuckle of grim pleasure was the only response he allowed himself as the rest of the party mounted up. As the men one by one hurled their torches into the surf, their dark forms blended with the rising fog once more. Jingling harnesses made but faint counterpoint to the waves as they quit the beach and headed south. Beyond the breakers, the ship lingered a moment longer, riding the long swells like a ghostly seabird, then was gone in the mist. Soon, the only sign of the predawn meeting was a scattering of burnt-out torch stubs drifting out to sea on the tide.

Their passage had not gone unmarked, however. The pair of bearded scouts observing from their bellies on a cliff above the cove had tracked the black-clad warband since just before midnight. The presence of any group of armed men on Transha soil would have been cause for suspicion; these seemed deliberately arrayed to disguise their identities and were certainly there without the leave of the MacArdry chief. The arrival of the ship had only increased the watchers' suspicions. One of them studied the landing party through a long spyglass, hissing in breath through his teeth as he watched the taller of the newcomers raise his hand in blessing.

"I dinnae know who he is, but I like not th' feel o' this," he whispered, handing off the spyglass to his companion. "Wha' d'ye think they're about?"

The other grunted and put the spyglass to his own eye, watching silently for several seconds before replying.

"Nae guid, an' that's for certain. We must tell th' laird."

"Aye."

They continued to watch until their quarry had mounted up and left, noting number, direction, and whatever other detail might be gained from such a vantage point. Soon they, too, had melted into the morning mist, settling quickly into a brisk, ground-eating pace as they headed back toward Castle Transha.

"I dinnae think they wore livery or badges, sair, but a band that well armed an' wi'out standard or banner smacks of treachery t' me," the stouter of the men reported an hour later, in the hall where the chief of the MacArdry and his heir broke their fast with a few other of their clansmen. "I'm wagerin' 'tis Mearan mischief."

"Mischief, aye. I'll grant ye that," old Caulay muttered. "But why *Mearan* mischief, Alexander? Have ye proof?"

Alexander shook his head. "Nae proof. A feelin' is all.

There's sommat else, tho': At least one o' the men who landed was a priest. He blessed th' escort before they rode out. Now, why would a priest be makin' secret rendezvous with rogue knights?"

Blearily Dhugal MacArdry rubbed sleep from his eyes and glanced at his father. The old man had had a bad night. Any physical leadership on the part of the ailing chief had been out of the question for some time; this morning, Caulay was barely even able to follow the conversation—and knew it. As an almost imperceptible nod passed between father and son, Dhugal stood, tossing off the last of his morning ale.

"I think we'd best find out why," he said, wiping the back of a linen-clad forearm across his mouth. "You say they're headed toward Carcashale?"

"Aye—unless they turn east at Colblaine, which I doubt."

"'Tis Carcashale for us as well, then. Caball, how many men can we muster in time to head them off?"

"Mayhap a dozen," his father's castellan replied. "I wish I could give ye more, but two patrols are out already—an' many hae headed to their ain hames for th' winter. It's a bad time o' year, lad."

"Aye, but there's no help for that. We must ride wi' what we have." Dhugal sighed. "Tomais and Alexander, I'll ask that ye join us—an' Ciard as well. Will ye see to it, Caball?"

"Aye, Dhugal."

As the men left to do his bidding, leaving only the clan piper and Kinkellyan the bard in the hall with the old chief and his heir, Dhugal turned back to his father. The old man's eyes were troubled beyond his physical pain as he reached out a hand to clasp Dhugal's.

"This does nae sound guid, lad. I dinnae like it. Th' priests an' bishops hae been at Culdi all th' past month. What cause has another priest tae come in secret this way? An' tae come by sea this time o' year—"

Tight-lipped, Dhugal nodded, stripping off linen and kilts to don riding leathers and light armor which his gillie brought.

"Aye, I dinnae like it either, Da. An' the king would've told me if he'd known of it. This smacks of treachery. But we've no choice but to investigate."

"Aye, ye have not. But—be careful, lad. Th' clan needs its chief."

Dhugal forced a grin as he squeezed the old man's hand.

"We'll hear no more o' that, Da. The clan *has* its chief, an' will for many a year, the Lord willing. Besides, I've nae finished my apprenticeship with ye."

The old man nodded and smiled as Dhugal pulled away to let Ciard finish arming him, but both of them knew it was a charade. Dhugal pretended to adjust a strap on his brigandine while Ciard looped a sword baldric over his head and brooched a heavy, furlined cloak at his throat.

Then Dhugal was drawing on gauntlets and striding out of the hall, raising a hand in final farewell as he went. Minutes later, the Transha warband rode out the castle gates toward Carcashale.

Two hours later, Dhugal and his men sat their shaggy border ponies stirrup to stirrup across the mouth of Carcashale pass—a position which would bring the approaching foreigners within a dozen yards of the Transha line before they were even aware they were not alone. Dhugal held the center of the line, Ciard at his left with his personal standard and Caball far to the right with the Transha banner. The silks were almost gaudy against the grey December sky.

From the point above, the signal came. As Dhugal drew his sword and raised it, steel slithered from a dozen other scabbards in answer. He shifted the leather-faced targe on his right arm and collected his pony's reins. As the first of the black-clad intruders rounded the curve and faltered at the unexpected array awaiting them, Dhugal kneed his mount a few steps forward.

"Stand, in the name of the king, and state your business!" he said, letting his sword rest lightly against his left shoulder. "You trespass on the Earl of Transha's lands."

But the men ahead were not inclined to parley. Even as Dhugal realized that, wheeling his pony in strategic retreat, they were spurring their larger mounts from trot to gallop, bunching around the two unarmored men in their midst and drawing weapons as they came.

Dhugal signalled his men to scatter as he fled, trusting that the quickness of their border ponies and intimate knowledge of the terrain would at least enable them to escape. The charging men did not fan out in general pursuit, however. To Dhugal's astonishment and horror, the men at the head of the band made directly for him, the outriders brushing off his more lightly mounted and armed men with devastating results while the leaders drove straight toward him.

"MacArdry, to me!" he cried.

His men tried to rally. Ciard got separated from him by a man on a particularly large and nasty bay which kicked and tried to bite, and Tomais darted desperately behind to take his place and shield him. But the strangers cut down the scout with hardly a wasted effort and then crashed their mounts into Dhugal's, bowling it off its feet. Dhugal fell hard. He lost his helmet, but somehow he still had his sword in his hand as he scrambled to his feet. He glanced around wildly to find himself totally surrounded by the enemy.

He threw away his targe. Catching at the reins of one of his attackers with his free hand, he jerked and forced the animal to its knees, spilling its rider even as he blocked another man's sword blow.

But his astonishment at the Trurill badge on the surcoat beneath the fallen man's mantle threw him off stride; and before he could collect his wits, the steel-shod hoof of another man's horse caught him in the thigh with near bone-crushing force. Even as he gasped with the pain of it, trying not to fall under yet another horse's hooves, another rider kneed him in the chest, knocking the wind out of him and cracking ribs. Dimly he recognized his attacker as the Trurill sergeant with whom he had ridden only a fortnight before.

"Gendon!" he gasped, stunned.

Wheezing desperately for air, and feeling horribly betrayed, he staggered to his feet and managed to deliver a bloody but shallow cut to the arm of another attacker, but already injured, he was too slow to avoid the hooves of another horse which tumbled him to the ground—or the sword hilt which struck his temple with a solid, sickening thump as the Baron of Trurill himself grabbed him by the neck of his brigandine and yanked him up across the saddle. He tried to struggle through the fog of pain which shrank his vision to a narrow tunnel, but his fingers uncurled from his sword hilt and let it fall as the pain pounded with every heartbeat.

"Pull back, or I kill the boy!" his captor bellowed, jerking him up straighter in the saddle before him and laying the flat of his sword against Dhugal's throat. "Will your chief thank you for a dead heir? I swear, I'll kill him!"

Dhugal's eyes would no longer focus, and he could feel the bitter bile burning in his throat as waves of nausea pulsated with the pain. Even drawing breath sent jagged fire lancing through his chest, and his slightest attempt to struggle only made his captor's arm clamp tighter over his broken ribs, adding to the agony. Dimly he was aware of the sounds of battle ceasing, and then Caball's voice, breathless and desperate.

"Yield yer prisoner, sir, in th' name of King Kelson of Gwynedd! Ye have attacked th' king's just representative wi'out cause."

"A heretic king!" an irate voice behind Dhugal shouted. "And the heretic king has forfeited his rights by making heretics his allies. Stand aside and let us pass, or the boy dies!"

Weakly, Dhugal tried again to struggle despite the pain it cost him. He could not think clearly, but instinctively he sensed that to allow these men to escape was a thing which must be prevented at all cost, even his life.

"No!" he managed to cry out. "Don't let them—"

But the sword hilt crashed into his head again before he could finish, and he felt his world going dark around him, his body totally refusing to obey him any longer. He knew more pain as his captor pulled him higher across the saddle to thrust a gauntleted hand through the back of his belt, and he heard Clan MacArdry's warcry as they tried to answer his command.

But then consciousness was slipping away even as his captor charged into the fray again, and he knew no more.

Caball MacArdry and the remnants of Dhugal's command limped their way back through the gates of Castle Transha just at dusk. They brought two dead with them, and not a man among the living had escaped unscathed. One prisoner they had managed to take, lashed to the saddle of Dhugal's protesting pony, but only because he had been too badly injured to ride with his comrades. Were it not for the fact that they hoped to question him, Caball gladly would have cut his throat without further ceremony.

All during the slow, painful ride back from Carcashale, the devastated Caball had rehearsed the possible ways of telling old Caulay that his son was captured. In the end, he could only let Dhugal's absence speak for itself. He dared not meet the old man's eyes as he and the five other survivors still able knelt at the foot of the chief's chair in the great hall. Caulay stiffened as his rheumy eyes searched the faces of the six and did not find Dhugal.

"We met them at Carcashale, sair," Caball said in a low voice, blood seeping between his fingers where he clutched at a wound in his right shoulder. "Brice of Trurill led them. He has turned traitor."

"And my son?" Caulay managed to rasp.

"Taken," was all Caball would whisper miserably.

He tried to tell Caulay that they believed Dhugal still to be alive, though wounded—and that Caball would send out the fiery cross to summon the clan and pursue—but the news was the final blow to Caulay's already frail health. Without uttering a sound, the old man clutched at his chest and sagged in his chair, eyes rolling up and out of sight. He died within seconds, cradled in the arms of Kinkellyan the bard, his helpless kinsmen able to do nothing.

Though numbed almost beyond further reaction, and weak from his own injuries, Caball had the alarm rung

and summoned the remaining clansmen at Transha to the
great hall—young boys and old men, for the most part,
though some of the women came to tend the wounded.
Stripped to the waist so his own wounds could be cared
for, Caball sat on a stool beside the slumped body of the
dead chief as the others gathered before him, one hand
gripped tight on the edge of the table against the pain. As
castellan and next in succession after Dhugal, it had
become his grim duty to assume the leadership of the clan
until Dhugal's condition should be learned. He winced as
his wife and Kinkellyan began washing out his wound,
trying to ignore the bard's troubled muttering.

"Young Dhugal is our chief now," he told the assembled
men, "*if* he lives. I dinnae know what his captors will do
wi' him, but since they didnae kill him when they first
threatened, we must hope he is still alive."

"We should go after!" one of the men rumbled. "If
young Dhugal still lives, then he must be rescued—an' if
he be dead, then he must be avenged!"

"Aye, an' where is the prisoner?" another demanded.
"Before we gae chargin' off tae take on rebel knights, we
should first find oot wha' we be dealin' with."

"Ciard, bring him," Caball ordered, waving off those
tending his wound as the gillie and another clansmen went
to do his bidding.

The prisoner's face was pale as whey, his sword arm
splinted and bound to his chest, but he managed to stay
on his feet as he was marched roughly to the dais. Though
they had stripped him down to woolen singlet and boots
and breeches beneath his black mantle, he still wore a
rust-stained arming cap on his head. He bit back a groan
as he was shoved to his knees before Caball, only barely
catching himself on his good hand.

"On yer knees an' uncovered before yer betters, man!"
Ciard barked, yanking back the man's coif and shoving
his head closer to the floor.

The man's lank hair was cut in the bowl-shaped hair-
style favored by many warriors, but a tonsured spot
gleamed at the crown. As the significance registered, Caball
seized a fistful of hair and yanked the man's head up to

look at his face, heedless of the blood streaming down his wounded arm.

"By the good God, he's a cleric an' come armed among us!" Caball breathed. "Look a' the tonsure! What's yer name, priest? Wha' master d'ye serve, who sends priests armed into the king's lands?"

The man merely grimaced and closed his eyes as Caball twisted the handful of hair harder.

"Speak up, priest! I hae little patience t'day."

"I have nothing to say," the man whispered.

"Dinnae waste yer time wi' such slime, Caball!" one of the clansmen snarled. "He's a traitor. Let's gie 'im a traitor's reward."

"Aye, hang him, Caball!"

"Touch me and your lands go under Interdict the instant my master hears of it!" the prisoner responded, opening blue eyes defiantly. "He'll excommunicate the lot of you. I claim benefit of clergy and the right to ecclesiastical trial. You have no authority to judge me."

"Interdict?" one of the men murmured, as several others crossed themselves.

Caball gave the man's hair another vicious twist.

"Mind yer tongue, priest! Yer traitor master cannae save ye here! Speak up. Who are ye?"

Consternation flickered across the man's face for just an instant, but still he shook his head stubbornly.

"I do not have to answer to you."

"No, but ye may well wish ye had," Caball replied, releasing the man with a shove that overbalanced him into a groaning heap on the floor. "An' there is one to whom ye *will* answer."

Caball backed off unsteadily and leaned against the edge of the table, catching Ciard's eye as he let his wife and Kinkellyan return to their ministrations.

"Ciard O Ruane, as gillie to our young laird, I give ye the charge o' tellin' the king what has occurred. Spare neither self nae steed, sae lang as ye reach Rhemuth quickly. If the king is nae there now, he will arrive shortly, so wait."

"Aye, Caball."

"As for the prisoner," he smiled menacingly as he turned his eyes back on the defiant captive, "a suitable escort shall follow ye tae Rhemuth on the morrow. 'Tis only for this that we spare ye, priest. An' know that th' king is bloodkin to our young laird, an' will be greatly wroth if any further harm should come to him. Ye'd best pray that yer master does nothing rash. Take him out."

As the prisoner was jerked to his feet and led none too gently from the hall, a grim Ciard following, Caball collapsed back against the edge of the table. Behind him, a gillie handed Kinkellyan the cloth-wrapped end of a glowing iron.

"Devlin, send out the fiery cross to summon the seven chieftains," Caball said to the clan's gleeman, who stepped forward at his name. "An' let th' piper sound the *corranach* tae speed Th' MacArdry on his way." He steeled himself as Devlin and another man moved in to hold him for Kinkellyan's work.

"An' let the women prepare The MacArdry's body for his final rest," he went on. "Until we hear otherwise, young Dhugal is our new chief, an' I shall direct the clan only in his—"

The hiss of the hot iron searing flesh cut off further speech, and Caball's body arched with the agony, though he uttered not a sound. He slumped into merciful unconsciousness before it was done, so he did not hear the lone piper begin his lament for the dead chief, or the women keening as they drew around the body to take it away.

Those who had ridden with the new chief heard it, however; and Ciard O Ruane, as he mounted a fast horse to ride for Rhemuth, hoped desperately that the *corranach* was not for the young laird as well as the old.

Dhugal MacArdry would have deemed the piper's lament wholly appropriate in the days which followed, though he stubbornly refused to die. Nor, it seemed, did his captors wish him dead. He vaguely recalled shouted threats to do him harm, when he first had been taken, but he sensed that his captors considered him a hostage of some value. When he first regained consciousness, they were bandaging his head, though nothing was done about his cracked ribs.

He passed out again when they made him stand to put him on a horse of his own, however, and he drifted in and out of consciousness often in the days which followed. Even when he was awake, swaying groggily in the saddle of the rough-gaited mount they had given him, his head throbbed and his broken ribs burned with every breath and jolt. Sometimes, the very effort of trying to focus on the world around him made him pass out.

Unconsciousness was something of a blessing initially, for there was no part of his anatomy which did not hurt. He could not fall off his horse, for his feet were bound to his stirrups and lashed beneath the animal's belly, but whenever he fainted, which was all too often, his already battered body sagged limply against the ropes and strained tortured muscles anew.

But his head was the worst. As often as not, when they roused him from one of their infrequent rest stops and made him stand, he passed out again. No matter how he reckoned that, it meant a serious concussion—for which the only cure was rest. And so long as his captors continued to press onward toward their unknown destination, he knew he would simply have to endure.

In such manner did the days pass—four since his capture, so far as he could calculate. He had learned the identity of the men his captors escorted, but that was hardly more reassuring than his condition. That the notorious Archbishop Loris had somehow managed to escape his sea-girt prison was chilling. He wondered whether Kelson knew. He suspected Loris' escape somehow had to do with the Mearan question Kelson had been worrying about, but he could not seem to put it all together. His head started aching anew everytime he tried to think about it.

He worried about his head and about Loris as they rode through the snow on that fourth day. The first snowstorm of the season had swept down upon them with the morning's first light, and he shivered with the cold of it, despite the extra mantle they had wrapped around him.

Exhausted and bordering on delirium, wrists chafed raw from days of riding with his hands tied in front of him, he laced his fingers in his horse's mane and concentrated on staying conscious as they seemed to float in a sphere of silence through the still-falling snow. When their pace eventually slowed and he weakly raised his head far enough to see why, they were approaching the ghostly blackness of city gates.

He thought it was Culdi at first, for the guards who admitted them wore the Bishop of Culdi's livery. But even as he thought it, he realized it could not *be* Culdi. Culdi was loyal to Kelson; Loris would never go there. They had ridden west and south. He decided it might be Ratharkin.

They rode for what seemed like hours through the silent streets, pulling up at last in a darkened courtyard where he was unceremoniously hauled from his horse and half-dragged, half-carried inside a formidable-looking stone building. Being supported under his arms put excruciating pressure on his cracked ribs, but worse by far was the jolting of his head. He passed out as they manhandled him down a narrow, ill-lit stair.

The next thing he knew was the warmth of a fire not far away and the play of firelight on his closed eyelids. He lay curled on his left side with his bound hands partially shielding his face. There was fur underneath him, besides the fur lining of his cloak. Voices buzzed low in the background, occasionally discernable as words and phrases, punctuated by the muted clank of men disarming and the snap of mantles being shaken out. He caught the scent of mulled wine behind him, but the sound of others arriving warned him to feign continued unconsciousness. Cautiously he eased his eyes open to the merest slits to see two men in clerical attire entering the room. The elder he recognized as Creoda, Bishop of Culdi.

"Your Excellency," Creoda murmured, bowing to kiss Loris' ring. "Welcome to Ratharkin. May I present Father Judhael of Meara, whose family is responsible for arranging your escape."

As Creoda stepped aside, a younger man with silver

hair came forward to bend in homage before the renegade archbishop, remaining on one knee when he looked up and Loris did not release his hand.

"So, Father," Loris said, "I see I must thank you for my freedom."

"In truth, it is not I, personally, who am responsible, Excellency," Judhael replied, gazing up at him raptly. "My Lord Creoda felt it wisest if I knew none of the details of my family's involvement. Apparently that was a wise precaution. When General Morgan questioned me about the attempt on Duncan McLain's life last week, I was honestly able to say that I knew nothing. 'Tis said the Deryni can make a man speak the truth whether he will nor no."

"The Deryni. Aye." Loris' eyes took on a dangerous, preoccupied glint. "They also say the traitor archbishops plan to make McLain a bishop at Eastertide. A Deryni bishop! Blasphemy! Blasphemy!"

"Yes, Excellency," Judhael murmured meekly.

His tone seemed to remind Loris where he was, and the archbishop's expression softened as he looked down at Judhael again and smiled, raising him to his feet.

"But more of the Deryni and their accursed race later. 'Tis also said that your bishopric has been given to another, my son. Do you intend to stand for that?"

Judhael looked a little taken aback. "I am not certain I have any say in the matter, Excellency. I am eager to serve, of course, but Henry Istelyn now holds the See of Meara directly from Archbishop Bradene and the king. What of him?"

"What *of* him?" Loris replied. "*I* am Primate of Gwynedd—not Bradene. Are you willing to accept a slightly less pretentious title than Bishop of Meara, to unsettle these dissident bishops who have usurped my position and yours?"

Creoda's brow furrowed in question. "What title did you have in mind, Excellency?"

"Bishop of Ratharkin," Loris said. "Because the Meara you know today is not the Meara which will exist when we are finished. We will take back the ancient Mearan lands when I confound the heretic Duncan McLain—who

shall never enter into his lands as prince and prelate while
I breathe—and you, Creoda, shall be Patriarch of the new
Mearan state," he finished pointedly. "Does that please
you?"

Creoda flushed with pleasure. "A promotion for all of
us, my lord. Of course I am pleased. And allegiance to
the rightful queen upon the throne of Meara?"

"Perhaps to a queen of far more than only Meara,"
Loris said softly. "It is not only in the episcopate that the
Deryni taint has cast its pall."

Creoda blanched. "The king?"

"He is Deryni, is he not?"

Dhugal, following their conversation with growing horror, nearly gasped aloud at the implications. It took all
his strength simply to close his eyes and force his body
not to tense in outrage. The three clerics continued to
discuss minor details of the flight to Ratharkin for several
minutes, while Dhugal lay there numbly and tried to think
what he could do to stop them. The clink of goblets jarred
through the buzz of their further discussion, almost directly
behind him, and suddenly he *knew* that their eyes were
on him.

"Who is that?" Judhael asked.

"A hostage," Loris said casually. "My Lord of Trurill
tells me he's the Master of Transha, Clan MacArdry's
heir. You'll want his support when Transha is reintegrated
with Meara."

Dhugal felt hands rolling him face upward, and the
pressure on his ribs made him moan and actually black
out for just a few seconds.

"—want him to witness Judhael's consecration, then,"
Creoda was saying, as consciousness returned. "Is he
badly injured?"

"Brice?" Loris called.

The Baron of Trurill came away from unbuckling his
armor and knelt to peel back one of Dhugal's eyelids.

"He's no worse than he was, Excellency," the traitor
baron said, pressing his fingertips to the pulsepoint in
Dhugal's throat. "He has some cracked ribs that nothing
could be done about while we rode, and probably a con-

cussion, but you're mainly seeing exhaustion. He's a strong lad; he'll mend."

"Well, if he's that strong a lad, we'd better put him in a secure place, hadn't we?" Creoda said. "Gendon, take him to one of the chambers below and have someone tend to him in the morning. I don't think he'll be causing anybody any trouble before then. After that, you can see to your men. Excellency, if you and Father Gorony will follow me, please, I'll show you to quarters where you'll be secure from prying eyes until we're ready to confront Bishop Istelyn in the morning. I expect you're in need of sleep yourselves."

"A few hours will suffice," Loris said, as they headed out the door. "I wish little delay before informing Istelyn of the error of his ways. Perhaps we can..."

Dhugal lost the thread of Loris' words in pain, groaning anew as Gendon and one of Trurill's knights lifted him between them and began slowly walking him toward the door. His only thought, as he tried to make his feet move with theirs through the fog of anguish, the pounding in his head, was that Kelson must be informed of what was happening here. But he did not know how he was going to accomplish that.

# CHAPTER EIGHT

*Thou art wearied in the multitude of thy counsels.*

—Isaiah 47:13

Kelson and his warband swept into Rhemuth the following forenoon on the fringes of a thunderstorm, half-frozen and soaked to the skin despite oiled riding leathers and fur-lined cloaks. Prince Nigel met them in the castle yard, bare-headed and heedless of the rain pelting down, and set his hand urgently on the king's bridle. The ill tidings he conveyed set a chill on Kelson which had nothing to do with the storm.

"Loris? But that isn't *possible*."

The words carried to the others of his close circle— Morgan and Duncan, Cardiel and Arilan—despite the downpour. Young Baron Jodrell was the first to spring from his horse when the others would have sat there dumbly in the rain, all but immobilized by shock. His movement jarred the rest of them to action. Kelson beckoned his intimates to follow as he dismounted and splashed up the steps to the shelter of the great hall, anger warring with despair.

"I expect you'll want to question the messenger yourself," Nigel said, handing off Kelson's sodden cap and gloves to a page and hurrying to keep up.

"Yes, but tell me briefly what he said right now, so I'll be prepared."

He listened tight-lipped as he stalked through the great hall, unclasping his wet cloak with one hand while his other fumbled at the buckle of his sword belt. Morgan collected cloak and sword as he shed them, passing them to another page in exchange for a towel which Kelson used on his dripping face and hair. Nigel left king and company in a small withdrawing chamber while he went to get the messenger.

They sought the meager comfort of the fire while they waited, heaping sodden outer garments in a corner and exchanging guarded glances, no one wanting to be the first to break the silence. Jodrell played squire to the tight-jawed Kelson, removing vambraces and spurs and helping him shinny out of his mail shirt, while Payne and Rory, Nigel's younger sons, moved among the others with cups of mulled wine. The king stiffened at the approach of footsteps outside the door, hastily drawing a dry robe over his clammy undertunic.

"This is Father Bevis, my liege," Nigel said, ushering in a nervous-looking young priest in the sea blue robes of Saint Iveagh's *Fratri Silentii*. "He has been given dispensation from his abbot to speak aloud."

The man had the courage to come forward alone, but he could not bring himself to meet Kelson's eyes as he knelt at his feet. Glancing at the others to draw them nearer, Kelson wrapped his robe closer and sat with his back to the fire, stretching one leg slightly to the side so Jodrell could pull off a soggy boot.

"Be welcome at our court, Father Bevis," he said formally, "though I fear I cannot say that your news is welcome. Forgive me if Baron Jodrell continues to disarm me while we speak, but I should rather not take a chill—especially if, as it seems, my old enemy is once more at large."

The priest's tonsured head bobbed even lower.

"Nay, it is I who must ask to be forgiven, Sire—I and my brethren. We have failed you." His voice was hardly above a whisper despite his dispensation. "We made every effort to keep the Lord Loris secure as you commanded, but he—got out." He looked up fearfully. "Please do not hold us entirely to blame, Sire. Father Abbot says he *must* have had help from outside."

Morgan, warming his backside to Kelson's right, snorted

contemptuously, but Kelson only shook his head and sighed, bracing himself so Jodrell could pull off his other boot.

"Please rise, Father," he said patiently. "My uncle has told me the gist of your message already. We are certain that your noble Order did all within their power to ensure the former archbishop's safe detention. Did you find no trace of him?"

"None, Sire. And an itinerant preacher calling himself Brother Jeroboam was also missing. We think he may have had some part in it. Archb—I mean Father Loris specifically asked that the man be allowed to hear his confession a few days before. We thought he simply had been moved by the man's preaching."

"Moved right out of Saint Iveagh's," Cardiel muttered. But Kelson ignored the remark.

"I see. And the escape occurred when?"

"Six days ago, Sire—the Eve of Saint Andrew's—sometime after Compline, we think."

"Saint Andrew's Eve," Kelson murmured. "While we were in Ratharkin. That's been six days," he added, glancing aside at Morgan. "He could be anywhere."

"Would it were in hell!" Morgan said bitterly.

Kelson sighed again and started to turn toward Cardiel and Arilan, then remembered the priest still standing before him.

"Ah, thank you for bringing us this news, Father Bevis. We may wish to question you further, but for now you have our leave to wait outside. The pages will show you where."

As his cousins escorted the priest from the room, clearly disappointed to miss what might happen next, Kelson pivoted on his stool to face the fire, waiting while the others found seats. Nigel and the bishops claimed the remaining stools, so Jodrell hunkered down on the edge of the raised hearth. Duncan chose to remain standing, his arms folded across his chest as he leaned against the wall to the left of the fireplace. Morgan, too restless to sit or stand, paced a short, fidgeting path between Duncan and the king.

"Very well, gentlemen. Any ideas where Loris might be headed?" Kelson asked.

Cardiel pursed his lips and exchanged a glance with his brother bishop, who had not yet said a word.

"Toward the source of his aid, of course, Sire. He cannot have acted alone in this—and all Gwynedd knows and understands why he was relieved of his office and sent to Saint Iveagh's. That means his help must surely come from outside Gwynedd. Two possibilities come to mind immediately: Meara or Torenth."

"Not Torenth," Arilan said. "Not while Deryni hold the Torenthi throne."

"Meara, then," Cardiel said, when Arilan did not go on. "The implications, while quite different, are hardly more reassuring, however."

"How so?" Kelson asked.

"Secular and ecclesiastical politics are very closely intertwined in Meara, Sire, as we are all aware. Loris is very much a political creature. He has always found his support among the conservative clergy—and such clergy were very much involved in the dispute over who should be Bishop of Meara. He garners support from rebel factions as well. Two years ago, it was Warin de Grey; today—well, why *not* the Mearan Pretender? So long as it suits his plans to regain his position, I should think Edmund Loris would support just about anyone."

"A sad commentary on the man who once was Primate of All Gwynedd," Duncan muttered.

"Let's talk about Meara, then," Kelson said. "Who in Meara might profit from Loris' release?"

"That's simple," Nigel said. "The Mearan Pretender and her kin."

"Especially ecclesiastical kin," Cardiel agreed, glancing at Arilan, who still was oddly quiet. "Like Judhael. Denis and I had quite a discussion about him after the attempt on Duncan, Sire. My brother in Christ made light of my notion that Judhael might have been functioning as an agent for his aunt."

Morgan, noting Arilan's sullen expression, decided he had best reveal what he had learned.

"He's innocent of that, at least, Excellency," he said quietly. "Or if he is involved, it's without the direct knowledge or assistance of his aunt. Nor did he know anything about the attempt on Duncan. I—ah—questioned him about it that evening."

Arilan's reaction conveyed both surprise and anger. "You questioned him after I forbade it?"

"I didn't set out to disobey you," Morgan countered, before the other could raise more specific objections in front of the human Jodrell. "Besides, I only Truth-Read him. He wasn't sorry to hear about the attack—which is hardly unexpected, given Duncan's position relative to the Mearan royal house—but he was shocked. When I asked how long it had been since he'd heard from his aunt, he said last Christmastide. I ended the conversation after that."

"A conversation you should not have begun in the first place."

"But one which does not rule out Judhael's political interests in all of this," Cardiel interjected. "Denis, you surely can't still believe he's totally innocent."

Arilan's lips compressed in a thin, pinched line. "I never said he was totally innocent."

"Let's not wander off the subject," Kelson said patiently. "Just now, I'm far more concerned that Loris may, indeed, have gone to Meara. Uncle, you said the abbot's men found no trace of him in the surrounding countryside, didn't you?" Nigel nodded. "That may mean he made his escape by sea, then. Jodrell, could he sail around the head of Ballymar this time of year?"

Jodrell, scion of an old seafaring family, wobbled his open hand in a yea-nay gesture.

"It would be risky, Sire—but no more risky than sailing the Kheldish coast to reach Torenth by sea. If he *is* making for Meara, however, my guess is that he'd not go as far as Ballymar. If I were Loris, I'd land somewhere farther east along the coast, probably in Kierney, and go overland to Ratharkin."

"Why Ratharkin?" Morgan asked. "The Mearan pretender's in Laas."

"Ah, but Ratharkin is the episcopal seat of Meara," Cardiel said, glancing at Arilan and almost daring him to contradict, "and the good Father Judhael is there, just aching to be a bishop. In addition, Ratharkin is only a few days' ride from Laas and the rebel factions, even in the dead of winter—but more than a week's ride for us. Oh, he's picked his ground wisely, if he's gone to Ratharkin," he finished bitterly. "The Devil take him for a false and forsworn knave!"

With a dour scowl, Kelson set his balled fists on his thighs and sighed. He was not sure he liked the apparent enmity building between the two bishops. Nor did he understand the reason for it.

"This is getting us nowhere, gentlemen," he said briskly. "Speculation is cheap. God knows I fear Loris' intentions as much as any of you, but unless we have some direction, any action we take will only be wasted motion. If he's tried to round Cassan, nature may solve our problem for us. The same applies if, by some odd chance, he's headed for Torenth after all."

"I doubt that," Nigel said. "My instinct says Meara— not that we necessarily know he's gone by sea, however. But whether by sea or by land, someone is going to see him and report to us eventually. Loris is too proud a man to hide for long."

"What about Bishop Istelyn?" Duncan asked. "Shouldn't he be warned? If Loris *is* headed for Meara, Istelyn could be in great danger."

"You're right, of course," Kelson agreed. "Uncle, will you see to it? I think it might also be wise to have Archbishop Bradene join us—and any other of the loyal bishops you think should be involved, my Lord Cardiel. Once Loris' intentions are known, it's vital that we present a united front, secular and ecclesiastical. I want none of the confusion which marked the beginning of our last campaign against him."

Cardiel inclined his head in agreement.

"It shall be done, Sire."

Kelson sighed and rose. "Very well. Loris has to surface sometime—and until we hear where, I don't suppose there's much else we can do for now. Uncle, please let me know as soon as you learn anything else. Meanwhile, I'm for a hot bath and some dry clothes. Morgan, Father Duncan, would you please attend me?"

The king said little while his bath was drawn, leading Duncan to wonder why they had been asked to come along, but Morgan suspected he knew. His suspicions were confirmed when the three of them sat down before the fireplace in Kelson's bedchamber. Kelson yawned and stretched, propping his slippered feet nearer the fire's warmth, and sipped at a warm posset of milk and honey his squire had left.

"So, what's the matter with Arilan?" he asked after a moment. "He was as sullen as a schoolboy who's been caught in a lie. And don't tell me it was just because you disobeyed him."

Morgan smiled. "He's angry with me because I questioned Judhael against his orders, yes. But he is also angry with himself because he championed Judhael's innocence—or at least he played the Devil's advocate in telling Cardiel and me why we ought not to suspect Judhael in the attempt on Duncan's life. And maybe he's right. But if he isn't, then the powerful and somewhat self-superior Camberian Councillor has made a grave misjudgment of a human's character—and he especially doesn't like having that pointed out by a mere Deryni half-breed."

"Do you think he's right?" Kelson asked. "Or *has* Judhael played us false? I swear I'll crush him, if he has. I don't need anyone stirring up trouble when Loris is on the loose. And if he helped Loris, then God help *him*."

"Amen to that," Duncan said, "*if* he's guilty. But if he hadn't any part in the attack on me, Alaric, and if he hasn't been in contact with Caitrin—"

"He still would have been glad to see you dead," Morgan interrupted, leaning forward to put another log on the fire. "And simply because he had no literal knowledge of the attack and hadn't heard personally from his aunt doesn't mean he isn't involved up to his ears. That's one of the limitations of mere Truth-Reading: one has to ask the right questions."

Kelson pursed his lips. "Then you think Judhael *is* involved?"

"I don't know. Someone certainly could have been working in his behalf, though. And Loris—"

"*Damn* Loris," Kelson muttered under his breath. "And damn the circumstances that let him escape. It all connects, Alaric, I'm sure of it! He's planning something terrible. I can feel it crawling up my spine! Here it is, noon, and I'm as jumpy as a page listening to ghost stories at midnight. I knew I should have had him executed!"

As he drained his cup and sat back to stare moodily into the fire, fingertips drumming vexedly against the chair arm, Morgan exchanged a concerned glance with Duncan. Casually his cousin rose and came around behind the king, beginning to massage Kelson's tense shoulders. Kelson sighed appreciatively and closed his eyes, making a conscious effort to relax.

"That feels wonderful," he said after a moment. "I hadn't realized how tired I was. Don't stop."

"We're all exhausted," Duncan said easily, reaching out a little with his mind as his fingers continued to knead at steel-taut muscles. "Don't let your righteous anger tie you into knots, though."

"If I'd killed Loris while I had the chance, I wouldn't have to worry about getting tied in knots," Kelson said dreamily.

"Indulge your fantasy, then, if it makes you feel better. I'll grant that if you *had* killed him, things certainly would be easier now."

Kelson yawned hugely and relaxed even more against Duncan's touch, mental as well as physical, tipping his head back to loll against the priest's chest and glance up.

"You aren't supposed to agree so readily," he murmured. "I'm sitting here contemplating murder. What kind of a conscience are you, anyway? If Loris has a conscience like you, I don't wonder that he strayed." Kelson turned his gaze toward Morgan. "What do you suppose *did* make him stray?"

"Pride," Morgan replied. "The belief that his notion of truth was somehow superior to anyone else's."

"So he sold his honor to serve his pride."

"It's said that every man has his price, my prince," Morgan said. "Some are simply too high to be met."

"And is yours that high?"

Duncan faltered just an instant in his ministrations, but Morgan merely smiled.

"High enough that no man could ever pay it but you, my prince," he replied without hesitation. "I am your man, as I was your father's before you. You have bought me with your love. Nor can I ever be resold."

Chuckling delightedly, Kelson yawned and closed his eyes once more, aware that Duncan was urging sleep on him and not fighting it.

"You always know the right thing to say, don't you? Here." Kelson handed his empty cup to Morgan. "And Duncan, you needn't nag; I was planning all along to have a nap."

"That's one of the more reasonable things you've said all day," Duncan replied. "You ought to go lie down in your bed, however. You'll get a crick in your neck if you fall asleep here."

"Nag, nag, nag," Kelson whispered around another yawn. But he smiled as he rose to obey. He was asleep almost as soon as his head touched the pillow. Duncan pulled a fur coverlet more snugly around him and closed the bed curtains, then returned to the chair the king had just vacated.

"He's in quite a mood," Morgan observed. "Anything we should worry about?"

"I don't think so. He's just tired. And shocked far more than he wants to admit, over Loris' escape. What do *you* think he's up to, Alaric?"

"Loris?" Morgan shook his head and glanced into the dying flames. "Damned if I know. As Kelson said not long ago, however—something terrible."

"And Judhael?"

"The same, I fear."

\* \* \*

Even as Morgan and Duncan spoke, Loris was making good their suspicions in Ratharkin. Bishop Istelyn, after celebrating the noon Mass, was seized by armed men wearing the livery of the Bishop of Culdi and, still vested, was conducted to the chapel adjoining his apartments. Creoda and Judhael waited near the altar. A third man wearing the same episcopal purple as Creoda knelt close by the altar steps with his back to Istelyn, who could not see his face. Something in the line of the shoulders and bowed head struck a cord of both familiarity and danger.

"What is the meaning of this?" Istelyn demanded, approaching the three as the guards released him and withdrew.

Creoda and Judhael moved diffidently to either side as the stranger rose and turned.

"Hello, Henry," the stranger said.

Istelyn froze in the center of the aisle and blanched nearly as white as his alb.

"Loris!"

The renegade archbishop folded his hands complacently across his narrow waist and gave a thin smile.

"Why, Henry, you seem surprised," he said softly. "But I would have thought that after so many years in Orders, you would know better how to greet your Primate."

"Primate?" Istelyn's jaw dropped. "You must be mad! How did you get in here? You were at Saint Iveagh's, the last I heard."

"Obviously, I am no longer at Saint Iveagh's," Loris said in a low, dangerous voice. "Nor was I pleased at my accommodations there—accommodations which you had a part in forcing upon me."

For the first time, the true danger of Istelyn's situation registered. Calling for the guard would do no good, for the men "loaned" him by his supposed benefactor, Creoda, were the same who had brought him here. Nor was Judhael's presence reassuring. The Mearan priest who had sought the office which Istelyn now held would have no reason to champion his former rival.

He was totally in their power, with no way to summon help or even to distinguish whose help could be trusted.

He supposed that the men left by Bradene were still loyal, but they were probably under guard by now as well. He hoped they had not been harmed. And Loris' reference to himself as Primate bespoke a far greater treachery than simply the escape of an imprisoned exarchbishop and his exaction of vengeance against a man who had helped to unseat him from his previous glory.

"What do you want of me?" Istelyn said carefully. "Your pretense to the Primacy is treasonous and your very presence in Ratharkin illegal. And Creoda—" He shifted his gaze to the betraying bishop. "You and Father Judhael also tread on extremely dangerous ground if you harbor this man. Was all your offer of assistance merely a sham to gain my confidence until this fugitive could join you in your betrayal of Mother Church?"

Judhael said nothing, though his jaw tightened in resentment, but Creoda smiled pleasantly and inclined his head.

"We perceive no betrayal of Mother Church," he said amiably. "Rather, we perceive the actions of the consistory and the king as a betrayal of the Mearan people. Father Judhael should have been bishop here—not you. It's as simple as that. And Archbishop Loris ought never to have been relieved of his office and imprisoned like a common felon. We feel that the time has come to rectify the error, Henry."

"What *error*?" Istelyn demanded. "His own brother bishops pronounced judgment on him, Creoda. You were there. Nor do I recollect any outbursts of righteous indignation on your part at the time."

Creoda raised an unconcerned eyebrow. "I was ill-informed."

"You mean you've since been bought! What did he offer you, Creoda? You're Bishop of Culdi, for God's sake! What could a disgraced archbishop possibly have offered you that was better than that?"

"You would do well to remember who and where you are, Bishop," Loris said pointedly. "And you will either cooperate or pay the price reserved for traitors. We shall begin with Meara: the seating of a Mearan priest upon an episcopal throne in Meara, the restoration of the legitimate Mearan royal line, and the extension of Meara's borders to her previous boundaries. Meara shall be an independent princedom once more, with her own ecclesiastical hierarchy—"

"Headed by yourself, no doubt," said Istelyn.

"Yes, headed by myself. And then we shall cleanse error from the land in Meara and eventually in Gwynedd and the rest of the Eleven Kingdoms. Deryni heresy has corrupted even the mighty. It must be obliterated. This time, we shall not fail."

"But the *king* is part Deryni," Istelyn murmured.

"A crown does not confer immunity from the just wrath of an offended God!" Loris thundered, drawing himself to self-righteous attention. "The king has erred; the king must be chastised. If it would change the past, I would strike off my own hand which poured the sacred oil upon his head! His error must be burned from him, *even unto death, if necessary*, for the sake of his immortal soul! The Lord's trust has been betrayed. The Lord will repay!"

"He's gone mad," Istelyn murmured under his breath, shaking his head as he turned half away. "They've all gone utterly mad."

He heard the rustle of episcopal silk coming nearer and glanced back to see Loris almost within reach of him, Creoda and Judhael flanking him to either side.

"I give you one chance and one chance only for clemency," Loris said, raising a single finger to illustrate his point. "If you will assist Creoda and myself in consecrating Father Judhael a bishop, I shall permit you the same kind of 'honorable retirement' to which you so generously consigned me for the past two years. It is more than you deserve."

"And all I must do to be granted this magnanimous favor is betray my archbishop and my king by raising a traitor in my stead," Istelyn said. "I decline the honor."

"I should not be too hasty, if I were you," Loris warned. "Do not let misplaced loyalties lead you to your death."

"Do not threaten *me*!" Istelyn snapped. "I'll not turn traitor for offices or riches or even to save my own life.

Nor will I lift one finger to assist your illegal consecration of that man."

"I beg of you, Henry, be reasonable," Creoda said.

"Oh, I am. I'm being quite reasonable. And it occurs to me that there's only one reason you'd be courting my assistance to consecrate your Mearan traitor. You need another bishop's hands to make it valid, don't you?"

Eyes narrowed and dangerous, Loris slowly shook his head. "There is nothing I *need* from you, Istelyn. Judhael shall have his sacring whether you will it or no."

"Not by *my* hand."

"If defiance gives you comfort, then so be it," Loris replied. "But do not make the mistake of thinking that your refusal will make it impossible to consecrate Judhael. Surely you do not think I would embark upon this holy crusade if I did not have further support among the episcopate of a reunited Meara? The Bishop of Cashien and two itinerant bishops are within Ratharkin's walls even as we speak, and Lachlan and Calder arrive with the Lady Caitrin's party within a few days—so we will have *twice* the number needed to make Judhael's consecration valid."

"Twice the number of traitors," Istelyn countered.

Loris' eyes narrowed. "You are as stiff-necked as ever, Istelyn. I believe I am becoming bored with this conversation. Judhael, ask the guards to come in, please. Father Istelyn will be going to his new quarters now."

"In the dungeons?" Istelyn asked, as Judhael bowed and moved past him to obey.

Loris returned him a prim smile. "I am not a man wholly lacking of a sense of propriety, Henry. Out of respect for the office you still technically hold, you shall be detained in reasonable comfort until after Judhael's consecration as bishop." He signed to the entering guards to wait just inside the doors. "For the sake of propriety, however, I shall require that you remove your vestments before going to your new quarters. We should not want sacred raiment soiled, should you decide to resist your escort."

The mere suggestion that guards might lay hands upon him while still vested for the altar sent a chill up Istelyn's

spine, but he knew the threat was not an idle one. Loris'
hard eyes had convinced him early on that there would
be no quarter, even had he agreed to terms. Slowly he
removed the violet chasuble with its somber symbols of
Advent and laid it across the waiting arms of Judhael,
followed by maniple, cincture, stole, amice, and alb.
Finally he stood before them clad only in the violet cassock, slippers, and skullcap of a bishop, clasping the jewelled pectoral cross on his breast in silent affirmation of
his continued defiance. A guard came from behind and
laid a fur-lined cloak around his shoulders, and Istelyn
nodded surprised thanks as he drew it around himself
against the cold.

"Bishop Istelyn is to lodge temporarily with the young
Master of Transha," Loris told the guard captain. "Please
escort him there with such respect as his behavior war-
rants. He is to receive no visitors. He has our leave to
celebrate Mass privately and to minister to the boy, and
may have what he needs for either intention. You may go
now."

The guards started toward him, but Istelyn ignored
them to shoulder numbly past Loris and Creoda and make
a reverent obeisance before the altar. He wore his dignity
like a mantle as he rose and went to his captors, even
though he was sick with fear inside, but the guards
responded to the outward nobility of the man and fell into
step as a true escort rather than a custodial force. He
managed not to start shaking until they had closed the
door of his prison chamber behind him. He did not know
how long he stood there with his back against the door,
trembling and fighting down the nausea of defeat, until
gradually he became aware of eyes watching him from
the shadows of a fur-covered pallet near the pleasant fire.

"Who's there?" he called softly.

"Forgive me for not rising to greet you, Excellency,"
a young voice answered, "but my ribs hurt me if I move
too much. You must be Bishop Istelyn."

"I am."

Cautiously Istelyn moved closer. The boyish face the
firelight revealed was far younger than he had been

expecting. Below a greyish bandage tied around the boy's forehead, tawny eyes gazed up at him with disconcerting directness, though a reddish smudge of mustache marked him as a little older than Istelyn had first thought—perhaps fourteen or fifteen. Dark circles stained the fair skin underneath the eyes. It was evident the lad had lived with pain for some time.

"You must be the young Master of Transha," Istelyn said, crouching down beside the pallet.

"Almost the *late* Master of Transha, thanks to Loris' escort," the boy replied, offering a hand from underneath his sleeping furs and essaying a tentative smile. "I'm called Dhugal by my friends. This hardly seems the place for overmuch formality."

Istelyn took the extended hand briefly and returned the smile. "Then I shall call you Dhugal, young laird, since we seem to be destined at least to be colleagues. Did they hurt you very badly?"

"The horses hurt me about as much as the men, I suppose," Dhugal admitted, settling back against his mound of pillows with a barely bitten-back grimace. "After I got knocked off my pony, I was kicked a couple of times and nearly trampled. The men only hit me in the head. I've some cracked ribs, but at least the headaches seem to be letting up. What day is it?"

"The fifth of December," Istelyn responded. "We're in Advent season. Shall I look at your injuries? I haven't much skill in such matters, but perhaps I can do something."

Dhugal closed his eyes briefly and managed a slight nod. "Thank you. I can tell you what to do. I've had training as a battle surgeon myself, but there's only so much one can do on oneself as patient. Have a look. My ribs are the worst just now."

Dhugal was nude beneath the sleeping furs, his slender torso and limbs displaying the number of old scars one might expect of a lad trained in warrior disciplines, but Istelyn sucked in breath between his teeth at the massive bruising across the left ribcage. Another bruise purpled the top of the right thigh in the precise outline of a horseshoe. Istelyn could even see the prints of the nails which had held the shoe in place.

"That one looks much worse than it is," Dhugal said, brushing the bruise lightly with his right hand. "Which is not to say it doesn't hurt, or that I won't limp for a while, but at least I didn't break my leg. If they'll give you bandages, or if something can be improvised, I need you to bind my chest. Without support, even breathing can be an agony if I move the wrong way. And coughing—"

As Dhugal braced both hands over his ribcage to draw a deeper breath carefully, Istelyn looked alarmed.

"You haven't punctured a lung, have you?"

Dhugal shook his head and winced as he pulled the furs back up to his waist. "I don't think so. I'm not coughing blood. I'd give a lot for a good night's sleep, though."

"Loris said I might have medical supplies," Istelyn said. "Perhaps they'll have something to help you sleep. What about your head? Any actual wounds?"

Dhugal flinched as the bishop pulled the bandage from his head and began probing gently beneath the reddish hair.

"No—and I don't think I've missed any fractures. It's just the headaches, and they're letting up."

"All right." Istelyn managed a shaky smile as he rose and glanced apprehensively at the door. "Let's see whether Loris meant what he said about medical supplies."

An hour later, bundled in a cloak against the cold, Dhugal was sitting gingerly in a chair beside the fire and feeling more comfortable than he had since before his capture. So long as he did not breathe too deeply, the bandages Istelyn had bound around his chest gave him enough support so that his ribs no longer hurt beyond a dull ache—and that was fast receding as he sipped at the cup of wine he had directed Istelyn to prepare.

"This should make me sleep at least through the night," he told the bishop, as he took another swallow of the drugged wine and let the bitter undertaste roll over the back of his tongue. "If they'll let you have more, I want you to keep me sedated for at least another day and night beyond that. I don't like leaving myself so vulnerable, but unfortunately sleep and rest are still the best treatments I know for head injuries like mine." He sighed dismally. "It's too bad Kelson isn't here. He could—"

He broke off and glanced at the bishop furtively as he realized what he had almost said, afraid even a veiled reference to the king's newfound powers might offend the human Istelyn. To his horror, Istelyn seemed to know exactly what he had been about to say.

"He could do what?" the bishop asked. "Help you in some way with his magic?"

Dhugal swallowed audibly, trying to stay on guard. The drug was loosening his tongue as well as damping the pain. Istelyn seemed trustworthy, but this was hardly the time to begin so controversial a discussion with a man whose sympathies were unknown.

"I—don't want to offend you, Excellency, but most clergy aren't altogether tolerant of—ah—magic. Please forget I said anything."

"Ah, then his magic frightens you."

"I—I'd rather not talk about it," Dhugal whispered, feeling trapped.

Istelyn cocked his head, then glanced back at the closed door before leaning closer to Dhugal.

"Why not?" he asked. "You spoke of the king with affection and familiarity, as if you were his friend. Do you think there's something wrong with his—ah—let's call them 'talents,' if you don't like the term 'magic,' shall we?"

"It isn't that," Dhugal murmured.

"Is it that you aren't sure of me, then?" Istelyn persisted. "You've already trusted me with your life."

"That trust is mine to give; Kelson's isn't."

"I can appreciate that."

The bishop's eyes did not leave Dhugal's as he sipped at his wine—which made Dhugal increasingly anxious—but after a few seconds the man sighed and gave a tiny smile, raising his cup in resigned salute.

"I don't blame you for trying to shield the king, son, but why don't you let me tell you how *I* feel about him? I can't prove that I'm telling the truth, but you're smart enough to judge for yourself. I wasn't present at Dhassa when Loris and the rebel bishops split off from the Curia, but I sided with the king as soon as I learned of it. I was with his army at Dol Shaia. It was I who had to bring him the news that Loris had excommunicated him and placed the kingdom under Interdict."

He sighed again, then went on. "Now I've put myself on the line again where His Majesty is concerned. Loris wants me to help him consecrate Judhael of Meara a bishop. I've refused, and he'll probably kill me for it. I swear by all I hold sacred that I'm not lying, Dhugal. I don't care that the king's Deryni—not the way Loris does, at any rate. It seems to me that Kelson's done only good with his powers. Or are you going to try to tell me differently?"

"Of course not."

Dhugal looked away into the flickering flames and made himself take another swallow of the drugged wine, even though he knew it would make him only more vulnerable to the bishop's questioning. He believed Istelyn. And even if the bishop were no better than the others ensconced here at Ratharkin, it could do little further harm to Kelson's already checquered reputation for Dhugal to report that he had seen the king put an injured man to sleep with magic. Far worse had been alleged in the past two years, and by far more important people than a fifteen-year-old border lord.

"About a fortnight ago, Kelson rode out from Culdi to pay a surprise visit on one of his local barons," Dhugal said carefully. "It was Brice of Trurill. Trurill borders on Transha lands, so I was riding with a Trurill patrol." He grimaced. "That's another story. Those same men, including the baron himself, were the escort that met Loris when he landed on the coast near my father's castle, hardly a week later. They're probably still here in Rhatharkin."

"*Brice of Trurill* supports Loris?"

Istelyn sounded genuinely surprised and shocked, which reassured Dhugal.

"Aye. It was Brice himself who captured me. He had the audacity to hold a blade to my throat."

At Istelyn's low whistle under his breath, Dhugal took another pull at his wine, making a face at the increasingly bitter taste as he got closer to the bottom. He could feel himself becoming more and more detached as the drug gently entered his system.

"Anyway, when the king met us a fortnight ago, we were in the middle of routing a band of brigands who'd been stealing sheep." He paused to yawn. "Afterward, it was my job to patch up the wounded. One of our lads was in a pretty bad way. Kelson—put him to sleep so I could work on him. It was like a miracle."

Istelyn's eyes had grown as round as the moon at full.

"Did he *heal* him, then?

"No. He only laid his hand on his forehead and made him go to sleep. He says that General Morgan and Father Duncan can heal sometimes, though." Dhugal forced himself to look Istelyn in the eyes. "That can't be wrong either, can it, Excellency?"

"No," Istelyn whispered. "No, son, I don't see how it *could* be."

The bishop seemed troubled by his question, however, and soon rose to seek the comfort of prayer. Kneeling at a prie-dieu set in one of the window embrasures, he signed himself, then bowed his head in his hands and was still. Dhugal stared after him for several minutes, forming a prayer in his own mind that Istelyn was what he appeared, but when he caught himself starting to nod off, he drained the last of his wine and lowered himself gingerly to his pallet once more, grimacing at the bitterness of the dregs.

It was becoming harder and harder to concentrate with the full dose of the sedative in him, but as he settled himself under the sleeping furs, he tried to think of ways to better his situation when he awoke. He wondered vaguely whether Kelson knew yet of his capture.

Not that there was much hope Kelson could do anything about it. The fate of one man balanced ill against that of an entire realm. But perhaps Dhugal could find a way to help himself, once he had regained some of his strength.

That they regarded him as a valuable hostage was

apparent, not only from the fact that they had taken him in the first place but from his continued treatment since arriving in Ratharkin. Had his usefulness ended once they were safely out of Transha, they would have cut his throat long ago. He also recalled some reference to wanting his support when they reunited Transha with old Meara—an unthinkable defection for one loyal to the king—but perhaps that meant that no one was aware of his renewed friendship with Kelson. Nor was anyone likely to connect the young Master of Transha with the then second son of Transha's chief who had served at King Brion's court as a page.

Also in Dhugal's favor was his boyish appearance. Given anything approaching luck, he thought he might play on that to convince them that he was as naive and pliable as he looked—a mistake even Istelyn had made at first. It was a dangerous game, but if he could play it well, he might mislead them enough to lower their guard. Then he could escape to warn Kelson.

He was thinking of ways that might be accomplished as he finally abandoned himself to sleep. Unexpectedly, he dreamed not of Kelson but of his father, and a lone MacArdry piper skirling a lament atop a snow-covered hill.

# CHAPTER NINE

*But thou, mastering thy power, judgest with equity, and orderest us with great favor: for thou mayest use power when thou wilt.*

—Wisdom of Solomon 12:18

Ciard O Ruane, the advance messenger from Clan MacArdry, arrived in Rhemuth late the following afternoon, stunning the court with his doubly woeful news.

"The young laird does nae know about his father, m'lord," the man concluded, nodding exhausted thanks to a young page who handed him a full tankard. "That's assuming he's still alive himself, of course."

The intimation that Dhugal might *not* be alive was like a blow to Kelson. Before that instant, he had not allowed himself even to consider the possibility. Shuttering down the shadow of fear that flickered at the back of his eyes, the king glanced to Morgan and Duncan for reassurance, his fingers tightening viselike on the arms of his throne.

"He has to be alive," he murmured, almost to himself. "I *know* he is! Ciard, you're sure it was Trurill's men who took him?"

The gillie gave a deprecating flourish with one hand as he took a long pull at his ale. If his own son had been taken, he could not have been more devastated.

"We hae ridden wi' those men all summer, sair. D'ye think I would nae recognize them? It were the Laird Brice himself wha' had my young master o'er his saddlebow."

"And this prisoner that's coming is a priest?"

"Aye, m'lord. And an impertinent an' close-mouthed

137

rascal he is, too. But Caball has warned him he il sing for
ye!"

"And I'll wager I can tell you at least one of the things
he'll sing," Morgan murmured so that only Kelson could
hear, as laughter tinged with menace rippled through the
chamber.

"What's that?"

"That Loris was one of the men Trurill was escorting.
Remember, Jodrell *told* us he'd land on the coast."

"That isn't funny, Morgan—even in jest," Kelson
whispered.

"Do you really think I'd jest about a thing like this?"
Morgan returned. "Watch the priest confirm that it's Loris.
Who else would dare to call you a heretic king? And if
you want my guess, they're headed for Ratharkin, just as
we suspected. It's on a direct line from Carcashale and
the coast where they landed, and the landing itself was a
day-and-a-half's sail from Saint Iveagh's."

Only the knowledge of the prisoner on the way, surely
to arrive in the next twenty-four hours, kept Kelson from
ordering their departure for Ratharkin then and there. He
was snappish and preoccupied by turns all through dinner,
inwardly mourning old Caulay even as he fretted about
Caulay's son, and let his anger build against Loris.

"You're right, it *has* to be Loris," he told Morgan later
that evening, after Duncan had excused himself to confer
with the other bishops and Nigel had retired for some
much needed sleep. "I hold him personally to blame for
Caulay's death. And if Dhugal—"

He would not let himself finish the thought, shaking
his head in fierce denial as he leaned both elbows on the
mantel and stared down into the crackling fire. Morgan,
looking out over Rhemuth's rain-slick rooftops from a
window embrasure, glanced sharply at the king, then
returned his gaze to the darkness outside. His breath had
misted the blurred grey glass, and he burnished a clear
spot with his fingertip to peer outside once more. If it was
raining this hard on the Gwynedd plain, then Meara was
probably experiencing heavy snow.

"Brice of Trurill's defection hurts, too," Kelson said

after a moment, breaking into Morgan's more practical introspections. "I was going to visit him—I'm sure I would have seen the signs if I had—but I let personal pleasure call me from my duty. I never should have gone to Transha with Dhugal. Now he's been taken and it's all my fault."

"It *isn't* your fault, and if you insist upon blaming yourself, you're only going to make yourself less effective. What possible difference could your visit have made?"

"I still should have gone to Trurill," Kelson said stubbornly. "If I had—"

"If you had, there's no guarantee you would have noticed anything was wrong," Morgan interrupted. "You may be Deryni, but you aren't omniscient."

"I recognize treason when I see it!"

"From our perspective, yes. On the other hand, I would venture to guess that the Mearans see what they're doing as patriotism. After all, the Mearans regard themselves as a subjugated people. They have since your great-grandfather married the daughter of the last Mearan prince. If Loris has found supporters in Meara, I suspect it's because he's told them they're crusaders in the cause of a free Meara."

"A free Meara?" Kelson's savage kick at the nearest log on the fire produced a shower of sparks. "Free Meara indeed! Meara has *never* been free! Before my great-grandfather wed the silly Mearan heiress whose marriage was supposed to resolve all of this, Meara had been ruled by petty warlords and despots for centuries. Before that, it was no more civilized than The Connait."

"The Connait, whose warriors are among the most prized mercenaries in the known world?" Morgan asked.

Scowling, Kelson retreated from the fire and stalked across the room to join Morgan in the window embrasure.

"You know what I mean. Don't confuse me with fine points of distinction."

"It isn't my intention to confuse you with anything, my prince," Morgan replied patiently. "The point is—"

"The point is that Loris is in Meara, stirring up dissention—maybe even spearheading a civil rebellion, for all we know—and winter is setting in and there isn't a bloody lot I can do about it until the spring."

"There is also the point that Loris has one of your closest friends to hostage," Morgan said softly. "And you would be far less the man I have come to love and respect if you were not deeply concerned over his fate."

Kelson lowered his eyes, the gentle rebuke well taken.

"He really is like a brother, Alaric," he said softly. "He's far closer than my cousins. He's—almost as close as you, if you were my age—or Duncan. He even—"

As he broke off and drew cautious breath, shifting his unfocused gaze to the fogged window between them, Morgan raised an eyebrow.

"He even *what*, my prince?"

"Dhugal," the king murmured. "Sweet *Jesu*, I'd forgotten to mention it to you." He glanced at Morgan sheepishly. "Do you remember that night you contacted me in Transha, and how I had to break off suddenly because Dhugal was panicking?"

"Of course."

"Well, it wasn't wholly my idea. Dhugal pushed us out of the link—with shields."

"Shields? But that's impossible. He isn't Deryni."

"Then what is he?" Kelson countered. "He's certainly got shields a lot like ours. He can't lower them, though."

"He can't—" Morgan broke off and forced himself to take a deep, steadying breath, putting out of mind the increased danger to Dhugal if he *were* Deryni and in Loris' hands, and Loris found out.

"He has shields, but he can't lower them," Morgan repeated more calmly, glancing back at Kelson. "Are you sure?"

"I tried to read him. I couldn't get through. All I did was give him a demon of a headache. And it hurt him, Alaric. It isn't supposed to hurt."

"No, it isn't," Morgan murmured.

After a few seconds, he shook his head and set his hands on Kelson's shoulders.

"I want you to show me exactly what you did and saw

and felt," he said. "Don't hold back a thing, even the pain. This could be very important."

Breathing out with a sigh, Kelson let his hands fall to his sides and closed his eyes, willing the familiar channels to open. He would not have thought of arguing. Morgan's touch on his forehead plunged him at once into rapport, the link unclouded by any separation of miles or differences of intent. He took Morgan at his word and sent the undiluted memory surging across the link in the space of a few heartbeats, not letting up even when Morgan gasped and staggered under the intensity. Morgan looked a little dazed even after he withdrew.

"I don't think I've ever felt anything like that," Morgan murmured, focusing with an effort, "I still don't understand. You should have been able to read him."

"Maybe he has something like my Haldane gifts," said Kelson. "Some potential for Derynilike abilities. Or maybe he's like Warin de Grey."

Morgan shook his head, voicing his thoughts aloud as he wandered in the direction of the fireplace.

"No, his shields have a . . . a flavor, for want of a better word, that's quite different from Warin, who has shields and can even heal, but definitely isn't one of us."

"Then, maybe he's fey," Kelson quipped, biting back a chuckle. "He said he was—Dhugal, I mean. He says hill people have the Second Sight—whatever that is." He paused a beat. "Why *couldn't* he be Deryni, Alaric? If the strain had come into his family several generations ago—perhaps during the worst of the persecutions— mightn't there be descendants who had no idea what they were, whose occasional odd quirks of talent were simply explained as 'Second Sight,' or 'fey'? My mother didn't know, after all."

"That's what she *said*," Morgan replied. "I'm sure she at least suspected, however. And there was certainly no doubt in *my* mind what she was, when I threatened to read her and she backed off. But nothing in your contact with Dhugal points to anything but shields." He sighed. "I wish I could give you better answers. I suppose that's one of the disadvantages of getting one's training in bits and snippets the way Duncan and I did. Arilan might know better what to do, but—"

"But you don't wholly trust him," Kelson finished.

Morgan shrugged. "You've seen his attitude. Do you trust him? In spite of everything that's gone on between us, he never lets go of the fact that Duncan and I are only half Deryni. Maybe his precious Camberian Council won't let him forget it—though he seems to set that aside in your case."

"They see me in a different light," Kelson said quietly. "I'm—not supposed to talk about it."

"You mean you've had contact with them?" Morgan asked, surprised.

"Not with the Council as a whole, but individuals have made overtures." The king lowered his eyes. "It isn't for me to say anything further yet. Please don't press me for details."

Morgan longed to do just that, for this was the first he'd heard of any such contact, but he forced himself to push curiosity aside and instead flung himself down in a chair beside the fire. If the Council *had* been making overtures, if only to Kelson, that was a positive step for them. He must do nothing to jeopardize the possible dialogue.

"Very well. I shan't belabor the issue. I'm glad to hear that something's happening in that regard, at any rate."

Kelson nodded idly, leaning both hands against one of the finials on the back of Morgan's chair. From his expression, Morgan wondered whether he'd heard a word he'd said.

"Morgan, have you ever done any scrying?" the king asked after a few more seconds.

"What do you want to scry for?"

"Dhugal, of course. *Have* you?"

"In a manner of speaking. I've worked visualizations using a *shiral* crystal, though I doubt that's quite the same. One usually needs something belonging to the person one wants to scry about. Do you have something of Dhugal's?"

"Not really—wait a moment. Yes, I do."

He went to a small casket set on a table beside his bed

and rummaged inside for several seconds, finally returning with a short length of black silk ribbon.

"I borrowed this when I was at Transha," the king said,
perching on the arm of Morgan's chair and offering it for
his inspection. "Is it enough?"

"It might be." Morgan let the ribbon trail across his
hand and gave it a tentative probe, but he could detect
nothing special about it. "I don't suppose you have a
*shiral* crystal?"

Kelson's face fell. "No, do we need one? Don't you
have one?"

"Not in Rhemuth." Morgan sighed. "However, it's said
not to be impossible without one." He cocked his head
at Kelson. "You're sure you want to do this?"

"Morgan..."

"All right. I can't promise any results, though. All you
may get out of it is a splitting headache."

"I'll take that chance."

"And if he's dead?"

Kelson ducked his head, tight-lipped and all but blinking back tears, and Morgan instantly regretted his blunt-
ness.

"I'm sorry, my prince," he whispered, giving the king's
arm an awkward pat as he drew a breath and got to his
feet. "That was tactless of me. Change places with me
and we'll give it a try. I didn't mean to feed your fears."

Kelson did not look at him as he obeyed, nor did he
answer. He sensed Morgan's awkwardness, and that the
Deryni lord understood how frightened he really was for
Dhugal's sake. Morgan sat gingerly on the right arm of
the chair facing him and took his nearer wrist as soon as
he had settled, twining an end of the tightly clutched ribbon through his own fingers.

"Let's use the flames as your first focus," Morgan said
softly, himself locking on the king's eyes. "Let yourself
slip into trance and stare into the fire. I'll not share your
vision, but feel free to pull energy from me as you begin
to build an image of Dhugal in the shifting patterns of light
and dark. Draw on his essence that remains in the ribbon
and start to reach out across the miles and See him. Let

your eyes unfocus. That's right. Use the flames as a background for your Vision, but know that the flames themselves are not your goal. See Dhugal as you last saw him,
and now bring that image forward in time. Let yourself
flow with it. Good . . ."

Kelson did his best to follow Morgan's instructions,
extending his mind through the length of black silk between
his fingers as his eyes gazed at and through the flames,
but his own fears hampered his concentration. He could
feel the support of Morgan's power augmenting his own
as he sought the captive Dhugal, but he was never sure
he made a real contact. His head ached as he came out
of trance, and it hurt to breathe.

"Nothing," Morgan guessed, taking the ribbon from
his fingers as Kelson forced himself back to equilibrium.

Kelson shook his head dispiritedly. "I can't tell. I really
do think I'd know if he were dead—but I couldn't separate out anything else that I'm sure was Dhugal. Maybe
we needed a *shiral* after all."

"Perhaps."

Despite their failure to locate any tangible clue to
Dhugal's whereabouts, Kelson became convinced in the
next hour that Dhugal almost had to be in Ratharkin—
and with Loris.

"And if that's what's happened, Istelyn is in danger,
too," Kelson reasoned. "Morgan, we've got to help them."

"You mean, go to Ratharkin?"

"Well, we might be able to surprise them. How strong
can Loris be?"

But reason prevailed where sheer emotion might have
won out, for Morgan reminded the king of the prisoner
due from Transha, who might be able to shed a great deal
more light on the situation. Loris might *not* have been
headed for Ratharkin. Kelson reluctantly agreed to delay
any decision until the prisoner arrived and had been questioned, but he slept only fitfully for what remained of the
night, despite the rain drumming against the mullioned
windows.

The rain continued without cease through the morning,
delaying the arrival of the expected prisoner until early

afternoon. At Kelson's order, the drenched and shivering bordermen who had brought him whisked their prize directly to a private withdrawing chamber, before anyone at court even got a close look at him. Only Morgan, Duncan, and Nigel were invited to attend the king.

"Someone give him a dry cloak," Kelson said, as the bordermen half-pushed and half-dragged their charge to a chair Kelson indicated by the fire. "Mind his arm."

The strain of the ride from Transha showed in the prisoner's every move as he collapsed into the chair before the fire, bracing his bandaged forearm against his chest. The man did not protest as Duncan removed his own cloak and laid it around his shivering shoulders, perhaps taking comfort from his benefactor's priestly garb, but he showed an instant's panic when Kelson dismissed the guards and Nigel closed the door behind them. The eyes beneath the warrior's shock of close-cropped hair mirrored suspicion and uncertainty along with physical discomfort.

"I claim benefit of clergy," he whispered hoarsely, his glance darting nervously among the four of them. "You have no authority to try me."

Kelson leaned an arm along the mantel and studied his captive with a mixture of curiosity and anticipation.

"I don't intend to try you," he said. "I simply plan to ask you a few questions. Father Duncan, do you suppose you and Morgan might be able to do something about his injury?"

The two names triggered the expected response— Kelson had been fairly certain their prisoner did not know Morgan or Duncan by sight. As Duncan bestirred himself to reach toward the bandaged arm, Morgan approaching him from the other side, the man shrank back in his chair.

"Stay away!" He did his best to watch both of them at once and fend off Duncan with his one good hand. "Don't touch me! I want no Deryni sorcerers—"

Before he could decide who was the greater threat, Morgan glided in slightly from behind and clamped the desperately swiveling head between his hands, extending control.

"Don't fight me," he ordered, sounding almost bored

as hands and mind compelled obedience. "It isn't going to do any good. And if you relax and cooperate, we may even be able to make you a little more comfortable."

The man's struggles subsided jerkily, much against his will, and his free hand fell away as Duncan began unwrapping the splinted arm. He winced as the priest's sensitive fingers brushed the angry-looking flesh over the broken forearm, his body arching with new pain as Duncan encased the damaged area between his two hands.

"What are you doing? No magic! No! Please don't!"

At Duncan's nod, Morgan drew his controls tighter and pushed the man into unconsciousness, shifting one hand to cover Duncan's two as he reached for the healing mode he and his cousin now achieved with increasing reliability. Building the rapport with Duncan, he felt himself sinking into that odd, other-wordly sensation which he had come to associate with the rogue healing talent—and felt the fleeting, familiar press of Another's hands atop his own as the connection was made and the bones began to knit beneath their touch. He withdrew when the healing was complete, blinking and partially releasing control to let their patient regain consciousness.

"No," the man murmured weakly, as his eyes fluttered open. "No magic, *please* ..."

"It's a little late for that," Morgan replied, settling on a stool that Nigel pushed closer, so he could keep one hand casually on the man's shoulder for future control. "Suppose you tell us your name now."

Dazed, the man flexed the fingers of his sword arm and rubbed where the break had been, glancing furtively at Duncan, not daring to look at Morgan or acknowledge the Deryni hand still resting on his shoulder.

"You—healed me," he whispered reproachfully.

"Yes, they healed you," Kelson replied, looking a little disgusted. "You're not contaminated, you know. Answer the question. Who are you?"

The man swallowed with difficulty. "I still claim benefit of clergy," he said weakly. "I—"

"The only benefit of clergy that you're going to receive right now," Nigel said pointedly, "is the fact that Monsignor McLain is here to witness your interrogation. Now answer your king's question."

As the man set his lips in a thin, defiant line and started to shake his head, Morgan exchanged a glance with Kelson and extended control again, imposing the compulsions of Truth-Saying.

"Tell us your name," he said patiently.

"Nevan d'Estrelldas," the man replied, his eyes widening as the words tumbled from his lips despite his intention to keep silent.

"D'Estrelldas?" Kelson repeated, glancing at Duncan in surprised question as Duncan, too, started. "That's an unusual name—Bremagni, isn't it?"

Duncan nodded, pursing his lips in grim suspicion. "It is also the name of one of the itinerant bishops working in Kierney, isn't it, Nevan?"

Nevan nodded, again much against his will, and Duncan scowled even harder. Kelson looked astonished.

"You mean this man is one of our bishops?"

"Unfortunately, I fear he is, Sire," Duncan replied. "I *thought* he looked familiar. I wonder how many other bishops Loris has managed to subvert."

"Let's see if he knows," Morgan said, turning pale eyes on his subject and locking his attention. "You *are* Bishop Nevan, are you not?"

"Yes."

"Yes, what?" Morgan insisted, touching further control.

Nevan moistened his lips and inclined his head in unwilling respect.

"Yes, Your Grace."

"That's better. And as a bishop, to whom do you feel you owe your obedience?"

"To the Bishop of Culdi."

"Culdi?" Kelson blurted, glancing from Nevan to Duncan in dismay. "Does that mean there were Culdi men with those of Trurill? Assisting Loris in his escape?"

"Only one question at a time, my prince," Morgan reminded him, returning his attention to the fidgeting Nevan. "Remember that he's very literal-minded in this state. Bishop Nevan, are you saying that the Bishop of Culdi was aware of the escape plans of Archbishop Loris?"

"Yes, Your Grace."

"I see. Did he, perhaps, instigate them?"

'No, sir."

"Someone else approached him, then, with a proposition?"

"Yes, sir."

"Who was that?"

"I'm not sure, Your Grace."

"Then, who do you *think* approached him?"

Nevan seemed to fight the response, but the name came out nonetheless.

"Monsignor Gorony, Your Grace."

"Gorony!" Kelson breathed.

With a glance, Morgan silenced him and returned his attention to their reluctant informant.

"Was Monsignor Gorony in your company, then?" he asked.

Nevan nodded.

"And Brice of Trurill?"

Again, the nod.

"How many men?"

Nevan thought a moment. "Fourteen now."

"Because you were taken?"

"Yes, Your Grace."

"And where were you bound?" Kelson asked.

"Ratharkin, Majesty."

"For what purpose?"

"To consecrate the Lord Judhael Bishop of Ratharkin."

"Not of Meara?" Duncan interjected.

"No, sir."

"Why not?"

"Meara is to be a patriarchy under Bishop Creoda."

"Under Creoda," Morgan repeated, exchanging glances with the astonished Kelson and Duncan. "And Loris?"

"He will become Primate again, of course."

"Not while *I* live and breathe," Kelson muttered under his breath. "Tell me this, then, Nevan. Does Bishop Creoda owe his obedience to Loris or to Bradene?"

"To Archbishop Loris, Majesty."

"And there are other bishops who feel the same way?"

Nevan nodded agreement.

"How many?"

Nevan thought a moment. "Six, Majesty."

"Six besides yourself and Creoda?"

"Yes, Majesty."

"And I suppose you know who they are?"

"Yes, Majesty."

"Name them."

"Bel—" The pattern of obedience had been well set, but Nevan stopped in midsyllable, fighting the command. Impatiently Morgan twitched at his controls, taking up just a fraction more of Nevan's ability to resist.

"Name the other bishops, Nevan," he said softly. "We haven't all day."

The eyes closed, but the lips parted once more.

"Belden, Bishop of Cashien; Lachlan, Bishop of Ballymar; and the four itinerant bishops, Mir de Kierney, Calder of Sheele, Gilbert Desmond, and Raymer de Valence."

"And he's consecrating Judhael—he'll have a whole rival hierarchy!" Duncan muttered. "*Damn* his impertinence."

"His impertinence doesn't bother me nearly as much as the fact that he's succeeding," Kelson said grimly. "He thinks he's scored the advantage, that there isn't a thing I can do to stop him until the spring. Well, maybe he's made a fatal miscalculation. Guards!"

Kelson's council judged that their king was making a fatal miscalculation at first.

"It's sheerest folly, Sire," Ewan argued, from his place three seats down from the king at the council table. "You can't hope to mount a successful campaign this late in the season! It's December, for God's sake!"

"Which is precisely why I'm going now," Kelson replied. "They won't be expecting me. Ratharkin is well fortified, but I won't believe the citizenry could have been won over that completely to Loris' leadership already. At best, he probably has control of the episcopal forces and nominal control of the city. A show of royal force, especially in December, when he thinks I can't do it, may be sufficient to break his strength."

"Perhaps he hasn't even gone to Ratharkin," ventured Saer de Traherne, sitting opposite Ewan. "If he has the support of the Mearan Pretender, he may be heading straight for Laas."

Kelson shook his head. "No, Nevan said Ratharkin. Loris has episcopal business to settle before he takes the time for secular politics. And I have a bishop in Ratharkin that I've sworn to protect."

"And you also have a friend in hostage there, Sire, if Loris has indeed gone to Ratharkin," Archbishop Bradene observed. "Might that not be clouding your judgment?"

"I have a duty to protect them both, Archbishop," Kelson replied. "And Loris must not be allowed to gain any more of a toehold than he already has. I shouldn't have to lecture you, of all people, about Loris."

"I still don't like it, Sire," said Arilan, who had already made it quite clear what else he did not like, when he heard of the manner of questioning Nevan. "Loris is clever—"

"Even if he has Ratharkin fully garrisoned, which I doubt," Kelson interrupted pointedly, "he does *not* have sufficient strengh to come out from behind the city walls and defeat a force the size I plan to bring. We would have heard of any large massing of troops. Even in Laas, there's been no report yet of anything larger than a household guard. At worst, it's a standoff and we come back home."

"I can think of worse, Sire," Cardiel sighed, "but be that as it may. Perhaps you're right. I shall pray that you are. But suppose that you aren't? If you were to be captured or killed—"

"If it will ease your mind, Archbishop, then be assured that my uncle is remaining here as regent," Kelson answered. "If anything should happen to me, he will be your king—and he has three sons to succeed *him*."

"And you should have sons to succeed *you*," Ewan

muttered petulantly, "before you go charging off on such harebrained ventures."

Kelson grinned, almost glad for the old argument.

"Don't I need a wife for that, Ewan?" he quipped.

"Then stay home an' *take* a wife, lad!" Ewan returned. "Spend the winter in bed with a bonnie queen, making bairns—not dashin' about in the snow, taking on rebel archbishops and God knows what else! There'll be time enough in the spring for making war."

Chuckling, Kelson motioned Duncan to take up pen and parchment, shaking his head in affection.

"I wish I *could* stay home, Ewan. Nothing would please me more. Now, I'll need the household troops, Nigel— and gentlemen, precisely because it *is* winter, I'll need to raid each of your personal guard units to augment my own. I'll want a hundred knights, lightly mounted for maneuverability and speed, and the minimum support force. I'll take Morgan, of course, and Jodrell and Traherne; the rest of you I'll leave to begin preparing summons of array for the spring, in case this doesn't resolve everything. Duncan, as Duke of Cassan I'd take you as well, but Nigel may need your good offices here in Rhemuth."

He did not *say* that Duncan would also be his Deryni link back to his capital, but Arilan seemed to sense it.

"Shouldn't you take a bishop to represent the legitimate episcopal hierarchy, Sire?" he asked, as prelude to including himself in the campaign.

"The matter is best handled by secular authorities at this point, Excellency," Morgan answered for the king, before Kelson had to stumble over a reason not to include Arilan as that bishop. "Unless His Majesty particularly wants to risk one of his loyal bishops in this venture—?"

He glanced at Kelson, ready to back down if the king had strong reasons for wanting to include the disputed Arilan, but to his relief Kelson shook his head.

"That won't be necessary. If anyone holds Ratharkin besides Istelyn, my sworn man, it's out of ecclesiastical jurisdiction. Now, does anyone have a major objection that hasn't already been stated?"

No one had.

"Then, I suggest we all set about making the necessary preparations. I suspect Loris has agents here in Rhemuth, so I want to leave tonight, under cover of darkness, before anyone has a chance to send word ahead and warn him. Morgan, let's get started."

As he rose and headed toward the great double doors leading from the chamber, the others stood and made their bows, Morgan exchanging a resigned glance with Duncan before falling into step behind the king.

# CHAPTER TEN

*Therefore the prudent shall keep silence in
that time; for it is an evil time.*
—Amos 5:13

Two days later, as Kelson and his battle force rode
toward Ratharkin in an icy rain, the Pretender of Meara
entered the city gates with her husband and children.
Snow had been falling since before dawn, discouraging
casual travel, so her party passed largely unnoticed through
nearly deserted streets. Only the guards keeping the gates
at the bishop's palace recognized the old Mearan colors
her captain carried, and hailed her as she passed.

She took their homage as her due; she rode like a
queen. The Lady Caitrin Quinnell of Meara had never
been a beautiful woman; nor had the years been kind.
But at sixty-one, she was compelling in that cool self-
possession that sometimes comes of the promise of power
and the unquenchable belief that one has been wronged
by one's station in life but eventually will be vindicated.
The white palfrey she rode was not a large animal, but
the top of Caitrin's immaculately coifed head barely
reached its shoulder when the Baron of Trurill handed
her down in the snow-covered palace yard. When he kissed
her hand, she acknowledged the salute like a queen receiving homage, polite but aloof as she waited for the rest of
her entourage to dismount around her.

"Welcome to Ratharkin, Your Royal Highness," Trurill
murmured. "Or perhaps I shall be privileged to greet you
as the Queen's Grace, ere long. I am Brice, Baron of

Trurill, your most humble servant. Your hosts await you inside."

She favored him with a quick smile, distracted and distant as she tapped a riding crop gently against her gloved hand, nodding toward the bearded man in border tartan who joined her from behind. He was plain of face and a little thickset, but robust and fit, his costly riding leathers cut to enhance muscular legs.

"My husband, the Lord Sicard MacArdry," she said, by way of introduction. "And these are my children: Prince Ithel, Prince Llewell, and the Princess Sidana."

Brice's jaw dropped a little as the three approached, for in addition to being far younger than he had been led to expect, Caitrin's offspring were strikingly handsome. He had no idea where they had gotten their aristocratic looks—neither Caitrin nor Sicard could have been described as more than pleasant looking, even in their youth—but it seemed the couple had thrown three of the comeliest offspring Brice had ever seen. The two boys, only slightly younger than King Kelson, compared very favorably with the king himself for poise, bearing, and fairness of feature; and the young princess—

Brice had to consciously remind himself that he was contentedly married, and such a lass not for the likes of him in any case. Short but sapling-slender, with curling locks the color of chestnut burrs escaping from beneath her travel hood, Sidana seemed the embodiment of Brice's every feminine ideal, dark eyes holding the dreamy mystery of some creature from another realm: worldly yet innocent, wise but naive. She inclined her head politely in his direction as she noticed his rapt interest, but she did not resort to the condescension so often shown by other girls of rank in similar circumstances. Her kindness enabled him to shake off her spell without making too much of a spectacle of himself.

"Ah, you find my daughter attractive, my lord baron?" he heard Sicard saying, the border lord's face creased with faint amusement as he extended his hand in greeting.

Brice looked the girl's father in the eyes and blurted out the truth.

"I' faith, my lord, she is exquisite. I had no idea. She will bring great honor to the man fortunate enough to win her hand."

"Aye, she will that," Caitrin said a little impatiently, "though she is not for just any lord, as I am sure you can appreciate." She took her elder son's arm and peered past Brice toward the doors. "But may we go inside now? Our attendants will see to the horses and baggage. It has been hours since our last warmth and refreshment."

A short time later, when an embarrassed Brice had shown the royal guests into the bishop's receiving room and the usual amenities had been exchanged, refreshment taken, royal and episcopal conspirators settled down to serious discussion. Sidana had made her apologies and retired to rest with her ladies, but her two brothers sat expectantly to either side of their parents, keen to be included in the exchange of recent happenings.

"I like not this news of the Duke of Cassan," Caitrin said grimly, as Loris took a chair directly opposite her, with Creoda, Judhael, and Brice flanking him. "Cassan is to be Ithel's, when McLain is dead. With McLain a bishop, it's conceivable he would try to leave it to the Church."

"And Kierncy as well," Ithel said, from his mother's right. Brice thought the boy's dark eyes made him look a little like a vulture in that instant.

Sipping delicately at a cup of mulled wine, Creoda shook his head.

"Not to the Church, Highness. To the Crown. McLain is the king's man. We did try to eliminate him, however."

Caitrin shrugged. "A poor try, I hear. He was fit enough to attend Mass the next day."

"The archfiend Morgan came to his aid," Loris muttered. "He used his Deryni sorcery to heal him."

"That was after the fact," said Sicard, with a disparaging wave of his hand. "'Tis said that McLain himself warded off the attack. Did you send a child to do a man's work?"

Anger flared briefly in Loris' face, but his response was temperate and controlled.

"The boy was young, yes, but he had been trained in McLain's own household. He knew what he was doing. A man could not have gained access as readily. McLain *was* wounded—"

"But to no avail, it seems—"

"My Lord Sicard, the drug on the blade should have rendered anyone with Deryni blood quite incapable of effective defense." Loris explained patiently. "And for a priest, conditioned not to kill if it can be avoided, the added hesitation should have been fatal."

"No matter now," Caitrin murmured, toying with her goblet. "It wasn't fatal, so we shall have to eliminate McLain some other way. Before that, however, there is the matter of my nephew." She favored Judhael with a fond smile, which he returned. "How soon are you prepared to proceed with his consecration as bishop, my Lord Loris?"

Loris inclined his head. "Tomorrow, if you wish, Highness. It is regrettable that Bishop Istelyn continues to resist the inevitable, but Bishop Creoda and several others will be honored to assist me in that happy task."

"So you said in your letter," Caitrin replied, glancing at her husband. "You said also that the Master of Transha is in your custody. Would you care to explain that?"

Blinking in surprise, Loris glanced from one to the other of them, husband and wife, then at Creoda, who shrugged.

"I landed near Transha, Highness, as I am certain I informed you," Loris said cautiously. "The boy led a patrol which tried to intercept me. My Lord Brice took him hostage to insure our escape, and we kept him because Transha's support could be valuable in the future. The boy's young; he might be won over. If you don't agree, it isn't too late to kill him."

"Kill him?" Sicard gasped, half-rising from his chair.

As Loris jerked back in surprise and Brice and Creoda poised to intervene, Caitrin caught at her husband's hand.

"Peace, Sicard. He obviously does not know. Peace, my lords—please."

As all of them subsided, Caitrin returned her attention

to Loris, at the same time gently stroking her husband's hand.

"In all the intensity of your own escape, you obviously have forgotten my husband's clan, Archbishop," she said carefully. "The young Master of Transha is my husband's nephew. My Lord Sicard has not spoken to his brother, the boy's father, for many years, but you must realize that blood is very important to border folk. The fact that Sicard and Caulay had a falling out does not lessen my husband's affection for his only surviving blood nephew."

Loris smiled and relaxed, nodding his understanding. "Ah, then, we have no quarrel, dear lady, since young Dhugal is in good health and waits upon your pleasure. Would you like to see him?"

"Immediately," Sicard murmured.

"But, of course—though I assure you, he is honorably detained. He presently shares quarters with Bishop Istelyn, who has been seeing to the injuries he received when he was captured. Nothing too serious, I assure you. Come. I'll take you to him."

Dhugal MacArdry stretched carefully, then moved one of his archers on the gameboard set between himself and Istelyn, glancing up to see the bishop's reaction. Istelyn raised an eyebrow and passed a ringed hand across his mouth and lower jaw as he studied the new tactical situation, deep in thought.

It was now more than a week since Dhugal's capture, and his injuries were healing with the swiftness often granted to the young and healthy. His head still throbbed a little if he moved too quickly or tried to stay awake for too long at a stretch, but the constant ache of his ribs had eased to only an occasional twinge. Nor did it hurt to breathe. For the last day or two, he had even begun light exercise to start getting back into shape.

He flexed his sword hand and made a fist, heartened by the increased strength he felt, then stiffened and looked up as footsteps approached the outer door. Istelyn pursed his lips in resignation but rose as the door opened, ges-

turing for Dhugal to rise as well. Dhugal obeyed, for it
would do no good to antagonize their captors.

"You have visitors, Lord Dhugal," Loris said, moving
through the doorway as the guard stepped back. "I assured
them you've been treated with all the proper respect due
your rank."

As Dhugal's eyes darted to the figures entering behind
Loris, his heart sank. The rather plain-looking older woman
he did not know, but he could guess her identity from her
company. Even had the man at her side not worn a shoulder plaid of MacArdry tartan, Dhugal would have recognized the unmistakable stamp of kindred blood. It could
only be his black-sheep uncle, Sicard MacArdry, and the
woman, the Pretender Caitrin.

"Kinsman," Dhugal murmured neutrally, in case he
was mistaken, inclining his head in a polite bow.

White teeth flashed in the man's heavy beard and mus-
taches as he chuckled delightedly.

"So, my brother's son has grown to manhood, eh? We
hear you gave His Excellency's escort a hard time, lad."

Dhugal merely inclined his head again. "I but did my
duty to my father, sir. As his heir, I could do no other."

The woman raised an eyebrow and glanced over at her
husband, apparently pleased with his answer.

"The boy speaks well, Sicard, and seems to know how
to guard his tongue. Perhaps blood will show him his new
duty as well. Will you introduce my nephew?"

Sicard gave her a little bow and called Dhugal closer
with a gesture. Dhugal approached slowly, all too aware
why they had sought him out.

"An' it please my Liege Lady," Sicard murmured, "I
beg leave to present my brother's son, Lord Dhugal
MacArdry: heir to the Earldom of Transha and tanist of
Clan MacArdry. Dhugal, Her Royal Highness The Princess
Caitrin of Meara. If you are wiser than your father, I hope
you will acknowledge her as your future liege. Transha
was once part of Old Meara, and shall be again, if the
fates are kind."

Dhugal's heart was chilled by the implication, but it
was only what he had expected. Putting on what he hoped

was one of his most wide-eyed and naive expressions, he took the hand Caitrin extended and brushed the knuckles with his lips in polite salute. He could feel Istelyn stiffen behind him in disapproval.

"I am honored to make your acquaintance, Lady," he said, turning earnest eyes shyly upon her. "Often while I was growing up, I mourned the fact that my father's quarrel with his brother had robbed me of uncle and aunt and cousins. I hope you will not hold his quarrel against me."

"A wise lad," she replied, taking him by the shoulders to formally kiss him on either cheek. "We shall talk more of this after your cousin Judhael's consecration tomorrow, if you comport yourself as the well-bred lad you appear to be." She drew back to glance at Istelyn, who returned her gaze stonily, then nodded to Loris.

"I wish Lord Dhugal to have an honored place at the ceremony tomorrow, my Lord Archbishop. He is family. I wish him treated as such."

Loris bowed. "If the Lord Dhugal will give his word not to interfere with the proceedings, I am certain that can be arranged, Highness."

"Well, Dhugal?" She glanced at him pointedly. "Can we trust you to conduct yourself befitting your blood?"

Dropping to one knee, Dhugal bowed his head and murmured his wholehearted agreement. If *that* were all the oath required, he could give it in clear conscience—for his blood and honor bound him to his king and brother above all. And by gaining their trust, he might yet escape to warn Kelson.

"Swear on the Cross, then," Loris said, not unexpectedly, starting to extend his pectoral cross for Dhugal to kiss, "Nay, on second thought, you shall swear on Istelyn's cross, lest you harbor some scruple about the one I wear. Istelyn, attend."

As Loris snapped his fingers toward Istelyn and held out his hand, Dhugal thought the bishop might refuse at first—Istelyn was looking thoroughly disapproving at what must surely appear to be a defection. But Loris' command left no room for disobedience. Defiance would only mean the taking of the cross by force. Unlooping the chain from around his neck, Istelyn averted his eyes and held out the sacred relic. Loris glanced at the kneeling Dhugal and complicated the matter.

"I think Bishop Istelyn should administer the oath as well," he said softly, seizing Istelyn's wrist and bringing the hand and cross down to Dhugal's eye-level. "Place your hand on this holy symbol and swear the oath to Istelyn, young Dhugal. And know that if you are forsworn, you will burn in hell for your sin!"

Dhugal's jaw dropped in very real misgiving, but he knew he had already made his decision as he laid his palm on the cross in Istelyn's hand: his first obedience was to God and the king, and that obedience superseded all other oaths which he might be required to make under duress.

"Swear that you will take no action to disrupt tomorrow's proceedings," Istelyn said softly, at Loris' impatient buffet of his imprisoned wrist.

The words were precisely what Caitrin had specified, and Dhugal thought he could still give his oath in good conscience. Perhaps Istelyn had even recognized that the wording left room for interpretation. But before Dhugal could bend to kiss the cross in confirmation, Loris' free hand clamped around their joined ones, pressing the metal of the cross cruelly into their flesh.

"Swear also that you will make no attempt to escape," Loris demanded. "Give me your parole, and you shall be accorded all the honor due your rank."

"I swear it," Dhugal murmured, dragging the words reluctantly from the depths of his soul as he raised frightened eyes to the rebel archbishop's.

"Say the actual words of the oath," Loris insisted.

Dhugal squirmed inside, but he had no choice but to obey.

"I give my parole that I shall not attempt to escape," he said steadily.

"And that I shall do nothing to disrupt the proceedings..." Loris prompted.

"And that I shall do nothing to disrupt the proceedings," Dhugal repeated.

"So help me God...."

"So help me God."

"And may my soul burn in hell if I keep not this solemn oath—say it!" Loris ordered.

Chilled despite his intentions, Dhugal turned genuinely frightened eyes on Caitrin in appeal, but the woman only smiled and nodded.

"And—and may my soul burn in hell if I keep not this solemn oath," he managed to choke out.

"Now kiss the cross," Loris said, releasing his cruel grip.

Blindly Dhugal obeyed, adding his own fervent prayer that God would forgive him for taking the oath in vain. He was shaking with the exertion the act had cost him as he stood, but Caitrin looked pleased and even Loris seemed satisfied. Istelyn's expression revealed nothing as he put the cross back around his neck, meeting Loris' gaze defiantly as archbishop and then pretender turned their attention on him instead of Dhugal.

"And what of you, Bishop?" Caitrin said softly. "I am not so naive as to think you can be won as easily as my young nephew, but you *shall* be present at Judhael's consecration tomorrow. Whether you attend in the honor due your station is up to you."

Istelyn bowed his head. "I will not be a party to any of this, Lady. I do not recognize the authority of this man whose escape you apparently have fostered—and you are foolish to think that the king will do nothing while you usurp *his* authority in his own lands."

"Meara is mine, not Kelson's," Caitrin answered.

"It is a part of Gwynedd, and was lawfully joined to it generations ago," Istelyn said stubbornly. "If you stand with this renegade priest, you join in treason against your lawful Lord."

"History will decide whether it is treason," Loris retorted, "just as history will decide whether your decision was wise. You may have overnight to reconsider your position—but you *will* witness Father Judhael's consecration tomorrow, even if you must be drugged and bound to your throne half-conscious. Do not make the mistake of thinking this an empty threat. It can and will be done."

"Then, the legitimacy of what you are doing *does* matter, doesn't it, Loris?" Istelyn turned his gaze on Caitrin. "My lady, I pray you to reconsider what you are about to do. It still is not too late to reverse what you have begun and beg the king's pardon. Loris is a fugitive, and will be dealt with, but you have committed no grave offenses if you back off now."

Outraged, Loris lifted a hand to strike him, but Sicard blocked his wrist at Caitrin's quick signal.

"We shall take your advice under consideration, Bishop," Caitrin said smoothly, "as we hope you shall take ours. Archbishop Loris, we have more to discuss in private, I think." She glanced at the silent and wide-eyed Dhugal as Sicard moved to open the door. "Nephew, if you value the life of this foolish priest, you would do well to try to convince him of the error of his stand. You shall dine with us this evening and report your progress."

She turned and swept through the open doorway after Sicard even as the astonished Dhugal made a hasty bow. Loris cast Istelyn one lingering, venomous glance, a more calculating one in Dhugal's direction, then followed. Dhugal exhaled softly as soon as the bolts had snicked shut on the other side, glancing uneasily at the now-shaking Istelyn.

"So that's my Aunt Caitrin," he murmured.

Istelyn shot him a look of undiluted disgust and turned away, making his way blindly to the prie-dieu to collapse with his head cradled on his folded arms. After a moment Dhugal followed, kneeling awkwardly on the bare stone beside him.

"Please don't be angry with me, Excellency," he whispered, trying to will the bishop to raise his head. "You don't think I *really* mean to do anything that would help Loris, do you?"

Istelyn's whisper could barely be heard from behind his folded forearms.

"You swore an oath, Dhugal—in terrible terms. Do you mean to be forsworn?"

"I—I had no choice."

Istelyn looked up coldly. "You had a choice: the same choice that I did. And you gave him your *word*!"

Dhugal swallowed painfully. His ribs were aching again from the pounding of his heart.

"I gave the *king* my word," he murmured. "And if it costs me my soul, I'll *keep* my word—to him." He folded his hands carefully, interlacing the fingers, and pressed them tightly clasped to his chin.

"But I can't escape to warn him if I'm too closely guarded," he went on very softly. "Maybe I can't escape anyway—but at least I have to try. And if I'm going to try, I owe it to him to give myself the best possible chance of succeeding."

"Even at the cost of breaking your sacred oath?" Istelyn asked.

"*Whatever* the cost," Dhugal whispered.

He could not convince Istelyn that the wisest course lay in pretending to cooperate with their captors, however. He tried until a servant came to fetch him for dinner, but the bishop maintained his stand: to allow the appearance of cooperation was as damaging as actually capitulating to the enemy. Istelyn would not be moved.

"But they mean to have you there, Excellency— probably even if they have to prop up your dead body on its throne!" Dhugal had said at last. "You can't help the king if you're dead!"

"Perhaps. But I will die knowing that I was true to my office and my God. Loris will never have that satisfaction."

Dhugal thought about what Istelyn had said as he followed the servant into the bishop's great hall, his spirits temporarily dampened by the heavy weight of duty, but he had all he could do to keep his wits about him once he sat down to supper. They put him at the far end of the high table with a man-at-arms to watch as well as serve him, and he knew that many others watched for errors as well.

Increasingly conscious of the dangerous charade he played, he kept his peace and did his best to stay wide-eyed and awed-looking in the presence of the Mearan Court. No one seemed to remember that he had been fostered to a finer court in Rhemuth, but if anyone had, Dhugal planned to shrug it off as time ill spent for a borderman. In fact, he had not been at court for several years, so it took little effort to slip into the more relaxed border manners common in his father's hall: loud and boisterous, hearty in appetite and more uninhibited in behavior than would have been seemly in Rhemuth.

Once he got into his role, however, maintaining it was easy. He was soon introduced to his cousins, Ithel and Llewell, both about his age, and the stunningly beautiful Sidana.

"I don't suppose you see many ladies to compare with this in Transha," Prince Ithel said proudly, pouring his sister another cup of ale. "Meara will be the center of the civilized world when we're done—you'll see."

He was just drunk enough to mistake Dhugal's nervous laughter for awe, Sidana also joining in the mirth.

Only Llewell kept himself aloof, staring furtively at Dhugal when he thought Dhugal didn't notice and brooding over his cup. Ruthlessly Dhugal set about to win all their confidence, drawing out the taciturn Llewell, hearing accounts of the princes' martial exploits with feigned awe, and eventually joining in the goodnatured teasing which Sidana endured from her older brothers. He was nearly one of them by the time dinner was over.

One of the children, however—not one of the men. Over stronger wine, after the ladies had retired, a possibly intoxicated Sicard drew his stool close beside Dhugal's and began sounding him out about old Caulay's politics, hinting that once Caulay was gone, Meara was in a position to better Dhugal's lot considerably.

Dhugal suspected his uncle was far more sober than he seemed. He hid his true feelings well, however, even pretending pleased interest in Sicard's offer of a dukedom when the secession was accomplished. He gathered that he gave the right answers. He drank with Sicard and his sons for another hour, somehow managing to consume far less than they thought he did. Ithel, a tipsy Llewell, and the watchful and still sober man-at-arms walked him to his room when the reveling was done, the two princes singing him a noisy salute as future Duke of Transha before giving him a playful buffet through the doorway of his room.

Istelyn was still cold to him, however. Dhugal found him on his knees in the little oratory, but the bishop would not look at him after an initial, disdainful sweep of him from head to toe, turning a contemptuous back on him after that. Nor could Dhugal elicit any verbal response.

He crept under the sleeping furs on his pallet feeling like a snake, tears streaming silently down his cheeks until he at last slipped into uneasy sleep. His dreams edged almost immediately into nightmares:

Judgment Day. Naked and afraid, he cowered at the foot of the great golden Throne of Heaven as a wrathful Istelyn raised one hand toward the Light in mute appeal, stabbing accusingly at Dhugal with the other. Hosts of weeping angels bore the supine form of Kelson before the throne, his body bleeding from a dozen wounds.

Frantic, Dhugal tried to explain. Kelson could not be dead, and Dhugal certainly was not to blame. But the king suddenly lifted his head and raised one gory hand to also point in Dhugal's direction, the flesh melting from the bones as Dhugal watched in horror, the eyes but empty sockets in a masklike skull.

The nightmare wrenched Dhugal out of sleep. Gasping for breath, he woke in a cold sweat, terrified that it was real, that he had already killed his brother and his king.

But the room was dark, Istelyn no longer kneeling in the oratory but wrapped in his sleeping furs on the other side of the room, his back to Dhugal, only a dark blur in the dim light of dying fire. It had only been a dream after all.

Dhugal's head pounded from the wine, however, even after the terror of the dream had passed, and he slept no more. Nursing his apprehensions and his hangover, he searched his conscience all through the rest of the night, hands clasped to his lips in intermittent prayer. The hours seemed to crawl until grey dawn at last streaked the sky and he could rise to wash and dress, a much sobered young man.

The object of Dhugal's prayers also saw the dawn that morning, a day's hard ride south of Ratharkin. Letting his horse blow at the top of a high pass, Kelson hunched down in his fur-lined cloak and gnawed on a lump of tough brown journey bread, glancing aside as Morgan drew rein beside him. They had been riding this leg of the journey since midnight, and planned no further pause until they reached Ratharkin. The rain had given way to a light snow during the night, with promise of more to come. Behind them, stretching back along the trail by twos, the hundred knights of their escort adjusted girths and bridle buckles and took advantage of the brief stop to eat or sleep or relieve themselves. Conall dozed on his horse behind and to Kelson's left, nodding in the saddle.

"He *has* to be alive," Kelson murmured, so low that even Morgan barely could hear him. "He *has* to be. If he were dead, I'd know—wouldn't I?"

"I honestly don't know, my prince."

"But we're closer now!" Kelson protested. "If he's still alive, shouldn't I have been able to touch *something* during the night? We were so close that night in Transha."

"Until you triggered the shutdown of his shields," Morgan reminded him gently. "You also had physical contact that time—and you know how much more difficult it is to establish rapport without it. A deliberate shielding—"

"It isn't deliberate. Not from me."

"Very well—not from you. But if he *is* shielded . . . ?"

"Are you saying he isn't?"

Morgan sighed patiently. "Touchy this morning, aren't you? Kelson, I haven't even *seen* the boy since he was—what?—nine or ten? How would I know?"

Shaking his head, Kelson shrugged again dispiritedly. "That long ago, how would *either* of us have known? He has shields now, though."

"Very well. And that's undoubtedly the reason you haven't been able to reach him." Morgan reached across to clap the king's shoulder in reassurance. "In any case, we should know something soon. We'll be at Ratharkin before dark."

"Before dark—yes. But will it be in time?" Kelson wondered.

# CHAPTER ELEVEN

*They fall into many actions and*
*businesses, and are void of sense, and*
*when they think of things pertaining unto*
*God, they understand nothing at all.*
                                    —II Hermas 10:12

The sparse noonday sun turned the stained glass of Saint Uriel's to darkly glowing jewels, but the cathedral's glory brought little comfort to Dhugal, kneeling meekly in the choir with the Mearan royal family. The consecration of Judhael as Bishop of Ratharkin was about to begin— and there was nothing Dhugal could do to stop it.

Nor could Henry Istelyn. He had spoken not a word on his awakening, to Dhugal or to the priest sent to inquire a final time whether he would assist with Judhael's consecration. Later he still stood mute as two deacons vested him, not resisting their ministrations or the cup which a cold-eyed Gorony commanded him to drink when they had done. Dhugal could see the drug's effect in Istelyn's eyes even as the two deacons walked him out of the room between them, Gorony following, and thought he knew what they had given him. He could expect no help from Istelyn for many hours, if then.

Dhugal was alone, then. He could depend on no one's resources but his own. Those kneeling around him claimed to have accepted him as family, and promised much in return for his support, but he knew they did not trust him yet; he had given them no cause to trust him other than the face value of his apparent opportunism. His very position in the seating, between Sicard and Llewell, the younger prince, placed him where he could be easily and quietly subdued, should he attempt a disruption despite his word. Dressed in the princely raiment they had brought him that morning—Ithel's, by the length of the richly embroidered cloak—he did look like one of them. Even his borderman's braid did not set him much apart, for Sicard and several of his personal attendants wore them as well, even if the two princes did not.

Far at the back of the cathedral, the choir began to chant the entrance antiphon. The nave was packed. Great liturgies of state were always popular with the common folk, with their chance to at least glimpse the rich and the highborn, and the appetites of Ratharkin's citizenry had been whetted not a fortnight before, when Istelyn had been installed. Dhugal wondered whether they had flocked in such numbers for their rightful lord as they did for a usurper's kin. But perhaps they did not know.

As the procession entered the church and headed down the aisle, those around Dhugal stood, so he did likewise. Slowly the clergy approached them, led by a thurifer, incense bearer, servers with candles, and then a processional cross and the choir. A second thurifer came after them, followed by the entourages of the various bishops assisting in the ceremony, each preceded by his crozier bearer and followed by two boys with candles. Dhugal could not identify any of the bishops preceding Judhael by sight, but he had been told that one of them was Bishop Calder—brother of his mother and, therefore, another uncle. He had not expected that.

The prelates escorting the new bishop-elect were quite unmistakable, however: the forsworn Creoda, whom Kelson had trusted, and Belden of Erne, the youngish Bishop of Cashien, come up from the south. Dhugal knew him by the arms emblazoned on the back of his white cope, and wondered whether Kelson had suspected his betrayal any more than he had Creoda's, or the others.

And Judhael himself, yet another of Dhugal's hitherto only legendary Mearan cousins. The young bishop-elect glanced neither right nor left as he approached the high altar, but a tiny smile of satisfaction played about his lips—unseemly even in a righteous man on his way to his sacring, Dhugal thought. Bishop's purple showed slightly at throat and hem, but he was vested with a priest's alb and stole beneath his white cope, hands joined piously before his breast. Dhugal wondered how he had the courage to come before the altar thus, knowing that his election was against the will of the rightful primate and the king. Perhaps God would smite him for his insolence. Dhugal wished He would.

And if not Judhael, then certainly the despised Loris, following in the full habiliments of his usurped office, precious mitre sparkling like a crown above his costly golden cope. Servers bearing candles and his crozier preceded him, and close behind came Istelyn, leaning heavily on the arms of the two deacons Dhugal had seen before. Istelyn appeared still to be moving under his own power, but his eyes were heavy-lidded and vague; Dhugal suspected he would nod off despite any other intentions, once they sat him on his throne. The treacherous Monsignor Gorony brought up the rear.

Dhugal had never seen a bishop made before, so he was not sure when the ceremony departed from the form of the simple Mass he knew. It was difficult to follow the actions of half a dozen priests when he was accustomed to watching only one; and once-familiar words took on odd accents and emphasis when chanted by a full choir. Taking his cues from those around him, he stood and knelt when they did, swallowing his disgust and outrage when the traitorous bishops gathered before the throne Loris had no right to occupy and the chiefest traitor of them all delivered a short instruction on the responsibilities of a bishop. Judhael was then brought before Loris to respond to formal questions.

"Dearly beloved brother," Loris intoned solemnly, "ancient custom dictates that bishops-elect are to be questioned before the people on their resolve to keep the faith and discharge their duties justly. I therefore ask thee, Judhael of Meara, whether thou art resolved by the grace of the Holy Spirit to discharge to the end of thy life the office entrusted to us by the apostles which is about to be passed on to thee by the imposition of our hands?"

"I am," Judhael answered.

"And art thou resolved to be faithful and constant in proclaiming the gospel of Our Lord?"

"I am."

The ritual dialogue went on, but Dhugal had no stomach to listen closely. Whatever promises Judhael made under these circumstances, and however pious a man he might have been before the advent of Loris' plotting, Dhugal was as certain as he was of his own simple faith that Judhael of Meara was damned for participating in this mockery of holy rite. Why did God not strike him dead? Was there no justice, even in the very House of God?

He feared greatly for Istelyn, too, though it was the man's body which gave him greater concern than the man's soul. He could not but admire the man's courage—forced to condone the affair by the presence of his body but unyielding in his resolve that he would not support it in his heart—but Dhugal was made of more practical stuff. He did wonder whether he himself had taken the easier way, by pretending to go along with those he knew to be wrong—and whether Istelyn was right: that Dhugal *was* dishonored by going as far as he had gone already. And as for how far he intended to go, if there were opportunity—

"Beloved brothers and sisters," Loris chanted, standing to face the congregation, "let us pray for this man chosen to provide for the needs of God's Holy Church. Let us pray that Almighty God in His goodness will fill him with abundant grace."

Dhugal knelt with the others at that, watching the forsworn Judhael prostrate himself before the altar while the rest of the bishops knelt around him, even Istelyn being propped kneeling at his faldstool to the side. The choir sang a *Kyrie*, familiar to Dhugal even in its embellished form, then shifted deftly into a litany of angels and saints invoked to bless the man being consecrated.

"*Sancta Maria...*"

"*Ora pro nobis.*"

"*Sancte Michael...*"
"*Ora pro nobis.*"
"*Sancte Gabriel...*"
"*Ora pro nobis.*"
"*Sancte Raphael...*"
"*Ora pro nobis.*"
"*Sancte Uriel...*"
"*Ora pro nobis.*"
"*Omnes sancti Angeli et Archangeli...*"
"*Orate pro nobis...*"

The litany went on and on, the cadences lulling the senses, and Dhugal let his mind drift back to his own dilemma. Though he had given his word he would not try to escape, his duty to Kelson dictated otherwise, despite the terrible oath Loris had made him swear on holy relics. He knew Istelyn did not approve, and counted an oath on oath, regardless of the circumstances under which it was made—and perhaps he was right. Perhaps there was no compromising with evil.

But the greater evil, if Kelson did not learn of what was happening here today, seemed to Dhugal to outweigh the niceties of semantics. If he could escape, it was his duty to do so, regardless of his sworn oath. Time enough, if he succeeded, to seek absolution. He would *not* betray his brother.

Increasingly angry and indignant, he watched the traitor bishops go through the form of consecrating Judhael: the imposition of hands, the anointing with sacred chrism, the giving of ring, mitre, and crozier, the bringing of the gifts of eucharistic bread and wine by his family—Caitrin and Sicard and their children. At least they did not ask him to assist them.

But he *was* expected to go forward and receive communion with the rest of them, after the new bishop had ordained a deacon and concelebrated Mass with his new brothers. And he was spared receiving it from Judhael only to have Loris himself lay the consecrated wafer on his tongue. Dhugal had all he could do not to choke on it as he returned to his place with folded hands and downcast eyes, hating the hyprocisy which forced him to pretend the same traitor's game which they played in earnest. He prayed as he had never prayed before that God would forgive him for receiving the Sacrament with as much loathing in his heart as he felt for the treacherous Loris.

The final strains of a solemn sung *Te Deum* followed them out onto the cathedral porch when it was over. Surrounded by senior clergy and his family, the new bishop paused on the cathedral steps to impart his first episcopal blessings to the people outside. Dhugal was drawn along with them, by virtue of his kinship with Sicard, but surveillance seemed to have lessened in the general excitement of the event and he found it possible to ease into the background, almost blending in with the family's lesser retainers. The bite of a coming storm was in the wind, so he pulled up the fur-edged hood of his cloak against it and began a casual survey of the cathedral square while he pretended merely to savor the fresh air. Other than to enter the cathedral a few hours before, he had not been out of doors since his arrival in the city.

From what he could see, the physical layout was not entirely impossible. He did not know Ratharkin at all, but movement in and out of the square appeared to be unhampered and unregulated. The south gates of the city lay less than half a mile beyond the mouth of a narrow street opening off west of the square. He had marked the way well in his mind as they rode here this morning, and a possible alternate route through another side street.

Of more important immediate concern was the help or hindrance Dhugal might expect from the milling citizens, many of whom were making their way closer to kneel for the new bishop's blessing. From what he had overheard, no one seemed to see Judhael's creation as Bishop of Ratharkin as any encroachment on the recently installed Istelyn, for Istelyn was Bishop of Meara. Besides, was not Bishop Istelyn standing at the new bishop's side, affirming the new bishop's legitimacy by his mere presence? Clearly, Judhael was meant to assist the bishop installed by archbishops and king a fortnight before—and who would have informed them otherwise?

The presence of Caitrin and her family, standing beneath

a banner in the Mearan royal colors, only added local interest, for who of the common folk knew what lord had placed his hands between whose? If Meara's senior royal was here, publicly witnessing the elevation of her nephew in the presence of the king's duly appointed and enthroned representative, Bishop Istelyn, who could say she was not entitled? And a prelate of Mearan royal blood could not but please most residents of this ancient Mearan city, regardless of the lip-service professed to the Crown of Gwynedd.

Dhugal dared not expect support from Ratharkin's citizens, then. But at least the public acclamation of Judhael, distasteful as it was to Dhugal, perhaps gave convenient cover to explore escape options; for with attention centered on Judhael and the rest of the Mearan royal family, there was very little notice being taken of Dhugal. Foot soldiers mingled with the throngs in the square, lining the cathedral steps as well, but none were very close to Dhugal. Less than a score of mounted knights and men-at-arms patrolled the area. Two of them sat their mounts at ease near the gate leading back into the cathedral compound, only casually watching the crowd, but the nearest other men on horseback were clear across the square. If Dhugal could make his way close enough to surprise the men and secure one of the horses. . . .

Blowing on his gloved hands to warm them, he eased his way a few steps farther to his left, closer to the guards, casually eying the nearer horse—a wiry, fast-looking bay. Almost immediately the animal tossed its head and snorted, swinging its hindquarters against the sorrel beside it and dancing a little jig until its rider curbed it sharply. The other rider looked irritated and murmured something to his companion that Dhugal could not hear, as he jerked at his own mount's mouth, but when the two stood once more at ease, both of them were several horse-lengths closer than they had been. It occurrred to Dhugal to wonder whether the animals somehow had been aware of his scrutiny, but he dismissed the notion almost at once. He was good with horses, but not *that* good.

The pageantry of Judhael's acclamation continued on

the cathedral steps, but many of the Mearan folk were also hailing Caitrin now. From under his hood, Dhugal watched her bask in their homage, wondering whether they realized their treason—or if they cared. It was also beginning to snow again. Soon, despite the sweetness of public acclaim, they would all pack up and go inside, and his opportunity would be lost.

He sidled a little closer to the horses, trying his best to appear nonchalant—and nearly jumped out of his skin when he felt a tug at his cloak from the right.

"Ithel, it's getting cold. I think we ought to—oh, I beg your pardon."

The voice was Sidana's; and as he curbed his initial urge to whirl in response and slowly turned instead, he saw by her expression what had happened. He was wearing Ithel's clothes. Immediately he sensed a way to take advantage of the error—if only he were given time to carry through.

"No need to beg *my* pardon, fair cousin," he murmured in his best court accents, catching her gloved hand to press it to his lips. "You're the only one who's addressed a kind word to me all morning—even if it *was* meant for someone else."

She blinked uncertainly, too flustered to withdraw her hand.

"In faith, cousin, I had not known you pined for our kindness. You were merry enough last night, but wine will make even false men seem hale and earnest. My father was not certain you felt the bond of blood as strongly as we."

With a shrug, Dhugal let go her hand and wrapped his cloak more closely around him, stamping his feet against the cold and withdrawing turtlelike into the closeness of his hood.

"In faith, cousin, the cold out here is cold enough without the chill of family rejection. The ride from my father's lands taught me much of the realities of life. If my uncle your father can make my fortune in the new order, then it behooves me to listen to my blood—and especially to so fair a kinswoman."

The color rose in her cheeks at that, but she dared a tiny smile as she returned his gaze.

"Are you flirting with me, kinsman?" she asked, dark eyes teasing just a little. "We *are* first cousins, after all."

Dhugal decided not to pursue that line, though he let his eyes sweep her face in frank appraisal. With a tiny smile of his own, he shrugged and merely brushed a few snowflakes off the ruff of her hood. She paled a little and stifled a nervous giggle, poised to flee.

"Wh-what are you doing?" she whispered.

"Why, displaying cousinly concern for your well-being, my lady," he answered softly. "Did you not complain of the cold, only a moment ago?"

"Aye, it *is* getting colder."

"Then, allow me to act in your brother's stead," he said, taking her arm and gesturing gallantly toward the side gate—which also brought him closer to the unsuspecting guards. "I would not have so fair a flower as my cousin blighted by the chill. We can warm ourselves by the fire in the bishop's hall and have something hot to drink...."

He had kept his face averted in his hood as they walked, ostensibly against the wind; and as he set his hand to the gate latch and deliberately fumbled, the two mounted guards moved closer, the man on the sorrel dismounting with alacrity to give assistance—for he recognized Sidana, and thought her richly cloaked companion to be her royal brother. The man presented half a dozen open targets as he eased importantly between princess and supposed prince and bent to the latch—and likely never even felt the dagger which Dhugal filched from the man's own boot-top and jammed home underneath his ribs.

Before the stricken guard did more than wobble, eyes glazing even as a half-gasp died in his throat, Dhugal had wrenched the man's sword from its scabbard and was lunging to catch the startled bay by the reins, twisting the bit to yank it deftly to its knees and unseat its hapless rider. The exertion jabbed fire across his ribs, but he ignored the pain and vaulted into the bay's empty saddle, grunting as the animal lurched to its feet. He kicked it into motion, hunting for his stirrups. The horse squealed and lashed out with battle-trained heels at foot soldiers approaching from the rear. Sidana finally screamed.

He ignored her cry, for others were scattering and screaming all around him as well, parting before the plunging greathorse like a surging human tide. The bay's former rider snatched at his reins, but Dhugal whirled his mount on its haunches and sent the man staggering—in the direction of the snorting sorrel. Brutally, Dhugal kneed the bay between the man and his intended prize, knocking him to the ground before he could grab the dangling reins of either steed. The bay tried to bite him while he was down, and the man came up cursing it and him and slashing with a dagger, trying to hamstring horse or rider.

The man was bellowing for help now, still trying to catch the sorrel. Dhugal had to stop him, or his chance was lost. Swooping precariously low to slash at the man, he blocked another attempt to remount, at the same time praying that the animal would rear. To his astonishment, it did. The descending hooves slammed the man directly into one of Dhugal's swordblows. Blood sprayed from a hand-wide gash in the man's neck and reddened the trampled snow as his body disappeared under the sorrel's churning hooves. Sidana, cowering against the still-closed gate, stared at the carnage in mute horror as Dhugal grabbed a fistful of reins and glanced around wildly for the nearest escape route—which was fast being filled by foot soldiers and other mounted men pressing through the throngs. He suspected that most of them had no idea who he really was.

There was clear space around him now—except for the bloody body of the slain and trampled guard—but the panicked citizens fleeing his horse's hooves would block pursuit for only so long. He must take his chances now. Far across the square he could see archers approaching. If he could not break free at once, they would cut him down. Kneeing his mount closer to the gate and the petrified Sidana, he seized her upper arm and dragged her up to the saddlebow in front of him, to shouts of dismay from the approaching soldiers.

"Sorry, coz, but you must be *my* escort now," he gasped, fighting to keep girl, sword, *and* his seat as he made the bay rear in defiance. "Out of my way, if you'd not risk the lady's safety!" he shouted.

She squirmed in his grasp, elbowing him in the ribs hard enough to nearly make him drop her, but he only swore under his breath and held her the more tightly, clapping heels to the horse and incredulously watching the guards melt from his path as he bolted for freedom. Sicard and his sons were screaming frantically for horses, Caitrin half-fainting, Loris mouthing unheard orders as Dhugal shot by them. His passage through the city streets became a blur of screaming, scattering people and shouting soldiers in pursuit, the chaos heightened by the loose horse which plunged along just ahead of them, helping to clear a path. Only a handful of riders pursued them at first. The city gates stood open as they usually did during daylight, and Dhugal and his still-struggling passenger careened past the gate guards and out across the snow-slick draw before anyone could do more than stare in surprise.

His pursuers were heavier than he in their war harness, so Dhugal managed to pull away slowly for the first few miles—but only at the expense of his gallant bay, running out its heart for him. Double-mounted, he could not sustain such a pace for long—but neither could his pursuers. He had temporarily lost sight of them when he pulled the blown bay to a shuddering halt and slid from its back, thrusting his sword upright in the snow. The horse staggered at the sudden lessening of weight and nearly went down, and Sidana clutched at the saddle, white-faced.

"Easy, good friend," Dhugal murmured, laying hands on the bay's heaving chest and soothing with his voice. "Better service a man could not ask, but you have earned your rest. Your stablemate shall carry us from here."

Still stroking the spent animal with one hand, he turned and held out his other to the sorrel, whistling low. The second horse was also lathered and breathing heavily, steaming in the cold air, but still with spring in its step for having run unburdened. Whuffling softly, it pricked

up its ears and came to butt its head against his chest and
present a sweaty face for scratching.

"There's a good fellow," Dhugal said with a grin as he
obliged, glancing up at Sidana as he continued to stroke
both animals.

Her expression brought him to her side at once, to lift
her down and let her sink onto the snow in a heap of fur-
lined cloak, weeping.

"I'm sorry for your rough treatment," he said, easing
to a crouch beside her. "I had to get away, though—
whatever the cost."

"Whatever for?" she sobbed. "Didn't my father offer
you enough? Can you betray your blood so easily?"

"To have stayed would have been to betray it far more,"
he replied. Nervously he glanced back the way they had
come. "What your father is doing is wrong. He usurps
the rights of King Kelson."

"Kelson?" Sidana hiccoughed and tried to stop her
sobbing. "What obedience do you owe *him*?"

"I am the heir of Transha," Dhugal replied. "My father
is King Kelson's liegeman."

"Your *father* is his liegeman. *You* have sworn no oaths."

"Have I not?"

"Well, you are free to give your allegiance where you
will," she said, staring up at him with great, accusing eyes.
"But how *could* you, with your family's blood joined to
Meara's? Your uncle is my father, and the father of future
kings. My brother will someday rule a reunited Meara.
You could have been a part of it—*would* have been a part
of it. Father had promised you a dukedom!"

Sadly Dhugal shook his head. "Only my king may give
me that, Lady," he said, standing to rest his hand on the
bridle of the bay. "And it is not *your* brother who shall
rule a reunited Meara, but *mine*."

"But—I thought you had no brothers."

He shrugged and smiled. "None yet live who were born
of my mother—but I have a brother, fair cousin: a brother
of blood, to whom I owe total allegiance; one worth for-
feiting my very soul to protect and serve—which I may

have done, by breaking my oath in escape, and taking you with me." He sighed.

"But having risked that, I don't intent to waste it all by being taken now," he said, offering his hand to help her rise. "Your hand, please, my lady," he added, when she drew back in protest. "Don't force me to add another offense to the litany of my crimes. Despite what you may think, I was taught to honor and revere women."

Rebellion and indignation flared again in her dark eyes, but Sidana was too much the daughter of nobility not to recognize an untenable position. Spurning his offer of assistance, she gathered the shreds of her pride around her with the fur-lined cloak she wore and wobbled to her feet, though she did allow him to lift her onto the sorrel's saddle. She sat woodenly as he scrambled up behind her and reached around her to gather up the reins.

A moment to retrieve the sword set upright in the snow, and then he set heels to their mount and urged it forward, glancing back over his shoulder at the dark specks of their pursuers. The bay followed them for a while, but gradually fell behind and was lost as the sorrel settled into a modest but steady pace.

They managed to keep moving for another hour, until the shadows were long and weak on the virgin snow of the Cùilteine Road, but their horse was nearly spent as Dhugal drew rein at the top of a rise and turned to look back. Their pursuers could be discerned as three or four score horsemen now, drawing inexorably nearer. Sidana stirred in his arms and gazed after him, the wind whipping a tendril of her dark hair against his face.

"My father will kill you," she said softly, not turning her head "*After* my brothers finish with you."

A tightness spreading beneath his aching ribs, Dhugal swallowed and shifted his gaze in the direction they had been fleeing—toward Gwynedd, and safety. They would never reach it now. Their horse would be lucky to make it down the hill, much less carry them beyond. And whether or not Dhugal were calloused enough to threaten harm to Sidana when they caught up to him—and even if he followed through—they would kill him for what he had done.

Whether quickly or painfully hardly mattered, under the circumstances. Dead was dead.

But as his eyes darted longingly back toward the east and safety, he caught a trace of unexpected movement: more horsemen approaching, perhaps even more than pursued him. He drew in breath sharply as he strained his eyes in that direction, for they could not be Sicard's men, and have ridden fast enough to circle round this way. But if not Sicard's, then it mattered little *whose* they were. Anyone was preferable to being taken by the Mearans.

He did not pause to analyze it further. Setting his heels to their trembling mount, he forced it down the hill, holding Sidana close against him as the animal stumbled and lurched, near to foundering.

He might still die. He might break his neck falling from this fool horse, if it didn't watch where it was putting its feet. Or the men ahead might be no more merciful than the ones behind.

But he was not going to wait for the Mearans to take him.

# CHAPTER TWELVE

*All the men of thy confederacy have
brought thee even to the border: the men
that were at peace with thee have
deceived thee, and prevailed against thee.*
                                    —Obadiah 1:7

"Uh-oh, we have company," Kelson murmured.

He reined back to a walk and stood in his stirrups for a better look, pointing at a snowy ridge far ahead where a mounted horse had just appeared, silhouetted against the twilight sky.

"D'you see him?"

Morgan, with a curt signal to halt the column of knights riding four abreast behind them, also drew rein and peered into the distance, casting about with other senses than sight, lest the rider not be alone.

"Aye, and he's undoubtedly seen us by now as well," he replied. "So much for approaching Ratharkin unob— what the—?"

He broke off in astonishment as the horse suddenly broke from the top of the hill and began plunging down the snow-covered slope, each ponderous lurch threatening to send both rider and steed tumbling.

"Is he *trying* to break his neck?" Kelson gasped.

The horse stumbled and nearly went down even as Kelson spoke, then suddenly both he and Morgan saw the reason for at least a part of the animal's labor.

"He's carrying double!" Kelson exclaimed in amazement.

"Aye, and to be riding double at that speed and on a

182

horse that spent, the Devil himself must be chasing them," Morgan agreed. "Care to give the Devil some sport, Sire?"

Kelson raised an eyebrow at the borderline blasphemy, but he needed no second invitation. He had been spoiling for just such a skirmish all day. With a grin which had nothing to do with mirth, he unsheathed his sword and raised it over his head, glancing back to where Conall was already shaking out the folds of the Haldane battle standard.

"Forward at the canter and fan out!" he ordered, standing in his stirrups and pointing with his sword. "Whoever's chasing that fellow is going to have a surprise, I think!"

Immediately Conall and Saer de Traherne spurred forward and to Kelson's left, folds of scarlet silk billowing on the wind as the battle standard unfurled. Jodrell led another detachment to the right. The deadly hiss of steel slithering from scabbards joined the jingle of bits and spurs and the creak of leather as the knights broadened their line, outriders spurring ahead on the flanks. They were nearing the start of the hillrise now, the fleeing horse nearly upon them—close enough for Morgan to see that the front rider on the horse was a girl, dark hair whipping in the wind. And the other—

"It's Dhugal!" Kelson cried, even as the other rider's arm flailed in a frenzied wave of recognition.

Dhugal was in their midst then, laughing aloud despite his exhaustion, Kelson and Morgan reining in to bracket his faltering mount as the rest of the warband swept on up the hill. Morgan caught the horse's near rein and drew its head close to his stirrup, his own mount scrambling for footing as the sorrel staggered and nearly fell.

"Steady!"

"Here, take her!" Dhugal gasped, helping lift his protesting companion to a new perch in front of Morgan's saddle. "She's Sidana, the pretender's daughter. Her father's men are right behind me."

"How many?" Kelson demanded, as he gave Dhugal a hand up behind him.

Dhugal hooked a hand in the back of Kelson's belt to steady himself and shook his head happily.

"Not enough to give your men any trouble, Sire. Am I ever glad to see you!"

"And I." Kelson wheeled his stallion on its haunches and glanced after his knights nearing the crest of the hill. "But let's make sure you counted correctly. Morgan, stay out of the fighting unless we're needed, but come along with me. Oh, and welcome to Gwynedd, my lady!"

Morgan felt the girl stiffen in his arms as she heard his name, but he only shifted her closer into the curve of his shield arm as he urged his horse up the hill after the king, naked sword still ready in his gloved right hand. Ahead of them, the warband spilled over the crest of the hill with shouts of glee. He could hear the answering cries of consternation as Dhugal's pursuers saw the Haldane standard in the midst of their attackers.

The sortie was all but over by the time Morgan drew rein at the top of the hill with Kelson. Down on the plain, a handful of Haldane knights were in pursuit of a few stragglers, but the rest of the opposition were on the run far ahead. Several men unhorsed in the encounter were scattered down the other side of the hill, picking themselves up shakily, but none of them wore Kelson's livery. Haldane knights stood guard over each one, Traherne and Conall marching another one back to join his fellows while the squires rounded up all the loose horses. A cheer went up from Kelson's knights as he started down the hillside, and at his signal the battle horn sounded to call back their knights still in pursuit. Grinning, Morgan urged his horse after the king's.

"A happy circumstance, Sire," he said as they drew abreast at the bottom of the hill and halted, glancing down in amusement at the girl now beginning to wriggle in his arms as he reached around her to sheathe his sword. "And a rich prize young Dhugal has brought us, too. There's no point in struggling, my lady. You'd best save your strength for the ride back to Rhemuth."

"My father will avenge me!" Sidana cried. "You took him by surprise."

"But, that's the whole point, isn't it, my lady?" Kelson asked with a grin. "To take the enemy by surprise? I would be a poor commander if I sent my men into battle in rebel territory without the best possible advantage. Your father would have done the same."

"My father is not a rebel!" Sidana said. "He seeks to restore my mother to the throne which is rightfully hers, and to give Meara back its freedom. We shall not be ruled by—by a Deryni heretic!"

The taunt was only an accustomed annoyance to Morgan, inured from childhood to ignore such affronts, but Kelson reacted as if he had been stung, apparently not expecting it from a beautiful young girl. Dhugal, sitting behind the king, could not see how the grey eyes flashed warning, but he obviously sensed the sudden tension before Kelson brought his anger under control. Even Sidana gasped as she realized what she had said, and to whom, and in whose arms. Morgan forced himself not to react, waiting to see how Kelson would handle this.

"In future, my lady, I should take better care for my choice of words," the king finally said, after permitting himself a careful sigh. "If the fact that we are Deryni is abhorrent to you, then you should be aware that at least some of what is said about Deryni is true—and we are not made of stone. Do not press our forbearance too far."

He glanced purposefully out at his returning knights for a few seconds, temporarily releasing Sidana from the intensity of his gaze, but the brief respite did nothing to reassure the girl, trembling in Morgan's arms like a sparrow in the clutches of a bird of prey. Dhugal's stiff carriage proclaimed him still stunned as well by the tight-leashed power he sensed in the man suddenly stranger sitting in front of him—even if Morgan had not been able to sense the fear behind the shields Dhugal should not have had. Kelson's expression was far more mild when he at last looked back at them, but Sidana still recoiled.

"You will not be harmed, my lady," Kelson murmured. "By my honor and my crown, I swear it. If my earlier words seemed harsh, I apologize, but we have ridden long and hard and I had not thought to have so gentle a captive in our company. My quarrel is not with you, but neither can I let you go. Now you must pardon me while I see to my men."

He turned his stallion down the slope toward the skirmish site without waiting for reply, white horse stark against the trampled snow, Dhugal shifting his grip from Kelson's belt to the horse's crupper behind him as the animal lurched down the slope. Morgan followed more slowly with the subdued Sidana, still pondering Kelson's reaction.

Dhugal's Mearan pursuers had not wholly abandoned the situation, Morgan saw, as he scanned the darkening plain before them. They milled in a tight knot a few hundred yards out, obviously trying to decide what to do next. Between them and the skirmish site, most of Kelson's knights sat their horses in a long single line, ready to repel any renewed attack. Behind the line, the remaining Haldane riders kept watch over the prisoners: six in all— four now standing bunched before Traherne and Conall, hands bound behind them, two more having minor injuries tended. None of the captives were heavily armored, and several wore only court attire—no armor at all.

"Did you interrupt some festive occasion, Dhugal?" Kelson asked over his shoulder, as they approached Traherne and Conall.

Dhugal grimaced, leaning around the king to inspect the captives as they drew rein.

"They would call it so, Sire. Archbishop Loris consecrated Judhael of Meara Bishop of Ratharkin this morning. And I suppose you've guessed they have Bishop Istelyn to prisoner." His face lit with surprise and then pleasure as he got a good look at the sullen young man standing closest to Conall's horse, hands bound behind and a rope halter running from his neck to Conall's hands.

"Well, fancy that!"

"Someone you know?" Morgan asked, feeling Sidana's silent gasp of horror.

Dhugal laughed and clapped Kelson on the shoulder, his earlier uneasiness apparently past.

"Know him? Aye, indeed, Your Grace. Oh, this is rare luck. Sire, may I be the first to commend to your acquaintance Prince Llewell of Meara, the younger of this lady's brothers." He gestured grandly in her direction. "Well done, Conall. Did you capture him?"

Conall drew himself up importantly, uncertain whether to be more pleased at the status of his prize or annoyed at Dhugal's omission of his proper title.

"Of course I did. Llewell of Meara, you say?" he repeated, prodding disdainfully at Llewell's back with a booted toe.

Llewell bore the affront without physical resistance, but his brown eyes blazed as he twisted to glare up at Conall.

"You never would have taken me if my girth hadn't slipped," he said hotly. "My father will return for us!"

"Yes, under a parley flag," Kelson retorted, directing their attention to the party heading toward his line. "Hardly a dashing rescue mission, I think, but we'll hear what they have to say."

Sick at heart, Llewell whirled to crane his head in that direction.

"My sister and I have done nothing wrong," he said desperately. "You have no right to hold us!"

"Have I not?" Kelson leaned his forearms casually on the high pommel of his saddle. "And what *should* I do with subjects who defy my laws and usurp my authority in my own lands?"

"But ours is the better claim," Llewell began. "Our line comes from—"

"I know all about the line from which you spring," Kelson interrupted. "The matter was settled nearly a hundred years ago." He glanced up at the squire riding back from the defending Haldane line, the knot of Mearan riders slowly approaching under a white flag, then stood in his stirrups and shaded his eyes to peer farther out on the darkening plain.

"I see them," Morgan said, noting the numbers of the torches another approaching body bore, perhaps half an hour's hard ride away. "Sicard's reinforcements. We'd best make this brief, Sire."

"My thought, precisely." Kelson kneed his horse over

to the new mount another squire was bringing up for Dhugal and helped him shift across. "Llewell, I'll oblige your father for a few minutes, but I think you can see why I don't intend to stay around. Jodrell, prepare the men to ride out as soon as we've parleyed. Conall, we'll need a horse for your prisoner as well. And Morgan—bring the girl partway. They may be more inclined to reason if they see she's safe."

Torches hastily lit sputtered in the falling snow as they rode out. Kelson and Dhugal led, Sidana still sitting stiff and frightened before the silent Morgan, half a length behind. Conall and Traherne flanked the mounted Llewell, with an escort of four knights behind. Among the dozen riders who approached from the Mearan side, Dhugal identified Sicard MacArdry and his son Ithel in the lead. All but the four principals drew rein within hearing distance of a central point between them, Kelson and Dhugal riding on to meet Sicard and Ithel. They stopped a horse-length apart.

"I have never done you any harm, Sicard MacArdry," Kelson said quietly. "Why have you broken faith with me?"

Sicard turned a cold, disdainful look on Dhugal, holding a torch beside the king, then glanced back at Kelson.

"I never swore you any oaths, Kelson of Gwynedd. My young kinsman, on the other hand, betrayed his blood and broke oaths sworn on holy relics, before many witnesses. Do not speak to me of faith with an oath-breaker sitting at your side as counsel."

"He serves far older faith than oaths sworn under duress," Kelson answered. "But I think you did not come to argue my Lord Dhugal's shortcomings, if such they are. I assume you wished to verify your children's safety. As you can see, they have not been harmed."

Sicard's tight-lipped glance flicked to his son, anxious but hopeful in his bonds between Conall and Traherne, then more briefly and painfully to Sidana.

"I want them back, Haldane," he muttered, forcing himself not to look at them again.

Kelson inclined his head gracefully. "A father could

not want otherwise, my lord. And that is easily arranged. I have no quarrel with children."

"And the price?" Sicard asked.

"For a beginning, the return of my bishop, Henry Istelyn."

"I do not have him."

"Not with you, no. But you can get him."

Sicard shook his head. "He is Loris' hostage, not mine."

"Loris' treason is old. I do not hold you answerable for that. *Your* treason is more recent, and might be forgiven if I received sufficient surety of your future loyalty. If Istelyn is returned unharmed and you deliver Loris into my hands, I would be willing to discuss a general amnesty for all your family."

"You would never do that!"

"I have said that I would."

"And what if I refuse?"

"You will never see your children again. And in the spring, I shall lead an army into Meara and scour the land until I have found you, your wife, and every other living member of the Mearan royal house and put them to the sword."

"You would never do that!" Sicard gasped.

"Do you wish to test that belief?" Kelson countered. "If, on the other hand, you present yourself, your lady wife, and the rest of your family before my court by Christmas, delivering the traitor Loris and his supporters into my hands and pledging your true homage as dutiful vassals of my crown, then this all may be resolved most happily for all concerned."

"Those are no terms at all!" Sicard said with a contemptuous spit into the snow beside him. "You must take me for an idiot! No sane man would agree to that."

"Then perhaps you had best go a little mad, Sicard!" Kelson retorted, glancing at the torches now closer by half the original distance. "And I should be mad if I remained to debate the issue with you. I did not expect you to give me your answer without more sober reflection."

"But what of my children?"

"You have a fortnight to tell me what will become of them," Kelson replied, gathering up his reins in preparation to leave. "I must have your decision by Christmas Court. In the meantime, I give you my word that they shall not be harmed—and I trust you will make me the same assurances regarding Bishop Istelyn."

"I told you, that is not within my power. . . ."

"Then find a way to *make* it so!"

"I cannot!"

"A fortnight!" Kelson repeated. And as he and Dhugal wheeled their horses and started back, the Haldane line edged forward, curtailing any thought Sicard might have entertained of following after. With a glance backward at the approaching reinforcements, still a quarter-hour too far away to make a difference, Sicard cast one final, longing glance at his son and daughter being drawn back among their captors, then reined his mount around and rode off at the gallop with his remaining son. Llewell took the turn of events stoically enough, only bowing his head and biting back a sob as father and brother receded into the dusk and the nearer torches moved off; but Sidana burst into distraught weeping.

"No! They can't leave us!" she gasped, struggling to wiggle from Morgan's grasp. "Father! Father, come back!"

The attempt was futile, of course, but a hysterical woman was the last thing Morgan wanted on his hands if they were going to have to make a run for it. Pulling off his right glove with his teeth while he restrained her in his shield arm, he caught Kelson's eye and communicated his intention. Kelson agreed. Pinning the struggling girl firmly against his mail-clad chest, Morgan pressed his hand over her eyes and willed her to sleep. Immediately, she went boneless and relaxed in his arms, head lolling against his shoulder.

"What have you done?" Llewell gasped. He wrenched at his bound wrists helplessly as he tried to kick his horse closer to see. "Oh, God, what have you done to her?"

"She's not been hurt; he's only made her sleep," Kelson said sharply, plunging his horse between Llewell's and Morgan's to seize Llewell by the shoulder. "And if you keep your head, I'll not use on you what's been used on her."

"Was it magic?" Llewell managed to whisper around an almost tearful gulp.

"No, but I haven't the time to explain the distinction just now. Agree to cooperate, and I'll even have them bind your hands more comfortably. It's a long ride to Rhemuth with your hands tied behind you."

"You'll pay for this," Llewell muttered through clenched teeth. "May your Deryni soul rot in Hell!"

"You're about to try my patience too far," Kelson warned. "Don't push me. If you believe me damned already, then it follows that I have nothing to gain by personal restraint—though despite your belief, it is my intention to deal with you as honorably as possible. Now, is this to be easy or difficult?"

Llewell maintained his glare of tearful defiance for a few seconds, measuring it against Kelson's calm, passionless gaze, then broke the contact and bowed his head, shoulders slumping dejectedly.

"I cannot stand against a demon," he whispered. "I am not fool enough to seek my death deliberately."

"Nor I," Kelson replied. "Conall, see to his hands, but keep a close guard on him." With another glance at the approaching Mearan force, he reined his horse around and raised a gloved fist in signal.

"'Tis time we made a tactical withdrawal, my lords!" he shouted, to answering shouts of approval from his men. "We have accomplished at least part of what we came for. Now we return to Rhemuth!"

Thus did they ride from the plain of Ratharkin, richer for two royal prisoners and a rescued earl, Dhugal not yet aware that he was poorer by a father. Darkness and the increasingly heavy snowfall soon enabled them to elude the pursuing Mearan host; and when human and Deryni senses confirmed that they were out of danger, Kelson allowed a brief stop to rest. Only then did he draw Dhugal a little aside and tell him about old Caulay, giving what meager comfort he could as he shared Dhugal's grief at the news of the old earl's death.

* * *

Grief and futile comfort were served up in full measure that night in Ratharkin as well, when the desolate Sicard returned without daughter, forsworn nephew, or second son. Caitrin and Judhael heard his halting report in stunned silence, Judhael lamely holding his aunt's hand but unable to give a word of reassurance.

"How could the Haldane have known to be there just then?" Caitrin whispered when her husband had done. "'Tis foul, wicked sorcery! And he has my babes to hostage."

"We were wrong to trust young Dhugal," Judhael muttered. "To betray his own kin—but who could have guessed he would break his sworn word, given on holy relics? He is damned, damned...."

"I should have struck him to the heart with my own dagger when first I saw him," the miserable Sicard whispered. "I should have known my brother would poison him against us after all these years. And my son... my little girl... in the hands of Deryni!"

They sent for Loris and Creoda a little later, when they had recovered some of their composure and reviewed the terms of Kelson's demands. By the time Sicard had repeated his account for their benefit, Loris was all but foaming at the mouth.

"He offered you amnesty if you would abandon *me*?" he raged. "He dared to demand Istelyn's release? The insolence! The very cheek! How *dare* he think he can threaten *us*!"

"He *does* think he can," Caitrin replied irritably. "What is more, he has done a very credible job of it. I would be naive in the extreme if I thought he expected us to accept his offer, but he almost had to make the attempt. Still, we are not without our own resources. Nephew, please have Bishop Istelyn brought to us."

"He is still my prisoner, not yours, Lady," Loris warned.

"I am quite aware of that. I wish to question him. See to it, Judhael."

Loris let him leave to do her bidding, but he continued to rant and mutter under his breath all the while Judhael was gone, hardly touching the wine which Ithel poured to bolster all their courage.

"God curse the Deryni!" Loris spat, as Judhael brought Istelyn in a short time later. "Curse the Deryni king who pretends piety and honor and continues to consort with magic! And God curse doubly any bishop who would keep counsel with him!" he added, glaring at Istelyn. "You are no better than the Haldane you serve, Istelyn. I should have you executed as the traitor you are!"

"There will be no executions in this city without my leave, Archbishop," Caitrin said mildly, as she signed for a stool to be brought for Istelyn. "A dead bishop is hardly a strong bargaining point. The Haldane wants him back unharmed. By the same token, he will not harm the children so long as he believes we are willing to negotiate. Negotiations could drag on until the spring."

"You credit him with too much honor, Madame," Loris said. "These Deryni are treacherous. Kelson is most treacherous of all."

"He is still hardly more than a boy," Sicard said contemptuously. "Children do not kill children."

"Do not underestimate him, my lord," Loris replied. "I did so before, but I shall not make that mistake again. He is a man, with all a man's cunning and treachery increased because he is Deryni." He paused a beat. "And given that he *is* a man, has it not occurred to you that he may have a man's appetites—he who now has your daughter in his power?"

Caitrin pursed her lips tightly together, saying nothing, but Sicard's knuckles whitened on the arms of his chair.

"If he touches her—"

"Of course, he might marry her," Loris continued, watching Sicard's reaction especially and choosing his words. "That would confirm his claim to the Mearan throne after he eliminated the rest of you. Union of the two crowns—the same logic that his great-grandfather used with your great-grandmother, Your Highness. Then again, he might simply use her and cast her aside—or let his men have her, once he had done. Such things—"

"I don't want to hear it!" Sicard cried.

"And then there is Llewell," Loris went on relentlessly. "He's a pretty boy. Soldiers sometimes—"

"Stop it!"

Uncurling his fingers from their deathgrip on his chair arms, Sicard took his wife's near hand blindly in his while he lifted his cup and drained it with a single-minded deliberation. Caitrin winced at the pressure of his hand, but she kept stony silence. When Sicard had done, he set the cup aside and drew deep breath before looking back at Loris accusingly.

"That last was a low blow, Archbishop."

Loris shrugged. "Then I apologize for it. The danger to Sidana, however—"

"I am her father, Archbishop!" Sicard snapped. "Can you imagine that particular fear has been far from my thoughts these many hours? When I saw the cursed Haldane sitting his great white horse, young and hot-blooded and proud, and his Deryni henchman with his arms around—"

"Sicard—no!" Caitrin said. "Don't do this to yourself. Sidana will be safe, you'll see. We'll find a way."

"Then, we must show the Haldane whelp that we mean business, Highness—and that we do not intend to be intimidated," Loris purred.

Jerkily Sicard took up his cup again and held it out for Ithel to pour him more wine, letting Caitrin soothe him with little caresses stroked along his shoulder. She was looking at Istelyn rather then her husband, however. The bishop had done his best to be invisible while his captors argued, but now he could not escape her scrutiny. Dark circles smudged the fine-drawn skin beneath his eyes, but he appeared to have recovered from the drug given him earlier in the day. As Sicard tossed off half his new cup of wine, Caitrin returned her attention to Loris. A new determination appeared to have stamped itself on her plain features.

"Indeed, we are not intimidated, Archbishop," she said quietly. "My love for my children is no less than my husband's, but the brutal fact of the matter is that they are of age and were fully aware of the possible consequences

of supporting our claim to the throne. If God wills that
they should die at a tyrant's hands, then I must pray that
they be granted the grace to endure it with all the dignity
of their royal blood. It is as a queen as well as a mother
that I speak these harsh words. With God's help, none of
us shall have to make the sacrifice."

She rose to begin slowly pacing the space between her
chair and the room's fireplace, playing with the rings on
her slender hands.

"As a queen, however, it occurs to me that our young
Deryni king may have made a great tactical error when
he let us know he wants Bishop Istelyn back. He threatens
reprisals if we do not submit by Christmas, but so long
as he thinks we are considering his terms, I doubt he will
actually do the children harm. For all that he is Deryni,
he seems to prefer not to shed blood if there is another
way. Negotiations could take a long time—all winter, as
I said before. Long enough to ensure that we have all the
support we need to meet and defeat him in the spring."

"Winter itself will give us the time we need to build
our strength for the spring campaign," Loris said stubbornly. "We do not need to bargain with Deryni, Madame."

"Mother, may I speak?" Ithel interjected.

Regally Caitrin inclined her head.

"Thank you."

Ithel came to stand beside his mother's empty chair,
one hand on its back as he gazed at Loris.

"Archbishop, as my mother's heir, I stand to gain a
great deal if we are successful against the Haldane, but I
hope you will understand that I would prefer that my
brother and sister were still alive to share our victory
when it eventually comes. To that end, I should like to
point out a few practical considerations of tactics and
politics which may have escaped your notice."

"Don't lecture me, boy!"

"I'm not a boy, Archbishop—any more than Kelson
is a boy," Ithel retorted, but coolly, and without raising
his voice. "I'm a prince and I'll thank you to address me
as such. Hasn't it occurred to you that even if it isn't
possible for Kelson to mount an actual campaign during

the winter, he could still harass the lowland regions enough
to interfere with the raising of our levies? But he'll not
take drastic action so long as we're negotiating."

"You have a lot to learn about politics, *boy*," Loris
replied coldly. "And about Deryni. How can you even
contemplate giving him the satisfaction—"

Sicard cleared his throat dangerously. "My son is a
realist, Archbishop. His mother and I have brought him
up that way. And speaking as a realist, I know that there
is nothing we can do to protect Sidana and Llewell if the
Haldane decides not to keep his word. But by the first of
the year, only a short time past the Haldane's Christmas
deadline, even the lowlands will be all but inaccessible to
large bodies of troops from outside Meara. As long as we
pretend to be considering his terms, they will be safe—
and so will our borderlands."

"Neither the children nor the land will ever be safe
while Kelson lives," Loris said stubbornly. "He regards
the land as his—and he must eventually kill you and your
heirs or else keep you in perpetual imprisonment, as he
tried to do to me. He would be a fool to let you live, lest
potential rebellion always hang above his head. He will
use the children as bait to lure you to your destruction."

"Then let him think he will succeed," Caitrin retorted.
"Talk is cheap. Perhaps we can tantalize him with the
hope of Istelyn's return, since he seems to care for the
man's safety. Now that Judhael has been consecrated,
Istelyn is of little use to us here."

Loris raised an eyebrow disdainfully in Istelyn's direction. "Aye. Any worthy priest would have informed his
superiors that one under his charge intended to break a
sacred oath. Istelyn, I hold you personally responsible
for young Dhugal's escape."

Istelyn, notably grim and silent until then, shook his
head.

"I honestly regret that I cannot take credit for that,"
he said softly. "As for his oath-breaking, I suspect there
are far worse offenses before God than the breaking of
an oath taken under duress. Perhaps you have knowledge
of a few of them."

Loris' eyes lit dangerously.

"As for my worthiness as a priest," Istelyn went on, "you have no authority to judge that—and have had none since the bishops removed you from office and sent you into confinement."

As much from reflex as volition, Loris was on his feet and raising his hand to strike the defiant Istelyn, a wordless growl rumbling in his throat, careless of the goblet which toppled from his chair arm to smash on the stone flags.

"Don't!" Caitrin gasped, as Sicard simultaneously launched himself between the two to block the intended blow.

The word and the sound of shattering pottery served to deflate Loris' blind fury, and he drew himself up indignantly before Sicard could touch him, pointedly dropping his hands to his sides and inclining his head in a grudging bow to Caitrin as he seated himself once more. Sicard, with an explosive sigh, tugged his tunic into place and also sat. Ithel, who had moved to his father's defense, warily resumed his place behind his mother's chair. Judhael clasped his hands tightly before him and tried not to look torn between loyalty to his aunt and obedience to the man who had made him a bishop. Istelyn had never moved from his stool or flinched throughout the interchange.

"Please accept my apologies, Your Highness," Loris murmured contritely. "I don't know what came over me. His insolence is—unbecoming in a priest."

"Indeed, it is," Caitrin replied coldly. "However, I doubt he sees his behavior in quite that light. Be that as it may, the Haldane will need some reassurance of Istelyn's well-being. His ring, I think—and perhaps a letter from his hand, which you shall dictate, Archbishop."

"I will not write it," Istelyn said quietly.

"And if he will not cooperate," Caitrin continued, her face hardening, "I shall leave it to you, Archbishop, to decide what measures should be taken to assure the king that we have his bishop and will deal with him as he intends to deal with my children, if agreement cannot be reached." She smiled grimly at Loris. "I shall ask my nephew to assist you, and rely on your joint good offices to see that our intention is carried out."

Loris nodded slowly, a grim smile coming across his face.

"Very well, Madame. I will be quite pleased to carry out your wishes. I think you will not be disappointed."

# CHAPTER THIRTEEN

*Yet was she carried away, she went into captivity.*

—Nahum 3:10

A weary but satisfied Kelson led his warband back through the gates of Rhemuth less than a week after his departure, none of his men with so much as a scratch, Dhugal's presence at his side proclaiming at least the partial success of his mission. As the column clattered across the bridge and into the castle yard, several elated Transha bordermen darted out to greet their new young chief with raucous highland yells. Dhugal's previous injuries had been aggravated by his escape and the enforced march of the past three days, but he managed a grin and a few words for each man before sliding painfully from his horse.

Nor was Dhugal the only addition to Kelson's company. Six glum prisoners rode with the warband; the youngest, a dark-haired, aristocratic-looking boy, was doing his best to put up a brave front, his wrists bound before him and his horse's lead secured to Conall's saddle. His cheeks flamed with embarrassment under the stares of the curious, but he kept his eyes pointedly ahead, disdaining assistance as he climbed down from his horse. The most intriguing addition of all sat limply in the circle of Morgan's arms, apparently asleep—a heavily cloaked female form with tangled chestnut hair escaping from beneath her hood.

"They're the pretender's younger children," Kelson told Nigel, as he dismounted in the snowy courtyard and helped Morgan hand the sleeping girl into Duncan's arms.

"Now all we need are Caitrin, Sicard, and the remaining son. And Loris, of course. The girl's name is Sidana. Dhugal stole her out from under their noses."

"She isn't hurt, is she?" Nigel asked.

Morgan, relieved of his burden, swung one leg over his horse's neck and vaulted to the ground, shaking his head.

"She'll be fine by morning. I—ah—had to put her to sleep. She started to get hysterical when she realized she wasn't going to be rescued. I doubt she'll even remember most of the trip."

Nigel nodded slowly, accepting Morgan's use of his powers without batting an eye.

"Aye, that was probably kindest. Duncan, why don't you take her to my wife? Unless you wish otherwise, of course, Kelson. She'll want the comfort of another woman's company when she wakes—and a lady's bower seems a more fitting setting for this Mearan rose than a cell."

"A briar rose, I think," Kelson said, smiling, "with proper thorns, I'll warrant. But no matter. Aunt Meraude will be a suitable companion, I'm sure. Father Duncan, would you take her, please?"

"Of course."

"And as for our other unexpected guest," Kelson went on, with a glance back at the sullen Llewell as Duncan withdrew, "you'll be proud to learn that it was your son Conall who captured him, Uncle. His name is Llewell. He's been a little belligerent from the start, so I think he'll want closer guard. No cell, though. He's a noble hostage, not a criminal."

Kelson took a few more minutes seeing to the disposition of his other prisoners and to the provisioning of his men and horses, then went with Dhugal and Morgan into the hall. While all three of them washed down mouthfuls of venison pasties with mulled ale, he gave a hastily gathered privy council his impromptu account of the venture. Dhugal was beginning to nod over his food by the time they finished, and even Morgan was beginning to slow down as food filled empty stomachs and ale lulled aching muscles. Within the hour, after scheduling a formal meeting of the full council for the following afternoon, Kelson dismissed the court and retired for the night. The torches in Rhemuth hall burned late that night as Nigel and the others tried to digest what the king had told them.

Kelson woke with the dawn, however—not yet fully refreshed, but unable to sleep longer. He felt the need to do *something*, but there was nothing he could do until Caitrin replied to his demands. He sat in a window and watched the snow fall for a while, hoping he might ease himself back into drowsiness, but he only grew more restless. After a while he gave up the notion of sleep and got dressed, pulling on plain grey breeches, boots, tunic, and fur-lined overrobe.

Like a silent ghost he prowled the precincts of his castle, inquiring after the men and horses that had returned with him from Ratharkin, checking on his prisoners and hostages, and breaking his fast with Morgan, who was also unable to sleep into the day. When he returned to his own apartments a few hours later, still on edge, he found Dhugal also awake and dressed, wondering where he had gone.

"I couldn't sleep," Kelson told him. "I talked to Morgan, but that didn't seem to help much. I thought I might pay a visit to my father's tomb before the council meeting. Sometimes doing so helps me clear my head—almost as if I could still ask him for advice. Would you come with me?"

They chose the most common-looking horses they could find in the royal stables, for Kelson did not want his going to be noticed. Cloaked and closely capped, as much for anonymity as for warmth, they rode the half mile to the cathedral along silent, nearly deserted streets and alleys. The weather held cold and clear; the snow was still mostly white from the previous night when they dismounted in the cathedral yard. Their breath fogged on the air before them as they made their way through a slype to skirt the northern side of the cloister garth, Kelson bounding up steps to a side door, Dhugal hobbling a little stiffly from the still-painful bruise on his thigh.

"I used to hate this place," Kelson said as he led the

way down the south aisle. "The royal crypt, I mean. Archbishop Cardiel has done a lot to make it more bearable in the two years he's had the cathedral, but it's still a little creepy. Did I ever bring you here before?"

"If you did, I don't remember."

"You'd remember." Kelson paused to open a high, gilded brass gate far enough for himself and Dhugal to slip through, then pulled it to behind them. "I suppose the best part about it is that it's one place where I can almost always be sure I'll not be disturbed," he continued. "Such places are rare when one is king."

Dhugal allowed himself a noncommittal grunt as they followed the corridor around a left-hand turn and started down a flight of marble steps, hanging back to ease his aching leg. By the time he reached the bottom, he found Kelson already kneeling beside an ornately carved sepulcher, head bowed in prayer; so he eased himself to a sitting position on the lowest step and breathed a prayer for his own father's soul. When he finished, he glanced around the dimly lit chamber, noting the rows of stone sarcophagi and the smooth marble of the walls. The stylized stone effigy atop the tomb where Kelson knelt was snowy-new and stiff, very little like the King Brion whom Dhugal remembered.

"I suppose this is the way most people will remember him," Kelson remarked, when he had crossed himself and stood to glance back at Dhugal, one hand lingering on the stone king's hand. "The stern Lord of Justice, who kept the peace for nearly fifteen years." He sighed and glanced at his feet. "It isn't the way I like to think of him, though. My father laughed a lot, but King Brion—well, he did what he had to do, as king. Kings don't get to laugh as much as ordinary folk. That's but one of the things I've learned in these three years I've worn the crown."

Dhugal nodded and glanced around the subterranean chapel again with idle interest, remembering the old king's kindness to a confused young page of eight, still fresh from the less sophisticated ways of his father's highland hall. Like many eight year olds, Dhugal's command of his rapidly growing body had been intermittent, with disastrous results the first time he was required to serve the high table. Only the king had refrained from laughing when Dhugal tripped and sent a tray of steaming pheasants and gravy skittering and sloshing down the steps of the royal dais.

The memory merged with recollections of old Caulay seated in the hall at Transha, training his own fosterlings with the same sort of firm but loving discipline that Dhugal had enjoyed at Brion's court, and Dhugal started to smile. The smile faded as he glanced again at Brion's effigy, however; for the man at Transha was only newly dead, and the shock of his passing was unnumbed by the passage of years. Dhugal could feel the tears threatening to well up in his eyes, despite the fact that, in some ways, old Caulay's death still seemed quite unreal.

"It's all right to miss him, you know," Kelson said softly, reading his mood, if not his thought. "I still miss my father, after all this time. I cried when it happened, too. And sometimes late at night, when I'm feeling especially alone and burdened, I still cry."

Dhugal had all he could do to swallow, not daring to look at Kelson lest he loose a whole floodgate of ill-timed grief. He focused on one of the torches burning in a brass cresset instead, forcing himself to raise his eyes to the chapel's vaulting.

"This isn't such a creepy place," he managed to say, in an awkward attempt to change the subject. "It's rather nice, actually."

Kelson gave him a sympathetic smile, well aware what his foster brother was trying to do and hardly blaming him.

"It's only been this way the past year or so. All the stone facing on the walls is new." He gestured casually toward the nearest stretch of burnished marble as he moved toward it. The slap of his open palm against the stone made Dhugal start.

"There are tomb niches carved in the living rock behind here," he went on. "It used to be that only kings and queens were buried in free-standing tombs like my father's. Other members of the royal family were simply wrapped in their shrouds and laid to rest on the shelves in these walls. They didn't rot for some reason; they just dried out and eventually crumbled away—something about the air, I'm told. I'd hold tight to my mother's hand and hide my eyes when my parents brought me here to pray on feast days. The fellow behind this wall, in particular, used to scare me half to death."

Ready to seize on any topic in preference to his own grief, Dhugal rose to approach the panel Kelson was touching.

"*Dolonus Haldanus, Princeps Gwyneddis, 675–699,*" Dhugal read, stumbling a little over the fine, archaic script. "*Filius Llarici, Rigonus Gwyneddis. Requiem in pacem.*" He glanced at Kelson in question. "Prince Dolon—didn't his own father execute him?"

Kelson nodded. "And his younger brother as well. It was thought at the time that they were plotting treason."

"Were they?"

"Who knows?" Kelson glanced at the next row of wall inscriptions. "His brother is over there. I can remember being terrified of the two headless skeletons. My nurse told me that their father had cut off their heads because they displeased him."

"What a thing to tell a child!"

Kelson grinned. "I think I'd been especially trying that day. Still, it was years before I gained a more objective perspective." He glanced back at his father's tomb wistfully.

"That wasn't my most frightening experience down here, though," he went on softly, not sure whether he should risk frightening Dhugal as well by recounting the old nightmare. "It happened the night before my coronation."

"My father heard rumors. . . ." Dhugal said cautiously.

Kelson smiled and moved back to Brion's sarcophagus, leaning both hands along the edge.

"I'll bet he did. Well, I shan't go into details that might alarm you overmuch, but as you may know, Morgan wasn't here when my father died. He was in Cardosa."

"And came back the day before the coronation," Dhugal supplied.

"That's right. My father had been buried for over a week by then: my mother's doing—she hates Morgan for being Deryni. Anyway, as I talked with him and Father Duncan that afternoon, it soon became apparent that— well, something we needed to make my kingship complete had been buried with my father."

"Then you *did* open the tomb!" Dhugal breathed, wide-eyed with horror. "My father said there'd been rumors of vandals—"

"We weren't responsible for that part," Kelson countered. "We think it was Charissa or her agents, trying to discredit Morgan and Father Duncan. We were looking for the Eye of Rom."

As he brushed a strand of hair behind his right ear, exposing the crimson gemstone, Dhugal nodded.

"I remember him wearing that."

"Aye, I never saw him without it. But when we opened this," Kelson tapped the stone cover of the sarcophagus with one hand, "it wasn't my father inside—or, it was, actually, but it didn't look like him. We thought someone might have switched bodies at first, so we started searching the rest of the chapel. I wasn't strong enough to push back these stone lids by myself, so Morgan and Father Duncan did that part. I had to look in the tomb niches. It—wasn't pleasant."

"I—don't think I understand," Dhugal said in a small voice. "You mean, it was your father's body in the coffin after all?"

Kelson nodded. "I still don't totally understand, but apparently Charissa had placed some kind of a—a binding spell on the body, which also changed its appearance. Father Duncan got rid of it, but he said that—" He hesitated as Dhugal got an odd, tight look on his face. "He said that Father's soul had also been bound up in the spell somehow...that he hadn't been...entirely free. I've frightened you again, haven't I? I'm sorry. It still bothers you to hear me talk so casually about magic, doesn't it?"

Dhugal managed to swallow, forcing himself not to avoid Kelson's gaze, but it was true.

"Yes," he whispered. "I don't want to be afraid, but I guess it's an old reflex. And when you talk about souls being bound up—"

"That isn't the usual kind of Deryni magic," Kelson said in a low voice, laying a gloved hand on the other's shoulder. "That's dark magic—and you have every reason to fear it, as I do. What I do—and what Morgan and Father Duncan do—is of the Light. I *know* there's no evil in it. Would I endanger my soul?—would I endanger *yours*?—if I thought it was evil?"

"No. Not if you knew. But what if you're wrong?"

"Was my father wrong?" Kelson asked. "You knew him, Dhugal. Was Brion an evil man?"

"No."

"And is Morgan evil? Is Father Duncan evil?"

"I don't think so."

"Is Bishop Arilan evil, then?"

"Arilan? Arilan's Deryni?"

As Dhugal's jaw dropped, Kelson nodded slowly.

"Arilan. And you are one of less than a dozen men who know that," he replied. "I'm told he comes from very, very old Deryni lineage, long hidden away—and he probably knows more about magic than Morgan, Father Duncan, and myself combined. I'm in awe of him—but I know he isn't evil. *Loris* is evil; and he isn't even Deryni."

"I—won't argue with you on that count," Dhugal murmured. "It's just that—" He passed a hand across his eyes in futile attempt to clear a growing fuzziness from his vision, suspecting that his treatment at the renegade archbishop's hands had taken a more serious toll than he had thought. "I'm sorry. I'm afraid I'm not thinking very clearly."

"No need to apologize," Kelson replied. "You've been through a lot in the last week or so, and you're still not well. I should have had Morgan and Duncan see you, instead of bringing you here."

A flicker of even greater foreboding supplanted Dhu-

gal's burgeoning discomfort, and he looked up at Kelson
with a sick, queasy sensation in the pit of his stomach.

"You mean, to heal me?"

"Yes."

"But—" He swallowed painfully. "Kelson, I'm—not
certain I'm ready for that yet."

"Because of what happened in Transha?"

"Yes," Dhugal admitted. He rubbed both hands across
his eyes. "God, my head is throbbing. I can't think."

"That's why I'd like to have them take a look at you,"
Kelson replied. "They might be able to heal your injuries
without touching your shields, you know. And maybe you
won't react the same way you did with me."

"Maybe. For now, however, I—think I might prefer to
let nature take its course, if you don't mind. I'll be all
right."

"If that's what you want," Kelson said. "They may ask
you themselves, though. I haven't told Duncan about
Transha yet, but Morgan may have. He knows."

Dhugal looked down at his hands clasped tightly
together and forced them to relax, drawing a deep breath.

"Well, then, I'll wait to see what they say. I just can't—
ask them myself, Kelson. And I don't want you to ask
them. Maybe I—won't be afraid, if they ask me." He
winced and rubbed at his temples again. "It's too bad
your probe hurts worse than the headache I've got anyway—though I wouldn't mind having my ribs healed,
that's for certain. I haven't drawn a proper breath without
pain for days. And the riding didn't help matters."

"We'd better get you back to rest then," Kelson said,
in a tone that conveyed nothing of his disappointment.
"It'll be time for the council soon anyway, and I could
use a snack before we settle down for the meeting."

"You could talk me into that without half trying," Dhugal answered with a game grin.

Their spurs jingled against the polished marble of the
steps as they ascended from the crypt to the level of the
nave, and the gate of gilded brass creaked noisily as Kelson pulled it shut behind them.

"I must ask the sacristan to have that oiled," he said,

making small talk as they moved along the transept arm heading toward the nave. "Remind me one day to tell you about *his* part in the confusion the night before my coronation. I wish you could have been here for the day itself."

Dhugal returned Kelson's sunny grin uneasily.

"My father told me about the part he saw. He said you fought some sort of magical duel, right here in the cathedral."

Kelson gestured grandly toward the transept crossing, trying to diffuse some of the magical drama of the incident while still conveying the wonder.

"Right there at the foot of the altar steps," he replied. "What really saved me, though, was one of those seals set in the floor. Without it, I wouldn't have had a clue what to do." He led Dhugal to one near the center of the transept and removed his right glove as he knelt beside it.

"All of these are seals and sigils of various patron saints of this cathedral," he explained, gesturing to include the entire circle of mosaic designs beneath the crossing. "Part of the kingmaking I had from my father called for a 'Defender's Sign.' We had assumed—not unreasonably, at the time—that the Defender's Sign was Morgan's signet ring, since he was my defender, my champion."

He brushed his fingertips almost reverently over the worn design beside his knees. "It wasn't, though. It was this: Saint Camber's seal."

"The Deryni heretic saint?"

"Yes. I know his name doesn't appear on it, but somehow I knew this was it—don't ask me how. Maybe the ability to recognize the true seal when it was time was part of the knowledge that passed to me with my father's magic. Here's the robed and hooded figure holding up the crown—see? Because Saint Camber restored the crown of Gwynedd to the Haldanes. And here, worked into the design, you can trace out most of the letters of his name, if you know where to look: C—M—B—R—S. The vagueness of the identification may be what saved the seal from obliteration when Camber's cult was stamped out, two centuries ago."

Dhugal nodded distractedly, steadying himself with gloved knuckles against the floor as he stared down at the swirls of colored mosaic, his eyes tracing out the sigil of *Sanctus Camberus* as Kelson's fingertip showed him where to look.

"You don't believe that Saint Camber was evil, then?" he finally asked.

Kelson shook his head and stood, giving Dhugal a hand up. "Not at all. And I don't want to sound naive, but either Saint Camber or some present-day disciple who wants us to *think* he's Saint Camber has come to *our* rescue more than once—Morgan's and Duncan's as well as my own. I think I'd like to restore his cult someday," he added wistfully. "Most folks would disagree, but I think he was a great man, as well as a powerful saint. I'd like to find out more about what he was *really* like; and then I think I'd like to go on a quest to try to recover some of his relics, and build a proper shrine to house them. He deserves that."

"I suspect the Church might take exception to that notion," Dhugal murmured.

"I suspect you're right," said a voice from behind them, "if you judge the Church by some of her more stodgy leaders. By that definition, the Church takes exception to a great many notions of far less controversial nature. I can personally vouch for that."

"Father Duncan!" Kelson said, as he and Dhugal both whirled to see Duncan standing behind them with an armful of manuscript scrolls. "Oh, bother, I didn't mean for you to overhear the part about Camber. It's probably silly to even think of it."

"Not silly, my prince," Duncan said mildly. "No genuine act of piety and faith is ever silly. This is not to say that your dream is necessarily *realistic*," he added. "At least not now. But who knows what the future may bring? After all, who would have thought the bishops would approve the appointment of a known Deryni to their ranks?"

Nervously Kelson glanced around the transept to be certain there was no one else within earshot, a little annoyed that even Duncan should have crept up on him unawares.

"Shhh!" he hissed under his breath. "The bishops may know, and a lot of other people, but *everybody* doesn't. You needn't make things any more difficult than they are."

Duncan raised an eyebrow. "I am what I am, Sire, as we all are. Denying serves no useful purpose."

"And what am *I*, then?" Dhugal whispered, turning sick, fearful eyes on Kelson. "Go ahead and ask him, Kelson. He's right. I need to know. And I can't properly serve you and what you've become, until I do."

Kelson glanced up at Duncan to find the Deryni priest incredibly still, glancing back and forth between him and Dhugal with taut question in the blue eyes.

"Dhugal has shields," Kelson murmured, at the same time touching his fingertips to Duncan's hands and imparting a quick mental impression of what he and Dhugal had experienced. "I told Alaric about them before the expedition, but there wasn't time to tell you. Now he needs to be healed, but I'm a little afraid to have either of you try it alone. I suspect you're going to have to get around the shields to do it, and that could be very tricky. He shut down in terrible pain when I tried to read him in Transha."

Duncan's eyes betrayed no emotion as he assimilated Kelson's words and thoughts; but when the king had finished, Duncan slowly turned his gaze on the apprehensive Dhugal, looking slightly wistful.

"Shields, you say? Shields that even you can't breach, Kelson?"

The king shook his head. "I don't want to hurt him any more than I have already, trying to force the issue. I have the technical knowledge, but you and Alaric have far more experience. If necessary, I thought you might draw on—other expertise, as well," he added, thinking of Arilan, and seeing that the thought had occurred to Duncan as well, though he suddenly did not want Duncan to know that he had told Dhugal.

"No," Duncan said softly, "I'd rather not involve anyone else, if we can handle this ourselves." He flicked his attention back to Dhugal, shifting his armful of scrolls to free one hand. "Do you mind if I try a light probe, Dhugal?" he asked, reaching casually toward the boy's forehead before Dhugal could back away. "I'll pull right out if it distresses you."

As he touched Dhugal, he sent out a cautious tendril of thought, recoiling almost immediately as rigid shields slammed into place and Dhugal blinked.

"Was that painful?" Duncan asked, not withdrawing his hand.

Dhugal gave a cautious shake of his head, too amazed to even think of pulling back. "Not painful, no. But I felt—*something*."

"With shields like that, I should imagine you did." Again Duncan extended a cautious probe. "Can you feel that?"

Dhugal got an odd, not-quite frightened look on his face.

"I don't exactly—*feel* it. It isn't a physical sensation at all. Kind of like a . . . an itch inside my head."

"Shall I stop?"

Dhugal swallowed. "Well, it doesn't really *hurt*. It isn't even that unpleasant, but—"

"Let me help," Kelson said, adding his hand beside Duncan's and trying a contact.

But at Kelson's first psychic touch, Dhugal gasped and recoiled, clapping hands to his temples and doubling over with pain. Both Kelson and Duncan withdrew immediately, Duncan letting his scrolls fall to the floor as he helped Kelson support his tottering foster brother. Dhugal gasped for breath, letting Duncan ease him to a crouch and push his head between his knees, trying not to jostle his sore ribs or kink the bruise on his thigh. His head was throbbing again.

"That's exactly what happened in Transha," Kelson murmured, leaving Dhugal to Duncan's ministrations while he awkwardly gathered up the dropped scrolls. "It didn't happen right away, but it's been that way ever since. I wonder why you don't get the same reaction."

Duncan shrugged, gently kneading the back of Dhugal's neck and trying a tentative probe again. "I don't know. He's still shielded, though. The harder I push, the stronger it gets."

"But it doesn't hurt when you do it," Dhugal managed to murmur.

"And damned if I know why," Duncan replied, helping the boy to stand. "I confess it's beyond me, at least on casual investigation. We're due back at the council meeting very shortly, but why don't we closet ourselves with Alaric afterward and get to the bottom of this? I'll be fascinated to see whether you react the same to him as you do to me, Dhugal—though I warn you, you could react just as easily as you did to Kelson's probe."

Dhugal grimaced, but he hobbled gamely between them as they started back down the nave.

"Just warn me before anybody else touches me, Father. If General Morgan—"

But he was not given time to complete the thought. As the three of them reached the narthex, pulling up cloak hoods against the snow falling outside the postern door, Morgan himself came through the narrow doorway, accompanied by a worried-looking Nigel. Morgan gave them all a grim, distracted smile and sketched a bow to Kelson as he pulled a parchment packet from inside his tunic. Nigel brushed snow from his shoulders and stamped his feet as Morgan handed the parchment to the king.

"This arrived within the present hour, my prince," Morgan said, scanning the narthex as he signalled Nigel to pull the door shut behind them. "I had a little difficulty finding where you'd gone. It's a reply from Ratharkin, though I fear it isn't the answer any of us would have wished."

The parchment was heavy with pendant seals and dark with the meticulous script of someone who had favored a broad nib to his pen. Kelson skipped over the first few lines, with their expected formulae of titles and assumed titles. The crux of the message was contained in only a few terse phrases.

*. . . that We do not intend to surrender ourselves; and*

*further, that if you do not immediately give indication of
your willingness to return our son and daughter, Bishop
Henry Istelyn will suffer for it. As earnest of our determination, We send you his ring....*

The missive was signed by Caitrin and Sicard, as co-
rulers of Meara, and witnessed by Prince Ithel, Archbishop Loris, and a host of other bishops, expected and
unexpected, eight in all.

"I can't say I'm surprised at the demand," Kelson
observed, scanning the script a second time, "though I
*am* surprised at the amount of support Loris managed to
gather in so short a time. He must have been laying his
groundwork for several years—all the while he was in
prison. He almost got enough names to set up a counter-
synod like last time. Do you think he will, Duncan?"

"I should think it almost inevitable, Sire," Duncan
replied, peering over his shoulder.

"There's more to it, I'm afraid," Morgan said, drawing
a small wooden box out of the front of his tunic. "This
was with the letter. It's going to put you in a very unenviable position."

"I'm already in an unenviable position," Kelson said,
taking the box and turning it to worry at the clasp, "though
I fail to see what Caitrin thinks she can offer that would
make me trade Sidana and Llewell for Istelyn."

"I suspect we have Loris to thank for this little piece
of work," Morgan said quietly, as Kelson opened the box.
"The note, at least, is his. The rest, I fear, is from Istelyn.
And more than just his ring."

Kelson's eyes widened and he recoiled so violently that
he nearly dropped the box.

"Sweet *Jesu*!" he gasped, his eyes darting to the others
as if to seek denial of what his eyes saw. "Look what
they've done!"

Lying on a curl of closely inscribed parchment inside
was Istelyn's bishop's ring, with the cut-off finger still
inside.

"And Loris threatens to send ever more important parts
of our captive bishop until you relent," Morgan said
quietly.

# CHAPTER FOURTEEN

*Let our strength be the law of justice: for
that which is feeble is found to be nothing
worth.*

—Wisdom of Solomon 2:11

"I had begun to suspect Loris had no conscience, but I never dreamed even he would be this ruthless," Archbishop Bradene said a short time later, when the king had presented his council with Caitrin's ultimatum and Loris' grisly postscript. "Certainly I never thought the Lady Caitrin would be a party to such an act."

"You underestimate the lady's desire to be queen, Sire," Ewan muttered.

Cardiel nodded grimly. "His Grace is right, Sire. Nor should we forget how persuasive Loris can be when it suits him. God knows he nearly fooled many of us, two years ago. And he's certainly fooled the other bishops who've joined him this time, in Ratharkin."

"Just now, my concern is with the bishop who *didn't* join him," Kelson said, "and whose finger lies in that box."

His curt gesture between himself and Morgan, where the box weighted a corner of the offensive letter, renewed the anger which had flared in every heart at his first reporting of the outrage.

"Unfortunately, I fear this is only a taste of what Loris has in store for Istelyn," Kelson went on after a studied pause. "Be that as it may, I cannot agree to the Mearan terms. Nor may I sacrifice my kingdom for the sake of one man, however precious he may be to all of us. As my council, you must know that at the outset."

They were not his full council, for several important members had not yet arrived from their outland holdings to keep the compulsory Christmas Court with the king, but they represented some of Gwynedd's finest minds. Kelson knew some of those minds in quite a literal sense; but without making unwarranted use of his powers, he could only guess about the others.

Morgan was no mystery, of course—at least in his feelings on this matter. Seated as usual at the king's right hand, he was as close as a touch, whether of hand or of mind. Morgan had spent his outrage on his first inspection of the letter and the box, so that now only cool purpose remained—that his old adversary should not have the ultimate victory.

Duncan occupied the next chair, where once his father and brother had sat as Duke of Cassan and Earl of Kierney; and after him came Ewan, senior of Gwynedd's three nonroyal dukes. Kelson sensed an uneasiness in Duncan which was as much an aftereffect of their interplay with Dhugal as a concern about Istelyn, but Ewan required no Deryni reading at all; he would say what he thought, when he thought it, as he always had.

Beyond Ewan sat Bishops Arilan and Hugh de Berry—the Deryni Arilan, whom Kelson could not have read even if he dared to try, and the earnest and faithful Hugh, touchingly human. Arilan had resigned a council seat on taking up the See of Dhassa, but Hugh had never been a member. Hugh *had* been secretary to Loris' deceased colleague, Patrick Corrigan, however, which meant he knew Loris as well as any man present.

Dhugal knew Loris, too—not as intimately, but certainly more recently—and he was acquainted with the Mearan royal family as well, which none of the rest of them were. He was not an official member of the council either, though Kelson planned to remedy that once Dhugal had been formally confirmed as Earl of Transha. Now that they had been reunited, the king wanted his foster brother at his side—especially in light of Dhugal's unexpected but intriguing shields. The recent probing of those shields, as well as Dhugal's on-going discomfort from his aggravated injuries, had left the young border lord a little shaky, but he was at Kelson's side now, perched self-consciously on a stool between Kelson and Archbishop Bradene.

Archbishop Cardiel sat next to Bradene, and Jodrell and Saer de Traherne beyond them, all four new to the council since Kelson's accession. Nigel occupied the chair at the opposite end of the table, as heir presumptive, with Conall as an unofficial observer at his right.

"No one questions your position, Sire," Bradene said quietly, when a few of the others began to fidget at the lengthy silence. "Least of all would Istelyn question it. According to what young Dhugal has told us, Istelyn is totally resigned to the consequences of his loyalty." He sighed. "I fear we can do nothing save to offer up our prayers for his deliverance."

"Prayers will not deliver him from the agony Loris intends for him," Arilan murmured under his breath. "If I could give him the coup and save him Loris' spite, I would."

Arilan's open espousal of an act the Church forbade as murder startled Bradene and Hugh, each only recently emerged from the relative shelter of cloister or academia. But the *coup de grâce* was an acknowledged if reluctantly practiced fact of life to the battle-seasoned—a human mercy to friend or foe when only pointless suffering lay between a man and death. Other than the two bishops, only Conall was yet unblooded in that regard. Even Dhugal had not escaped the grim initiation. Most of the young border lord's experience had been limited to animals sick or injured past healing, but once it had been one of his own clansmen shattered in a fall from a river cliff, and no one else was nearby to take responsibility. The man had been beyond speech already by the time Dhugal reached him, hardly a bone unbroken in his twisted body, but the pain-glazed eyes had begged for release, all the suffering ending as Dhugal drew his dirk across the pulsing throat. Dhugal had just turned thirteen.

As Nigel cleared his throat impatiently and sat forward, Dhugal jerked himself back from memory and suppressed a shudder, glad that the decision about the unfortunate Istelyn was none of theirs to make. He knew no one blamed him for not bringing Istelyn out of Ratharkin, but he regretted his inability nonetheless. The bishop had been a brave man and a welcome friend for the short time Dhugal had known him, even if they had disagreed over points of conscience.

"We serve neither Istelyn nor ourselves by brooding on this further," Nigel said quietly, breaking the awkward silence. "No one regrets his situation more than I, for he has been a good friend as well as a faithful shepherd to the Church, but I think we must address more constructive concerns." He looked directly down the table at Kelson. "Sire, Loris may seem the greater threat at the moment, but his importance is directly related to the influence and support of the Lady Caitrin. Break her and you will break him as well."

Kelson inclined his head in wry agreement. "I should like very much to do both, Uncle. Unfortunately, I fear that any meaningful forcing of that issue must wait until the spring."

"Well, thank the heavens for that bit of wisdom," Ewan muttered under his breath. "I thought he might be intending to gallop off to Meara again tonight!"

"In *this* weather?" Bradene asked, shocked.

Morgan, sensing the disapproval under Ewan's gruff aside, flashed a warning look at Kelson.

"I think His Majesty is quite aware of the situation, Ewan," he said easily. "In any case, even were it not for the weather, we've lost our element of surprise. Our foray into Meara went unchallenged because no one expected us to venture forth on the edge of the season's first storm. They'll be ready for us next time."

"They'll be ready for a military offensive, yes," Nigel countered. "However, I have in mind an offensive which requires no military action whatsoever. The means of accomplishing that offensive is already in your hands, Sire."

Expressionless, Kelson sat back in his chair and lowered his eyes, tracing the carving on the chair arm with one fingertip. He suspected he knew what was coming. He had hoped to avoid the question indefinitely.

"If you're referring to our hostages, Uncle, I don't make war on women and children."

"Nor am I asking you to do so," Nigel said. "I would remind you, however, that not all wars are won on the battlefield."

Before Kelson could frame a reply, Ewan's bearded face creased in a lecherous grin.

"He means the marriage bed, lad. Now, *there's* a merry winter's sport! I *told* ye a bride was what ye needed. An' wouldn't *that* frost her mother?"

"Ewan, please!"

Kelson's rebuke stilled the old duke's tongue, but it did not wipe the grin from his face or extinguish the gleam in his eyes. Nigel was studying his royal nephew with a mixture of compassion and resolution, not liking the suggestion any more than Kelson did. To Kelson's left, Archbishop Bradene looked dubious, Cardiel thoughtful. As Bradene cleared his throat, all eyes instantly turned toward him.

"Sire, it appears that between them, Their Noble Graces have just suggested a marriage with the Lady Sidana," Bradene said quietly.

"The *Princess* Sidana, by Mearan reckoning, Excellency," Nigel amended, "and heiress to what they regard as the legitimate royal line."

"But it *isn't* the legitimate royal line," Kelson pointed out. "And even if it were, she has a mother and two brothers ahead of her."

"The mother is not a young woman," Nigel countered. "Even if she were to escape us, you have time on your side. You can easily outwait her. Of the brothers, one is in our hands already and the other eventually will be taken or slain in battle. Eliminate the two of them and marry Sidana—not necessarily in that order—and the Mearan royal line will *become* the legitimate line in your children's generation, as should have been done in your great-grandfather's time."

From the animation of the discussion that followed, it soon became apparent that the notion had already occurred to at least a few of them, probably from the moment Sidana rode through the city gates in Morgan's arms. Kelson mostly listened for the first few minutes, occasionally exchanging uneasy looks with Morgan, Dhugal, or Duncan; but when at last he held up a hand for silence, he had shuttered his true feelings behind a facade which even Morgan could not pierce.

"There is a certain logic in what my uncle has proposed, my lords," the king said carefully. "I will tell you from the outset that this is not the first time the lady in question has been proposed as a potential royal bride. When I was in Transha a few weeks ago, Lord Dhugal's late father also extolled the lady's suitability—not as an uncle seeking rich dowry for his niece, but as a loyal liegeman suggesting a possible way to ease the tension which has been increasing along the Mearan border for the last several years."

"Old Caulay offered you her hand and you didn't tell us?" Ewan blurted, eyes flashing above his bushy beard. "Why, that old fox!"

"He didn't offer me her hand, Ewan!" Kelson retorted, allowing himself a sigh of exasperation. "He wasn't in any position to make me such an offer. He simply pointed out the obvious advantages of such a match. Sidana was still in Meara at the time."

"And now that she is in Gwynedd?" Nigel asked.

Kelson closed his eyes briefly and drew a deep breath, then let it out with a patient sigh.

"Frankly, the idea terrifies me. I don't even know the girl. But I'm a king first and a man second. If such an alliance would ease the tension along the border and help secure peace, then I would be less than true to my coronation oath if I did not give it my wholehearted support."

"It might just do that, Sire," Jodrell said thoughtfully. "I know the Mearans. My patrols go back and forth across the border constantly. Caitrin's sons or Sidana's sons—

it would make no difference to most folk. They've been sending sons and husbands and brothers off to war with Gwynedd for over a hundred years."

"I doubt a marriage with Sidana would stop *that*," Saer de Traherne said. "Unless Caitrin does submit by Christmas, which I think highly unlikely in light of that," he gestured curtly toward the letter and box, "there's still going to be a war in the spring—at least until we take her and Ithel."

Bishop Hugh, silent until then, sat forward and raised a hand for recognition.

"Sire, forgive me if I speak out of turn, but might not a marriage with Sidana be used to negotiate a true peace? Perhaps Caitrin would be willing to renounce her claim, if she were assured that her daughter would be queen of a united Meara and Gwynedd."

Dhugal shook his head emphatically. "Not a chance, Excellency. Even if *she* would, Ithel wouldn't. He's full of plans for when he's king. Llewell's little better, though at least we have him in custody."

"The lad is right, Sire," Jodrell agreed. "Marriage with Sidana might provide an ultimate solution, but we'll still have to take Caitrin and Ithel—and any other Mearan heirs, while we're at it—before it would be meaningful. Judhael, in particular. Mearan partisans might pass over Sidana if another male heir could be persuaded to take up the cause."

"*We* will deal with Judhael, my lord," Arilan said pointedly. "You need not worry about a renegade priest. The marriage does have its merits, though. Sire, from what has been said, I assume that you would be willing to enter such a union. Is that a correct assumption?"

Kelson shrugged, making a game attempt to appear casual. "If I must. However, a great deal depends upon the lady. She may not want to marry me."

Ewan snorted. "She'll do as she's told, if she knows what's good for her!"

"And suppose she doesn't?" Kelson asked.

Jodrell shrugged. "She *is* your hostage, Sire. If such

is your desire, I hardly think she has much choice in the matter."

"Oh? And if I drag her to the altar against her will, how then for the sanctity of our marriage vows?" Kelson retorted. "What say you, Archbishop?"

As Bradene squirmed under the royal scrutiny, Arilan shook his head. "It is not required that the bride be eager, Sire, only willingly resigned. And if the wooing is carried out with—the proper delicacy," he arched an eyebrow knowingly at the king, "I think she would not be unwilling."

His glance at Kelson conveyed all the potential of a Deryni king's ability to persuade, without even resorting to his own Deryni abilities. Kelson read his meaning instantly, a little sick at heart, and knew by Morgan's quickly damped flare of indignation that he had read it, too.

With a chill smile, Kelson leaned back in his chair and allowed himself a resigned sigh.

"I take your meaning, Bishop," he said quietly, trying to put out of mind the temptation Arilan had just presented him. "If wooing's to be done, however, I'll do it in my own fashion. For the sake of my kingdom, I'll even take her by force if I must. I'm sure a priest could be found who would turn a blind eye to her protests," he added dryly. "But if peace can be secured some other way, without much loss of life, then I would as soon *not* wed for now. We still have time."

"And does Istelyn have time?" Bradene demanded. "How do you intend to answer that?"

As he gestured angrily toward the box across from him and Kelson, the king slapped his open palm against the table in consternation.

"Obviously I cannot answer it, Archbishop! I have already said that I can do nothing for Istelyn. I shall reiterate our demand that Caitrin and her son submit to me by Christmas."

"And if she does not?"

Kelson sighed heavily, his momentary anger deflated.

"If she does not, then I shall take the Princess Sidana

to wife at Twelfth Night and send out summons of array for a spring campaign."

"Alas, I fear that will mean Istelyn's death," Cardiel said, as murmurs of concurrence rippled around the table.

"We must count Istelyn as dead already, my lords," Morgan said softly. "And if he dies, then we must make his death count for something. I know he would support the king's wish to settle all as bloodlessly as possible, but if necessary, the spring shall see his murderers confounded with the sword."

"Very well," Bradene replied. "I see that there is no appeal for that. Fortunately, the Church has weapons other than the sword with which to confound Loris and his would-be Mearan queen. Nor need we wait until the spring to use them."

As Bradene swept his fellow bishops with his hard glance, almost in challenge, Kelson knew with a chill certainty what was coming next.

"I propose a rite of general excommunication," Bradene went on. "That we formally strip Loris of his rank and priesthood—something we should have done two years ago—that we suspend the bishops who have taken his part, and that we excommunicate the lot of them, including the Mearan royal family."

The other bishops nodded gravely, murmuring among themselves; but Kelson's stomach did a slow, queasy roll, even though he had been half-expecting someone to bring up the subject before they were done. Having been excommunicated himself at one time, if only for reason of Loris' spite, Kelson could not but feel pity for those about to incur the same fate. He glanced at Morgan and Duncan, who had felt the cold breath of excommunication even more directly than himself, and caught their similar recoil at the very notion; but it needed to be done. Excommunication was a language Loris would understand, though it would also enrage him.

"I agree," Cardiel said quietly. "The measure comes after much provocation. Do you also recommend a general Interdict of Meara, my lord?"

As the others drew in breath—for Interdict would bar

everyone in Meara from all sacraments and solace of the Church, even the innocent—Bradene shook his head.

"I would not place that burden upon the entire Mearan people at this time—though it may prove necessary in the future, if excommunication does not bring the principals to heel. No, what I have outlined is sufficient for the present, I think—unless you have some valid objection, Sire?"

Kelson bowed his head. "I would not presume to dictate the conscience of my bishops, Excellency," he whispered. "If you feel this action warranted, then so be it."

"It should be done as soon as possible, then," Bradene said decisively. "Tonight, I think, after Compline—so that our response may go to Loris and the Lady Caitrin along with His Majesty's."

Cardiel nodded. "The necessary documents can be drawn up by nightfall. My monks will assist us. Sire, we would count it a particular favor if you and the rest of the lords of state could lend us your support by your presence."

"We shall attend you," Kelson replied.

Bradene nodded, relieved. "Thank you, Sire. I should like your support in a happier matter as well. I have had no opportunity to consult with my brother Cardiel, but I feel certain he will concur with what I should like to propose."

As he turned his glance across the table to Duncan and smiled, his intention immediately became clear.

"Father McLain, you know that I was in complete sympathy with your wish to delay your consecration until the spring, so that you might better prepare yourself for your increased responsibilities, but our changed circumstances are such that I feel we need you now. Confirmation of your rank will also underline the authority of the bishops who elected you and help to strengthen our present position regarding Loris' bid for power. Will you consent to be consecrated immediately? Or as soon as may conveniently be arranged?"

As Cardiel nodded agreement, Arilan and Hugh also turning expectant eyes on Duncan, Kelson allowed himself to relax just a little. This he could support without a qualm. He sensed Morgan's support as well, as he turned his keen Haldane gaze on Duncan. The Deryni priest folded his hands precisely on the table before him and let out a long, resigned sigh before looking up at his superior.

"I will consent, Excellency, but I would ask one indulgence on your part: I wish to be invested with Bishop Istelyn's ring." He glanced around defensively. "It would mean a great deal to me. We may be helpless to save his physical body, but I would at least do honor to the courage and conviction of his soul."

"Well said," Kelson murmured, as Bradene and Cardiel exchanged approving glances.

"It shall be done as you have asked," Bradene said. "We shall set your consecration for three days hence. But for now, Sire, by your leave, I think we must all retire to prepare our various answers to Loris and his cohorts."

The bishops' answer was given substance later that night. Kelson did not relish his part in it, but he attended as he had promised. Kneeling in the front row of the south choir stalls, Dhugal and Morgan to either side of him and the rest of his council behind, he listened to Bradene sing the opening invocation, answered by the circle of cowled monks and priest-bishops around him. Duncan stood among them.

"*In nomine Patris et Filii et Spiritus Sancti....*"

"*Amen.*"

The cathedral was darkened save for the candles in the hands of the gathered clergy and the red glow of the Presence Lamp above the altar behind them. A draft curled down the nave and through the choir, making the candlelight dance fitful shadows on vestments, choir screens, and stalls. Bradene stood with Cardiel on the lowest altar step, both of them wearing black copes and mitres and also holding a candle apiece. A long strip of parchment trailed from Bradene's other hand, ragged at the bottom with heavy pendant seals.

"My lords and my brothers, it is my unpleasant duty to pronounce the following judgment, to which all of you have subscribed," he said. "Be it duly witnessed, here before the altar of the Lord and in the Presence of the Hosts of Heaven, that we do what we do without malice, and for the good of the souls of those involved, in hopes that they may come to recognize the error of their ways and repent, returning at last to the loving bosom of Mother Church."

Clearing his throat a little nervously, he handed his candle to Cardiel and brought the parchment within the range of its light, beginning to read in a voice which carried through the choir and all along the nave.

"Whereas Edmund Loris, priest and former archbishop, hath fled the just penance of a duly constituted synod of his equals and thus rejected the authority of those set above him; and whereas said Edmund Loris hath consorted with rebellious subjects of his lawful liege and king, forswearing his own sacred vows by such action, and exhorted them to treasonous acts; and whereas the said Edmund Loris hath resumed authority to which he no longer hath claim and hath used that authority illicitly to consecrate a bishop neither elected by a properly constituted synod nor approved by the king; and whereas said Edmund Loris hath usurped the authority of a brother bishop in his own diocese, and forced him to witness illicit acts, and caused him grievous physical harm, and used threats against his life in an attempt to sway others to his treasonous ways.

"So therefore do we, Bradene, by the Grace of God Archbishop of Valoret and Primate of All Gwynedd, pronounce said Edmund Loris deprived of his episcopal rank and degraded from the fellowship and office of the priesthood throughout the land. We do further excommunicate the said Edmund Loris and suspend and excommunicate all bishops claiming to owe him obedience, especially Creoda of Carbury and Judhael of Meara. Likewise do we excommunicate Caitrin of Meara, Sicard MacArdry, and Ithel of Meara, and bar them from all solace of Mother Church. Let no church of God be open to them, but let every sacred temple and sanctuary be shut against them. . . ."

Squirming inwardly, Kelson sat back on his heels as the rite continued and made himself rest his chin quietly on his folded hands, unable to put from mind his own excommunication and the blind panic it had first evoked. He sensed a similar discomfiture in Morgan, kneeling motionless at his right, but outwardly the Deryni lord was as composed as always. He dared not try to read Dhugal. Behind, he was aware of Nigel and Conall, quiet and awed, and Jodrell and Saer de Traherne to their left, only a little less affected for never having been directly exposed to this aspect of the Church's power before. Ewan sat alone behind them all, indulgent, dozing a little; he had never been much for formal ceremonies. Out on the choir floor, Duncan seemed to be holding his own reactions in tight check; but Kelson had no doubt that he, too, was remembering a time, not so long ago, when it had been they, not Loris, who had been the subjects of anathema.

".... We will neither give them the right hand of fellowship, nor eat at the same table with them, and much less will we communicate in sacred mysteries with those who choose to take part with Edmund Loris...."

They were twenty-six gathered before the altar tonight, the black-coped archbishops set like twin stones in the ring of somber-garbed bishops, priests, and monks. Duncan was a vague, indefinite form between Arilan and Hugh de Berry, more evident by his psychic presence than by sight. Bradene's voice rose in volume as the words of condemnation rolled from his tongue, the tension of the ecclesiastical magic building as the rite neared its climax.

".... And unless they speedily come to a better mind and make satisfaction to us, we confound them with eternal malediction and condemn with perpetual anathema. Curst be they in the house, curst in the field; curst be their food and drink and all that they possess. We declare them excommunicate and numbered among the thrice-damned. May they have their portion with Dathan and Abiram, whom hell swallowed up quick, and with Pilate, and Judas, who betrayed the Lord. So do we strike their names from the Book of Life. So may their light be quenched in the midst of darkness. Amen. So be it!"

And with his final words, and as the others responded, "So be it!" Bradene took back his candle and, with Cardiel, stepped down from the altar step and moved to the center of the circle, the others closing the gap behind them. In silence the two archbishops raised their candles aloft and held for several heartbeats, then reversed them end for end and snuffed the flames against the floor. The others followed suit, the hollow clatter of the falling candles echoing ominously in the darkening choir.

When the silence settled, no light shone save the Presence Lamp glowing above the high altar. Not a word was spoken as participants and witnesses filed slowly from the heavy dark.

# CHAPTER FIFTEEN

*But now it is come upon thee, and thou
faintest; it toucheth thee, and thou art
troubled.*

—Job 4:5

In the days that followed, the worsening political situation claimed increasing amounts of time and energy on the parts of everyone at court, forcing Kelson to shift his personal concerns for Dhugal into a place of secondary importance. Still, he worried. But the constant demands of his royal station left no opportunity to seek out the intimate counsel he might have asked of Morgan and Duncan in less harried times—and that seemed to content Dhugal very well. The young border lord carefully avoided any mention of what had happened in the cathedral, but his behavior made it clear that he was not yet ready to venture a repeat of his experience. Though Kelson tried to broach the subject several times, suggesting that Deryni ministrations might ease Dhugal's discomfort and perhaps even speed his recovery, Dhugal always managed to sidestep the issue without ever alluding to it specifically.

It was just as well, perhaps, for both Kelson and Morgan had spent nearly every waking hour bound up in meetings of one sort or another, first hammering out the terms of the royal reply to Caitrin and Loris and then cloistered with Nigel and the other commanders, preparing the writs of summons that must go out to all Kelson's liegemen if Meara could not be coaxed back into the fold by peaceable means. Duncan was predictably preoccupied with preparations for his suddenly imminent consecration. Even Morgan saw little of him during those two days.

The morning of the third day marked a temporary suspension of war preparations, however, for Duncan's consecration was to take place at noon. In honor of the occasion, Archbishop Cardiel announced a relaxation of the usual dietary restrictions of Advent, to which Kelson responded by declaring a celebration feast for that evening. The opportunity for respite from the past days' tensions lent the court a festive air to which even Morgan responded, putting aside the serviceable but plain leathers and homespuns of the past few days in favor of a rich court robe and cloak of fine sapphire blue wool. He had not been expecting a summons to attend the incipient Bishop Duncan before his consecration, however, and hurried to his cousin's quarters with some apprehension when a servant came to fetch him.

"Duncan?" he called, when he had dismissed the deacon who admitted him and glanced around the room.

"In here," came the muffled reply.

A tremor was evident in hand as well as voice as Duncan emerged partway from behind a heavy curtain screening the oratory beyond. Freshly barbered and shaved, he was clad in the expected priestly vestments of alb, amice, and crossed stole over a purple cassock, wanting only the white cope on a nearby stand to complete his attire for the entrance procession not an hour away; but his face wore anything but the serenity and calm which should have been his when approaching episcopal consecration. He kept his eyes averted as he backed against the curtain to make the opening larger, flinching when Morgan brushed past him to enter.

"What's wrong?" Morgan whispered, stunned.

Duncan shook his head, his voice almost inaudible as he answered.

"I'm sorry to bother you, Alaric. I'm—afraid I've taken on more than I realized. I thought I could deal with it myself, but I was wrong. I—can't even pray."

"What in the world are you talking about?" Morgan said. He set his hands on Duncan's shoulders and tried to get him to raise his eyes. "Look at me! Isn't this what you want? You're going to be a bishop—the first known Deryni bishop in—what?—two hundred years? What's the matter with you?"

Duncan kept his head bowed and turned half away. "I don't think I can pay the price, Alaric," he whispered. "It's because I *am* Deryni that makes it so difficult, don't you see? When they put that ring on my finger, how can I ever hope to measure up to *him*?"

Only as he gestured blindly toward the altar behind him did Morgan see the small wooden box resting at the foot of the standing crucifix. Suddenly Morgan thought he knew what was terrifying Duncan.

"Good God, don't tell me you've still got Istelyn's finger!" he muttered, crossing the few short steps to snatch it up before Duncan could stop him. "What kind of morbid nonsense is this? He'd beat you about the head and shoulders if he knew you were behaving this way."

"If he's still alive." Duncan crossed his arms on his chest and studied one slipper-shod toe morosely. "Maybe I shouldn't become a bishop, Alaric. Every time a messenger arrives at court now, I wonder what Loris will send us next. A hand? An eye? Or maybe a head, next time."

"And not accepting consecration will keep him alive?" Morgan countered. "You know it won't. As for messengers, I'm afraid I'd welcome delivery of a head."

"What?"

"At least it would mean he was beyond Loris' ability to hurt him anymore. You don't really think Loris means to let him live, do you? Not after he's gone this far."

Duncan bit at his lip and sighed heavily. "You're right. I know you're right. I suppose that's why I asked for Istelyn's ring in the first place. I knew he'd never wear it again. But it was different three days ago. Now, taking the ring from a martyr's hand seems—well—presumptuous, to say the least."

"Not presumptuous. An act of homage to a brave man who would not succumb to the enemy."

When Duncan did not respond, Morgan opened the

box and extracted the ring, carefully avoiding contact with Istelyn's shriveled finger. The gold seemed to tingle as he closed it in his palm. That confirmed what he had guessed Duncan feared—and that the fear would have to be faced before Duncan left for the cathedral. Tight-lipped, Morgan closed the box and replaced it gingerly on the altar.

"I know what's bothering you as much as anything," he said after a slight pause.

"No, you don't."

"Duncan, I can't *not* know—and neither can you. We're Deryni. Just holding this is enough for me to sense that it isn't just any ring."

"Of course not. It's a bishop's ring."

"And it's *Istelyn's* ring, taking from him in a most brutal fashion," Morgan countered. "Some of that is bound to be clinging to it. And you're going to have to face what's on it—if not now, then later today, in front of all those people in the cathedral, when you'll be far more vulnerable than you are now."

"I'll keep my shields up," Duncan whispered.

"Is that really the way you want to experience your consecration as a bishop?" Morgan asked quietly. "You remember your ordination to the priesthood—God knows, *I'll* never forget it. Do you really want to shut yourself away from that kind of magic, Duncan?"

He watched the tonsured head jerk up, the white-clad shoulders stiffen, though Duncan did not turn around.

"That's what you'd have to do, you know," Morgan went on. "And I don't think that's really what you want. Give me your hand and let's be done with it."

Slowly, stiffly, Duncan turned, his face nearly as white as his vestments, emotions completely shuttered save through the light blue eyes, where fear and reason warred for precedence. When reason won out at last, Duncan let out a long-held breath with an audible sigh. All at once, the eyes which met Morgan's were the mirrors of the soul which Duncan bared now to the man closer than any other living being.

"You're right," he whispered. "If I don't face it, I'm no bishop and no true Deryni. Stay with me, though."

"I shouldn't think you'd even need to ask," Morgan answered softly, smiling.

Taking Duncan's slack right hand in his, he held Istelyn's ring poised at the tip of the ring finger, bracing for both of them as Duncan, without further hesitation, thrust his finger into the band of gold. A little shudder went through Duncan's body as the cold metal slid across the skin, but he only shook his head and closed his eyes at Morgan's sound of question, bringing his clenched fist to his lips to touch the cold amethyst in oath confirmed. As he shuddered again, Morgan slid his hands up Duncan's arms to rest on his shoulders again and pushed himself quickly into trance, reaching out for rapport. He joined Duncan just as memory began to course, pulsing from the metal and amethyst on Duncan's hand.

Fire and ice, golden and violet—intimations of the forge which had shaped the ring and the setting of the stone which marked its sacred purpose. It had been crafted especially for Istelyn and worn by no other until this instant. Recollection stirred of its sacring by water and incense at Istelyn's consecration—words of blessing pronounced above it as it lay on a silver salver: holy ritual binding it to the service of a servant of the servants, binding the servant himself to the service of a higher Lord.

Nor had the servant disgraced the ring, through all the years it had graced his hand. The lips of the great and the lowly had brushed it in salute, most with honest respect, some perfunctorily, a few with duplicity in their hearts—but the man and his function remained true to the higher Lord. Only at the end was other than respect shown to the servant of the servant.

Honest human fear, resignation—and then the echo of sharp, burning pain as a bright blade flashed, severing the ring from its owner. Even though Morgan was prepared for it, he gasped at the shock, holding Duncan tightly in support as the new wearer of the ring shivered in more direct recollection of the deed, even crying out a little at the transmitted pain.

But then, with a shudder, Duncan was sinking even deeper into trance as the ring continued to beckon, Mor-

gan following hesitantly to brush even earlier images of
the gold itself, before the ring was forged. It had been
something besides a ring in the beginning, when first it
took form from virgin nuggets purified in the flames—an
impression of unearthly radiance and a warmth which was
not physical. Consecrated hands had lifted it toward an
even greater Glory—two pairs, the one merely priestly,
the other something more. A flash of an old, familiar
presence intervened for just an instant—and then nothing.

Roughly Morgan yanked himself back to normal consciousness as the contact ended, staggering as Duncan
became a dead weight in his arms for just an instant. But
before he could react, Duncan stirred and got his feet
under him, allaying his concern with a weak grin and a
wave of the hand with the ring.

"What in the world—?" Morgan began.

Duncan shook his head and smiled more sedately,
propping himself against the edge of the altar while he
slipped the ring from his hand to lay it reverently beside
the box.

"Not entirely *this* world," he managed to whisper,
glancing back at Morgan. "I assume you caught the part
about it being made for Istelyn?"

Morgan nodded. "And about him losing it."

"I think that's the *least* important part of what we saw."
Duncan gave the ring another long, respectful look. "How
about before it was a ring?"

"Something else was melted down to make it," Morgan
ventured. "Do you know what it was?"

Duncan nodded wistfully. "A piece of altar plate, I
think. Maybe a chalice or a paten." He shivered. "I'm
not sure I want to say aloud whose I think it was."

"Well, I'll say it if you won't," Morgan said carefully.
"I caught two separate and distinct identities. One was
only a priestly presence, but the other—well, who could
it have been besides Saint Camber?"

Duncan nodded, leaning the heels of both hands on the
edge of the altar to gaze down at the ring again. "It wasn't
a manifestation this time, though—just a memory." He

flashed a smile. "But it may be the only true relic of Saint Camber that we have—something he actually touched. I wonder what it was."

"Well, if Istelyn's ring really was made from melted-down altar plate, maybe it could be traced," Morgan said. "It's said Camber's son was a priest. Perhaps the chalice or paten belonged to him. Perhaps Camber gave it to him—an ordination gift or something of that sort. In any case, it might be possible to find out where they got the gold to make the ring."

"Perhaps." Duncan smiled again. "Incidentally, did I tell you that Kelson's keen to restore the cult of Saint Camber?"

"Oh? He's never mentioned that to me."

"Me either. I just happened to overhear. Perhaps it's only just begun to take shape in his own mind. He was telling Dhugal about it when I met them in the cathedral, just before you found us. And Dhugal—has Kelson told you about him?"

"About his shields? Oh, yes. I was on the receiving end when he pushed Kelson out of the link, the night you nearly got killed. There hasn't been time to investigate further, since we got back."

"Well, I've had a go at him, if only briefly," Duncan said. "Oddly enough, he doesn't recoil from my probe the way he does from Kelson's; I simply can't get through. I've no idea where he got shields like that. Unfortunately, Kelson tried to join in on my probe after the first few seconds—with rather devastating consequences for poor Dhugal. If you've gotten the impression he's been trying to avoid us these past two days, that's undoubtedly why."

Morgan nodded. "I can't say I blame him. I'll try to speak with Kelson about it this evening, though. I suspect you're going to be too busy for the next few days to do too much about it."

"If it's important, we'll make time somehow." Smiling, Duncan scooped up the ring and hefted it in his hand. "Meanwhile, I seem to recall I have an appointment with some bishops—and you, with a king, I think."

"The next time I see you, you'll *be* a bishop," Morgan

quipped. "I, on the other hand, shall never be a king."
Grinning uninhibitedly, he took Duncan's right hand and
dropped to one knee. "Still, I should like to be the first
to greet you as a bishop, even if it is a few hours premature. We'll repeat this officially later this afternoon,
Your Excellency."

When, over Duncan's exasperated but smiling protests, he had kissed the soon-to-be episcopal hand, Morgan left to join the king's party for the ride to the cathedral.
The interlude with Duncan had given him much to ponder.

As it had been three days before, Morgan's place was
at Kelson's right hand when they knelt in the cathedral a
little while later. It was the same stall they had occupied
for the excommunication, though a few places closer to
the altar, with Morgan on the end. Nigel and his wife and
three sons knelt behind them this time, but Dhugal was
again to Kelson's left. Others of the royal household occupied the stalls farther west and on the north side of the
choir, along with such other nobles as could be accom-
modated. As the minutes passed and the cathedral filled,
Morgan prayed for the man about to be consecrated to
even greater work, asking mercy and guidance both for
himself and for Duncan in the times ahead. Beyond the
still, vigilant flame of psychic strength and control which
was Kelson, at his left, he could sense the darkly shuttered presence of Dhugal. As the entry procession began
and all of them stood, Morgan resolved to speak to Kelson
about him before the night was over.

The ceremony proceeded without notable incident,
so far as Morgan could determine, though he readily
acknowledged his relative ignorance of liturgical intrica-
cies. Everyone seemed to be in the right place at the right
time and to know the proper responses, no one dropped
anything, and Duncan looked genuinely moved as he made
his responses to Archbishop Bradene's ritual questions.

"Beloved brother, art thou resolved by the grace of the
Holy Spirit to discharge to the end of thy life the office
entrusted to us by the apostles which is about to be passed
on to thee by imposition of our hands?"

"I am."

"Art thou resolved to keep faith with our Holy Mother the Church, and to guard and guide her children as thine own?"

"I am."

As the dialogue continued, Morgan put the words aside and let his mind extend gently toward Kelson beside him. It was not their part to share directly in what Duncan was about to experience, but it occurred to him that Kelson probably ought to be aware of what had happened when Duncan put on Istelyn's ring, just in case something else unforseen occurred when the action was repeated. Kelson felt the light tendril of his thought and glanced at him in question, but Morgan only gave a slight nod and opened the contact further as all of them knelt for the litany of blessings for the now-prostrate Duncan. What he had to say was not the sort of thing which might even be whispered safely in a church.

"*Kyrie eleison.*"

"*Kyrie eleison.*"

"*Christe eleison....*"

*What's wrong?* Kelson's thought drifted into his mind.

Morgan leaned his elbows on the prayer desk in front of him and bowed his head, resting his forehead on the heels of his hands as he let the link deepen.

*Nothing's wrong, so far as I know*, he returned. *I thought you'd like to know about something that happened a little while ago, however. Apparently Istelyn's ring is more than it seems.*

*Istelyn's ring?*

He shared the vision of the forging then, and all he could recall about what Duncan had experienced when he put the ring on his finger. When he had finished, he felt Kelson shiver a little beside him.

*Camber, eh?* Kelson sent.

*Maybe. It was certainly an impression of great power. Where did Istelyn get his ring?*

*I don't know. Maybe Duncan can find out.*

*Maybe.*

The litany had ended while they conferred, and as both of them raised their heads, physical vision was superimposed over psychic Sight, though both remained in rapport. Now Duncan knelt before the archbishop's throne, head bowed and hands joined in prayer as Bradene, Cardiel, and then each of the other bishops silently laid their hands on his head, willing him the fulfillment of total and perfected priesthood which was a bishop's portion. Morgan could sense the heightened energy levels pulsing from their midst as Cardiel stood and took the open Gospel book from an attending deacon, holding it ceremonially over Duncan's bowed head like a sheltering roof as he began the prayer of consecration.

"Lord God, merciful God, bringing comfort to all, now pour out upon this chosen one that power which floweth from Thee, the perfect spirit which Thou gavest to Thy beloved Son, the Christ, the Spirit whom He gave to the apostles. Inspire the heart of Thy servant whom Thou hast chosen to make a bishop. May he feed Thy holy flock and exercise the high priesthood without blame, ministering to Thee day and night to reconcile us with Thee and to offer the gifts of Thy Church. By the Spirit of this priesthood may he have the power to forgive sins, as Thou hast commanded. May he assign the duties of the flock according to Thy will and loose every bond by the power Thou gavest the apostles. May his gentleness and singleness of purpose stand before Thee as an offering through Thy Son the Christ. Through Him glory and power and honor are Thine, with the Holy Spirit, now and forever."

"Amen."

Even twenty yards away, Morgan could feel Duncan's anticipation mounting as Cardiel removed the Gospel and Bradene prepared to anoint his head with chrism. All in an instant, though he had not tried to do it, he was in Duncan's mind, feeling what he felt, seeing what he saw. The impression was blurred by the double perception of Kelson in the link with him, also one with Duncan in that instant.

"God hath made thee a sharer in Christ's priesthood," Bradene said, pouring the holy chrism on the crown of Duncan's head. "May He pour upon thee this oil of mystical anointing and make thee fruitful with spiritual blessing."

As Bradene cleansed his hands, first with scraps of fine white bread and then with a linen napkin, Morgan basked in the joy welling over from Duncan, feeling a little of the warmth even as a physical thing.

"Receive thou the Gospel and preach the word of God," Cardiel said, putting the great book briefly in Duncan's hands, "always teaching with the greatest of patience."

The book was taken away, to be replaced by a silver salver bearing the ring. As Bradene traced a cross above it, Morgan thought he saw it glint from more than candlelight. It flashed with a fire of its own as the archbishop held it briefly before Duncan's extended right hand.

"Take thou this ring as a seal of faith; and keeping faith, guard and protect the Holy Church which is the bride of God," Bradene said.

Morgan was not surprised, as Bradene slid it onto Duncan's finger, to sense reiteration of the images he and Duncan had seen before: the placing of the ring on another hand, in days gone by—and vague impressions of a ghostly Other, clad in priestly vestments of a deep, royal blue, offering up the ring—no, a cup—in ritual sacrifice of the Mass.

But there was more—a misty aureole of silver shimmering around Duncan's head for just an instant, its boundaries contained between half-sensed hands which Morgan had known half a dozen times before, and Duncan as well. It vanished as Bradene and Cardiel placed the mitre on Duncan's head, leaving Morgan to blink and glance at Kelson in question, wondering whether the glimpsed vision had been only his imagination.

If imagination, however, it had not been his alone, or even his and Kelson's. From the king's other side pulsed a more discordant note of shock and stark panic: Dhugal, his face drained of color, shoulders rigid with blind fear. Kelson caught the echo of Dhugal's distress in the same instant and immediately slipped to Dhugal's other side, supporting him between himself and Morgan. Behind them, Nigel half-rose in concern, but Kelson shook his head.

"It's all right, Uncle," he whispered lamely. "He's a little ill, is all. He'll be all right."

As Nigel subsided, shushing Conall and the curious Payne and Rory and no doubt suspecting there was more to it than that, Morgan slid his arm around Dhugal's shoulder and tried to shield him from curious eyes.

"Are you in pain, Dhugal?" he whispered.

Shuddering, Dhugal broke his rigid stare at the pageant still proceeding before the altar and ducked his head.

"What's happening to me?" he managed to gasp. "My head feels like it's about to burst."

"Take a deep breath and try to let go what's frightening you," Kelson urged softly. "Try to flow with it."

"Oh, God, I can't! Didn't you *see* it?"

*Alaric, he picked up the same thing we did!* Kelson whispered in Morgan's mind. *We've got to get him out of here—and I can't leave until it's over.*

His thought was mixed with consternation, caution, and even a little joy, but Nigel was jostling Morgan from behind, gesturing toward the altar. With the consecration itself completed, the bishops had rearranged themselves to continue with the Mass—and Morgan had a part in what came next.

*It's time for the offertory*, Morgan sent back, glancing sidelong at Kelson and the still trembling Dhugal and rising as the choir monks began the hymn which was his cue. *If I don't go forward, it will look even worse than this. Keep him quiet until I can get back.*

With eyes averted and hands folded as was seemly, Morgan moved down into the aisle and paused before a small, white-draped table, gracefully returning the solemn bow that a waiting deacon gave as he handed over a crystal cruet of wine and a lidded chalice of gold. The crystal was cold and sleek in his hand, the ciborium seeming oddly light for all its contents of pale, unconsecrated hosts. He could feel Duncan watching him as he slowly passed to the foot of the altar steps and knelt before him and the two archbishops, aware that something was amiss. The sense of what he planned passed between himself and

Duncan like a spark as he offered up the gifts and their hands touched.

*Dhugal Saw something. I'm taking him to your old study. Come there with Kelson as soon as you can break away*, Morgan sent.

He felt Duncan's startled agreement like a caress as he rose and bowed and turned to go back to his place. The stark, disruptive pulse of Dhugal's distress welled up almost like a wall as he knelt once more and slipped a supporting arm under Dhugal's elbow.

"Say that Dhugal became ill," he whispered across to Kelson, "and meet us afterward in Duncan's old study. I'll do what I can until then. I've already told Duncan."

He did not look back as he led Dhugal stumbling from the choir. The words of Archbishop Bradene's prayer chased them in hollow echo, embracing with depths of meaning which neither could appreciate at the time.

"Lord, accept these gifts which we offer for Thy chosen servant, Duncan, Thy chosen priest. Enrich him with the gifts and virtues of a true apostle, for the good of Thy people. Amen."

# CHAPTER SIXTEEN

*In the valley of vision...*
—Isaiah 22:5

With Dhugal clinging dazedly to his arm, so pale that his freckles seemed painted on in blood, Morgan managed to navigate the curved aisle around the back of the cathedral apse without arousing any more attention that was his usual wont. Several monks not involved in the ceremonies eyed them curiously, but Morgan's grim expression precluded any offers of assistance. Morgan was known and at least grudgingly respected even by most clergy after three years' active and visible service with the new young king, but he still inspired a certain amount of fear in some.

But Dhugal's fear worried Morgan far more than that of any anonymous monks lurking in the shadowy aisle—and it was likely to get worse before it got much better. He could feel the stark terror throbbing just beneath the surface like floodwaters only barely held in check by a failing dam, and realized Dhugal's awareness of the precarious balance was only adding to the pressure. The only way Dhugal was managing to hold his panic in check at all was by watching his feet, concentrating all his attention on the simple act of putting one foot in front of the other.

"We've got to get you away from here," Morgan muttered, guiding Dhugal toward the door to the sacristy. "Can I trust you to do exactly as I say?"

Dhugal stumbled and nearly fell as he gave Morgan an odd, pinched look.

"You're—assuming I have a choice," he managed to

whisper, as Morgan braced him and reached for the door latch. "What's happening to me?"

"That's exactly what I'd like to know."

Morgan had hoped that the sacristy might be unoccupied during the ceremony, but the presence of Saint George's elderly sacristan was not unexpected. The old man had been nodding in the meager sunshine of an oriel window at the other end of the room when they entered and woke with a start as the door closed behind them.

"Who's that?"

"Ah, Brother Jerome, is that you?" Morgan said, shifting his grip on the tottering Dhugal. "The boy's been taken ill. He needs to sit down."

Frail and failing of eyesight, the old monk shuffled closer to squint quizzically at Morgan and his obviously ailing companion.

"Why, 'tis the Duke o'Corwyn—an' who's this?" the old man said, his tone conveying just a trace of wariness along with surprised respect. "Here, laddie, sit ye doon. Ye look a trifle peaked. What's wrong with the boy, Yer Grace?"

"Nothing serious, I hope," Morgan replied, letting Jerome help him seat Dhugal on a low settle next to a vestment press. "I think it was just the closeness of the air in the choir. Maybe the incense was too much for him." He ventured a sidelong glance at Jerome as he felt for the pulse in Dhugal's wrist. "I'm sure he'll be all right in a few minutes. Do you think the archbishop would mind if you raided his sacramental wine for a wee dram?"

"Ach, o'course not, Yer Grace. 'Twill be just th' thing. Wait ye here."

As the old man shuffled across the room, fumbling with a ring of keys hanging at his waist, Morgan leaned closer to Dhugal's ear. The boy's breathing was shallow, his head leaned against the side of the press, eyes closed.

"Dhugal, sit still and don't be surprised at anything you see," he whispered, touching a forefinger to his lips for silence as the boy opened his eyes. "I think Brother Jerome is going to take a little nap."

Morgan could sense Dhugal's startled question through

the fog of his distress, but he put it out of mind as he crossed to where Jerome was trying to match a key to the lock on the wine cabinet.

"I know I hae th' key here somewhere," Jerome was muttering.

"Why don't you try that one?" Morgan said, deftly slipping one arm around the stooped shoulders as if to point one out, before he pressed his other hand over the old man's forehead and eyes.

"Never mind, old friend. Just go to sleep and forget all this," he whispered. "That's right . . ."

The old man was no challenge at all. As he started to buckle at the knees, already deep asleep, Morgan shifted control and steadied him enough to walk him carefully back to the seat in the oriel window. Soft snoring followed Morgan as he returned to the dazed and awestruck Dhugal.

"Don't touch me," Dhugal whispered, going rigid as Morgan took his hand and pulled him to his feet. "Please. What did you do to that old man? Where are we going?"

"I didn't hurt Brother Jerome, and I'm not going to hurt you," Morgan said, only tightening his grip on Dhugal's wrist. "Come stand here with me. If you don't cooperate, it will only be more difficult for both of us."

"No. Please!"

Shaking his head sympathetically, for there was no time to explain, Morgan half-dragged the reluctant Dhugal to the center of the room where the floor tiles marked out a squared cross just large enough for two people to stand side by side. As he spun Dhugal away from him, clamping his hands on the boy's shoulders, Dhugal tried again to pull away.

"If you can let yourself relax, this will be a great deal easier," Morgan murmured, slipping one arm around the boy's neck from behind for a choke hold if he did not stop struggling. "One way or another, I'm going to take you through something called a Transfer Portal. It's a Deryni way of getting somewhere in a hurry."

"It's—magic?" Dhugal gasped, panic flaring around him with an almost physical resistance.

Morgan sensed him drawing breath to cry out. The last thing they needed was to attract more attention. Biting back his annoyance, for it was hardly Dhugal's fault he was frightened, he tightened his arm across the boy's throat and clapped his other hand over the gasping mouth, reaching out with his mind for the controls that would bring unconsciousness. Dhugal only struggled harder, his fear and his now wildly pulsing shields making psychic control all but impossible unless Morgan wanted to risk really hurting him. He nearly had to wrestle Dhugal to the floor before he could feel the choke hold starting to take its toll.

"I'm sorry son," he murmured, as he felt the dark start to swoop down on the boy's mind and Dhugal ceased his squirming. "But I told you, one way or the other, you're going. I don't have time for niceties. That's right," he finished, as Dhugal slumped in his arms.

He could feel the Portal tingling beneath his feet as he straightened once again, shifting both arms to a firm hold around Dhugal's chest. Drawing a deep breath and closing his eyes, he visualized his destination and opened his mind to the energies binding the two locations, reaching out to shift their balance. Abruptly he was standing elsewhere in close darkness, Dhugal a dead weight in his arms.

Cautiously he felt along one corner of the comparment for the stud that would let them out, conjuring handfire with an impatient gesture when he could not readily locate the stud by touch alone. By the greenish light, he found the stud at last—he had been searching the wrong corner initially. When he pushed it, the adjacent wall pivoted away from him with a soft hush of still air stirred, also pushing back a heavy tapestry that ordinarily concealed the door's outline.

The room beyond was deserted, softly lit by daylight filtering through the amber glass mullions of the window to their right. A fireplace dominated the left-hand wall, with a thick carpet covering the stone floor before it. There Morgan laid the unconscious Dhugal, making a pillow of his cloak to cushion the boy's head. A few soft-spoken words closed the door to the Portal chamber and brought flame to torches set in wall cressets. As an after-thought, as Morgan knelt down beside the boy, he quenched the handfire hovering at his shoulder; no sense having *that* frighten Dhugal when he came to.

And there was certainly enough to frighten him without that. Even in unconsciousness, the reaction triggered in the cathedral continued to pulse around Dhugal's tight-locked shields. An added complication was the constant ache of his injuries, only aggravated by Morgan's less than gentle handling—but for that, at least, Morgan might have a solution.

"Let's just see if I can heal around those shields," he muttered to himself, quickly unlacing the thongs closing Dhugal's tunic front and the shirt beneath.

A wide bandage bound the bruised chest, but if Morgan took the time to remove it, Dhugal might regain consciousness before he was finished. No matter. He could work around it. Laying his palms on Dhugal's chest above and below the turns of greyish linen, hands rising and falling with Dhugal's shallow breathing, he slid his fingertips as far under the bandage from either side as he could, already reaching out with his mind to read the damage as he closed his eyes and let out a long, slow breath. Dhugal's shields *were* avoidable at this level—perceivable as an annoyance, a distraction, but they did not interfere. Without further hesitation, Morgan shifted into the healing mode which had become more and more second nature in the past three years, letting his senses extend through his hands and into Dhugal's body.

The damage was not great. This healing would require very little drain of him, for life energy was not threatened. Smoothly, Morgan set the healing process in motion, mending torn cartilage and muscle, knitting bone, sending rich, life-bearing blood to melt away the bruising, not only in Dhugal's chest but in all parts of his body. He felt it in himself as a tingling and a resonance which reached to the furthest corners of his being, evoking such a surge of joy that the pleasure was almost pain. With that came the fleeting but familiar impression of unseen hands superimposed on his own—the Camber touch, as he had come to think of it.

Then the flow was slacking and he was opening his eyes, a little light-headed until he remembered to take a few deep breaths; he sometimes forgot to breathe as much as he should, when in his healing trance. He blinked and settled back into normal consciousness, heaving another deep sigh, then began slowly undoing the bandages which still bound Dhugal's chest. As he gently eased his patient to a half-sitting position against his knee, to unwind from behind, Dhugal's eyelids fluttered and he groaned.

"Just take it easy, my young friend," Morgan murmured, bracing the boy with one arm while he continued to unwind the bandage. "You'll be fine in a few seconds. I'm sorry I had to take you out the way I did, but it was either that or hit you. It seemed to me you'd had enough of hitting lately. And it was obvious I wasn't going to be able to use the approach I used on Brother Jerome."

"On Brother Jerome—" Dhugal repeated groggily. "What did you—what're you *doing*?"

"Taking off your bandages."

"But—"

"Well, you don't *need* them anymore," Morgan replied, pulling the last turn free of Dhugal's shirt and sitting back on his heels to begin winding the linen into a roll as he saw that Dhugal was capable of sitting on his own.

Dhugal blinked and glanced down stupidly at his bare chest inside his shirt, touching tentative fingertips to the once-bruised ribs, then shivered as he looked up again, his face pinched and still.

"Did you—heal me?" he whispered.

Morgan finished winding up the bandage and tossed it onto a chair behind him, not taking his eyes from Dhugal's.

"I did. Would you rather I'd left you in pain?"

Confusion played on Dhugal's face for an instant, old fear warring with new curiosity, and then the boy warily lay back on his makeshift pillow, gaze shifting deliberately to the fireplace.

"You used your magic on me, didn't you? And on that monk."

"Brother Jerome?" Morgan shrugged. "I don't know that I'd really call *that* magic. It's one of the things I can do as a Deryni, but—" He shrugged again and managed a tentative smile.

"As for the healing, I don't *think* that's magic—but I suppose I'd be hard-pressed to tell you what I do think it is. So far as Duncan and I can figure out, it's a rare talent even among Deryni. Other than ourselves, we haven't found anyone else who can do it—except for a human named Warin de Grey. And *he* thinks that his gift comes from God. Maybe it does. Maybe that's the source of our healing as well."

"And that's what makes you say it isn't magic?" Dhugal asked. "Because someone who isn't Deryni can do it, too?"

Morgan cocked his head tentatively. "I don't know that I've ever given it much thought. I consider most of what I do as a talent—that's all. Magic is mostly—oh, something that Charissa did to kill King Brion, or what Wencit of Torenth did. You've at least heard rumors about those, I'm sure."

"But those were evil things," Dhugal objected. "Are you saying that if powers are used for good, they're talents, but if they're used for evil, they're magic?"

Morgan could not help chuckling at the simple logic.

"I suppose I *have* come off sounding as if that's what I meant," he admitted, shifting to a sitting position on the carpet to ease his cramped knees. "Actually, I suppose I was reacting to your negative view of magic—the negative view most people have, for that matter. Magic simply has to do with harnessing power which is not accessible to most people. The power itself—Let me try to put it to you another way. Power exists. Correct?"

"Of course."

"I think you'll even grant me that many *kinds* of power exist—that power can come from many sources. Yes?"

Dhugal nodded.

"Good. Let's take fire as just one example of power,

then," Morgan went on, rubbing his hands together briskly and holding them toward the cold hearth as he glanced back at Dhugal. "Fire can be used for many beneficial purposes. It can give us light, like those torches on the walls," he gestured vaguely with his chin, "and it can warm a room."

A mental nudge sent flames springing up bright from the kindling already laid, and Dhugal scrambled to a sitting position to stare.

"How did you do that?"

"I think it's sufficient for now to acknowledge that I did it," Morgan replied, "and that providing light or heating a cold room are good things. But fire can also be destructive when out of control or when turned to evil use. It can burn down a house—or heat hot irons to take a man's sight."

His expression hardened as the memory surfaced of a Deryni lord who, half a century before, had allowed himself to be blinded to ransom captive Deryni children: Barrett de Laney, one of the most venerable members of the Camberian Council—the same Camberian Council that scorned Morgan and Duncan for being only half Deryni, even though the two "half-breeds" could heal.

As Morgan's old bitterness welled to the surface, Dhugal suddenly became very still and stared at him, the rigid shields blurring just a little for the first time since Morgan had become aware of them. Clear as sunlight, compassion surged across the intervening space: pure, clean, untainted by fear or mistrust.

"Did you see someone blinded that way?" Dhugal asked softly.

As Morgan glanced at him in surprise, the shields tightened down immediately, but Morgan thought he saw a new note of acceptance in the tawny eyes which continued to meet his bravely—perhaps an echo of Dhugal's own interest in healing, if only from the limited sphere of his training as a battle surgeon. Suddenly Morgan wondered whether Dhugal *was* Deryni, and perhaps a potential healer, at that.

"No, I never saw it done," he said hesitantly, "and

thank God for that—but it's been a common enough practice, through the centuries. I have a—an acquaintance
who lost his sight that way." He blinked. "But this is not
the time to digress. I've pointed out some of the things
that fire does. Does that make the fire good or evil?"

"It isn't either," Dhugal replied carefully. "It's how the
fire's used. The same hot iron that cost your friend his
sight also could have been used to cauterize a wound."

Morgan nodded, pleased. "So it could. And what does
that tell you about power in general?"

"That it isn't the power—it's how the power's *used*
that makes it *con*structive or *de*structive." Dhugal paused
for just an instant. "Are you saying that magic is the
same?"

"Precisely the same."

"But the priests say—"

"The priests say what they have been told to say for
the last two hundred years," Morgan returned briskly.
"Deryni have not always been persecuted, and not all
'magic' has been anathema until fairly recently. *Black*
magic—extraordinary power applied to destructive or
selfish ends—has always been condemned by the righteous. But those who could harness extraordinary power
for the aid of man— for healing and for defending against
the abuse of power—traditionally have been called miracle workers and saints. They were also once called
Deryni."

"But there *were* evil Deryni!" Dhugal objected. "And
there still are. What about Charissa and Wencit?"

"They were Deryni who used their gifts for evil. The
gifts themselves . . ." Morgan sighed. "Do you think I'm
an evil person?"

Dhugal's face went very still. "No. But they say—"

"They say *what*, Dhugal? Morgan whispered. "And
who are *they*? And do *they* ever give an accounting of
what I've *done*, or is it all because of what I *am*?"

"I . . . never thought about it that way before."

"No, I don't suppose you did." Morgan glanced at the
Haldane signet on his right hand, balanced by the Corwyn
gryphon on his left. "I'll make you a bargain, Dhugal. I

can't speak for Duncan or Kelson, but if you can name one specific instance in which you think that I've misused my powers, I'll submit to whatever justice you think is appropriate. Should I not have helped Kelson defeat the woman who killed his father and would have killed him to seize his throne? Should I have let the former archbishops continue the lie and bring down Gwynedd by undermining her rightful king? Should I not have healed *you*?"

Dhugal shook his head, unwilling to meet Morgan's eyes.

"Dhugal, I may have access to more and other kinds of power than most men," Morgan continued softly, "but I must answer for the use of that power to the same God and king that you do—or that any of the priests and bishops do—and to my own conscience as well, which can be a far sterner taskmaster. Because I've been given far greater abilities, I've had to contend with far greater responsibilities. I didn't ask for either—but I have them. All I can do is serve the best way I know how. Kelson's father taught me honor and chivalry, and I've tried never to betray the trust he put in me. I hope I've not been too unsuccessful—despite the fact that I'm Deryni."

But he was to be given no chance to hear Dhugal's judgment, for at that moment a fumbling at the door latch announced visitors. As Morgan came to his feet, already aware of their identities, the door opened and Duncan peered around the edge and entered, standing aside to admit Kelson and Bishop Arilan. Dhugal got to his feet more slowly as Kelson came to give him a hand up and search his face questioningly. Arilan came straight to Morgan, his lean face set in tight-checked disapproval.

"Why wasn't I told you'd found another Deryni?" he said through his teeth, drawing Morgan aside. "And what the devil was he trying to do out there?"

Morgan sighed and picked up his cloak, far more concerned for Dhugal, deep in whispered conversation with Kelson and Duncan, than with an opinion of Arilan.

"First of all, Bishop, we don't know that he's necessarily Deryni—only that he has shields that we can't breach and he can't control," Morgan murmured, slinging his cloak around his shoulders and fastening the clasp. "As for what he was trying to do, I can only guess that he was trying to shut out the psychic overflow from Duncan's consecration. Surely you're aware that such a ritual generates a great deal of energy, especially if the central participant is Deryni."

"Don't be impertinent," Arilan muttered. "And what do you mean, you don't know that he's Deryni?"

"Just that, Bishop. There's nothing in his family to account for any of this—unless you can count that rather undefinable talent the border folk refer to as the Second Sight. Dhugal does have shields, though, and he doesn't have the first clue what to do with them. As Duncan's consecration gathered momentum, it must have seemed like an enormous pressure beating against those shields he only recently learned he had, and which he doesn't know how to lower."

"You say 'recently.' *How* recently?"

Morgan tried to curb his impatience. "Three weeks ago, while we were in Culdi for the convocation. It happened the night you asked me to try to contact Kelson and let him know about the attack on Duncan. Kelson put him in the link to augment his power, but Dhugal felt something that frightened him enough to kick both of them right out of the link. Then he nearly went into convulsions when Kelson tried to read him."

"Has anyone tried since, or anyone besides Kelson?" Arilan asked, a little subdued after listening to Morgan's account.

"I tried," Duncan said as he joined them. "He didn't seem to mind my probe as much as Kelson's, but nor was I any more successful at getting through. It was like going up against an obsidian wall. The harder I pushed, the stronger it got. And when Kelson joined in, thinking he might be of help, Dhugal had another violent reaction."

"I see." Arilan sighed resignedly. "And you, Alaric?"

"I wasn't able to bring him through the Portal without roughing him up physically," Morgan replied. "My touch seems to fall somewhere between Kelson's and Duncan's on a comfort scale. I *was* able to get around his shields enough to heal his injuries, but only while he was unconscious. I wouldn't have wanted to try it otherwise."

Arilan glanced at Dhugal, letting Kelson help him to a seat at the table set back from the fireplace, then shepherded Morgan and Duncan with him as he moved purposefully to join them. Dhugal started to rise, courteous even in his confusion and apprehension, but Arilan stayed him with a gesture and pulled out a chair for Kelson to sit, only then taking a seat himself. At Duncan's sign, Morgan took the remaining chair to Dhugal's right, across from the king.

"With your permission, Sire," Arilan said, nodding to Kelson, "I should like to get right to the heart of this matter. Dhugal," he conjured handfire in a softly glowing blue-white sphere which he set in the center of the table, "I think this should answer any question about what I am and why I presume to take charge in this matter. Will you trust me?"

Dhugal had jerked back as the fire materialized, new apprehension flaring around the still pulsing shields, but a glance at Kelson lent him sufficient courage to push his anxiety to a lower level. Morgan was amazed. As Dhugal drew a deep, steadying breath, he folded his shaking hands in deliberate mimicry of Kelson's, setting them but a handspan from the handfire glowing in the center of the table, and made himself look squarely into the eyes of the Deryni bishop.

"I'd be lying if I said I'm not afraid, Excellency, but my—friend Duke Alaric has taught me a great deal in the last little while. And Kelson told me of you before. I'll try to do as you ask."

Arilan's mouth quirked upward in grudging response—even he could not deny the boy had pluck—but Morgan caught his disapproval of Kelson's indiscretion quite clearly. He was glad it was directed at the king instead of himself.

"Very well. We shall see just how much you *have* learned," Arilan said. "I assume I shan't have to go into long, involved explanations of what I should like to do."

"N-no, sir."

With a sigh and a glance at the rest of them which bespoke impatience only barely held in check, Arilan flexed his fingers and lifted one hand toward Dhugal's forehead. The startled Dhugal started to draw back in reflex avoidance; but then he took another deep breath and leaned closer so that Arilan could touch him. He flinched at the contact, but he did not draw away even when Arilan began to probe, though the process obviously caused him some discomfort. After a moment, Arilan dropped his hand and sat back, sighing again.

"Well, there's no question of the shields. Given time and the right support, I could probably breach them, but it might do permanent damage. I see no need to risk that. Duncan, you said he didn't seem to mind your touch as much. Are you willing to give it another try?"

Duncan, standing between Arilan and Morgan, looked at Dhugal in question. "That depends. Are *you* willing, Dhugal? I'll stop whenever you want, if it gets too bad."

Licking his lips nervously, Dhugal swallowed and gave a nod. Without further ado, Duncan came around to stand behind his chair, resting his hands lightly on Dhugal's shoulders.

"Has Kelson taught you how to relax by using deep breathing?" he asked, easing Dhugal's shoulders back against his chest and sliding his thumbs up to rest on the pulse points in his throat.

"A little."

"Good. That will make things much easier for both of us. Take a deep breath, then, and let it out, and try to concentrate on your heartbeat. You should be able to feel it against my thumbs. Do you?"

"Aye."

"Excellent. Take another breath, then—that's good— and now close your eyes and let all your muscles go limp. And another deep breath. Good . . ."

Morgan dared not follow Duncan's probe for fear of spilling over into the precarious balance he was building, but he could see physical signs of Dhugal ceasing his resistance. The boy did not tense or even seem to notice as Duncan shifted his fingertips up to overlap temples and forehead. He relaxed even more as Duncan bowed his head to rest his lips against the reddish hair. They stayed that way for most of a minute, still and balanced, until finally Duncan slowly raised his head and opened his eyes, coming back to normal consciousness with a blink. Dhugal, too, looked up and blinked as Duncan slipped his hands back to Dhugal's shoulders.

"Well?" Arilan asked.

Duncan shook his head. "No clash—and no pain, I don't think, was there Dhugal?"

Dhugal shook his head, twisting around to stare up at Duncan in awe. "What did you do?"

"Well, I didn't get through," Duncan replied. "I just went round and round. Any suggestions, anyone?"

With a perplexed sigh, Arilan sat back and folded his arms across his chest. "Fascinating. He's either one of us or another damned Warin de Grey. I don't suppose one of you has a *shiral* at hand?"

As Duncan nodded and went across the room to rummage in a desk drawer, Dhugal whispered, "What—what's a *shiral*?"

"It won't hurt you," Kelson said quickly. "It's a clear amber stone. One finds them in streambeds—and sometimes along the seashore."

"Well, wh-what does it do?"

Morgan smiled. "It's sensitive to the kind of power that Deryni can draw upon. That's all. Remember how we talked earlier about power not being good or evil of itself, but only the *use* being good or evil?"

Dhugal's nod was still very apprehensive.

"Well, all a *shiral* crystal does is serve as a focus," Morgan continued. "If you have the ability, or even the potential ability, to wield the kind of power we do, the crystal will glow."

"But, I'm not D—"

"Dhugal, you don't know *what* you are right now," Kelson muttered under his breath. "All we know for sure is that you've got those bloody shields!"

Duncan returned to the table, undoing the strings of a

small leather bag, and withdrew a wad of age-yellowed silk. As he carefully unwrapped it and Dhugal craned his neck to see what was inside, loops of a fine leather thong sprang free, strung through the center of a honey-colored lump the size of an almond.

"I've had this since I was younger than Dhugal," Duncan said, holding it to the light by its thongs as he tossed bag and silk on the table. "It isn't the clearest of crystals, but it's always been sufficient for my purposes."

As Dhugal stared, half afraid and half intrigued, Arilan caught the dangling stone against his sleeve and peered at it more closely, quenching his handfire with a gesture, then released it and sat back, giving Duncan a nod.

"I'd hoped for better, but it will do. Go ahead and test him. You know what's involved."

"But *I* don't know what's involved," Dhugal protested, as Duncan moved back behind his chair and extended the crystal over his shoulder.

"I assure you, there's even less chance of discomfort from this than there was from what we just did," Duncan murmured. "Just hold the stone in your hand—either hand. Physically, it won't feel different from any other stone."

Hesitantly, Dhugal reached up, flinching when the stone first touched his skin. But then he closed it resolutely in his palm and dared another questioning glance at Duncan.

"What next?"

"Close your eyes and try to ignore what's in your hand," Duncan said with a smile, slipping his hands to Dhugal's shoulders and bearing him back in the chair again. "I'm not going to do anything different from what I did before, so there isn't a thing to be anxious about. Take a deep breath and let it out slowly. This won't take long."

With a nervous nod, Dhugal obeyed, gradually calming again as Duncan droned on, soothing and reassuring. When Arilan at length reached across the table to touch the boy's closed fist lightly, the hand relaxed enough for all present to see golden light streaming from the crystal clutched inside. Arilan pursed his lips as he glanced at Morgan and Kelson, then nodded for Duncan to bring the test to an end. The light in Dhugal's hand flickered and died, but not before Dhugal's eyes fluttered open and he caught just a glimpse.

"It was glowing! I saw it!"

As his hand jerked open in reflex, Duncan leaned down to snatch the crystal before it could be spilled onto the table. Kelson nodded, a grin creasing his face.

"We saw it, too. You're not going mad. Guess what it means."

"It means that he's probably another rogue Deryni like the rest of you," Arilan muttered, pushing back his chair with a jarring scrape of wood on stone floor before Dhugal could reply. "And where does *his* power come from?"

As he stood and turned to face the fire, Kelson laid a protective hand on the awed Dhugal's shoulder.

"I can't answer that, Arilan, but I don't think I really care right now," the king said pointedly. "Nor do I think we should pursue this more right now. He's been through enough for one day."

"I agree, my prince," Morgan said, following Kelson's lead. "Not only that, I seem to recall we're supposed to be celebrating the creation of a new bishop this evening."

"The feast, I think, does not begin until well after sunset," Arilan answered curtly. "We still have time to—"

"We still have time for Dhugal to have some rest before the feast, if he wishes," Kelson said as he rose. "Right now, that takes precedence."

"But the Council will want—"

"What the Council wants is not at issue here," Kelson replied sharply, eliciting a near-gasp from Arilan and an exchange of stunned glances between Morgan and Duncan. "Nor do I think this is the time or the place to discuss it further, do you?"

Arilan could have no answer to that, with the others in the room. As the king drew Dhugal to his feet and they started toward the door, Arilan made a sparse bow.

"I apologize if I seemed to press the issue, Sire."

Kelson paused with Dhugal in the open doorway to look back at all three of them.

"Apology accepted. And Father Duncan, I suspect you

could also use some rest. This has been a long day for you as well."

Duncan shrugged. "I have no complaints, Sire."

"I see. Nonetheless, we'll all plan to meet again at the feast. Morgan, Arilan, are you coming?"

Morgan would have stayed, for his curiosity about the afternoon's varied events was far stronger than any real need for rest; but if he had, Arilan also might have wanted to—and if Arilan stayed, conversation was sure to come round eventually to the old disagreements about half-Deryni and the Camberian Council. Besides, the king's tone put the question almost in the form of a command. Both Morgan and Arilan went, the Deryni bishop all but muttering under his breath.

When they had gone, Duncan sat back in the chair Dhugal had just vacated and closed the *shiral* crystal in his hand, letting his mind wander back to boyhood and the giver of the stone. The memories were sweet, and he sat dreaming into the firelight until the shadows lengthened and the golden light died from behind the amber glass at his back.

# CHAPTER SEVENTEEN

*He that justifieth the wicked, and he that*
*condemneth the just, even they both are*
*abominations to the Lord.*

—Proverbs 17:15

The news of Duncan's consecration to the episcopate came as no great surprise to the would-be Mearan court in Ratharkin. Creoda had warned them to expect that. It was merely another justification for war, so far as Caitrin and Sicard were concerned, though it vexed Loris and Judhael greatly. Equally anticipated was Kelson's renewed demand for Caitrin's submission by Christmas, with its hints of dire consequences to his hostages if Caitrin did not comply or if further harm came to Istelyn.

But Archbishop Bradene's writ of excommunication, read aloud with increasing disbelief and horror by an appalled Judhael, came as a total shock. So enraged was Loris that he overturned his chair in his haste to get to Judhael and snatch the offending document.

*"How dare they?"* he gasped, his breath coming in sharp, rasping wheezes as he scanned the signatures and seals appended at the bottom, little droplets of spittle spattering the parchment and his purple cassock. *"Who do they think they are?"*

Brandishing the writ as if he wished it were a physical weapon, Loris stalked across the room to where Caitrin and Sicard stood staring blindly out an oriel window, arms around one another's waists for comfort, devastated by the treble blow. Back a few paces, a pasty-faced Ithel divided his attention between watching his parents, Loris, and Judhael, and nervously twisting the end of one of his cloak strings.

"How dare they?" Loris repeated. "Excommunicated, by God! *Me!* And by my own former subordinates! I am outraged! I am speechless!"

"Hardly that," Sicard muttered, though Loris did not hear him, caught up as he was in further diatribes against the bishops in Rhemuth and the Haldane royal house. But Sicard shared the tight-lipped anxiety of his wife and liege lady, and the helpless confusion of his son. When Loris at last ran out of expletives and holy oaths, Sicard let fall the drapery he had withdrawn to gaze out at the morning snowfall and turned back into the room, taking Caitrin's elbow to guide her back to the chairs before the fireplace. At his gesture, Ithel hurried to upend the chair Loris had overturned.

"Enough of self-indulgence—on *all* our parts," Sicard said, glancing pointedly at Loris and signing for Judhael to join them. "We have heard the response from Gwynedd. Now we must decide what to do about it. Sit here, my dear."

Composing herself deliberately, Caitrin sat, carefully spreading her fur-lined skirts around her feet and arranging her hands just so in her lap. When she looked up, Sicard had dropped to one knee beside her, one hand resting on her chair arm, and Judhael stood expectantly behind him. Ithel waited at her right. Loris, with ill-disguised resentment at Sicard's tone, came to stand in front of the chair Ithel had just set back in place—though something in the family tableau before him cautioned him not to presume by sitting until invited.

"My queen," Sicard said softly, before Loris could choose a suitable remark, "we are yours to command, as you know well, but I fear the Haldane has struck a telling blow this time. Is it your wish to continue as we have thus far, knowing that we lie under the ban of the Church?"

"Not the ban of the Church!" Loris snapped. "The ban of a handful of outlaw bishops who have betrayed their oath of obdience to *me*!" He remembered himself sufficiently to bow slightly in apology. "Forgive me, Highness, but there can be no question of capitulating simply because of a bit of parchment and wax. *This* is what I think of it!"

With a grandiose flourish, he flung it into the fireplace, but at Caitrin's urgent gasp, Ithel scrambled onto the raised hearth and rescued it, pinching out the embers along the edges where it had started to burn and stifling an oath as molten wax dripped on his hand from one of the seals.

"That is not the answer," Sicard said, rising to pull a straightbacked chair beside his wife's. "And that bit of parchment and wax, as you call it, seemed to give *you* cause for consternation, Archbishop. Nor does denying it make it cease to exist, unfortunately."

He took Caitrin's hand in his as he sat, chafing at it in futile attempt to comfort. Loris scowled.

"The writ is an annoyance. It has no force," he said. "Those who issued it had no authority to do so."

"What matters authority?" Caitrin whispered. "One needs no authority to make a curse—and that is what it is, for all its highflown language. We folk of the hills understand such things, Archbishop. You cannot dismiss a curse as lightly as that."

"Then we must counter it as you think appropriate," Loris said, easing into the chair behind him and studying them both carefully. "Shall I curse them back? It would give me great personal satisfaction. I can and shall countermand the writ and proclaim the same against the House of Haldane and her outlaw bishops. But you must do your part as well, Highness. This needs must be the spur which drives you to give the king the answer he deserves. We must not be intimidated by Haldane threats anymore."

"The Haldane has learned to threaten well, for all that he is hardly grown," Caitrin replied dully, picking up the other document which had accompanied the excommunication: Kelson's answer to her last defiance. "He repeats his demand for my surrender, Archbishop. And he still holds my Llewell and Sidana to hostage."

"You yourself pointed out not a fortnight ago that they are of age, Highness. They knew the dangers."

"But they are my children!" Caitrin said. "Shall I abandon them to their fate? Shall they suffer the wrath of the

Haldane usurpers and die the death so that I may wear a crown?"

Grim and determined, Loris slipped to his knees before her, lifting his palms in entreaty.

"Do you not think they would willingly give their lives to secure the throne of Meara for its rightful queen?" he countered. "This land has lain under the rule of foreign princes for far too long already, noble lady. Malcolm Haldane wrenched it from the lawful heiress a century ago, and he and his heirs have kept it in thrall ever since, despite the cries of your people. You have the means to bring an end to Haldane tyranny. For the sake of your people, you dare not shrink from your sacred duty."

White-faced, Caitrin listened to his words, fingers intertwined with those of her husband, her one remaining son crouched beside her with the scorched scroll of excommunication all but forgotten in his hands, her nephew standing silent and stricken behind them in his episcopal purple. When the archbishop had finished, Caitrin bowed her head. After a moment tears splashed on her and Sicard's joined hands.

"It appears that I must offer my children's lives on the altar of my aspiration," she finally said, shaking her head bitterly. "But you are right, Archbishop. I have a duty."

With her free hand, she reached across to take Ithel's and bring it to her lips, then held it cradled against her breast as she looked up.

"Very well. The writ must be reversed, and you shall pronounce the ban against the Haldane court and bishops. What else?"

Loris inclined his head in acknowledgment, folding his hands precisely on his upraised knee.

"You must give the Haldane your answer in terms that will leave no doubt of your resolve, Highness," he said. "And you yourself must carry through with the threats that *you* have made."

"What—threats?" Caitrin breathed.

Controlling a smile of triumph, Loris rose and returned to his chair, setting his hands precisely on the arms.

"Istelyn, Madame. He must be executed. You have

said you would do it. You must follow through. Istelyn is a traitor."

Caitrin blanched. Ithel gasped. Sicard looked decidedly uncomfortable.

"But, he is a priest, a *bishop!*" Judhael whispered, equally horrified.

"He has betrayed his oaths and is no longer fit to be regarded as other than betrayer," Loris retorted. "If you like, I shall degrade him from the priesthood and excommunicate him as well."

"Can this be done to a bishop?" Caitrin asked.

"I am the apostolic successor of Saint Peter, given authority to loose and to bind," Loris said haughtily. "It was I who consecrated Istelyn bishop. What I created, I can also uncreate."

"Then he would be executed as a layman," Sicard said.

"As a layman and excommunicate." Loris shifted his gaze deliberately to Caitrin. "You *are* aware of the penalty for treason, Highness?"

Caitrin stood, turning slightly away to wring her hands.

"Must he suffer *that*?" she whispered.

"He is a traitor," Loris said. "And the penalty for treason—"

"I know the penalty for treason, Archbishop," she said steadily. "To be hanged, drawn, and quartered—I know."

"And shall it be done?"

Shoulders slumping, Caitrin of Meara bowed her head in reluctant agreement.

"It shall be done," she said in a low voice. "And may God have mercy on his soul."

Sentence was carried out the following morning, just past dawn. Impressed by Loris with the importance of witnessing the execution, to underline the fate of future traitors, the Mearan royal family watched from a doorway overlooking the snowy castle yard. Loris and his bishops waited restlessly at the foot of the steps. Out in the wan sunlight, ranks of soldiers in the livery of Culdi, Ratharkin, and Laas lined up along either side of the execution area. Four teams of horses, restless under the hands of their grooms, stood ready behind the ranks nearest the stables, tossing their heads and stamping and snorting in the cold morning air, harness all a-jingle. Snow still lay thick in the center of the yard where black-clad executioners waited around a hastily erected scaffold, anonymous behind their masks.

Muffled drums rolled as the condemned man emerged from a doorway across the yard, surrounded by guards, blinking in the sunlight, barefooted in the snow. The cold December wind stood his hair on end and plastered his thin gown to his body. His hands were bound behind him. He stumbled a little as his escort led him toward the scaffold.

He appeared pale but composed as he walked to his fate. He had been stunned by the harshness of his sentence, but it had come as no real surprise, knowing Loris' spite. He had never expected to leave Ratharkin alive. He had known a brief, soul-wrenching moment of despair when he learned they had set aside his priesthood, for he had thought they would leave him that comfort, at least; but the excommunication which followed had only renewed his conviction that any pretense of episcopal authority on Loris' part held no validity whatsoever. Henry Istelyn was a priest and bishop despite anything Loris might say or do. His captors might kill his body, but his soul was answerable only to God.

He *had* been briefly troubled that they would not allow him the solace of another priest in those final, predawn hours, for a last confession and communion. It was an almost automatic reaction for any pious man facing death. But then he reminded himself sternly that it was only the outward forms of those sacraments which were being denied him. Just before the dawning, having made his own examination of conscience and act of contrition, he knelt and kissed the earthen floor of his cell in commemoration of the Body of his Lord, and drank of melted snow in remembrance of His Sacred Blood. Then he sat quietly to watch the lightening sky and await the earthly reckoning, all at peace.

He was calm when they came to fetch him, his escort

four smartly turned-out soldiers and one of his own former captains, none of whom would look him in the eyes. He bore their rough handling without comment or protest as they bound his hands behind, only wincing once when someone jarred the bandage on his right hand where once he had worn a bishop's amethyst. The stairs up from his cell were slick with melted snow and slush, but the men steadied him when he slipped and would have fallen. He hardly felt the snow beneath his feet as he emerged into the open courtyard, or the cold wind knifing through his thin gown. Nor did he give the scaffold more than passing notice, or the executioners and their shining implements.

Loris he did note, meeting the archbishop's frigid glare with a serenity and even compassion which made Loris drop the contact first, to gesture brusquely to the guards. Caitrin and Sicard likewise avoided his gaze, but young Ithel stared at him in confusion as Istelyn smiled gently to himself and shook his head.

The scaffold steps were wet and slippery. He stubbed a toe on the way up. His murmured apology put his guards off balance, and they backed off uneasily once he was standing in the center of the scaffold. The masked executioner who came to place the rope around his neck would not meet his eyes either, and himself apologized as he slid the knot snug against the back of the prisoner's neck.

"You must do what you must do, my son," Istelyn murmured, giving the man another gentle smile. "I forgive you freely."

The man retreated in confusion, leaving Istelyn alone in the center of the scaffold once more. Serenely, he turned his eyes toward the winter sky as the sentence was read, hardly even minding the pressure of the ropes around his wrists or the noose closed harsh around his neck.

"Henry Istelyn, formerly bishop and priest," the herald read, when the drums had given another muffled roll, "having been adjudged traitor, it is the sentence of the Crown of Meara that you be hanged by the neck and cut down while still living, your members cut off and your bowels taken out and burnt before you, and then to be rent by horses and your head and pieces of your body to be set on display at such places as the queen shall assign. Thus shall all know the fate of traitors to Meara!"

There was no plea for God to have mercy on the soul of the condemned, for excommunicants were judged to have forfeited all hope of that. Istelyn had not expected it, so he was not disappointed. As the drums rolled again, it became clear that he was not to be allowed any final statement, either—nor had he expected that. He kept his gaze lifted to the heavens as they stripped him naked and made sure of the rope around his neck, only a strangled little gasp escaping his lips as they hoisted him off his feet and the world began to go dark.

He prayed as long as he could. Only dimly did he feel the jolt as they shortly cut him down and pinned him spread-eagled in the snow. He let the cold and the shock claim him, slipping gently beyond the reach of his torturers, and was never even aware of the knives, much less the fire—or the snorting horses, maddened by the smell of his blood, who ripped his bleeding body limb from limb. The smile on his lips, even after they severed his head from what was left of his body, sent a cold chill through the heart of more than one witness to his judicial murder.

The following week saw the arrival of increasing numbers of Kelson's vassals in Rhemuth, all come to keep the feast of Christmas with their king as was customary, no one in Rhemuth yet aware of Istelyn's fate. Kelson held daily courts to greet the newcomers, with briefing sessions each afternoon, while Morgan, Nigel, and the other senior members of his staff continued their planning and preparation for the projected spring campaign. The bishops had their own affairs to attend to, but exchanged progress reports with the king and his chief advisors each evening after dinner. Tension grew as Christmas Day approached, for all their futures would be affected by the expected reply from Meara.

Burchard de Varian, Earl of Eastmarch since the conclusion of the war with Torenth two years before, arrived at midweek as expected with Generals Gloddruth, Remie, and Elas in his train, along with half a dozen barons and other lesser lords. A few days later, the Earl of Danoc came with two more of Kelson's generals, Godwin and Perris, and also the young Earl of Jenas, whose father had fallen with Jared McLain at Candor Rhea. Not at all expected was the man waiting for Morgan outside his quarters when he returned alone from Mass on Christmas Eve.

"What the—who's there?" Morgan demanded, hand reaching warily toward the hilt of his sword.

Sean Lord Derry, the young noble who once had been Morgan's aide and now served as his lieutenant in Corwyn, stood away from the wall where he had been leaning and held out empty hands, a sheepish grin flickering across his earnest face as he inclined his head in salute.

"Christmas blessings, Your Grace. I hope you don't mind that we didn't join you for Mass, but we only arrived just on midnight."

His blue eyes held a twinkle of mirth at Morgan's surprise, but also a note of apprehension. He flinched as Morgan seized him by the shoulders to stare at him, but he did not avert his gaze.

"Sean, what on earth are you doing here?" Morgan murmured, though he had an idea exactly what the younger man was doing. "And what do you mean, *we*?" Good God, you didn't bring Richenda, did you?"

Derry raised one eyebrow in an expression he had picked up from his former master. "Your lady wife decided she'd like to keep Christmas with her husband, Your Grace. If I hadn't brought her, I suspect she would have come on her own."

"Aye, she probably would have," Morgan muttered under his breath. "I wish you could have tried to talk her out of it, though."

"Do you think I *didn't* try?" Derry asked indignantly. "I know what your orders were. I can't say my heart was really in it, though. I think she's about had enough of Coroth for a while."

Morgan sighed, awareness of *that* situation catapulting

back to consciousness as it had not for several weeks, so far from home himself. For all the personal satisfaction his marriage with Richenda had brought him, there were still vast areas of their relationship which had not yet come into balance. Chief among them was the question of how much authority his new wife should assume during his all too frequent absences from his own court—and that decision, to Morgan's continued dismay, was not entirely his to make, for all that he was Corwyn's duke.

In the ordinary course of things, certainly within the first year of their marriage, Morgan's duchess should have become his chatelaine at Coroth and regent of Corwyn in his absence. Morgan had not granted Richenda that status. The fact was that many of his own men distrusted her—not because she was Deryni, for probably no one at Coroth even suspected that—or would have cared, if they had, since Corwyn's duke was Deryni anyway—but because her first husband had betrayed the Crown.

Perhaps she was tainted with treachery as well, they reasoned—perhaps even plotting revenge for her first husband's death, for the sake of her son by him. As Dowager Countess of Marley, she already had young Brendan's guardianship jointly with her new husband, with virtual freedom to manage the lands and income of the six-year-old earl as she chose. If anything were to happen to Morgan, Her Grace the Dowager Duchess of Corwyn and Dowager Countess of Marley would have access to Corwyn's vast wealth as well, until the infant Duchess Briony came of age. For such power and position, what might the former wife of a known traitor *not* do?

It was all utter nonsense, of course; but convincing his men of that, other than the few officers close to Morgan, had proven far more difficult than Morgan ever imagined. He had expected some controversy and suspicion when he first brought his bride home to Coroth, less than a year after Bran Coris' death, but he had thought the suspicion would diminish as they came to know and trust her. They had not.

They did not trust her because they did not know her. They did not know her because when Morgan was away, which was far more often than he would have liked, she kept largely to herself, having no authority to exercise in his absence. He could not give her authority, since they did not trust her—and they did not trust her because they had no opportunity to observe any behavior that might have confirmed her stated loyalty to her new lord. It was an unfortunate vicious circle that Morgan had not yet figured out how to break.

Hence, Richenda had remained a mere resident of his castle at Coroth, treated courteously enough by the immediate ducal household, but given no responsibility. Explanation had been easy enough in the beginning, when Richenda was at first new to Coroth and then pregnant with their first child—both good reasons for letting Morgan's seneschal and garrison commander continue to run things in his absence as they had for years; but Briony was eleven months old now, and Richenda had been Duchess of Corwyn for nearly two years. The old excuses had grown lame, and Morgan could not bring himself to admit the real reasons to his wife. Small wonder that the intelligent and capable Richenda chafed increasingly under what appeared to be irrational restrictions on her role as his wife.

"You know what the problem is, Derry," Morgan said with a heavy sigh. "There just hasn't been time to do much about it. I don't want to hurt her."

Derry averted his eyes and hooked his thumbs in his sword belt, chewing at his lower lip.

"Do you think it *doesn't* hurt her, not knowing why you shut her out of your affairs?" he said quietly, looking up again. "Forgive me, sir, but in the past year I've spent far more time with your wife than you have. She's far too well-bred to pry, even though she easily could, but she senses the distrust on the part of the men. And if you don't tell her that you don't share their distrust—" He swallowed. "Sir, I—thought being Deryni was supposed to make it easier to work these things out."

"Sometimes that makes it harder, Derry," Morgan whispered. "Don't you reproach me, too."

"I'm sorry, m'lord."

"It isn't your fault," Morgan said after a few seconds. "Maybe her coming here is for the best, though. With a spring campaign almost inevitable, I was already planning to have you bring her to court as soon as the weather broke again. Kelson has made it clear that she'd be welcome on his council as Brendan's regent—and I suspect her presence would be doubly welcome now that we have Sidana of Meara to hostage."

"Sidana?" Derry said. "Here? How did you manage that? Is he going to marry her?"

Morgan chuckled despite his concern over this new turn of affairs. "Odd how that proposition seems obvious to everyone but Kelson himself. He may. A lot depends on the answer we get from Meara tomorrow."

"Ah."

"I'll fill you in on all the details after court tomorrow, if you haven't already found out from other sources by then," Morgan went on. "I'm sure there'll be a briefing, once we've had the Mearan's answer. In the meantime, you should probably get some sleep—and I undoubtedly should go and greet my wife. I assume, by the way, that Hamilton and Hillary have things under control at home?"

"Aye, m'lord. And my mother has charge of the little ones."

"That's fine. How many men did you bring?"

"Half a dozen—and one maid for Her Grace. I hope you're not angry, sir."

"No, I'm not angry." Morgan sighed, then clapped Derry on the shoulder as he set his hand on the door latch.

"Go get some sleep, then. We'll see you at court in the morning. And thank you for bringing my wife here safely, Sean."

"My pleasure, m'lord."

As Derry sketched a bow and turned to go, obviously relieved, Morgan lifted the latch and slipped into his quarters, softly closing the door behind him.

Only firelight greeted him at first. Near the curtained entrance to the garderobe, he could make out a small pile of trunks and travel valises that had not been there earlier, a fur-lined cloak spread before the fire to dry, but there was no sign of the maid who should have accompanied them. Moving on through the room and into the adjoining bedchamber, a glimmer of candlelight caught his eye from behind the curtains of his canopied bed. He darted a quick Deryni probe inside as he approached, confirming the presence of Richenda and not some lurking assassin, but he resolutely shuttered off the part of his mind that dealt with the subject he most definitely did *not* want to discuss, on this first night back together in months.

"It was too late to join you for Mass," a soft, tentative voice whispered as Morgan parted the curtains with both hands, "but I've said my own prayers. Shall you come to bed now, my lord?"

Richenda lay in the middle of the bed with the sleeping furs pulled close under her chin, her face aglow in the light of the single candle set in a sconce at the head of the bed. Her eyes, bluer than any summer lake, mirrored a mixture of mischief and uncertainty as she gazed up at him, flame gold hair completely veiling the pillow beneath her head. The gold of his marriage ring on her hand glittered bright and chill as she fingered the edge of the sleeping fur at her throat. She was nervous. He knew she was expecting him to be angry.

"So. Just what do you think you're doing here?" he asked, his words cool but his eyes warming as her thought reached out in caress. "And stop that when I'm trying to scold you."

Lowering her eyes demurely, she obeyed, though as she raised up on her elbows to look at him again, the furs slipped down a little to expose a bare shoulder and shake his composure.

"I came to keep Christmas with my lord and husband," she murmured, letting another tendril of thought brush more lingeringly against his mind. "Should I not have come?"

The contact was excruciating pleasure after so long a parting. With a gasp, Morgan dropped his surface shields to her and lurched onto the bed, taking her in his arms and pressing his lips hungrily to hers as she embraced him. The touch of her flesh, intensified by the touch of

mind against mind, sent fire pulsing along every nerve.
He groaned as she pushed him far enough away to unbuck-
le his swordbelt, both of them trembling as she slipped
it from his waist with one hand and cast the sword on the
bed beside them while she worked at the clasp of his cloak
with her other hand, her lips continuing to nuzzle kisses
on his neck and throat.

"*All* the clothing, my lord," she whispered around the
kisses, starting on the laces of his overtunic. "Especially
the boots. I've brought our own linens from Coroth and
put them on the bed, and I won't have you ripping holes
with your spurs."

He raised up on his elbows in astonishment and burst
out laughing at that, causing her to begin giggling as well,
then shook his head and sat up all the way, still grinning,
the fire in his loins only banked, not slaked, as he drew
up his knees to unfasten low indoor boots.

"Fortunately for both of us, I didn't ride today, so I'm
not wearing spurs and I can manage the boots myself,"
he said, as the buckles came free. "It would take far too
long to call a squire."

"Oh, aye," she agreed, wide-eyed and dutiful.

Grinning, he kicked both feet through the curtain opening and heard the satisfying slap of leather hitting floor
somewhere outside. His overtunic quickly followed the
boots. She sat up to help him with his mail shirt, but the
sleeping furs slipped down around her waist, almost too
distracting even for Deryni self-control, and he had to
close his eyes and take several deep, shuddering breaths
while together they peeled the dead weight of the chain
up his torso and over his shoulders. His overtunic came
up partway as well, tangling around his neck with the
mail, and he could sense her mirth as his head got stuck
when she tried to pull both off at once.

"Just hold still until I get this sorted out," she whispered.

He could feel her body warm against his back as she
rose up on her knees behind to free him, every nerve
tingling at the touch of her hair trailing over one of his

shoulders. She tugged at the tunic and muttered as something started to rip. He yelped as one ear got bent.

More fumbling at the tangled opening, a grunt as she lifted the weight of the chain, and he was finally free. Drawing a deep breath, he pushed the mail and the rumpled undertunic out of the bed and turned to gaze at her again, doing his best to suppress a foolish grin.

"Thank you," he said softly.

Her smile was still just a little tentative as she nodded in answer, but her eyes never left his as she brushed one hand down his side to play at the waist of his breeches.

"And you are *sure* you're not angry, my lord?" she murmured.

"You know that I should be," he said, taking her in his arms and bearing her gently back onto the bed with the weight of his body. "But I'm not. That passed as soon as I saw you lying here. All I can think about is how long it's been since I've been in your bed. I think you must be some kind of witch—a Deryni witch, perhaps."

She laughed delightedly at that and drew him down to kiss him, lightly at first and then more lingeringly, as their speech shifted beyond mere words.

*A witch, am I?* she whispered in his mind. *And have I ensorcelled you, my love?*

*Totally and utterly*, he managed to reply, before losing himself in the growing urgency of what her hands were doing, working at the laces of his breeches. *God, how I've missed you, Richenda!*

But even in the sharing of minds as well as bodies, he was not *totally* ensorcelled. Some things he knew she understood he *could* not share, for he held the trust of other minds besides her own and might not grant those trusts even to a wife without leave.

But the thing he *would* not share remained a niggling frustration, doubly irritating to Richenda because Morgan would not really acknowledge its existence. To ease the rebuff, he gave her his perception of the events since their last reunion: the color and intrigue of the synod at Culdi; Loris' escape; the attempt on Duncan's life; Kelson's foray into the borderlands of Transha—and Dhugal and his shields.

*"Shields?"* Richenda whispered, drawing back to search his eyes even as her mind continued to read what he offered. "Is he one of us?"

"We think so," Morgan replied, "but we're not sure. No one can get past the shields, and he doesn't know how to lower them. Most attempts to read him have been so painful that he's become afraid for anyone else to try—except Duncan. Duncan doesn't hurt him, but Duncan doesn't get past the shields, either."

"Does Dhugal *want* to be read?" Richenda asked.

Morgan shrugged. "He *says* he does—though he hasn't gone out of his way to let us try. Not that any of us have had the time to pursue the matter. Maybe you'll have some ideas for new approaches. Duncan's actually the logical choice to do it, but he's been as busy as the rest of us."

By the time he had given her the rest of what he knew of Dhugal—the capture by Loris, Istelyn's mortal danger, the daring escape from Ratharkin, with its resultant royal hostages, and Dhugal's totally unexpected reaction to Duncan's consecration—Richenda was quite taken with the challenge the young border lord presented.

"I have a few ideas already," she said thoughtfully. "Be sure I get to meet him at court tomorrow."

"You'll hardly be able to avoid it," Morgan chuckled. "He's being formally invested as Earl of Transha. And then the real excitement begins."

"Caitrin's answer to Kelson's ultimatum," Richenda guessed.

Morgan sighed and nodded. "Aye. And since we really don't expect her to submit, it's almost certainly war in the spring—and a royal wedding for Kelson and Sidana at Twelfth Night."

Richenda stiffened in his arms and turned her face away at that, and Morgan could only hold her close in comfort and wait for the moment to pass, regretting the off-handedness of his last remark. He had never pressed her for the intimate details of her own first marriage, but he knew she had had no more say about it than Sidana would have. Unless they entered the religious life, marriages of state were almost inevitable for daughters of great houses. Richenda had been just sixteen when she married Bran Coris, and had never even seen her future husband before their wedding day.

"Oh, I understand all the dynastic reasons for a marriage between Gwynedd and Meara," she finally said, huddling back into the curve of his arm for reassurance. "They've been fighting for generations. It could finally resolve that old, old argument."

She gave a heavy sigh before continuing.

"But Kelson and Sidana—they're people, Alaric, not kingdoms. I don't know the girl at all, but I know Kelson. He's a kind and generous young man, and I know he'll do his best to make the marriage more than just a legal form for getting heirs, but—but—"

"But neither of them really has a choice," Morgan said, answering what she could not articulate. "I know. It doesn't make me very happy either. Unfortunately, such duties go with a crown."

"I suppose." She was silent a long time, her thoughts shuttered inside those private areas Morgan would not have thought of invading, until finally she sighed again.

"Well, if the marriage happens, you're going to have to take charge of Kelson," she said. "I don't know how a man feels about such things, but I do know how a woman feels. Despite whatever *she* may want, Sidana of Meara will probably be our next queen. She's bound to be afraid and unhappy and upset, but there's no reason it has to be as bad as it could be. I've been in a similar position; perhaps I can help her see the positive aspects. If you'll allow it, I'll ask to be a lady-in-waiting—and her friend, if she'll have me. I feel so sorry for the girl, Alaric."

"My beautiful Richenda," Morgan murmured, drawing her closer into the circle of his arms. "I am so very, very glad I found you."

He had also found, he reflected, as he drifted off to sleep, at least a temporary diversion for his wife's discontent—so long as she remained in Rhemuth, at any rate.

Early Christmas morning, Haldane scouts reported the approach of a Mearan herald and a man-at-arms, perhaps two hours away at their present pace. A page brought the news to Kelson in Dhugal's chamber, where king and border lord had been speculating on that very subject while Dhugal dressed for his investiture. The king himself wore an ankle-length court robe of Haldane scarlet, ermine showing at wrists and hem and along the deep slits front and back, but he had not yet put on his crown or the other accoutrements of his kingship.

"I don't like the sound of that, do you?" Kelson asked, when page and squire had been dismissed, watching Dhugal knot a narrow sash over his grey woolen tunic. "A herald and one man-at-arms. Not even a delegation. What do you suppose it means?"

With a snort, Dhugal shook out a cloak of fine MacArdry tartan and slung it around his shoulders, holding it closed with one hand while he rummaged in a wooden casket for a suitable brooch. The yellow, black, and grey plaid made bright contrast to the nubby grey wool beneath.

"Not a surrender, I'll warrant—but then, we never did really expect that, did we? I take it you *will* receive them?"

"I will—*after* we've finished with your investiture. It won't do them any harm to cool their heels for a while. That's part of what heralds are paid to do."

"That's true, I suppose."

As Dhugal threaded the pin of a heavy ring brooch through the two edges of his cloak, Kelson raised an eyebrow and leaned closer, tipping the carved silver toward the light with two fingers underneath the edge.

"That's a striking piece. Border silver?"

Dhugal nodded and turned the ring into place, fussing with the arrangement of the cloak's folds on his shoulders.

"Aye. This one's a MacArdry clan motif. It's been in the family for generations. I suppose I really ought to wear the chief's torc, too. Ciard said he'd put it in the bottom of the casket. Would you see if you can find it?"

With a grunt for answer, Kelson turned his attention to the wooden casket. He remembered the torc. Old Caulay had worn it when he came forward to swear fealty at Kelson's coronation. Underneath several other brooches and rings, something the right size and shape lay wrapped in the folds of a white rabbit pelt. Ornately chased end bosses in the shape of golden horses' heads protruded from the fur as Kelson slid it out from under the other things, but he handed it off without a second look as he continued to poke at what was left in the chest.

"It looks like Ciard brought you the entire Transha treasury," he said, pulling out a ring encrusted with granulated gold. "Is this a Transha seal?"

"That? Oh, aye. Transha, as opposed to MacArdry." Dhugal burnished the torc against his sleeve and then slipped it around his neck, pulling his braid free and adjusting the cloak and collar so they would not interfere. "It probably ought to be added to the rest of the regalia, actually. I think it goes with the coronet. Does someone have that?"

"Probably Ciard," Kelson replied. "One of your men, at any rate." He slipped the signet on his own finger, where he would not lose it, and poked in the casket some more. "Here, this one's nice—the cloak clasp with the lion's head. Why don't you wear that instead of the ring brooch?"

"That?" Dhugal gave it a perfunctory glance as he took it from Kelson, they shook his head and put the clasp back in the casket.

"Not today for that one, I think—though I promise to wear it to your wedding, if you end up marrying Sidana." He closed the lid of the casket with a hollow clunk. "I'm told my father gave it to my mother on their wedding day—which makes it far more suitable for a celebration of love than for the creation of a warlord, don't you agree?"

"Hmmm, I suppose. I still like it better than the ring brooch, though."

Dhugal, thrusting a sheathed dirk through the back of his sash, grinned and gave a sheepish nod.

"So do I, if you really want the truth. But if I didn't

wear the proper badges of my rank as chief, especially for my first formal reception at court, I might offend my clansmen. They think it's far more important to be their chief than it is to be your earl. You know how it is in the borders."

"Oh, aye," Kelson said, mimicking Dhugal's broad border accent and smiling as he bade him twirl around for inspection.

He was sober again by the time Dhugal finished turning, though, the grey Haldane eyes shadowed with just a trace of apprehension.

"What's wrong?" Dhugal asked.

Sighing, Kelson glanced at his boots. "I wish that all I had to do this morning was to make you an earl," he said quietly. "I'm not looking forward to the rest."

"Neither is anyone else," Dhugal replied.

"Then, why do we *do* it?"

"I suppose—because we have to."

"We have to," Kelson repeated.

Drawing a deep breath, he let it out explosively and looked up with a grin that was only a little strained.

"Well, if you put it *that* way, I suppose it's time I finished putting on the badges of *my* rank, don't you think? Can't make you an earl without them, you know."

"Certainly not!" Dhugal retorted, picking up the cue.

They continued to banter on that level all the while Kelson finished dressing, and even up to the very doors of the great hall.

# CHAPTER EIGHTEEN

*And I shall even betroth thee unto me in*
*faithfulness.*

—Hosea 2:20

Christmas Court: The tang of evergreen and cedar in
Kelson's nostrils—more pungent scent of pine knots
dipped in pitch, lighting his way through the packed, murmuring hall. Silver trumpet voices, a flourish of drums.
Bright-clad forms giving him obeisance as he moved among
them; rows of courtiers in holiday finery, some lightly
armed, ladies bright and graceful as songbirds.

As on most great feast days, he wore the jewelled state
crown of his coronation rather than the simpler circlet of
gold he usually favored. His black hair fell loose on his
shoulders. A belt of gilded leather girded his father's sword
at his waist; a jewel-encrusted sceptre lay cradled in the
crook of his left arm. Before ascending the dais to the
canopied chair of state, he passed to the left where
the bishops waited and knelt briefly for Bradene's Christmas blessing, hoarding the brief peacefulness as he took
his throne.

It was to be the only island of calm. No sooner was
he seated than the drums rolled to command attention to
a herald who proclaimed the opening of Christmas Court.
The loyal greetings of his vassals followed—mostly a rapid
blur. Head inclining to acknowledge their bows, hand
extending to receive the brush of lips in homage, murmured words of thanks, of inquiry after their families and
lands, each man replaced by the next in rapid succession.

He brightened at the unexpected approach of Derry—

278

for he had not known the young lord was coming to Christmas Court—then rose to kiss the smiling Richenda's hand when Morgan brought her forward, suddenly understanding Derry's presence. Still, one presentation ran into the next all too quickly, the pace slowing only when Dhugal came forward to be invested. And even that sped by too fast to really savor.

Border plaids and braids and silver-mounted dirks, the skirl of pipes. Dhugal kneeling before him. Words of condolence for the death of the old earl, welcome for the new. The act of homage and oath of fealty, Dhugal's hands between his own.

Dubbing with the great sword, bright line of silver gleaming between them—and girding Dhugal with another sword, Dhugal's own, on the gilded belt of his earldom. . . .

"With this sword defend the defenseless and punish evil, always remembering that honor, like the sword, has two edges: justice and mercy. . . ."

The presentation of banner and cauldron: tokens of Dhugal's authority to lead in war and his duty to feed and support his vassals . . . and the vesting with the ring and coronet.

"Though its worth in precious metal is token of thy rank and dignity, let its weight also remind thee of thy duty, and of the responsibility which thou sharest now with us. Arise, Dhugal MacArdry, Earl of Transha, and stand at our right hand, among our other well-beloved and trusty counsellors."

Pipers had skirled again in spirited interlude as Dhugal's clansmen paraded him around the hall on their shoulders, chanting a border salute, but all too soon the maelstorm began anew.

The Mearan herald coming forward, courteous in his own demeanor, but delivering words of defiance in behalf of his mistress—spurning the offer of clemency, abandoning the royal hostages to their fate.

And Istelyn's bloody, waxen head displayed aloft by a handful of matted hair, stark declaration of the fate of any man who broke faith with Meara.

And even then it did not stop. The hall erupted to howls

of outrage and shouted threats of retribution. Several women fainted. More than one of Kelson's retainers had to be forcibly restrained from taking out his fury on the herald before the man was whisked away into protective custody. When king and chief advisors had retired to the privacy of the council chamber, reaction exploded even more heatedly. Too stunned and sick-at-heart even to think about what he was going to do next, Kelson sat with his head in his hands and merely shut out everything for several minutes, letting the others get the anger out of their systems, only looking up when Bradene, close on his left, called him repeatedly.

"Sire? Sire, I beg of you! I am not a vengeful man, Sire, but this is an unforgivable affront," Bradene was saying, twisting his pectoral cross in nervous, agitated hands. "Surely there is no longer any question of marrying a Mearan!"

"If I don't marry her, my only other choice is to kill her," Kelson said wearily. "Would you have me vent my anger against an innocent hostage?"

"Innocent?" Jodrell snorted. "Since when did the guilt or innocence of hostages have anything to do with their fate? Beg pardon, Sire, but Henry Istelyn was far more innocent than any Mearan princeling. His fate cries out for vengeance!"

"Aye, and if I did allow vengeance to rule me, what kind of a king would I be?" Kelson countered. "I swore oaths, Jodrell! Oaths to uphold law—to temper justice with mercy—not to take vengeance!"

"I see no justice here," Jodrell muttered almost inaudibly, as he shifted angrily in his chair.

"What was that, Jodrell?"

"I said that it seems you intend to allow the offspring of traitors to go unpunished, Sire!" Jodrell said in a louder voice, his handsome face distorted by a scowl, "and to reward one of them with the very crown her mother tries to seize so treacherously! Mercy is *weakness* in this case, Sire. The Mearan bitch slew the hostage she took; it is our right to slay the ones we hold."

"An eye for an eye?" Kelson said. "I think not. And

you yourself admit that it is Caitrin who has rebelled against me."

"Aye, *rebelled*, Sire!" Bradene boomed. "And committed sacrilegious murder! Shall the sins of the fathers not be visited upon the children? She had a *bishop* executed, Kelson! A man anointed of God! And before they took his life, Edmund Loris had the audacity not only to excommunicate him, but to degrade him from the priesthood—Henry Istelyn: one of the godliest men I have ever known!"

As Kelson searched for a temperate reply, for this was getting quite out of hand, Cardiel shook his head and laid a restraining hand on Bradene's sleeve.

"Peace, brother," he said quietly. "No one will argue that Istelyn was not a godly man. But given that he *was* a godly man, he will not have faltered when faced with his martyrdom in the cause of king and faith. Loris' action was empty of substance."

"Of course it was empty," Bradene retorted. "That isn't at issue here. Empty or not, Istelyn had to face an unjust death—alone, bereft of the outward solace of his office. And to die so horribly," he finished lamely, anger dissolving away to grief.

Cardiel sighed and looked down at the table, tears in his eyes.

"Dear, dear brother, I beg you, do not torment yourself this way. In all things, Henry Istelyn was the king's and God's good servant. We *must* believe that he died in the faith—that he did what *any* of us would pray we had the grace to do, were we in his place—and that his faith sustained him through—"

"No!" Bradene gasped, anger flaring again. "Let the faith of the Mearan brats sustain *them*, as they meet their justly deserved fate as traitor's kin! Sire, I *cannot* find it in my heart to let this pass. One *crushes* a viper's brood— one does not *marry* it!"

Morgan, seated at the king's right hand with Richenda close beside him, could not fail to catch the overflow of shock and stomach-churning grief that flared for just an instant as the two archbishops argued. It was quickly damped, but he knew Richenda had sensed it, too. He could feel her trembling, her hand clenched tight in his. He knew also what it was costing Kelson not to lash out in his own anger and sense of helplessness. No matter what the king did, some would not agree.

Hurting with Kelson, Morgan turned pleading eyes on the two archbishops, letting his glance include everyone around the table.

"Let *be*, my lords!" he said, cutting off another heated exchange. "Do you think your railing makes his decision any easier? What are you trying to do to him? Do you think he does not *know*? How heavy must the crown *be*?"

"How heavy was *Istelyn's* burden?" Bradene muttered.

But any further outburst was forestalled by Arilan's withering glance and the pained, compassionate shake of Cardiel's grey head.

"*Please*, Bradene," Cardiel murmured. "Duke Alaric is right. However terrible and unjust may have been our brother Istelyn's fate, that is past. He is beyond our ability to help or hinder him. We must not let the wisdom of our future decision be clouded by our grief and outrage."

"Archbishop Cardiel is correct," Nigel agreed. "If we kill our hostages, we lose all hope of any peaceful resolution to the Mearan question. Spite will only breed yet more spite, and—"

"Aye, now *there's* a key word," Ewan butted in. "Breeding. Let the lad get on with his wooing, Archbishop. He needs to breed an heir."

A rumble of agreement from the other laymen around the table gave Ewan encouragement to go on.

"Go ahead and marry the lass, Sire. Wed her and bed her as quickly as ye may—and get her with child before the spring campaign! There are many in Meara who'll come flocking to yer standard if there's an heir to two crowns in the offing. But ye haven't time to waste."

As Bradene sighed and bowed his head, lifting a ringed hand in grudging acquiescence, a little of the tension seemed to leave the room. After a moment, Nigel gazed down the table at his royal nephew, attempting a strained smile.

"Wise counsel, Kelson," he said quietly, "though I should have phrased it a trifle more delicately. You need an heir of your own body and you need a Mearan alliance. And the heir born of a Mearan union would be the strongest asset of all. I know this marriage is not what you would have chosen, had things been different, but—" He shrugged. "What can I say, except to wish you the best of fortune and offer you every power at my disposal to facilitate this match?"

Kelson glanced up at Nigel listlessly, hands folded still and quiet. "Thank you, Uncle. Please do not mistake my lack of enthusiasm for lack of gratitude. All that you and Duke Ewan have said is perfectly correct." He sighed. "We must now pray that the Lady Sidana sees matters in a similar light."

"And if she does not—" Arilan said archly, his glance again conveying the implication of extraordinary methods of persuasion. "Will you marry her anyway, against her will?"

"I have already said that I would," Kelson answered a little sharply. "Will *you* perform the ceremony, Bishop, if I bring an unwilling bride before the altar?"

Arilan pursed his lips, nodding resolutely. Bradene and Cardiel looked shocked. Ewan snorted.

"Take him at his word, Sire. This is no time for too many niceties. If she will nae have ye at first, bed her and *then* wed her—or at least threaten to do it. She'll come around."

That remark elicited its own flurry of comment and indignation, principally among the clergy but also from Richenda and Dhugal, until Kelson finally cleared his throat and swept them all with his grey Haldane eyes, some of the old, hard fire of his father's day touching each one.

"I'll manage my own wooing, thank you, gentlemen," he said when they had quieted. "It will be conducted with as much honor as possible on both our parts, but there *shall* be a royal wedding at Twelfth Night, I promise you, one way or another."

"Why the delay?" asked Saer de Traherne. "If part of the purpose of this exercise is to get an heir before the spring campaign, Sire, you should be sowing the seeds as quickly as possible. The Mearan lass is young. It may take her a while to begin breeding."

As Kelson blushed furiously, at a loss how to answer, Duncan came to his rescue.

"If I read his Majesty's intentions correctly, my lord, I suspect he plans to crown the queen on the same day he marries her, which presents a somewhat different logistical problem than merely publishing the banns and bringing the intended couple before a priest."

As Kelson nodded and murmured, "Aye," obviously grateful for the rescue, Duncan went on, "Indeed, if the lady is to be enthroned in state fitting the consort of the King of Gwynedd, we shall all find ourselves hard-pressed to complete the preparations in so short a time. And as I'm sure the Lady Richenda will confirm, twelve days will be only barely adequate to prepare the gowns and jewels that our queen-to-be will require for this momentous event."

"'Tis true, my lords," Richenda said quietly. "Not only that, I beg you have some care for poor Sidana herself. Is it asking too much that she should have at least a little time to prepare for the role being thrust upon her?"

"She will hae guessed what's in store," Ewan muttered. "She has been bred to her duty. Dinnae coddle the lass too much, Sire."

"Indeed, do not coddle her at all," Richenda retorted, before Kelson could reply. "But I speak as one who was herself a bride of expediency, wed to the benefit of lands rather than any desire of my own. Give the girl a few days to realize her duty, to decide that this is what she herself wants, for the sake of her own land. She may thank you in years to come, when she is your queen."

"And I thank *you*, my lady," Kelson murmured. "You do right to remind us of Sidana's part in all of this."

She inclined her head gracefully.

"May I also ask you to serve her while you are at court?" he went on, with a strained, hopeful grin. "And

perhaps to supervise the feminine aspects of our preparations? I have no illusions that she will be any more
enthusiastic about this match than I am, but perhaps your
experience and sympathy can help her accept what must
be."

"I would be most honored to serve your intended queen,
Sire, both now and in the future," Richenda murmured.
"My lord and I discussed the very matter only this morn-
ing."

"Ah," Kelson said. "Well, that's a relief."

He glanced at the rest of them, drawing a deep breath
and letting it out audibly, then stood. Immediately the rest
stood as well.

"Very well, then, gentlemen—and my lady," he said.
"I go now to speak with your future queen. Lady Richenda,
I would be pleased if you would accompany me—and
Bishop Duncan as well. I leave the rest of you to continue
setting plans for the coming nuptials. Uncle, I shall ask
you to preside in my absence."

Kelson was glad, a little while later, that he had asked
Richenda and Duncan to go with him, for he found himself
more anxious than he wanted to admit, as he led them
along the dimly lit corridor. He had installed Sidana in
his mother's former apartments on her arrival in Rhemuth,
judging them the only suitable quarters for a princess of
however dubious seniority; now he wondered whether he
had been contemplating this visit all along.

His mouth was dry as dust as he approached the outer
door, and he cleared his throat nervously as he motioned
Duncan on ahead to announce him. The guards came to
smart attention and rendered royal salute as the three of
them approached, but he gave sign for them to be at ease
as he straightened a fold of his heavy court robe. He had
exchanged his state crown for a simpler, lighter circlet of
gold, and he glanced nervously at the shadow he cast by
torchlight as Duncan paused before the door. Richenda
waited slightly behind him.

"You're sure you're ready to go through with this,

Sire?" Duncan murmured, glancing aside at him with hand poised on the brocaded bell pull.

Swallowing awkwardly, Kelson nodded, conveying just a little of his sense of apprehensive duty in a lightning thought as Duncan's yank brought an answering chime of bells. The Deryni bishop glanced at him again in comradely support and compassion and composed his own expression as the door was opened by a serving maid. The girl gaped at his episcopal purple.

"The king wishes to see the Lady Sidana, child," Duncan said, quietly, putting on his most reassuring yet commanding demeanor. "May we come in?"

A little flustered, both by his rank and his mere male presence, the girl dropped him a curtsey and stood aside to let them enter, making another, deeper reverence to the king, whose eyes she would not even meet. As she closed the door behind them, Duchess Meraude appeared in the doorway to the next room, smiling as she saw who had arrived.

"Nephew," she said, coming forward to dip in formal curtsey. "You are most welcome. And Bishop Duncan—and *Richenda*! Ah, Richenda, what a welcome Christmas gift *you* are! Alaric neglected to tell me you were coming."

As the two women embraced happily, even Kelson managed a wan smile, murmuring his own greeting as Meraude brushed his cheek with a dutiful kiss. He was always surprised at how short Meraude was. The top of her head reached only to his chin. In his new awareness of things feminine, sweeping his glance over her deep green gown, he found his eyes drawn unabashedly to her slightly swollen abdomen.

"Ah, yes, there's finally to be another little one," she said casually, noticing his notice. "She's due late in the spring."

"*She*?" Richenda said, smiling.

"Yes, how do you know it's a girl?" Kelson asked.

"Well, with three boys already, I'm allowed to hope it's a little girl," Meraude replied. "Not that I would wish her the fate of *some* princesses." She glanced among the three of them speculatively. "*Is* there to be a royal wedding? Is that what you've come to tell her?"

Biting at his lower lip, Kelson nodded. "I fear it is, Aunt. And I—think it best if only Father Duncan accompanies me just now."

"Of course, Sire," Meraude murmured, suddenly a little cooler. "She's in the solar."

She held her head high as she led king and bishop across the room. She might have been a queen herself. The long hair coiled at the back of her head beneath her veil was black as any Haldane's, her complexion fair and smooth. As she paused at the entrance to the solar and turned to beckon him pass through, she looked hardly older than her royal charge—who turned and froze in the mouth of a deep window embrasure on the other side of the room.

"Good afternoon, my lady," Kelson said neutrally.

Sidana blanched at the sound of his voice, immediately turning away from him to stare out at the falling snow, her apprehension apparent even from where Kelson stood. The dying sun shining through the window beyond cast reddish highlights on her long chestnut hair and purpled the pale blue of her gown.

"The lord Llewell is visiting his sister, Sire," Meraude warned, restraining Kelson with a hand on one forearm as he started toward the girl. "Well, it *is* Christmas," she added, at his expression of annoyance as he stopped to stare down at her. "No one said they couldn't see one another—and it was only for an hour. Should I not have let him come?"

Sighing, Kelson shook his head and continued toward the embrasure until he could see Llewell sitting stiff and indignant at the far end. He had hoped not to have the Mearan prince present for this conversation, but perhaps it was for the best. If he could win Llewell's cooperation, it would be easier for Sidana.

But Llewell stood as their eyes met, defiance like a wall between them, hand going automatically to his belt for the weapon which was not there. For just an instant, Sidana looked like a trapped, frightened bird.

"No, there's no harm done, Aunt," Kelson replied easily. "What I have to say concerns Lord Llewell as well as the Lady Sidana. I must warn you, though, Llewell: I intend this to be a civilized, reasoned discussion. Any disruption on your part will be dealt with. Do I make myself clear?"

For an instant Llewell only stood there glowering, right hand flexing and unflexing where the hilt of his dagger would have been, and Kelson wondered whether he and Duncan were going to have to deal with a physical confrontation. He sensed Duncan tensing beside him in readiness, and knew Duncan wondered, too. But Llewell was stayed from any further indiscretion by Sidana's urgent touch on his arm, the slight shake of her head.

"Let be, brother," she whispered. "I would not be the cause of your hurt. If he wills, he will speak with me. There is nothing you can do to stop it."

"Your sister is very wise, Llewell," Meraude agreed. "You must accept what is. Do not make me regret I allowed you to come."

Sullenly Llewell turned a long, bitter gaze on Kelson and dropped his hands to his sides, forcing the wound-up tension from his body with visible effort. In answer, Kelson inclined his head in cool acknowledgment. Llewell continued to stare at him for several seconds before dropping his head to murmur something to Sidana that no one else could hear. Then the prince turned his back on his sister's royal caller, to stare out the window. Even Sidana looked embarrassed at his rudeness and wrung her hands worriedly as she stole a glance at the king.

"Please go and make the Duchess Richenda welcome, Aunt," Kelson said to Meraude, not taking his eyes from Sidana. "Father Duncan and I have matters well in hand."

As Meraude curtseyed and departed, closing the door behind her, Kelson tried not to give any outward sign that he even noticed the scared, drained look on Sidana's face, only gesturing mildly for Duncan to precede him up the steep steps to the embrasure. Llewell turned warily at their approach, and Sidana backed off, both of them standing finally in the right-hand corner of the compartment, she with her back pressed close against her brother's side, he with a protective arm around his sister's shoulders.

"Please sit down—both of you," Kelson said quietly, gesturing toward the cushions behind them, then taking a seat himself, Duncan to his left. "There's no need to make this more difficult than it already is. I don't intend to threaten either of you, but there are things which must be said. Sit down!" he repeated, when neither of them moved. "I'd rather not crane my neck looking up at you."

Blanching even whiter, Sidana eased herself onto a cushion, back ramrod straight, hands balled into fists at her sides, though she tried to hide them under the folds of her skirt. Llewell, sinking down beyond her, looked just as scared, but he did a fair job of hiding it behind a façade of bravado. Suddenly Kelson was aware how he must look to them, crowned and wearing his state robes of crimson and ermine, with a Deryni bishop at his side. He tried to soften his expression a little as he glanced from one to the other of them, but knew he must be firm. He was glad of Duncan's tempering presence.

"I've had word from your mother," he said to both of them, resting his hands awkwardly on his thighs. "Her emissary arrived this morning."

Sidana gave a little gasp, closing her eyes for just an instant. Her brother flushed scarlet.

"She still defies you, doesn't she?" Llewell crowed. "She's going to stand against you!"

"She executed my bishop, who was her hostage," Kelson said evenly, refusing to be baited. "Do you know what that means?"

As Sidana glanced fearfully at her brother, Llewell drew himself up even more haughtily.

"Do you intend to execute us as well, then? We are not afraid to die!"

"No one has accused you of being afraid," Kelson said sharply. "And I am trying to insure that *no one* else need die—though I think even you will agree that I would be within my rights to kill you."

"Deryni bastard!" Llewell muttered.

"I will admit to being Deryni," Kelson replied softly. "And I shall attribute your use of the other term to your anger and the brashness of youth. But do not interrupt me again, or I shall ask Bishop McLain to deal with you."

He sensed they knew the threat was not an empty one. As Sidana stifled another little gasp and both of them glanced automatically at Duncan, Llewell closed his mouth and sat back sullenly in his place. Duncan wore no weapons and presented no particular physical threat in size or even expression, but they must suspect he was also a "Deryni bastard." Neither had had a taste of his particular talents, but they had both felt Morgan's magic. The threat was sufficient for the moment.

"Very well, then. I trust we understand each other on that point," Kelson breathed. "Please believe that it is not my wish to execute *anyone*, especially my own kinsmen and women, but I would be less than true to my coronation vows if I allowed treachery to go unpunished. I am Meara's lawful, anointed king, as well as Gwynedd's. Your mother has risen in rebellion against me and taken an innocent life."

Sidana continued to stare at him numbly, and Llewell appeared to be on the verge of another outburst; but, at least for the moment, the threat of Duncan sitting across from him kept him silent as Kelson went on.

"But I wish to spend no further lives in this matter," Kelson said in a more conciliatory tone. "It is my earnest desire that Meara and Gwynedd may be one, as our great-grandfathers intended. And if that can be accomplished peaceably, then that is what I choose. You can help me do that."

"Us? Help a Haldane?" Llewell sneered.

Even as Llewell said it, Kelson was glaring at him angrily and signing to Duncan.

"One more word out of him . . ." he said with deliberate menace.

Casually but purposefully, Duncan moved closer to the end of the embrasure, within easy reach of Llewell. The boy subsided immediately, and Kelson turned his full attention on Sidana. He almost hoped Llewell did say something else; his constant interference was not making this any easier.

"What I say next must be directed to you, my lady," he said patiently. "I do not expect you to do anything for *me*, but I do hope you will do what you must for the sake of Meara. I offer you a way to resolve the conflict between our two lands without further shedding of blood. I ask that you join your royal line with mine—that our children may reign as undisputable rulers of a united Gwynedd and Meara."

He hardly flickered an eyelid at Llewell's strangled cry, only shooting out a hand to seize Sidana's right wrist when she would have tried to stop Duncan. The bishop was across the intervening space before Llewell could even leave his seat, imposing control so swiftly that Llewell had time for only a futile gesture in Kelson's direction. The prince's eyelids fluttered once and then closed as he crumpled into Duncan's arms, his head lolling against the episcopal purple without resistance. In repose, with the defiant lines erased from the face, he looked even younger than his fifteen years.

"He was warned," Duncan murmured, shifting Llewell's head and shoulders to a more comfortable position across his lap and glancing up at Sidana. "I haven't harmed him. He can hear what's going on around him; he simply can't react. I promise you, he felt no pain. Nor is he feeling any now. His Majesty has asked a question of you, my lady. I suggest you answer him."

With a startled gasp, Sidana jerked her wrist away from Kelson and stood, apparently only then remembering that he still had held it. She was too proud to cry, but Kelson could sense the effort it took her to bite back her tears as she retreated to the left-hand corner of the embrasure, as far from all of them as she could get. Hugging her arms across her breast, she stared blindly out the window for several seconds, her long hair cloaking her to her knees. When first she tried to speak, her voice broke. Embarrassed, she turned the strangled sound into a nervous cough.

"Do I—correctly discern a proposal of marriage?" she managed to ask at last.

"You do," Kelson replied.

"And does the king truly ask, or does he command?" she whispered bitterly. "If I refuse, will he take me by force?"

Kelson managed a mirthless smile, choosing to ignore the jibe.

"Here, in front of witnesses, my lady?" he said lightly. "And a bishop, at that?"

"A *Deryni* bishop," she countered, lifting her chin defiantly, "who has already bent my brother to your will. Why should he not do the same to me, if you desire it? Or *you* could do it if you wished. We have heard how you won your crown with black magic."

Duncan glanced at the king indignantly, but Kelson shook his head, his own denial already forming on his lips.

"Do you truly believe I would force you into marriage?" he asked softly. "Or that a bishop would countenance it, much less be part of such coercion?"

"You are Deryni—both of you. I do not know what you might do."

"I would not use *any* power at my command, whether physical or Deryni, to force you to an act against your conscience, Sidana. Marriage is a sacrament. That means something to me—something very important. But also important is what our marriage might mean to our two lands: an end to the bloodshed over disputes of succession; peace in our time. Is the thought of being a queen so abhorrent to you?"

She bowed her head, her shoulders shaking silently for just a moment.

"What of my parents?" she asked at last. "And my brothers?"

Kelson glanced at the motionless Llewell and sighed. "I would offer Llewell the opportunity to renounce his rights to the Mearan titles your family claims. Once I had his parole, I would honor him with all the estate appropriate to the brother of my queen."

"And Ithel? My mother and father?"

"I know what you desire to hear," he replied, "but I cannot offer you any false hopes. One way or another, if there is to be a lasting peace, I must break the succession ahead of you so that there will be no question of the right of our heirs to rule both Gwynedd and Meara. The fate of your parents and your brothers is dependent upon their further actions. I do not seek their lives, but I shall not hesitate to take them if it will save hundreds, perhaps thousands of others."

"I see."

Slowly she glanced at her brother and moved listlessly to the window itself, laying both hands flat against the glass as she gazed out at the freedom of the hills beyond Rhemuth, white-bronze in the dying sun.

"I have no true options, then," she said after a few seconds. "Whether or not I refuse you, my family is doomed, as is my country. We posture grandly, but we are a small land compared to Gwynedd—and human. We cannot stand against the might of a Deryni overlord. I have known that all along, I suppose. Our cause was lost before it began, even if my mother would not recognize it. And regardless of what *I* do, I know the rest of my family will die. They will not surrender."

"Then, think of your people," Kelson murmured, standing slowly to gaze at her and wishing he could offer further comfort. "Is it so terrible to be the instrument of peace? Could you not find some contentment in being queen?"

"Queen of a land besides my own—"

"Queen of a land which *encompasses* your own," Kelson amended. "And wife to a man who would do his utmost to make you happy."

"In a marriage of state and convenience, wed to the enemy of my people," she replied, lowering her eyes. "A pawn in the game of dynasties and kings, as has ever been the fate of women."

"As has ever been the fate of kings as well, my lady."

Trembling, Kelson removed his circlet and set it aside, sinking to one knee behind her. He longed to reach out to her, to touch even one strand of the shimmering hair, but he was too nervous, all too conscious of Duncan sitting silently to his right, with Llewell sprawled quiet but aware across his lap.

"I am—as much a pawn in this as you, Sidana," he continued softly. "Father Duncan will tell you that I always hoped to marry for love, or at least affection, but I have also always known that dynastic considerations must come before personal desires, when eventually I took a wife."

He cleared his throat nervously. "Still, even a marriage of state can be one of at least contentment. I cannot promise that you will be happy if you marry me. I do give you my word as a king and as a man that I will deal fairly with you, and try with all my might to be a kind and gentle husband—and pray that love might grow between us in time. Perhaps it is not all you would have wished for—it is not all *I* would have wished for—but it is all I have to offer. Will you at least consider my proposal?"

For a long moment she did not move, and he was sure she would refuse. Against all prudence, he reached out with his mind and read a little of her turmoil: helpless anger mixed with duty and honor and just a hint of compassion, which gave him cause to hope.

Withdrawing, for her emotions were too intense to bear for long, read unbidden and without her knowledge, he raised a hand to brush one errant chestnut lock caught in a fold of her gown, intending to beseech her further. Its touch was like captive lightning, jarring him so profoundly that he nearly gasped. As if stung, he jerked back his hand and stared up at her face set in profile against the darkening glass, swaying a little on his knees. He dared not allow the thoughts which went coursing through his mind, but he could not stop them. If she continued to refuse, he knew the possibility of force was *not* wholly ruled out, regardless of what he had said before.

He was saved from himself by Sidana's own action, however. After a few seconds, though she still did not look at him, her right hand dropped to her side and opened.

"I will marry you," she whispered, a tear at last trickling down her cheek.

Reverently, not daring to speak for fear of changing her mind, Kelson took her hand and kissed it, damping the surge of relief and pleasure which coursed through him anew at her touch. Even so, she felt some of it. As he turned her hand to press his lips against her palm, he felt her shudder. He rose with new confidence, keeping her hand in his as he turned awkwardly toward Duncan.

"Will you witness the lady's consent, Father?"

Nodding, Duncan shifted Llewell to a sitting position and stood, laying his priestly hands on their joined ones. Llewell stirred slightly and opened his eyes, but could not seem to summon sufficient will to do more.

"Have you a date in mind, Sire?"

"Twelve days hence, at Epiphany."

"A fitting day to crown a queen," Duncan said gently, with a compassionate smile for the trembling princess. "Sidana of Meara, do you promise and covenant, of your own free will and desire, to contract honorable marriage with Kelson of Gwynedd twelve days hence, according to the rites of our Holy Mother the Church?"

Her eyes brimmed with tears, but she swallowed and gave a quick dip with her chin.

"I do promise and covenant it, so help me God."

"Kelson of Gwynedd, do you promise and covenant, of your own free will and desire, to contract honorable marriage with Sidana of Meara twelve days hence, according to the rites of our Holy Mother the Church?"

"I do promise and convenant it, so help me God," Kelson said steadily.

"Then I do witness and affirm that a contract to marry has been solemnized between Sidana of Meara and Kelson of Gwynedd, to be joined in holy matrimony twelve days hence, according to the rites of our Holy Mother the Church. The banns shall be published on the morrow. And this covenant shall be as binding as the vows of matrimony, and shall not be put asunder." He made the sign of the Cross over their joined hands. "In the name of the Father and of the Son and of the Holy Spirit, Amen."

She drew her hand away at that, to turn and sink sobbing to the cushions by the window. Kelson would have tried to comfort her, but Duncan shook his head and summoned Meraude and Richenda instead, telling them briefly what had happened before leading Llewell and Kelson out of the room. The dazed Llewell he placed in the custody of a guard, to be returned to his own quarters.

Kelson he led back to the royal apartments, where Morgan, Dhugal, and Nigel waited. There he and Kelson told them what had been decided, and the king commanded preparations to go forward.

# CHAPTER NINETEEN

*A merry heart doeth good like a medicine:*
*but a broken spirit drieth the bones.*
                                        —Proverbs 17:22

During the week and a half that followed, Kelson avoided all further contact with his bride-to-be, hopeful that time for reflection would win her to less tearful acceptance of both their duties. Richenda's continued presense proved a godsend, for Sidana soon preferred her company over that of any other lady at court, despite the undisguisable fact that Richenda was wife to a Deryni. Kelson did not ask whether Richenda had helped the relationship along in any extraordinary way; the knowledge that his own wooing had been accomplished without Deryni advantage was sufficient for his own conscience.

However Richenda managed it, though, Sidana's fits of near-hysterical weeping gradually abated to stony endurance, resigned tolerance, and even occasional shy excitement as gowns were cut and fitted and Richenda began gently instructing her young charge in some of the privileges as well as the duties of her life to come. The only major setback occurred at midweek, after a private audience with her brother degenerated into a shouting and weeping bout. On hearing of it, Kelson forbade all further sibling contact until after the wedding day and asked that Richenda remain with the princess day and night for the interim. Morgan regretted his empty bed, but Sidana's progress after that was so tangible that he counted the sacrifice well worth while. Once, passing near the queen's

297

solar, he even heard Sidana singing with Richenda. When told, Kelson beamed for the rest of the evening.

On the military and ecclesiastical front, preparations also went forward as Twelfth Night approached. The morning after Christmas, the archbishops loosed the next offensive in their attempt to bring Loris to his knees, extending their earlier excommunication of rebel bishops and Mearan royal family to a general interdict of all of Meara. Kelson doubted the long-range usefulness of the measure, for it was unlikely that Loris would observe it, but he allowed it to be sent along with his formal declaration of war in the spring. As was only honorable, he also sent notice of his intentions regarding Sidana: a stark, official copy of the banns of marriage published in Rhemuth that same morning, witnessed by nearly a dozen bishops and lords of state as well as by both principals. There was no chance of Mearan interference with the latter, for no messenger could reach Ratharkin and return before the wedding took place; and as for the rest, spring would decide the future from that point.

"Her parents would probably rather she were dead," Kelson said gloomily, sipping rich Fianna wine with his closest friends the night before his wedding. "Maybe she would, too. I suspect Llewell would. I'm sure he wishes *I* were."

Dhugal, showing the effects of the evening's indulgence far more than the king, shook his head and chuckled, exchanging an exaggerated wink with Morgan and Duncan.

"Of *course* Llewell wishes you were dead, Sire," he said lightly. "Llewell is her brother. What brother ever thinks *any* man is good enough for his sister?"

"There was once one good enough for *my* sister," Morgan replied, glancing over his cup at Duncan with a sad, wistful smile.

The comment caught both younger men by surprise— Dhugal, who had no idea what Morgan was talking about, and Kelson, who understood the reference all too well. As Kelson lowered his eyes, obviously saddened by the memory, Dhugal turned puzzled gaze on Duncan, who sighed and raised his cup slightly in remembrance.

"To Kevin and Bronwyn: together for all eternity."

He grimaced and drank the toast, not looking up as Morgan and Kelson silently followed suit. Dhugal, even more mystified, turned to Kelson in question.

"Did they die or something?" he whispered, much sobered.

Kelson leaned his head against the back of his chair and closed his eyes. "Or something."

"What does that mean?" Dhugal persisted. "Weren't they—Deryni?"

Sighing, Morgan picked up the wine pitcher and began carefully refilling his and Duncan's cups, not meeting any of their eyes.

"Bronwyn was. She was my only sister. Kevin was Duncan's half-brother, and human. There was also at Duke Jared's court a young architect named Rimmell who'd taken a fancy to Bronwyn, though no one knew that at the time—least of all Bronwyn. In any event, Rimmell formed an insane jealousy of Kevin. Two days before Bronwyn and Kevin were to be married, Rimmell apparently decided he must eliminate his rival."

"You mean he killed Kevin?" Dhugal breathed.

Morgan paused with the wine pitcher in his hand to gaze unseeing at the fire.

"Not—directly," he said after a slight pause. "He obtained a love charm from an old witch woman up in the hills. She told him it would turn Bronwyn's love away from Kevin and toward himself. The charm was ill-set. It backfired. Bronwyn—tried to protect Kevin. Both of them died."

"How awful!"

With another sigh, Morgan shook his head and resumed pouring wine for the king, obviously trying to shake the mood as well.

"I'm sorry. I thought everyone knew. And I apologize to you as well, my prince." He set the pitcher on the hearth and glanced at Kelson. "This is hardly fit conversation for the night before your wedding. We should speak of less ill-fated unions: your aunt and uncle, your parents—"

"Your own marriage, perhaps?" Kelson asked with a faint smile, his lips red with the wine of which he had just drunk deeply.

As Morgan demurred, unreadable emotions flickering across his face, and Duncan chuckled politely, Dhugal gave a tipsy giggle and raised his cup in unsteady salute.

"Here, here, Your Grace! You're the only married man among us. Tell my virgin brother what he can expect on his wedding night!"

"I—doubt our lord the king needs any serious instruction in that regard," Morgan said after a slight pause, suspecting that Kelson might, but reluctant to go into too intimate detail in front of one of Kelson's apparently more experienced peers, and with all of them increasingly in their cups.

"What makes a marriage is not the wedding night, however," he went on, "but what comes after. I suspect that Kelson's marriage will be rather like everyone else's in that respect. Regardless of how much he and his bride eventually may come to care for one another—and God grant that love *will* grow between them—there will be good days . . . and days that are not so good." He shrugged and smiled. "One works things out."

Kelson looked at him strangely. "Is that the voice of experience, Alaric?" he said softly. "Odd, but it never even occurred to me that you and Richenda were anything but deliriously happy. You seemed so much in love—"

"And we're still in love," Morgan said, raising an eyebrow wistfully. "That doesn't mean there aren't occasional problems, however. She's an intelligent, headstrong woman, Kelson—and I'm as headstrong a man as you're ever likely to meet. I wouldn't lie to you and say we haven't had our bad days, but I *will* assure you that the nights are almost always good."

"I'll bet they are." Dhugal chuckled, raising his cup in oblivious salute as Kelson looked at him in astonishment. "I've heard about your wife, Your Grace!"

"*Have* you, now?"

Morgan's dry tone of affront was only in jest, for he knew Dhugal had not meant his comment the way it sounded, but the look of consternation which came over the boy's face as he realized what he had said could not be ignored. Better he learn about the consequences of too much drink while in the company of friends than among strangers, who might take genuine and perhaps deadly offense.

"Your Grace, I'm sorry!" the boy managed to whisper, his eyes so wide Morgan wondered how he could see. "I only meant—"

"What *did* you mean, Earl of Transha?" Morgan replied softly. "That my wife is beautiful?"

"Yes! And that's *all*!"

Before their very eyes, Dhugal turned a pasty shade of green, so quickly that even he was taken by surprise.

"Too much to drink!" he managed to croak, as he lurched to his feet and ran stumbling from the room to disappear into a garderobe cubicle, which shortly echoed with the sound of retching. Kelson, hardly less inebriated but in far better control, at least of his stomach, stifled an embarrassed giggle and hiccoughed.

"I'm sorry. I shouldn't laugh. I think I've had too much as well. Someone ought to make sure he's all right, though."

"I'll go," Duncan said, rising to join the unfortunate Dhugal.

Morgan glanced over his shoulder at the retreating bishop, then back at the still-snickering king.

"Are you sure *you're* all right?" he asked Kelson.

Kelson shook his head and pressed the cool goblet against his forehead as he closed his eyes.

"No. I'm scared silly about tomorrow. I'm going to have a *wife*, Alaric! She doesn't even *like* me. What am I going to do?"

"You're going to make the best of it, as you have with everything that's been dealt you," Morgan replied. "And as for whether she likes you or not, why not give her a chance before you decide she doesn't? You're going to discover a great change just since you last saw her. And you've already admitted that you're attracted to *her*. Make that work for you. It isn't that hard to fall in love. I've done it dozens of times."

Kelson snorted and opened his eyes. "Only once that's counted—and where did *that* get you? *Is* something wrong between you and Richenda, Alaric? Is there anything I— what a stupid thing to say!" He took another quick gulp from his cup and looked back at the surprised Morgan. "Well, here I am, scared witless about getting married, asking an old married man whether there's anything *I* can do to help *him*. I'm as drunk as Dhugal!"

"Not if you mean what you say," Morgan replied, eying the king wistfully.

"That I'm drunk? Oh—that I'm willing to help," Kelson answered, echoing Morgan's patient nod.

"Yes."

"Very well. What?"

"What?"

"What do you want me to do to help?" Kelson said, making a rolling gesture with his free hand to urge Morgan on. "Come on, tell me."

With a short, resolute sigh, Morgan leaned a little closer, toying with his goblet between his two hands as he gazed across at the king.

"I'd like Richenda to remain at court when we go on campaign in the spring."

"You mean here in Rhemuth?"

"Yes."

"What about the children. Aren't they still in Coroth?"

"I can have them brought here as soon as the weather lets up. They'll be fine where they are, through the winter months. Derry's mother has become their governess. And my staff have things under control otherwise."

Kelson grimaced, obviously having trouble following Morgan's logic.

"So the children join Richenda here in the spring and they all stay here through the campaign. I still don't understand why."

"Well, for one thing, your future queen has taken a fancy to my wife, as you well know," Morgan replied. "That would be reason enough, all by itself. She could also help your aunt. With a new baby on the way, Meraude shouldn't have to shoulder the duties of chatelaine indefinitely; and until you're sure you've won Sidana's loyalty, you won't be able to trust her with those duties."

Kelson nodded profoundly. "Aye, that's true enough. And I'm sure Aunt Meraude would welcome Richenda's company. But won't Richenda be needed at Coroth, with you away?"

Morgan bowed his head and toyed with the stem of his goblet, wishing desperately that she were.

"No," he whispered.

"*No?* But she's your duchess. Who else is equipped to manage things for that long in your absence?"

"Not the former wife of a traitor," Morgan said quietly.

"*What?*"

"They don't trust her, Kelson. I think they mean well, but I suppose they're afraid she'll betray me. Maybe they think she'll take revenge for my part in Bran's death."

"But *I* killed Bran—and partially for that very reason; so no one could later say you killed him to get his wife."

Morgan sighed. "I know. There's more. Hillary says they're nervous about her being co-guardian for Brendan—that if something were to happen to me, she'd have Corwyn *and* Marley at her disposal until Brendan and Briony came of age. And then, if she were to betray *you*—"

"Alaric, that's insane!" Kelson blurted. "She's loyal! She'd never betray either of us! There must be some other explanation." He made a vexed face. "It's probably Hamilton and Hillary's fault, not wanting to let go of the authority they've had all these years you weren't married. One can hardly blame them for being jealous."

Morgan shook his head. "I wish it were that simple, my prince. Actually, Hamilton and Hillary like her very much. They're as mystified as you and I. But a few of *their* officers have come right out and told them they can't be responsible for the men's behavior if I leave her in charge and something goes wrong—even if it isn't her fault." He sighed. "So I *haven't* given her any authority, and I haven't been able to bring myself to tell her why. It would make it seem like I agreed with them."

Kelson was sobering fast as he listened to Morgan's account, and he set aside his cup with a grimace of distaste as Morgan finished.

"You should have told me sooner."

"I didn't want to bother you. Before Carsten of Meara died and everything blew up, I thought I'd be home all winter and get things straightened out. Now it's going to be the end of next summer before I get home. I didn't know she was coming for Christmas court, you know, but I'm glad she did, under the circumstances. Rhemuth will be the best place for her until I get things sorted out."

"You still should have told me. Does Duncan know?"

"No. No one else." He broke off as Duncan appeared in the garderobe doorway supporting a weak and contrite Dhugal.

"He's going to be fine," Duncan called, grinning as he helped Dhugal cross the room and sit gingerly in his former place. "He isn't nearly as drunk now as he was a few minutes ago, are you, son? I think he's learned a valuable lesson, too."

"Aye. Never again," Dhugal nodded miserably. "What kind of wine *was* that, anyway? I've *never* felt this awful before, just from drinking."

Lazily, Morgan raised his cup to sniff at its contents. "Fianna red. It's quite good, actually. Does your head hurt?"

"Like a smithy's forging swords," Dhugal muttered, palming across both his eyes and tipping his head against the chair back. "I may die."

Duncan, perching casually on Dhugal's chair arm, slipped one hand behind the back of Dhugal's head and began to massage at the base of his skull, steadying him with his other hand on a shoulder as Dhugal sighed and immediately began to relax. Morgan, guessing what Duncan was about and sensing that Dhugal did not, glanced at Kelson and prepared to divert Dhugal's attention further. At least they might salvage something for Dhugal from this evening's work.

"Well, I suppose we all know *that* feeling," he said with a smile, sending the king a hint of their intentions. "Red wine is the worst offender, too. I remember one night with Derry in Jennan Vale—long before you were king, Kelson—when he and I got so drunk on the local vintage that I was sure it was the end of both of us. Derry can really drink, too. He got up on a table and sang a song...."

He spun the yarn for several minutes, he and Kelson watching Dhugal fall increasingly under Duncan's influence all unawares, the hands slowly sinking to rest on his lap, the lines disappearing from his forehead as he relaxed in sleep. After a few more minutes, Duncan shifted one hand briefly to cover Dhugal's closed eyes. When he looked up at Morgan and Kelson, he grinned.

"Well done. He isn't exactly controlled, but he's asleep. I didn't want to push my luck. The shields are still very much in place. And if he thought he had a headache just now, wait until morning!"

"I'd rather *not* think about that," Kelson muttered.

"Ah, but *you* have a choice," Morgan said, shifting back in his chair and setting aside his cup with a grin. "One of the side-benefits of having healing talents is being able to ease the morning after. Actually, we could probably help Dhugal, too, but it's much harder having to work around shields. Maybe that will be an incentive for him to learn to lower them."

"I hope *something* soon is!" Kelson murmured. Sighing, he stood and ran a hand through his rumpled hair. "But it's time we all got some sleep, I suppose. Duncan, why don't you bring Dhugal on into my room; there's plenty of room for two in my bed, at least until tomorrow night—and then you and Alaric can put me out of my misery as well."

A little unsteadily, but declining Morgan's offer of assistance, the king led the way into the sleeping chamber and shed his outer garments.

"Make everything be right when I wake up, Alaric," he whispered, as he lay back and Morgan sat down beside him. "Please."

"Close your eyes and go to sleep, my prince," Morgan said softly.

He let himself sink into trance as Kelson obeyed, spreading his hand across Kelson's forehead to touch the closing eyelids with thumb and middle finger, wrapping his consciousness lovingly around that of his king and guiding it into stillness. After a few seconds, Duncan joined him in rapport, the two Deryni gradually extending ease and healing upon the king, comfort to soul and mind as well as body.

Epiphany dawned cold but clear for the royal nuptials. Shortly after dawn, Morgan was already attending to the few remaining details that must be resolved before the start of the bridal procession, which would wind its way from Rhemuth Keep down to the cathedral below. He did not mind rising early, since his bed was empty anyway—though in a good cause. Richenda had spent the night with the nervous royal bride. Two hours before the wedding procession was to begin, heading down the corridor that led past Kelson's apartments, he met Duncan just emerging.

"How is he?" Morgan asked, as the two of them continued on down the corridor.

Duncan smiled. "Well enough. I've just heard his confession—and he's as nervous as I've ever seen him over something that isn't mortally dangerous—but he's in good spirits. 'Hopeful' is probably be the best word to describe him."

"Well, that's reassuring," Morgan said. "How about Dhugal?"

"I don't know. He'd gone to change before I arrived. I gather that loud noises and sudden movements are not his favorite things just now, however. Poor lad."

"Well, we all had to learn that the hard way, didn't we?" Morgan replied. "Incidentally, and on a far more optimistic note, did you know that Llewell's consented to lead his sister's horse this morning, and to stand witness to the marriage?"

Duncan chuckled. "I'm not surprised to hear it. I'm

told he had Bradene hear his confession yesterday. Apparently he's quite contrite."

"More likely, Nigel sat him down and had a little chat about the realities of being a hostage prince," Morgan snorted. "But—well, look who's still alive despite his hangover!" he added jovially, as Dhugal came around a corner at the far end of the corridor, headed in their direction.

The boy wore formal border garb this morning: bright MacArdry tartan pleated around his body and caught at the shoulder of his doublet with silver, hair braided and knotted in customary border fashion and tied with black silk. He sketched a half-hearted bow as they met, but the movement obviously distressed him. Morgan laid a comradely hand on his shoulder and leaned down to peer into the bloodshot eyes, giving him a speculative smile.

"What's wrong, Dhugal?"

"That isn't funny, sir," Dhugal whispered, grimacing. "It isn't fair, either. Kelson acts like he didn't have a thing to drink last night. I feel like the top of my head is going to come off."

Morgan raised one eyebrow and clucked his tongue sympathetically. "Well, when you learn to lower those shields of yours, we'll be able to cure your hangover, too, won't we, Duncan?" he quipped.

But Duncan's face was still and devoid of expression, his mind suddenly shut tight to Morgan's tentative and surprised probe. Morgan could isolate no one thing which made him aware of something not quite right, but the shadow was there. Duncan blinked as he felt their eyes on him, as if dragging himself up from contemplation of something grim and even soul-shaking.

"Duncan?"

"I'm sorry. I was thinking about something else. What was it you asked?"

"I was just teasing Dhugal about his hangover," Morgan said, trying to make light of Duncan's sudden change of mood. "Did you forget to do something?"

"Yes, I did," Duncan replied, seizing gratefully on the

excuse Morgan offered. "I need to go back to my quarters for a few minutes. Could you give me a hand?"

"Of course. Do you think it will take very long?"

"No. Just something I need you for." Duncan glanced back at Dhugal. "We're probably keeping you from your duties as well, Dhugal. I must say that it's pleasant to see formal border garb at court again, however. Is your cloak clasp a MacArdry design?"

"This?" Dhugal pulled the cloak clasp away from his body with a thumb and glanced down at it. "No, I don't think so. My father had it when he was a boy. I don't know where he got it. He gave it to my mother the day they were married, and she left it to me when she died. I don't wear it very often, but Kelson thought it was appropriate for a wedding. It *is* rather striking, isn't it?"

"Yes it is." Duncan glanced at Morgan even more urgently. "But, I really must take care of that errand. Alaric, are you coming?"

The Deryni bishop would say nothing else as he led Morgan not to his apartments but to the little study where they had met after his consecration. Nor would he lower his shields. Only when they were inside did he relax a little, though he still was like a tightly wound spring as he crossed to the little prie-dieu in the corner by the window and dropped to his knees. Morgan watched him curiously from the center of the chamber, not pressing a contact. Finally, Duncan crossed himself and stood, turning a grave profile toward the amber glass of the window.

"You're owed an explanation for the last little while," he said softly, beckoning Morgan to come closer. "I can only say that this is something that never occurred to me in my wildest dreams. It's—going to take some getting used to."

Morgan frowned as he stopped within arm's reach of Duncan, afraid to touch him.

"Would you please tell me what you're talking about? What's wrong? You look like you've seen a ghost."

"In a way, I suppose I have." Duncan chewed on his lower lip and sighed. "Alaric, I wasn't just being courteous when I complimented Dhugal on his border garb and asked about that cloak clasp. And then, when he told me where he'd gotten it—"

He sighed again, dropping his gaze to the violet slippers showing at the hem of his cassock.

"That clasp used to be mine, Alaric. I gave it to Dhugal's sister many years ago, under exactly the circumstances he described." He paused to swallow with difficulty.

"Only—now I think the 'brother' born a little while later may not have been her brother at all. I—think Dhugal may be her son—and mine."

# CHAPTER TWENTY

*Yet will I bring an heir unto thee.*
                                              —Micah 1:15

As Duncan raised his eyes to Morgan's, he did not need Deryni abilities to read the shock and astonishment written there. He knew that he must be projecting much the same feeling himself. He, like Morgan, was finding it hard to believe, but the clasp spoke for itself—and Dhugal would be *exactly* the right age.

The memories of those long-ago years started to well into consciousness, but Duncan pushed them down for just another moment as he gestured toward the two chairs facing the fireplace. He tried to keep his shields closed and not to think much at all as he made his feet move in that direction and Morgan followed, and could not quite decide whether it was elation or stark terror threatening to overwhelm him when he unleashed the memories at last. He sat, eyes unfocused through the fire on the hearth, and was only dimly aware of Morgan sitting down beside him, moving his chair closer to face him almost head-on, so that their knees were nearly touching.

"Suppose you tell me about it," Morgan said softly. "I'm not a priest, but I think you know that my word of confidence is just as binding to me as any sacramental seal."

Duncan allowed himself a wry smile. "If it's true, I doubt I'm going to be able to keep it secret very long," he said in a low voice. "If I could have chosen a son, he would have been very much like Dhugal. And if he *is* my son, then he has a right to know."

"Sometimes it's better not to know," Morgan said tentatively. "If he's illegitimate—"

"My son is not a bastard!" Duncan said emphatically. "His mother and I were free to marry at the time, and we exchanged vows which we considered binding. In our eyes and in the eyes of God, she was my wife."

"And in the eyes of the law?"

Duncan shook his head and sighed. "That I don't know. It's going to be a tricky point of canon law, at very least. It's called—" He dug for the term, forcing calm on his mind by the discipline. "I think it's called *per verba de praesenti*—a vow in front of witnesses, rather than a ceremony performed by a priest. At least in theory, it's as binding as a betrothal, which is as binding as a marriage."

"You can produce the witnesses?" Morgan asked.

Duncan hung his head, remembering that night so very long ago, shrouded in that twilight land of memory between childhood and maturity—he and Maryse kneeling in the chapel at midnight, fearful of interruption at any time, making their prayers before the only witness whose understanding they could count on, with her father's men preparing to move out of his father's courtyard at the break of dawn.

"*Before Thee as the Supreme Witness, my Lord and my God, I make this solemn vow,*" Duncan had said, eyes turned toward the Presence Lamp burning brightly above the altar. "*That I take this woman, Maryse, as my lawful wedded wife, forsaking all others until death do us part.*"

The pin of the clasp at his throat was stiff, and he had fumbled as he unfastened it and laid it in her hand, gazing down at her with all the desperation of love soon to be parted.

"*I give thee this token of my love and take thee for my wife, and hereto I plight thee my troth.*"

"The witnesses," came Morgan's soft prompting. "Can you produce them?"

Duncan's shoulders slumped and he shook his head. "We spoke our vows before the Blessed Sacrament, Alaric," he said softly. "There was none other we could trust. As I said, the strict legality will be considered to be hazy."

"I see." Morgan sighed. "Very well, let's not worry about that for the moment. How do you know that the clasp Dhugal is wearing is the one you gave—what was her name? Maryse?"

"Yes." Duncan swallowed painfully. "The—clasp that I gave as pledge was unique. The artisan who'd made it put a sort of locket compartment in the back. Unless one knew what to look for, it would never even be noticed. If that *is* my clasp, then in that compartment there will be one of my hairs intertwined with one of hers. She had very fair hair—almost white."

Morgan sighed again, even more heavily than before.

"Very well. What do you intend to do about this? Do you want to confront Dhugal now, or can it wait until after the wedding?"

"I don't think I can wait, Alaric," Duncan replied, looking up at his cousin's face for the first time since his confession. "I know it may sound strange, after all these years, but I have to know. I don't think I could stand up there, across from him, and celebrate Kelson's marriage, and not know whether my brief marriage bore fruit or not."

Morgan nodded slowly. "Being a father myself now, I can understand that," he said softly, then quirked an odd, lopsided grin back at him. "If Dhugal *is* your son, though, won't *that* throw consternation into the Mearan ranks? You'd have an heir of your body to succeed to the Cassan and Kierney titles—and so much for the hopes of re-uniting those lands with Meara for an independent kingdom again."

Duncan snorted. "That honestly hadn't occurred to me, but you're right. And all the more reason for finding out, and then figuring out how to acknowledge him so that there can be no question of the right to the titles." He glanced back at the fire. "I certainly could have asked for better timing, though. A bishop's son is going to raise more than a few eyebrows."

"You weren't a bishop at the time, or even a priest."

"No. It's still going to smack of conspiracies, however."

"I couldn't agree more. Would you like me to go and find him? We've not much time, but I'll do the best I can."

"Please do," Duncan whispered. "Don't tell him why I want to see him, though. I—need to do that myself."

"Believe me, that's the last thing I intend to do," Morgan murmured, as he rose and left the room.

Duncan did not move for several seconds. One hand over his face, he tried to push back the hope, the expectation, just in case he was mistaken. He told himself there were many ways Dhugal could have gotten the clasp— if, indeed, it really was the same one. He tried to tell himself it might not be. But deep inside, he knew it was, and how it had come into Dhugal's keeping.

Though neither he nor Maryse had thought about the possibility of issue, in that one, brief, tearful, fumbling union of innocents, he saw the scenario as it unfolded behind his closed eyelids: Maryse, months later, safe back at Transha for the winter, her father and elder brothers off to war with the king's troops, discovering that she was with child. Fearful, at first, to tell another soul, but then, as it became less and less possible to hide, the tearful confession to her mother, who was also expecting—and the plan evolving, so that Maryse might bear her child in secret and give it to her mother, to be raised as twin to the child due a month or so before. In the fastness of a border winter, with the menfolk wintering in Meara, and the circumspectness of a few serving women, who would have known?

And then, when Maryse died, whether of childbirth complications or the fever which was given out as the reason, who else was to know? Duncan, when he had heard of her death the following summer, certainly had never put two and two together. News of her death had only turned him back to his original plans to continue in holy orders and become a priest. Before too long, the brief, intense days at Culdi held only the poignant memory of a particularly vivid dream which now would never be.

He had never told a soul, save a long-dead confessor—not even Morgan.

Blinking back tears, Duncan rose and went to the desk beneath the amber window, taking out the *shiral* on its fine leather cord. It had been *her* gift—and all unwittingly, he had used it to test their son for sign of magical heritage which *certainly* existed; no doubt about that now. He held it by the cords as he returned to his chair and sat, holding it before his eyes like the talisman it had become.

*Shiral*.

As he closed it in his fist, he was taken back to that chapel again, and the vows they had made.

"*I take thee as my wedded husband*," she had said. "*I give thee this token as a sign of my love, and hereto I plight thee my troth*."

She had taken it from her own neck, still warm from her body, and placed it around his neck. Trembling, he placed it there again and pressed the stone to his lips, startling as a knock at the door intruded on the memory.

"Come," he called, slipping the necklace into the front of his cassock.

He rose as they came into the room, Morgan ushering a curiously expectant Dhugal.

"You wanted to see me, Father Duncan?" the boy asked.

Duncan hardly trusted himself to speak as he gestured for Dhugal to be seated. Morgan was looking very uncertain, but Duncan nodded for him to remain as well.

"Sit down, please—both of you," Duncan said, himself sitting as Dhugal complied. "I—realize this is awkward timing, but I didn't think it could wait. It—may get more awkward, yet."

"I don't think I understand," Dhugal replied, perching gingerly on the edge of his chair. "Is it something I've done?"

Duncan smiled despite his apprehension. "No, nothing you've done. Would you indulge me for just a moment?"

"If I can."

"Very well. Without asking me why, I'd like you to take off your cloak clasp and look at the back of it."

With a puzzled glance at Morgan, Dhugal obeyed, fumbling wordlessly with the pin. When he had given the back a cursory glance, he looked up at Duncan in question. The bishop was gazing into the fireplace, the flames reflecting from his light eyes.

"What am I supposed to see?" Dhugal whispered, after a slight hesitation.

Duncan swallowed visibly. "Along the top edge, you'll find a fine crack. If you'll pry it with a fingernail, it should open. If there's something inside, I'd like you not to tell me what it is, just yet. All right?"

With a shrug and a puzzled glance at the stony-faced Morgan, Dhugal grunted his agreement and worried at the clasp with a thumbnail. He jumped a little as something gave, then bent to peer more closely into the compartment he had just discovered.

"What the—how did you know? How did you know there was even a compartment?"

Duncan gave a resigned sigh and sat back in his chair, covering his eyes with the hand nearest Dhugal and leaning wearily on that elbow.

"May I tell you a brief story, Dhugal?" he whispered.

Mystified, Dhugal nodded and sat back in his chair, still glancing down at the clasp in his hand from time to time.

"Your description of how you came by the clasp struck the first chord," Duncan murmured. "How your father gave it to your mother when they were married. I've never told anyone about this before, but something like what you described happened to me when I was only a little younger than you. I fell in love with a beautiful and loving young girl, and all thought of becoming a priest went out of my mind. She was from your clan, and we planned to ask our parents' permission to be married as soon as our fathers returned from the campaign they were on. That's why she and her mother and sisters were at my father's castle.

"Something happened between the clans while they were on that campaign, however. Her eldest brother was killed in a drunken brawl with one of my father's men, and there was the very real possibility of a bitter blood feud, even though the guilty McLain man was duly executed. Her father and his men came back to Culdi just long enough to pack up the women and children and prepare to ride out the following dawn.

"In any case, to make a long story short, we realized that our fathers would never let us marry, under the circumstances—at least not for a very long time—so we exchanged vows in the darkened chapel. She gave me a token, and I gave her a cloak clasp very similar to the one in your hand. In fact, that could be the very one."

Dhugal had followed the entire story with increasing amazement, and now he glanced at the clasp in his hand again, suspicion beginning to niggle at the edges of consciousness.

"May—may I ask what her name was?" he breathed.

"Maryse MacArdry," Duncan whispered. "And if only in the eyes of ourselves and of God, she was my wife for that brief night."

"But—Maryse was my sister's name. She died the same winter I was born."

"Yes, I heard that the following summer," Duncan said, "and that her mother had borne twins about the same time. Until I saw you wearing that cloak clasp, it had never even occurred to me that one of those children might be mine."

"You mean, me?" Dhugal asked, in a very small voice.

Duncan dropped his hand to look full into Dhugal's eyes.

"Shall I tell you what you found inside the compartment of your cloak clasp?" he asked.

Solemnly, fearfully, Dhugal nodded.

"The afternoon before we made our vows, Maryse took strands of our hair and wove them into a ring, using longer strands from our ponies' tails to form the framework. I know that you don't remember her, if you ever even saw her, but you may have seen paintings. Her hair was silver blond, even lighter than Alaric's. The horsehairs were black. I think that's what you'll find, if you'll pull out what's inside."

Almost afraid to breathe, Dhugal prodded at the compartment in the clasp and worried loose precisely that: a mostly dark ring of hair, oval in shape from having been compressed, with a strand of purest silver braided into the design. As Dhugal held it tremblingly between his thumb and forefinger, not daring to speak, Morgan leaned forward and spoke for the first time.

"If one of the hairs is Duncan's, I'll be able to detect it, Dhugal," he said quietly. "And if it isn't, I'll tell you that, too. May I hold it?"

Wordlessly, Dhugal placed it on his outstretched palm, glancing fearfully at Duncan as he did so. Morgan closed his eyes for several seconds, the ring closed lightly in his fist then passed it across to Duncan.

"It *is* one of your hairs," he said softly. "But that doesn't prove that Dhugal is your son—only that you probably did have the relationship with Maryse that you've described. Dhugal could still be Caulay's child. You have a twin sister, don't you, Dhugal?"

"It—sounds like I have another aunt or niece," Dhugal breathed, "depending on which one of us was Maryse's child."

"That's true," Duncan murmured. "But I would be willing to wager everything I hold dear, including any slight chance I may have of salvation, that you are Maryse's child. Shall I tell you why?"

Dhugal nodded solemnly.

"Because Maryse's child by me would be part Deryni— and I think that's what we've been getting hints of, ever since you and Kelson got back together," Duncan said steadily. "I think that night at Transha, when you helped Kelson reach Alaric, was a catalyst that went awry. Your Deryni potentials started to be touched for the first time, but it was frightening, and you froze up. That would also explain why, when we later tried to read you and find out what had been going on, you felt most comfortable with me. Do you remember?"

Dhugal's eyes had been getting wider and wider as Duncan spoke; now his hands were trembling. Quickly he clamped them together to make them stop, not daring to take his eyes from Duncan's.

"I—want to believe you," he finally managed to whisper. "I mean no disrespect to my f—to Lord Caulay, but if—if you *are* my father, it would certainly explain a lot."

Slowly Duncan drew deep breath. The time was come to take the final chance.

"I know of only one way to prove that to you, beyond what I've already done, Dhugal," he said softly. "If I *am* your father, then you're Deryni, too. And if you're Deryni, then—if you're willing—I should be able to form a mind-link with you and show you exactly what I remember about your mother and me. I loved her very much, Dhugal, and I've come to care a great deal for you, over the years, before I ever suspected you might be my son. I can't make up for all the years you've lived in ignorance—and that's the fault of no one who's still alive—but I can try to bridge the gap now that I know it's there. Do you trust me?"

"Yes," Dhugal breathed.

"No, do you *really* trust me?" Duncan insisted. "You trusted me before and weren't able to let me in. Do you think you might be ready now?"

"Duncan, I'm not sure we really have the time," Morgan murmured.

"If it's going to work without a lot of trouble, it isn't going to *take* a lot of time," Duncan replied, not taking his eyes off the boy. "We'll be given the time, if that's what Dhugal really wants."

Dhugal swallowed and nodded. "He's right, Morgan," he breathed. "We have to try it now. Would you go to Kelson, please, and tell him I'll be there directly? Don't tell him what's happened. He has enough to think about just now."

"Duncan?" Morgan asked.

"Do as he asks," the priest replied. "We'll be all right."

# CHAPTER TWENTY-ONE

*I will be to him a Father, and he shall be to me a Son.*

—Hebrews 1:5

As soon as the door had closed behind Morgan, Duncan glanced at Dhugal.

"We haven't any time to spare," he said softly. "If you want your proof now, you're going to have to do exactly as I say, perhaps without as full an explanation as either of us would want."

Dhugal shook his head slowly. "I don't want to wait, Fa—" He lowered his eyes. "I just realized that maybe I've been calling you by the proper name all these years," he continued softly. "Strange, but it somehow feels so much more comfortable than when I used to call Caulay my father."

"He *was* your father, in all the ways that are most important to a boy growing up. I wish I'd had the chance to watch you grow. Of course, I did, in a way, knowing you at court and all—but I think I might have felt differently if I'd known you were my son."

"Maybe it was meant to be this way," Dhugal replied shyly. "Maybe I had to lose one father before I could find the other. If I'd known about you while Caulay was still alive, I wouldn't have wanted to hurt him."

"Nor I. And I hope you'll always honor his memory." Duncan smiled as he laid a hand lightly on Dhugal's forearm. "He gave you his name and his protection in the years when you were most vulnerable. Now that he's gone and you're a man, no one will be hurt by the truth." The smile broadened to a grin.

"You should know that there's at least one complication that could be—ah—awkward, at best. If I'm to acknowledge you, as is my intention—if you want it, that is—there are going to be those who will call you bastard in addition to Deryni, of course."

Dhugal smiled. "They've called you and Morgan bastards for years. Somehow I've never gotten the impression that had anything to do with your paternity."

"No." Reaching into the front of his cassock, Duncan rose and moved a stool in front of Dhugal's chair, withdrawing the *shiral* crystal on its leather thong as he sat.

"You remember this," he said simply, placing it in Dhugal's hand. "It was your mother's. She gave it to me the night I gave her the cloak clasp."

Dhugal ran a thumb across the rough-polished stone and nodded slowly. "What am I supposed to do this time?"

"I'll do most of what needs to be done. All I ask is that you try to be open and unafraid. We'll try to use the crystal as a link between us. You may feel some odd sensations, perhaps even some uncomfortable ones, but I promise I won't hurt you. To start, all I want you to do is concentrate on the crystal and try to seen Maryse in your mind's eye. *Have* you seen paintings of her?"

Dhugal closed the crystal in his fist and gave another nod.

"One miniature. That was a long time ago, though."

"Then let me paint a picture in your mind with my words," Duncan said softly, closing one hand around Dhugal's hand that held the crystal and resting the other on top of his head as if in benediction. "Close your eyes and try to see her, in as much detail as you can remember. Don't force it, though; try to coax it. See her fair hair, like molten silver flowing halfway down her back, bound across the brow with a fillet of tiny metal flowers . . . primroses, I think they were."

He could feel Dhugal relaxing under his touch, and he, too, closed his eyes, seeing the image of a long-lost love.

"There were tiny golden stones set in the centers of

the flowers, the exact shade of her eyes—almost the same shade as yours," Duncan went on quietly. "And she wore a gown of pink that matched her blush . . . fair, very fair skin. . . ."

As he spoke, gently insinuating thoughts along with words, he could begin to read the image forming in Dhugal's mind as well as his own, just on the surface at first, then gradually eroding the pulsing, troublesome shields.

"She had a laugh like silver bells . . . a serenity as still and deep as the lake at Shannis Meer. . . ."

Even as Duncan's voice trailed off and he tried a stronger probe, he was past Dhugal's shields and in his mind, driving the memories across the unconscious links and into Dhugal's consciousness, holding the channel open relentlessly when Dhugal sensed what was happening and would have drawn back in momentary panic. He felt Dhugal gasp as something psychic snapped, but he damped the sharp wrench of pain which followed even as he pulled Dhugal closer and gave him physical comfort.

All in an instant, all the barriers were down and Dhugal was with him, reliving those halcyon days with Maryse. Shy meetings in corridor and castle hall, wind-blown rides on the downs around the castle, shared meals of travel fare under the forest canopy of nearby Alduin, tender glances and shy, chaste kisses in the warm, earthy shadowspace between their ponies, sheltered from prying eyes—

And then the clans were home, the awful news spreading: how Ardry MacArdry, tanist of Maryse's clan, had quarrelled with a McLain retainer over a tavern wench . . . MacArdry blood spilling . . . the hangman's noose for the murderer and grim, silent escort for both bodies back to Culdi, just long enough for the MacArdry to gather up the rest of his family and go, before a blood feud broke out anew.

Maryse's panic as they realized the personal significance of what had happened . . . Duncan's despair . . . defiant agreement in a castle hallway to meet in the chapel later that night . . . the rendezvous itself—desperate, fearful at the presumption as they made their vows before God alone. . . .

And then the consummation, in a warm, sheltered corner of the stable loft—hurried, fumbling, only partially satisfying, but joyous, nonetheless . . . and parting so soon after . . . and parting for good, the next morning, as Duncan watched her and her family ride out of Culdi and out of his life, neither of them dreaming that she carried the child of their love. . . .

The sheer force of the emotion which surged with Duncan's remembrance flooded through Dhugal's mind with such a pressure that no resistance was possible; nor, once the pathways were in use, did Dhugal feel any further fear or apprehension. Duncan sensed almost the exact instant when Dhugal made that conscious choice to let the mind-link fill him—and the surge, as Dhugal opened to his father's mental touch, gave new impetus to the sharing Duncan now pursued even more.

Sparing only the areas of confidence which might not be shared with anyone—his priestly secrets and duties, the confidences of others—Duncan poured forth all the memories of the years he and Dhugal had lost, intertwining them with Dhugal's own—sparser, for sheer number, but no less potent and treasured, for his part. And Dhugal, once he sensed how it was done, entered joyously in the sharing.

Neither of them could later remember at what point Dhugal had lurched even closer to twine his arms around Duncan's waist, weeping, or when Duncan's own joyous tears began—only that, when the sharing at last began to ebb and normal consciousness gradually intruded, they found themselves huddled together for comfort, Dhugal half in his father's lap, Duncan gently stroking his son's hair and soothing as he withdrew mental contact, the old barriers gone between them.

"Are you all right?" Duncan whispered after a moment.

Sniffling contentedly, Dhugal drew away far enough to look at Duncan and nod, dragging a sleeve across his eyes.

"My head hurts a little, right behind my eyes, but it's probably just my hangover. It's all right."

"Let's see if I can make it better than all right," Duncan murmured, laying his hand over Dhugal's forehead and touching thumb and middle fingers to the quickly closed eyes. "Take a deep breath and let it out ... and feel the pain dissolving. That's right."

Only the lightest of healing touches was required to ease the afterache. Duncan could read it across the light rapport between them as easily as he could read Morgan, when they worked together. As he withdrew his hand, Dhugal opened his eyes to stare at him in awe. This time, all shadow of discomfort was gone from behind the almond-amber eyes.

"Was that your healing magic?" Dhugal asked.

"Just a little," Duncan smiled. "And if you don't get off my leg, I'm going to have to heal a terminal muscle cramp," he added, shifting Dhugal's weight and wincing as circulation started to return. "I'm afraid we didn't plan this very well. I should have made you more comfortable."

Awkwardly, and almost a little embarrassed, Dhugal staggered to his feet, weaving a little until Duncan guided him back to the edge of the chair.

"I'm only a little wobbly," Dhugal protested. "I'll be fine. Kelson must be waiting for us, though. I can hardly wait to tell him."

"I—think we'd better wait until after the ceremony for that," Duncan said, steadying him by the shoulder. "Your first instinct was very good. He has a few other things on his mind right now. This will keep."

"But, aren't we late?"

Duncan shook his head. "What we did took far less time than you think. You've got time to catch your breath."

"Oh." With a shy grin, Dhugal let himself relax a little, then impulsively snatched up Duncan's hand and pressed it to his lips.

"Father," he whispered wonderingly. "You really are my father—and that means I'm Deryni, too." He paused to swallow. "Do you know that I wished about the Deryni part, that first time I saw Kelson use his powers? He put a man to sleep, so that I could sew up his arm. I thought I was just dreaming at the time, but was I starting to realize, even then?"

"Perhaps," Duncan answered gently. "I expect your skill with horses probably comes from that, too. Bronwyn used to call the birds. Maybe you'll even make a healer some day."

"Me? A healer? Oh, but I could never learn it all. It must take years."

"We'll have the years now," Duncan murmured. "We'll be given the time and the teachers. You'll be amazed at how fast some of the skill comes, once you know what you are. And Alaric and I can teach you what we know— and Richenda."

"Lady Richenda is Deryni?"

"Aye, and trained in a far different tradition than Alaric and I were. You'll enjoy getting to know her."

Dhugal blushed. "If she'll ever speak to me. Do you think Duke Alaric told her what I said about her last night? I didn't mean it the way it sounded—honestly."

"I know you didn't, son. And if Alaric *has* told her, I'm sure she hasn't taken offense. Speaking of Alaric, however, I think it probably *is* time to join him and Kelson now."

"Aye, and see our king properly married!" Dhugal agreed. He remembered the *shiral* as he stood, and touched it to his lips almost reverently as he held it out to Duncan.

"Here. You probably ought to have this back."

"No, you keep it, in memory of your mother."

"But—that leaves you with nothing of hers," Dhugal began.

"It leaves me with everything," Duncan replied, touching a fingertip to Dhugal's cheek. "I have her son."

And in another chamber not far away, another, spiritual son prepared for his nuptials, fretting and impatient as his dressers made final adjustments to his wedding finery. The velvet of Kelson's full-length crimson cloak was powdered with scores of tiny Haldane lions worked in fine gold bullion, his tunic quartered in the same fabric for two panels and its reverse for the other two, silk-embroidered lions of scarlet on cloth of gold. As a compliment to his bride's highland ancestry, he had bound his hair at the nape of his neck with a golden cord, though it was not braided, border-style. A golden state crown of crosses and leaves intertwined had been brought out of the vaults of the castle treasury, said to have been worn by Malcolm Haldane at his wedding to another Mearan princess nearly a century before, and Kelson ran a careful finger along one of the leaves and glanced at Morgan as the dressers packed up the last of their accoutrements and left. Some even said the crown had once belonged to Cinhil Haldane, perhaps even the infamous Festils before him. If it had, perhaps Saint Camber had seen and even touched it.

"Do you think I'm doing the right thing?" Kelson asked Morgan, when they were alone at last. "It isn't what I always dreamed of, God knows—a marriage of state, with a girl I hardly know, much less love."

"Are you asking for a reiteration of all the objective reasons why the marriage should take place?" Morgan countered.

"God, no! We've gone over them so many times, I could recite them by rote, in voices appropriate to the councillors who made each particular point." Kelson sighed. "I suppose I'm really asking whether you think there's any chance of real love creeping in amid all those reasons of state. I know objections of the heart have to come second to duty when one is king, but I can't help envying what you and Richenda have."

Morgan smiled, remembering his own fears on *his* wedding day, even though he and Richenda had loved one another as only Deryni, who had shared minds and dreams and fears, could. He doubted Kelson would ever find that perfect meshing of souls with the human Sidana, but who could say? Couples often fell in love *after* marriage, and grew to cherish one another. If both Kelson and Sidana made an honest effort, their union should not be too oppressive. And with peace as the potential prize—

"I won't try to tell you that I *know* you'll live happily ever after, as the bards would have us believe," he said after a moment. "It won't be easy. On the other hand, Richenda tells me that your princess does grow wistful about you on occasion. Of course Sidana would never admit that she's at least a little excited about your coming marriage—she's far too proud for that. But she *is* a beautiful, healthy young girl—and you are the most eligible, puissant, and attractive prince in all Christendom. How could she not find you desirable?"

Kelson blushed furiously. "Alaric, stop that! You're putting it on such a—a carnal level! If she *can* come to love me, I want our love to be—well, spiritual, like yours and Richenda's."

"Spiritual?" Morgan snorted. "Kelson, do you think that Richenda and I spend all our time alone discussing the spiritual aspects of our relationship."

"Well, I—"

"That's a part of it, of course," Morgan went on, "but I assure you that the 'carnal level,' as you put it, is very, very nice, as well. Don't sell your body short. It's a part of who and what you are. Lofty love is well and good for monks, and a healthy measure of it gives marriage deeper dimension; but especially with a human wife, where you won't have the potential for such sharing of minds, you're going to find that the physical act of love is a very special means of communication and communion in itself. And of course, on a very practical level, it's essential for begetting heirs."

"Yes, well—" Kelson turned and paced back and forth several times, hands clasped nervously before him, his cloak stirring around his heels. When he finally stopped to glance aside at Morgan again, he was a little paler against his crimson raiment.

"Alaric, I—never have, you know."

"I know," Morgan murmured sympathetically, but Kelson went on as if he had not heard.

"There—just hasn't been time—not to do it the way I'd always dreamed," the king whispered. "Oh, there could have been casual couplings with any number of serving wenches and maids and even ladies of the court—and one can hardly live in the close quarters of a castle, or on campaign, and not have seen and heard enough to know what that's all about. If all we're talking about is the physical drive, then every page and peasant boy soon learns how to relieve that. Princes are no exception. But I *am* more than just my body, Alaric. And even though I've never—been with a woman, I know there has to be more to making love than just the physical relief."

As Morgan nodded wisely, sensing no need for a verbal response, Kelson paused only long enough to draw breath before racing on, justifications and logic jumbling all together with emotion and the natural apprehensions of the sexually uninitiated.

"There's another thing, too," the king blurted, starting to pace again. "I'm the king. What if there had been children? The last thing I need complicating the already convoluted family relationships in Gwynedd is a succession of royal bastards to muddy the waters twenty years from now—or to become pawns in my enemies' hands at any time. And I'm Deryni, Alaric. My children will be, too. That alone might have been enough to ensure their deaths and those of their mothers. It just seemed . . . safer to abstain, and avoid the risk."

"It probably was," Morgan agreed.

"So that leaves me in the very awkward position of being a virgin on my wedding night," Kelson concluded. "That's fine for a woman; it's essential in the woman I marry. But—what if I don't know what to *do*, Alaric? What if she laughs at me?"

Morgan had all he could do not to smile. Was there a man alive who had not had such fears, at least in the beginning? And some never really lost those fears—though Kelson, with his gentleness and his genuine concern for others, was not likely to be left with that dilemma.

With avuncular understanding, then, Morgan put an arm around Kelson's shoulders and did his best to reassure, reminding the virgin Kelson of his young bride's similar state and suggesting ways that the king might sense how best to please her. That idea had never even occurred to Kelson. By the time Dhugal appeared at the door with the rest of the king's wedding procession, Kelson could relax and even banter with his more worldly foster brother as he put on his crown and went out to meet his bride.

* * *

The horses and the bride's company were waiting in the castle yard under a sky of palest winter blue, Sidana gowned in slightly darker shades of the same and seated on a milk white palfrey with white and silver bardings. The fine wool of her mantle, a deeper azure embroidered with golden pomegranates all around the hem, had been spread over her horse's rump so that it nearly trailed the ground in the back. She was crowned with a wreath of white roses, her long, chestnut hair spilling down her back to nearly veil the mantle.

Llewell stood at her horse's head, nervously knotting and unknotting the animal's white leather lead-rein in gloved fingers—a brooding shadow in darker blue than Sidana's, scowling into the sun. A little way behind, Richenda and three other ladies waited on pale grey palfreys, ready to attend the bride. Others of the king's attendants were already mounted up as well, Derry holding the reins of his black stallion. To one side, four of Kelson's knights were readying a canopy of sky blue silk to carry over the bride. None of the four ranked lower than an earl's son.

"We are blessed with fair weather for our nuptials, my lady," Kelson said, inclining his head in tentative greeting when he, Morgan, and Dhugal had made their way through the horses and bowing courtiers and stopped before her. "I trust that my people have made you welcome and carried out the preparations to your satisfaction."

"Satisfaction?" Llewell said before Sidana could reply. "How can there be satisfaction when we are prisoners?"

"Your bondage has been light, I think," Kelson murmured, hoping desperately that Llewell was not going to make a scene. "You have not been ill-used."

"Ah, and you do not consider that you ill-use my sister by forcing her to agree to this marriage?" Llewell asked.

*I thought he'd agreed to cooperate,* Morgan said to Kelson, as Sidana drew in a breath of horror and Kelson's jaw tightened. *Do you want me to put him to sleep?*

*No, just shake him up a bit. Sidana wants him to escort her.*

*As you wish.*

Without a flicker of warning, Morgan reached across to seize Llewell's upper arm in a vise-grip, though his pleasant expression did not alter.

"The lady has agreed to an honorable marriage," he said softly. "Now, *will* you hold your tongue, or must I thrash you over my knee for the spoiled, ill-bred young boor that you are?"

"You wouldn't dare!"

"Wouldn't I?"

"Llewell, please—"

"Stay out of this, Sidana!"

"My prince," Morgan murmured, his hand clamping tighter on Llewell's arm, "by your leave, I shall escort this young fool to a place where he can do no one any harm—himself included."

"Now yet. Llewell," Kelson said quietly, "you have found me an uncommonly patient man so far. You may judge the truth of that by the fact that you are still alive, even though your mother treacherously slew my bishop and you yourself claim to stand between your sister and the Mearan crown. Out of concern for the feelings of my bride, I am willing to overlook a great deal. But I will not have your insolence, and I will not have you disrupting your sister's wedding and coronation. Now, are you certain you want to pursue this line of resistance?"

Llewell's eyes blazed with undisguised hatred, but after a few seconds, he turned his head away.

"You'd only use your black magic on me, if I tried," he muttered into the horse's mane.

"What did you say?" Kelson gasped.

As Morgan jerked Llewell around to face them, even angrier than he had been, Kelson moved closer incredulously.

"I—said that you'd only use your accursed powers on me, if I didn't agree to cooperate!" Llewell said haltingly, still defiant, though he winced at the pressure of Morgan's fingers digging into his biceps. "As your Deryni priest did before."

"Are you *trying* to goad me into an act we'll both regret?" Kelson whispered.

"Llewell, *please*!" Sidana begged. "For *my* sake. You can't stop the marriage. You promised you would stand beside me. If they take you away, I'll be all alone!"

Heaving a heavy, defeated sigh, Llewell drew himself up with as much dignity as he could salvage from the situation, though Morgan's hand remained clamped on his arm.

"I see I am also alone," he said evenly. "But I'll not deprive my sister of the escort to which her rank entitles her. I'll—play my father's part and give away the bride, if it's the proper form you're looking for, Kelson of Gwynedd. But I'll be loathing you for every second!"

"Ah—*loathing* me." Kelson raised an eyebrow and smiled with relief. "Well, I can put up with that, I suppose, if you do as you're told. Morgan, you can let him go. My lady, I'm sorry you had to witness this."

"Please forgive my brother, my lord," Sidana whispered. "He only means to protect me."

"Sidana, I don't need to hide behind a woman's skirts!"

"*Will* you shut your mouth?" Morgan muttered.

As he raised a gloved hand in threat, Llewell drew back in alarm.

"Enough, Morgan!" Kelson said. "He's young and he's proud and hurting. Let's not make those fatal flaws. I will make you one threat, however, Llewell of Meara," he went on, turning the full force of his quicksilver gaze on the Mearan prince again. "I will remind you only once that Morgan and other loyal friends and vassals will be right at my side during the ceremony. If anything happens that isn't supposed to, and it's your fault—*anything*—I am here and now giving them free license to take whatever action they deem necessary. That assumes, of course, that I haven't dealt with you first. Do I make myself perfectly clear?"

"You do," Llewell muttered under his breath.

"I didn't quite hear that."

"You make yourself perfectly, *abundantly* clear," Llewell repeated sullenly.

"Good. Then we understand one another. My Lady?"

He glanced up at Sidana again, tentatively extending his hand, and to his surprise, she responded. Much heartened, he bent to brush her knuckles with his lips, more confident as he straightened and released her hand.

"My lady, I apologize again. A woman's wedding day should be joyous and free from care. I'm afraid I've started it out on rather a poor note."

"You have done what you had to do, my lord," she whispered, "and I, too, must once more beg pardon for my brother."

"Sidana!"

Ignoring Llewell's outburst, Kelson shook his head. "This is neither the time nor the place to speak further of the matter, my lady. Later, after we are wed, there will be time enough for everything. But for now, the archbishops are waiting—and the people—to see their new queen go to her marriage and coronation. May I give the commands for our procession to begin?"

"Do you ask *my* permission, my lord?" she said, amazed.

"Of course. You are my lady and my queen."

One look at her brother glaring up at her, hanging on her every gesture and expression, apparently was sufficient to keep Sidana from answering with words, but she shyly inclined her head nonetheless. To Kelson, it seemed more than just dutiful agreement. As he withdrew to the head of the procession where his horse waited, he signalled the knights to bring the canopy—blue silk powdered all over with tiny stars and moons—but his expression was jubilant once his back was safely to the Mearan prince and princess.

"Alaric, did you see?" he whispered, as Morgan held his stirrup and helped him mount, and Dhugal spread the crimson mantle over the horse's rump. "I think she *does* like me. Once we get her out from under her brother's thumb, who knows *what* might happen! Maybe it's going to work, after all."

As they started to move out, Morgan glanced back at

the small, lonely figure on the white horse, led to her
destiny beneath a canopy of silk; all their hopes of peace
wrapped up in one frail girl. He dearly hoped Kelson was
right.

# CHAPTER TWENTY-TWO

*For the Lord delighteth in thee, and thy
land shall be married.*

—Isaiah 62:4

To Kelson's already heightened senses, the bright-
etched images of the procession route were almost over-
whelming: crowds cheering, banners rainbow-hued,
fluttering above the streets, showers of snowdrops and
other winter flowers carpeting his path—and cheers and
flowers also for the dark-haired bride who followed. The
sounds and the colors carried him higher on a wave of
hope, and he grinned at Morgan and Dhugal, riding to
either side of him.

The streets were narrow and winding, the procession
thick with celebrants between him and his bride, but on
the few occasions when the way was straight or they
passed through a square, he could glance back and just
catch the top of her rose-crowned head under its silken
canopy. Once, their eyes met, and he almost fancied he
could feel the current leap between them, kindling anticipation in his brain and a white heat in his loins.

He told himself that he was imagining things, that he
was letting himself read too much into their earlier meetings—a word, a glance—but it was not in his nature to
hold back, once a commitment had been made. His body
was eager to unite with hers already, but he was also
resolved to make theirs a union of hearts as well as lands,
if he could. He tried not to think too much about the
coming wedding night. He was much relieved when they
reached the cathedral at last and he could dismount, turn-

ing mind as well as body to less physically distracting contemplation.

Archbishop Cardiel received him at the great doors, golden cope and mitre almost blinding in the noonday sun, rich counterpoint to Kelson's crimson and gold and the crown of leaves and crosses. When the two of them had exchanged formal greeting, archbishop bowing, king bending to kiss the episcopal ring, Arilan and Duncan joined them for more casual interchange, lace-lavished surplices immaculate and pristine over purple cassocks, gold glistening on stoles of snow white silk. Kelson accepted their greetings in something of a daze, pulling Morgan to him psychically as he made nervous conversation with the bishops, drawing on Morgan's calm as he shaped his own thoughts into more suitable framework for the sacrament he was about to exchange with Sidana. As the bride's procession began to enter the cathedral yard, king and escort fell into place behind the three prelates and went inside.

More clergy waited just beneath the western portico—the crucifer with Cardiel's processional cross, candle bearers, a flock of choristers—men and boys with fresh-scrubbed faces above the white and scarlet of surplices and choir cassocks—two older boys gently swinging censers. As the archbishop and the rest of the royal party joined them and the procession began to move down the nave, musicians in the gallery above trumpeted a royal fanfare and salute.

Kelson held his head high as he walked, oblivious to the scrutiny of the congregation, eyes focused on the roundel on the back of Cardiel's cope. He recognized the choir's anthem as a solemn *Te Deum*. Flanking him, he could feel the solid, reassuring presence of both Morgan and Dhugal: Morgan his usual pillar of bolstering calm, Deryni senses extended just slightly to give Kelson psychic substance to lean against—but even Dhugal seemed somehow more solid, more confident, almost Deryni himself in the steadiness of his presence, either not feeling or not minding the distracted but curious feather touches that Kelson sent fleetingly in his direction.

They crossed the transept, passing directly over the Camber seal, and Kelson briefly wondered what the Deryni saint would have thought of what he was about to do. As he recalled, Camber had arranged a marriage between his own ward and Cinhil Haldane, even before the Restoration. The name of Cinhil's eventual queen escaped him, but he toyed with the notion that she might have been crowned with the same golden coronet resting on the alter before them, shimmering in the light of the altar candles. He eyed it wistfully as he followed the bishops into the choir to approach the altar steps, also taking in the wedding guests standing in the choir stalls.

Nigel and Meraude held the places of honor to his right, closest to the altar, they and their three sons ranged along the front row of stalls. Others filled in behind them and on the other side: Ewan and Derry, Jodrell, Saer de Trah-erne—all the senior members of his court—their faces reflecting all the varied expectations of the marriage. Just before Kelson reached the altar steps, he caught Nigel's quick smile of reassurance, the fond, approving nod of his aunt.

*Lord, forgive me if I approach Thy altar with reservations in my heart,* Kelson prayed, as he paused behind the bishops at the foot of the steps and bent his knee to the Divine Presence. *Let me love the woman I am about to marry—and let her love me. And help me to be a wise and compassionate husband to her.*

Then the bishops were turning to face him in anticipation, he and his supporters shifting slightly to the right to turn and await the bridal procession. In the loft above the western doors, Kelson caught the glint of the trumpets being raised again—silvery notes sounding Sidana's fanfare this time, sweet and lingering. The choir began to sing a Psalm to greet a queen.

As the doors opened outward to reveal her, she seemed for an instant to be floating on a cloud of sunshine, so light that she might have drifted away, were it not for the anchor of her hand on her brother's arm. As the canopy moved slowly inside, she and Llewell following under its splendor, the white roses on her hair seemed to glow with a light of their own, lending her an almost Deryni nimbus in Kelson's Sight.

*O God, she wears peace like a mantle!* he thought, watching her approach him, eyes demurely downcast. He hardly even saw the tight-lipped Llewell, or Richenda and the other attendants following behind.

*Please, Lord, let it be peace between the two of us, as well as our lands. I don't want to have to kill her people. I don't want to have to kill anyone else. I want to create life, not death. Please, Lord....*

Then she and Llewell were genuflecting at the foot of the altar steps, mounting the steps to stand beside him, Llewell scowling between them. Flanked by Arilan and Duncan, Cardiel waited for the canopy to move into position, setting apart the place where the marriage rite would be performed. Morgan and Dhugal remained just outside the canopy, Richenda and the other attendants ranged to the other side, as Cardiel read from the Mass book, addressing the pale, attentive king.

*"Kelsonus, Rex Gwyneddis, vis accipere Sidanam hic praesentem, in tuam legitimam uxorem juxta ritum sanctae Matris Ecclesiae?"*

*Kelson, King of Gwynedd, wilt thou take Sidana, here present, to thy lawful wife according to our Holy Mother, the Church?*

*"Volo,"* Kelson breathed, not daring to glance in her direction. *I will.*

Bowing gravely, Cardiel turned his attention to the bride, asking her the same question.

*"Sidana, Princepessa Mearae, vis accipere Kelsonum, hic praesentem, in tuum legitimum maritum juxta ritum sanctae Matris Ecclesiae?"*

Holding his breath, Kelson allowed his glance to flick just slightly to his left, past the tight-jawed Llewell to his bride. Part of her glossy hair fell like a curtain over her right cheek, so that he could not see her eyes, but after only a slight hesitation her lips parted.

*"Volo,"* she whispered.

Kelson could almost hear Llewell's mental moan of despair, but he forced himself not to read it further. The boy was bred to duty, even as Kelson was. What purpose, for Kelson to disturb the calm which should be his own as he exchanged this sacrament of marriage with his future queen?

"Who giveth this woman in marriage?" Cardiel asked.

Woodenly, Llewell placed his sister's right hand in the archbishop's, only allowing himself a cold glance in Kelson's direction as he stepped back a pace. As Cardiel joined Sidana's cold, slightly clammy hand to her bridegroom's, Kelson permitted himself a tiny sigh of relief.

"Repeat after me," Cardiel said. "I, Kelson, take thee, Sidana . . ."

"I, Kelson, take thee, Sidana," Kelson said steadily.

"To my lawful wife . . ."

"To my lawful wife . . ."

His eyes were riveted on her face as he repeated the ancient formula, not daring to use his Deryni abilities for fear of what he might read there, but increasingly hopeful at the warmth he thought he sensed. Only as he finished did she raise her eyes to his for just an instant—and what passed between them then was like a flash of summer lightning, bright and hot, surging into every nerve and sinew.

The dark eyes were quickly lowered—had she felt it, too?—but the sensation lingered as she repeated her own part of the vows, her voice as cool and still as the sacred well at Candor Rhea, the ripples of her words stirring hope and even gentle promise of what might be. Kelson kept her hand in his when she had done, and she did not flinch or try to pull away as they looked back to Cardiel for the blessing of the ring.

But it was Duncan's hand that produced it, and Arilan's that blessed it, sprinkling it with holy water and then passing it through incense smoke with a special prayer. An artisan of Arilan's acquaintance had wrought it of Cassani gold—a Deryni craftsman of Camberian Council connections, the bishop had confided to Kelson alone, in a rare moment of candor about that particular aspect of his own life. On a flat, oval facet pared from the curve along the top, the man had etched a delicate Gwynedd lion, the eyes set with tiny rubies—fitting token to seal a new queen to her lord and land. Kelson's hand was trembling only a little as he recited the words after Duncan, slipping the ring briefly over the tips of thumb, forefinger, and middle finger before ending with her ring finger.

*"In nomine Patris, et Filii, et Spiritus Sancti, Amen."*

Cardiel joined their inside hands then, binding them ritually with the stole from Duncan's neck, all three bishops laying their hands on the joined ones as Cardiel pronounced his confirmation of the marriage vows:

*"Ego conjungo vos in matrimonium: In nomine Patris, et Filii, et Spiritis Sancti."*

In that holy moment, lulled by the great *"Amen"* chanted and embellished by the choir, no thought of danger entered Kelson's mind. Head bowed and eyes closed, hand locked to his bride's, he was too intent on savoring the fullness of his new estate to sense Llewell's heartsick shift from thought to deadly action.

Only as Sidana gasped and was half jerked from his grasp did he become aware—far too late to prevent it! Far too late for *anyone* to prevent it! With his hand tangled in the stole binding him to Sidana, he could not whirl in time to stop Llewell—or the deadly little knife the Mearan prince inexplicably produced from somewhere. The lightning flash this time was bright-honed steel glinting in the candlelight, dyed by a pluming shower of crimson as Llewell slashed it across his sister's throat in a single desperate stroke.

It seemed to Kelson that everyone but Llewell was encased in thick honey, moving far too slowly to do anything but gape in horror at Llewell's ghastly act. Even the blood fountaining from the victim's mortal wound seemed to hang suspended in space, Sidana's lips frozen in a silent *O*, the light in the brown eyes already fading as Kelson's scream echoed in the cathedral, both physical and psychic:

*"Nononononononono . . . !"*

Then all at once, *everyone* was moving. Shouts of outrage and dismay ripped the silence as Dhugal and the knights who had held the canopy swarmed over Llewell

and dragged him to the floor, trying to avoid his knife—
trying to keep him from turning it on himself. Kelson,
stunned almost past function by the senseless horror of
the act, caught the sinking Sidana to his breast and eased
her to the floor, one futile hand clamped to the awful
wound in her throat even as his eyes sought Morgan and
Duncan and his mind screamed for them to save her.

Blood gushed from her throat as they crowded around
her, drenching the blue of her gown and pooling in the
hair spread under her head like a cloak, staining the white
roses. Duncan's white surplice turned red almost in the
blink of an eye, his and Morgan's hands slick with her
blood as they tried to staunch her wound.

"Don't kill him!" Arilan commanded, as Dhugal and
the knights finally brought Llewell under control and
yanked him to his feet, battered and bruised. "That satisfaction is for another!"

Still Morgan and Duncan fought to save the mortally
wounded princess, Kelson staring numbly at the blood,
Cardiel finally summoning the initiative to begin shepherding horrified witnesses out of the choir, Arilan assisting. The two Deryni continued their feverish efforts for
yet a few more minutes, until finally Morgan looked up
at Kelson and shook his head, bloody hands lifted in a
vanquished, futile gesture. Duncan murmured a silent
prayer for Sidana's soul, making the sign of the Cross
over her bloody forehead, then sighed and also raised his
eyes to Kelson's. His once white surplice was drenched
with her blood, his hands red with it, and he could only
look up at Kelson helplessly, unable to offer any solace.

"Kelson, we tried," he whispered. "God help us, how
we tried! But it happened so fast—she lost so much blood,
so quickly...."

Before Kelson could respond, Morgan's glance flicked
to the panting, triumphant Llewell, bloody himself from
his rough handling, standing on wide-spraddled legs in the
midst of the hard-eyed knights, Dhugal with the bloody
dagger in his hand. In a single motion, Morgan was on
his feet and seizing Llewell by the throat of his tunic,

wrenching him downward, grey eyes as cold and brittle as an ice-filled sea.

"On your knees before your king, Mearan excrement!" he muttered between clenched teeth. "What kind of animal would slay his own sister on her wedding day?"

"Morgan, don't kill him!" Kelson snapped, turning a colorless face toward the two of them and raising a hand to stay Cardiel's alarm. "It's clear what he's done. I want to know why." He turned the full intensity of his Haldane gaze on the captive prince, though he did not move from his crouched position beside his bride.

"I'm waiting for an answer, Llewell. Why Sidana? Why didn't you go for me? You had the chance."

The cords of Llewell's neck were knotted with tension, but he did not flinch from Kelson's stare.

"Kill a Deryni?" He spat contemptuously and glared at Morgan and Duncan. "*They* would have stopped me, somehow. And even if they hadn't, and I'd killed you, it wouldn't have saved Sidana from a Haldane marriage. *He* would have been king after you," he jerked his chin toward the shocked Nigel, standing directly behind Kelson, "and he has three greedy little sons. I didn't want my sister besmirched by Haldane hands."

Kelson started to rise at that, anger beginning to smoulder away the grief, but Duncan grapped his sleeve and stopped him.

"Kelson, no!"

"If you don't intend to kill him, then give me the pleasure!" Morgan muttered, a stilleto appearing in his hand as he twisted Llewell's collar tighter and glanced beseechingly at the king.

"No!" Cardiel interjected. More boldly than Kelson had ever seen him, the archbishop grabbed Morgan's wrist and put himself between the prisoner and the king. "Let there be no more bloodshed in this house of God! Couldn't you have let it be, Llewell?" he added, shaking his head in pity as Morgan released the Mearan's throat and put away his blade. "She would have been Queen of Gwynedd as well as Meara. It could have ended almost a century of bloodshed. Do you realize what you've done?"

"I've given my brother back the chance to take his crown," Llewell said doggedly. "With another Meara-Haldane alliance, his claim always would have been in doubt. Let the King of Gwynedd find another queen. My sister was meant for a better mate. She is with the angels now."

"And you shall see her nevermore," Arilan said quietly, joining Cardiel. "There's a special place in hell reserved for murderers, Llewell."

Llewell only shook his head. "Hell will be welcome, if I've saved my sister from what *you* had planned for her, Bishop. Better she die than be queen to a curst Deryni king."

"I wish you well of it, then," Kelson said in the stunned silence. "But curst or not, I was prepared to love and honor your Sidana—and I think she meant to try, at least, to love and honor me."

Llewell spat. "She never loved you!"

Kelson only shook his head sadly as Morgan, with cool efficiency, snatched the bloody stole that had bound the couple's hands and bade one of the knights to gag Llewell with it.

"You may be right, Llewell," the king whispered. "You may, indeed, be right. But she *was* my queen, if only for a little while, and she shall be honored as a queen, at least in her final sleep."

He glanced at Morgan, blinking back the tears, then lowered his eyes.

"Take that—*person* out of here, Alaric. I don't want to see him again until after my queen has been laid to rest. I'll sit in judgment then. There can be no doubt of the outcome, but even Llewell shall receive the full benefit of the law."

"It shall be done, my prince," Morgan murmured, signalling the knights to carry out the order.

"And now, if you don't mind," the king continued in a failing voice, "I'd like to be alone with her for a few minutes. Uncle, take the rest of the family out as well, please."

Soon only Morgan, Duncan, and Dhugal remained in

the blood-spattered choir with the grieving king, Nigel and his family lingering in sight but out of earshot near a side door, reluctant to leave completely. Meraude and Richenda wept quietly in one another's arms, and even the three royal cousins looked subdued: Conall genuinely regretful and the two younger boys wide-eyed and still a little frightened at the violence they had witnessed. Sighing, Morgan crouched down beside the silent king, where Duncan also knelt. Dhugal stood white-faced and mute behind his father, helpless to offer comfort.

"Is there anything else you'd like me to do, my prince?" Morgan asked, resting a brief, sympathetic touch on the rigid shoulders.

Kelson only bowed his head and closed his eyes, mind tightly shuttered against intrusion.

"Go to your wife, Alaric," he whispered. "Please. She needs you now, and I—need to be alone."

"Very well. Duncan, Dhugal, are you coming?"

"In a moment," Duncan answered. "We'll meet you in the sacristy."

Sighing, Morgan rose and joined the others waiting for him, embracing Richenda for a few seconds, then simply letting his wife hold him before shepherding Nigel and his family out a side door. Kelson opened his eyes as Dhugal eased down silently beside Duncan, but he did not look up.

"Kelson, we have a lot to learn about a lot of things," Duncan said softly. "We tried, Alaric and I, but there simply wasn't time. If we were better trained—but who knows how to train healers, these days?"

"No one could have saved her," Kelson whispered. "She wasn't meant to live. It was all too easy. The perfect solution: for the king to marry the fair princess and unite the two lands, bringing peace...."

Dhugal swallowed audibly, tears springing to his own eyes. "It's my fault," he said. "I should have been watching Llewell more closely. If I'd—"

"It wasn't your fault," Kelson dully. "No one could have known Llewell would kill his own sister, rather than see her wed his mortal enemy. But when we'd gotten through the vows, I thought he'd accepted it."

"Kelson is right, son," Duncan said softly. "You couldn't have known. I doubt even Llewell knew, before the actual instant. One of us would have caught some hint."

Kelson shrugged and gave a heavy sigh. "It doesn't matter now, anyway. We did our best, with the best of intentions—and it wasn't enough. The Fates obviously have something else in store for us."

"Perhaps," Duncan said.

A taut silence fell between them, Dhugal unconsciously easing closer to his father for comfort, but Kelson was oblivious to them. After a moment, Duncan slowly rose, gathering his blood-caked surplice in his arms and motioning for Dhugal to join him.

"We'll leave you alone for a few minutes, then, Sire," he said softly. "I'll be back when I've changed. Dhugal, will you help me?"

"In a moment," Dhugal whispered, not moving.

"Very well."

Without further words, Duncan retreated slowly up the altar steps and through the sacristy door, leaving only Dhugal still kneeling beside the king.

"Kelson, I'm so sorry," Dhugal managed to whisper.

"I know. So am I."

"Did—did you really fall in love with her?" Dhugal asked.

"Fall in love?" Kelson shrugged dejectedly. "How should I know? I never had the time to find out. I think I'd convinced myself that I *could* love her, and I was prepared to do everything within my power to make her a good husband. Perhaps a king hasn't the right to expect more than that."

"A *man* has the right," Dhugal said indignantly. "Is a king any different?"

"Yes, damn you! A king *is* different. He—" Kelson lowered his eyes, fighting back tears. "I'm sorry," he whispered. "I *am* a man as well as a king, and I grieve for both my brides today. This girl, who I might have come to love as wife as well as queen—and the thwarted union of our two lands, which might have brought peace a little sooner. I—"

His voice broke, threatening to sob, and he set aside his crown and buried his face in one bloodied hand.

"*Please* leave me, Dhugal," he managed to choke out.

He even managed to keep control until Dhugal had gotten up and left, shaking his head hopelessly as he let his eyes pass once more over the still, pitiful form before him.

*O God, they mean well, but how could they possibly understand?* he thought numbly. *It's over before it even had a chance to begin.*

Vision starting to blur, he reached out one trembling forefinger to lightly touch a lock of her hair that was not slick with her blood. He lifted it to his lips as the tears welled in his eyes, fighting back the sobs which threatened to reduce him to a weeping ruin.

*Sidana* ... he whispered only in his mind. *Sidana, my silken princess. I would have tried to make you happy. You might have been* ...

Tenderly he slid his arms under her shoulders and lifted her to rest against his chest, heedless of the blood, cradling her head against his shoulder and rocking her, whispering her name as the tears made him blind and the sobs shook both their bodies.

"*Sidana* ..."

And thus, set apart by his blood and his crown, as he would always be, Kelson of Gwynedd crouched in the ruin of shattered dreams and wept bitter tears, holding the dead hope of peace in his trembling arms.

Here ends Book I of *The Histories of Kelson the King*.
Book II, *The King's Justice,*
will continue the struggle of Kelson against the conspiracy
of Archbishop Loris and Caitrin of Meara,
bring the return of Jehana,
Kelson's Deryni mother, and develop new themes and
problems
for the young King and his counsellors.

# INDEX OF CHARACTERS

ALARIC   *see Morgan.*

ALEXANDER—a MacArdry scout.

ALROY, King—late King of Torenth, eldest son of Duke Lionel of Arjenol and Princess Morag, sister of Wencit; killed in a fall from a horse while hunting, summer of 1123, shortly after his fourteenth birthday; succeeded by his younger brother Liam, age nine. Many in Torenth believe the "accident" was engineered by Kelson to eliminate a rival who had come of age.

ANNALIND, Princess—twin sister of Roisian of Meara. After Roisian's marriage to King Malcolm Haldane in 1025, Annalind's adherents maintained that she, not Roisian, was the firstborn of the two sisters and, therefore, rightful heiress to the Coronet of Meara. Her descendants are Pretenders of Meara. Caitrin Quinnell is the current claimant.

ARDRY MacArdry—eldest son and heir of Caulay; killed 1107, age 20, in brawl with a McLain retainer.

ARILAN, Bishop Denis—formerly Auxiliary Bishop of Rheumuth, now Bishop of Dhassa, age 39; secretly Deryni and member of the Camberian Council.

BARRETT de Laney—elderly Deryni; blind co-adjutor of the Camberian Council.

BELDEN of Erne, Bishop—Bishop of Cashien.

BENOIT, Father—a candidate for the office of Bishop of Meara.

BERTIE MacArdry—young borderman wounded in skirmish and tended by Dhugal.

BEVIS, Father—messenger sent from Saint Iveagh's to inform Kelson of Loris' escape.

BRADENE, Bishop—former Bishop of Grecotha, now Archbishop of Valoret and Primate of Gwynedd.

BRAN Coris, Lord—traitor Earl of Marley and former husband of Richenda; killed by Kelson.

BRENDAN Coris, Lord—six-year-old Earl of Marley, son of Bran and Richenda.

BRICE, Lord—Baron of Trurill.

BRION, Donal Cinhil Urien Haldane, King—Kelson's late father; slain at Candor Rhea by the magic of Charissa, 1120.

BRIONY Bronwyn de Morgan, Lady—infant daughter of Morgan and Richenda, born January 1123.

BRONWYN de Morgan, Lady—sister of Morgan, slain by magic at Culdi with her betrothed, Duncan's brother Kevin.

BURCHARD de Varian, Lord—general and current Earl of Eastmarch, which he was awarded for his services in the Torenth War.

CABALL MacArdry—castellan of Castle Transha and a chieftain of Clan MacArdry; next in succession to the clan's chiefship after Dhugal.

CAITRIN Quinnell, Princess—the Pretender of Meara, age 61.

CALDER of Sheele, Bishop—one of the 12 itinerant bishops of Gwynedd, with no fixed see.

CAMBER of Culdi, Saint—outlawed Deryni saint of two centuries previous; patron of magic.

CARDIEL, Bishop Thomas—former Bishop of Dhassa, now Archbishop of Rhemuth, age 44.

CARSTEN, Bishop—deceased Bishop of Meara.

CAULAY MacArdry—*see MacArdry, The*.

CHARISSA, Lady—most recent aspirant to the Festillic claim to the Throne of Gwynedd; Deryni; slain by Kelson at his coronation by Duel Arcane.

CIARD O Ruane—Dhugal's old gillie.

CONALL, Prince—eldest son of Prince Nigel, and Kelson's cousin, age 16.

CONLAN, Bishop—one of the 12 itinerant bishops of Gwynedd, with no fixed see.

CORAM, Stefan—Deryni; deceased former co-adjutor of the Camberian Council.

CORRIGAN, Archbishop Patrick—former Archbishop of Rhemuth, deceased (heart) 1121.

CREODA, Bishop—Bishop of Culdi after dissolution of his former See of Carbury.

DANOC, Earl of—one of Kelson's nobles.

DELACEY, Bishop—former Bishop of Stavenham; died (pneumonia) 1122.

DERRY, Sean Lord—young military aide to Morgan and member of Kelson's Council.

DERYNI—(Der-ín-ee)

DEVLIN—gleeman of Clan MacArdry.

DHUGAL MacArdry, Lord—foster-brother to Kelson, age 15; Tanist of Clan MacArdry and Master of Transha.

DONAL Blaine Haldane, King—grandfather of Kelson; died 1095.

DUNCAN Howard McLain, Monsignor—Deryni priest-cousin of Morgan, age 31; Duke of Cassan and Earl of Kierney, following the deaths of his father and elder brother; incipient bishop.

ELAS, Lord—one of Kelson's generals.

EWAN, Duke—Duke of Claibourne and hereditary Lord Marshall of the Gwynedd Royal Council.

FULK—a boyhood friend and blood-brother of Michael MacArdry.

GENDON—a sergeant in service to Brice of Trurill.

GILBERT Desmond, Bishop—one of the 12 itinerant bishops of Gwynedd.

GILES—stuffy chief body squire to Kelson.

GLODDRUTH, General—aide to Kelson, formerly in service of Duke Jared McLain.

GODWIN, General—one of Kelson's generals.

GORONY, Monsignor Lawrence—aide to Archbishop Loris.

HAMILTON, Lord—seneschal of Morgan's castle at Coroth.

HILLARY, Lord—commander of Morgan's castle garrison at Coroth.

HUGH de Berry, Bishop—former secretary to Archbishop Corrigan and long-time colleague of Duncan, now one of the 12 itinerant bishops of Gwynedd.

IAN Howell, Lord—traitorous former Earl of Eastmarch, deceased.

IFOR, Bishop—Bishop of Marbury.

ISTELYN, Bishop Henry—former itinerant bishop; assistant to Archbishop Bradene.

ITHEL, Prince—elder son and heir of the Pretender of Meara, age 16.

JARED McLain, Duke—Duke of Cassan and father of Kevin and Duncan McLain; captured at Rengarth and executed by Wencit of Torenth at Llyndruth Meadows, 1121.

JATHAM—squire to Kelson.

JEHANA, Queen—Deryni mother of Kelson and widow of King Brion, age 35.

JENAS, Earl of—son of the Earl of Jenas who fell with Jared McLain at Candor Rhea.

JEROBOAM—preacher monk responsible for helping Loris escape from Saint Iveagh's.

JEROME, Brother—elderly sacristan at Cathedral of Saint George in Rhemuth.

JODRELL, Lord—a young baron in Kelson's entourage, holding lands in Kierney.

JOLYON, Prince—last sovereign Prince of Meara, father of the twin princesses Roisian and Annalind and a younger daughter.

JUDHAEL of Meara, Father—priest-nephew of Caitrin of Meara and a candidate for the office of Bishop of Meara, age 38.

KELSON Cinhil Rhys Anthony Haldane, King—son of King Brion and Jehana, now 17; Deryni.

KEVIN McLain, Lord—Earl of Kierney and half-brother to Duncan; killed by magic with Bronwyn at Culdi, 1121.

KINKELLYAN—clan bard at Castle Transha.

KYRI, Lady—Deryni, around 30, known as "Kyri of the Flame"; member of the Camberian Council.

LACHLAN de Quarles, Bishop—newly appointed Bishop of Balymar, in Cassan.

LARAN ap Pardyce, Lord—Deryni physician, 16th Baron Pardyce, about 58; member of the Camberian Council.

LEWYS ap Norfal—an infamous Deryni who rejected the authority of the Camberian Council.

LIAM, King—middle son of Duke Lionel and Princess Morag, age 9; King of Torenth since the death of his elder brother, summer of 1123; Deryni.

LIONEL, Duke—Deryni Duke of Arjenol and father of

Wencit's nephews and heirs; killed by Kelson at Llyndruth Meadows, 1121.

LLEWELL, Prince—younger son of the Pretender of Meara, age 15.

LORIS, Bishop Edmund—fanatically anti-Deryni former Archbishop of Valoret and Primate of Gwynedd; stripped of his offices and sent into forced seclusion at Saint Iveagh's Abbey by his fellow bishops in 1121.

MACAIRE—a scout in Kelson's warband.

MACARDRY—*see Ardry, Bertie, Caball, Caulay, Dhugal, Maryse, Michael, Sicard.*

MACARDRY, The—Caulay MacArdry, Chief of Clan MacArdry and Earl of Transha, age 62.

MAHAEL, Duke—Deryni younger brother of the slain Lionel, and his ducal heir; regent, with Princess Morag, of the young King Liam.

MALCOLM Haldane, King—great-grandfather of Kelson who married Roisian, the eldest daughter of the last Mearan Prince, intending by that union to join the Mearan Coronet permanently and peacefully to Gwynedd; died 1074.

MARLUK, The—Hogan Gwernach, father of Charissa; Deryni; killed by King Brion in magical battle, 1105.

MARYSE MacArdry—eldest daughter of Caulay MacArdry; died 1108, age 17.

MCLAIN—*see Duncan, Jared, Kevin.*

MERAUDE, Duchess—Nigel's wife, and mother of Conall, Rory, and Payne.

MICHAEL MacArdry—second son of Caulay; died 1119, age 29, making Dhugal the heir.

MIR de Kierney, Bishop—one of the 12 itinerant bishops of Gwynedd.

MORAG, Princess—Deryni sister of Wencit of Torenth and widow of Lionel; mother of the current king, Liam, and Prince Ronal.

MORGAN, Alaric Anthony—Deryni Duke of Corwyn and King's Champion, age 32; cousin of Duncan McLain and husband of Richenda.

MORRIS, Bishop—deceased itinerant bishop.

MORTIMER, Lord—one of Kelson's generals.

NEVAN de'Estrelldas, Bishop—an itinerant bishop working in Kierney.

NIGEL Cluim Gwydion Rhys Haldane, Prince—Duke of Carthmoor and Brion's younger brother, age 36; Kelson's uncle and Heir Presumptive.

PAYNE, Prince—Nigel's youngest son, age 8; royal page.

PERRIS, Lord—one of Kelson's generals.

QUINNELL—family name of Caitrin, the Pretender of Meara.

RATHOLD, Lord—Morgan's master of wardrobe at Coroth.

RAYMER de Valence, Bishop—one of the 12 itinerant bishops of Gwynedd.

REMIE, General—one of Kelson's generals.

RHODRI, Lord—Kelson's chamberlain.

RHYDON, Lord—Deryni; a former Baron of Eastmarch, member of the Camberian Council, and ally of Wencit; deceased.

RICHENDA, Duchess—widow of Bran Coris, Earl of Marley, and mother of the current earl, their son Brendan; now wife of Morgan and mother of his daughter Briony; Deryni; age 24.

RIMMELL—former court architect to Duke Jared McLain; executed at Culdi for his part in the deaths of Bronwyn and Kevin, 1121.

ROBARD—a scout in Kelson's warband.

ROBERT of Tendal, Lord—chancellor to Morgan, age 52.

ROISIAN of Meara—(Ro-sheén) eldest daugher of Jolyon, the last sovereign Prince of Meara, and queen to King Malcolm Haldane; died 1055; firstborn twin sister to Princess Annalind of Meara.

ROLF MacPherson—Deryni Lord of the 10th century who rebelled against the authority of the Camberian Council.

RONAL, Prince—Deryni younger brother of the current King of Torenth, age 5.

RORY, Prince—middle son of Prince Nigel, age 13.

SICARD MacArdry, Lord—Dhugal's uncle, younger brother of Caulay, and husband to Caitrin, the Pretender of Meara.

SIDANA, Princess—daughter of Caitrin and Sicard, age 14.

SIWARD, Bishop—former itinerant bishop, now in charge of the new See of Cardosa.

STEPHAN, Father—Creoda's secretary.

THORNE Hagen—Deryni, in his early 50's; former member of the Camberian Council.

TIERCEL de Claron—Deryni, in his mid-20's; youngest member of the Camberian Council.

TOLLIVER, Bishop Ralf—Bishop of Coroth, age 52.

TOMAIS—a MacArdry scout.

TRAHERNE, Saer de—Earl of Rhenndall and brother of Meraude, Nigel's duchess.

VIVIENNE, Lady—Deryni; elderly co-adjutor of the Camberian Council.

WARIN de Grey—self-appointed messiah who formerly believed himself divinely designated to destroy all Deryni; has healing power that does not seem to come from Deryni sources.

WENCESLAUS, Brother—a monk of Saint Iveagh's.

WENCIT of Torenth, King—Deryni sorcerer-King of Torenth and scion of the Festillic claim to the Gwynedd throne; slain by Kelson at Llyndruth Meadows in 1121.

WOLFRAM de Blanet, Bishop—former itinerant bishop, now in charge of the See of Grecotha.

APPENDIX II

# INDEX OF PLACE NAMES

ALDUIN—forest near Culdi.

ARJENOL—duchy east of Torenth; held, since the death of Lionel, by his brother Mahael.

BALLYMAR—newly created coastal see in northern Cassan, seat of Bishop Lachlan de Quarles.

CANDOR RHEA—field outside Rhemuth where King Brion was slain; also site of a sacred well.

CARBURY—north of Valoret, the former episcopal see of Bishop Creoda, now transferred to Culdi.

CARCASHALE—town near Transha where Dhugal was captured.

CARDOSA—often-disputed border city in the mountains between Eastmarch and Torenth; newly designated the episcopal see of Bishop Siward.

CARTHMOOR—duchy of Prince Nigel, bordering Corwyn and the Royal Honour of Haldane.

CASHIEN—newly created see on the Gwynedd-Connait border, seat of Bishop Belden of Erne.

CASSAN—duchy of Duncan McLain since the death of his

father, encompassing the Earldom of Kierney and bordering the Mearan Protectorate.

COLBLAINE—town near Transha.

COROTH—capital of Morgan's Duchy of Corwyn.

CORWYN—duchy of Alaric Morgan.

CÙILTEINE—marcher holding south of Droghera.

CULDI—site of the synod to elect a new Bishop of Meara, and see of Bishop Creoda, new Bishop of Culdi.

DANOC—A Gwynedd earldom.

DHASSA—free holy city and seat of the Bishop of Dhassa, now Bishop Denis Arilan; known for its woodcraft and the shrines of its patron saints, Torin and Ethelburga, that guard its approaches south and north.

DOL SHAIA—area in Carthmoor.

DROGHERA—marcher holding on the Meara-Gwynedd border, south of Culdi.

EASTMARCH—former earldom of Ian Howell; ceded to the Crown on his death and subsequently given to Burchard de Varian to reward his loyalty in the Torenth War.

ELEVEN KINGDOMS—ancient name for the entire area including and surrounding Gwynedd.

FIANNA—wine-growing country across the Southern Sea.

FORCINN BUFFER STATES—group of independent principalities south of Torenth.

GRECOTHA—university city, former site of the Varnarite School; seat of Bishop Wolfram de Blanet.

GWYNEDD—central and largest of the Eleven Kingdoms, held by the Haldanes of Gwynedd since 645.

HALDANE—crown duchy comprising the central portion of Gwynedd and traditionally held directly by the king.

JENAS—a Gwynedd earldom.

KHELDISH RIDING—northeastern portion of the old Kingdom of Kheldour, held directly by the King of Gwynedd; famous for its weavers.

KIERNEY—earldom and secondary holding of the Dukes of Cassan, now held by Duncan McLain.

LAAS—ancient capital of independent Meara and periodic center of separatist uprisings in Meara.

LENDOUR MOUNTAINS—mountain range delineating Corwyn and Haldane Crown Lands; located in this range are Dhassa, Saint Torin's, Saint Neot's, and the Gunury Pass.

LLYNDRUTH MEADOWS—grasslands at the foot of the Cardosa Defile; site of the final confrontation between Kelson and Wencit of Torenth.

MARBURY—seat of Ifor, Bishop of Marbury, in Marley.

MARLEY—former earldom of Bran Coris, now held by his son Brendan, under the regency of Richenda and Morgan.

MEARA—formerly a sovereign principality, now a possession of the Crown of Gwynedd, west of Gwynedd.

PURPLE MARCH, The—meadowlands north of Rhemuth; one of the Lordships of the Crown of Gwynedd.

RAMOS—site of the infamous Council of 917, which ruled stringent measures forbidding Deryni to enter the priesthood, hold office, own property, etc.

RATHARKIN—new capital of Meara after the union of Meara and Gwynedd in 1025, and seat of the Bishop of Meara.

RHELJAN RANGE—mountain chain separating Eastmarch from Torenth; site of the walled city of Cardosa.

RHEMUTH—capital city of Gwynedd, called "the beautiful."

RHENNDALL—mountainous earldom in the southern portion of old Kheldour, famous for the blueness of its lakes; held by Saer de Traherne, brother of Duchess Meraude.

R'KASSI—desert kingdom south and east of the Hort of Orsal, famous for its blooded horses.

SAINT ETHELBURGA'S SHRINE—shrine of the patroness of Dhassa, guarding the northern approach to the holy city.

SAINT GEORGE'S CATHEDRAL—seat of the Archbishop of Rhemuth, now Thomas Cardiel.

SAINT GILES ABBEY—convent in the lake region of Shannis Meer, near the Eastmarch border, where Jehana went into retreat before Kelson's birth and after his coronation.

SAINT HILARY'S BASILICA—ancient royal basilica within the walls of Rhemuth Castle, of which Duncan is rector.

SAINT IVEAGH'S ABBEY—mother house of the *Fratrí Silentii* (Brothers of Silence), on the coast in southern Kheldour, where Loris was sent into captivity.

SAINT SENAN'S CATHEDRAL—seat of the Bishop of Dhassa, Denis Arilan.

SAINT TORIN'S SHRINE—shrine of the patron of Dhassa, south of the city and Lake Jashan.

SAINT URIEL AND ALL ANGELS' CATHEDRAL—seat of the Bishop of Meara, in Ratharkin.

SARDEUX FOREST—between Trurill and Transha.

SHANNIS MEER—lake region site of the Abbey of Saint Giles, where Jehana went into retreat before Kelson's birth and after his coronation.

STAVENHAM—seat of the Bishop of Stavenham, Conlan.

TOLAN—duchy in Torenth, formerly held by Charissa.

TORENTH—major kingdom east of Gwynedd, now ruled by regents for the boy King Liam, nephew of the late King Wencit.

TRANSHA—seat of Caulay MacArdry, Earl of Transha, in the border marches between Kierney and the Purple March.

TRURILL—ancient border barony between Gwynedd and Meara, west of Culdi; held by Brice of Trurill.

VALORET—old capital of Gwynedd during the Interregnum, and seat of the Archbishop of Valoret (and Primate of Gwynedd), Bradene.

# PARTIAL LINEAGE OF THE HALDANE KINGS

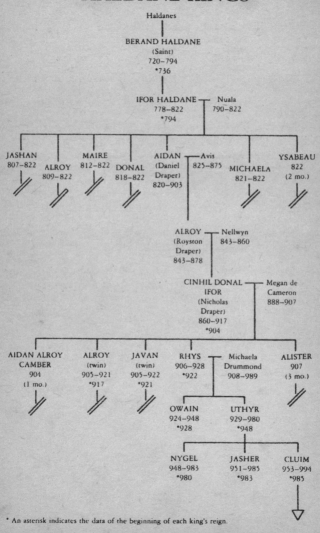

Haldanes

**BERAND HALDANE**
(Saint)
720–794
*736

**IFOR HALDANE** — Nuala
778–822    790–822
*794

**JASHAN**    **MAIRE**    **AIDAN** — Avis    **YSABEAU**
807–822    812–822    (Daniel    825–875    822
    **ALROY**    **DONAL**    Draper)    **MICHAELA**    (2 mo.)
    809–822    818–822    820–903    821–822

**ALROY** — Nellwyn
(Royston    843–860
Draper)
843–878

**CINHIL DONAL** — Megan de
IFOR    Cameron
(Nicholas    888–907
Draper)
860–917
*904

**AIDAN ALROY**    **ALROY**    **JAVAN**    **RHYS** — Michaela    **ALISTER**
CAMBER    (twin)    (twin)    906–928    Drummond    907
904    905–921    905–922    *922    908–989    (3 mo.)
(1 mo.)    *917    *921

**OWAIN**    **UTHYR**
924–948    929–980
*928    *948

**NYGEL**    **JASHER**    **CLUIM**
948–983    951–985    953–994
*980    *983    *985

* An asterisk indicates the data of the beginning of each king's reign.

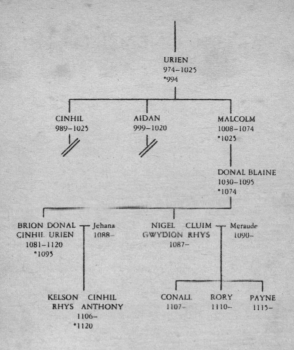

# ABOUT THE AUTHOR

Katherine Kurtz was awarded a B.S. in chemistry from the University of Miami and attended medical school for a year before deciding she would rather write about medicine than practice it. She earned an M.A. in medieval English history from UCLA while writing her first two novels, and worked as an instructional designer for the Los Angeles Police Academy for the next ten years. She is also a professionally trained hypnotist, an avid horsewoman, and an avowed cat person. She has a husband who wears kilts, a ten-year-old son named Cameron, a vintage Bentley motorcar once owned by HRH the Duke of Kent, and hopes soon to live in a castle in Ireland. Besides the Deryni Trilogy, the Camber Trilogy, and several short stories set in the Deryni universe, she has recently published a World War II thriller, *Lammas Night*, dealing with magic worked to keep Hitler from invading England in the summer of 1940. She is currently at work on the second and third books of the *Histories of King Kelson*, with at least two more trilogies planned.